P9-CMW-507
TURKMENISTAN
UZBEKISTAN
TAJIKISTAN
CHINA
Kabul
Peshawar
AFGHANISTAN
Islamabad
Kandahar
Lahore
Helmand
PAKISTAN
IRAN
Shamsi Air Force Base
INDIA
Karachi
Arabian Sea
200 miles
RUSSIA
KAZAKHSTAN
CHINA
KYRGYZSTAN
Tashkent
UZBEKISTAN
Caspian Sea
TAJIKISTAN
Dushanbe
TURKMENISTAN
Peshawar
Islamabad
Kabul
Tehran
AFGHANISTAN
BHUTAN
INDIA
Kathmandu
NEPAL
BANGLADESH
New Delhi
Varanasi
IRAN
PAKISTAN
Kolkata
Basra
Shiraz
KUWAIT
INDIA
Persian Gulf
Karachi
Bay of Bengal
QATAR
Dubai
Riyadh
UNITED ARAB EMIRATES
Hyderabad
Mumbai
RABIA
OMAN
Chennai
Arabian Sea
YEMEN
SRI LANKA
30°N
20°N
10°N
50°E
60°E
70°E
80°E
90°E

WARLORD

TED BELL

wm
WILLIAM MORROW
An Imprint of HarperCollins*Publishers*

This book is a work of fiction. References to real people, events, establishments, organizations, or locales are intended only to provide a sense of authenticity and are used fictitiously. All other characters, and all incidents and dialogue, are drawn from the author's imagination and are not to be construed as real.

HarperCollins books may be purchased for educational, business, or sales promotional use. For information please write: Special Markets Department, HarperCollins Publishers, 10 East 53rd Street, New York, NY 10022.

FIRST EDITION

Designed by Jamie Lynn Kerner

Library of Congress Cataloging-in-Publication Data

Bell, Ted.
Warlord : an Alex Hawke novel / Ted Bell. — 1st ed.
p. cm.
ISBN 978-0-06-185929-8 (hardcover)
1. Hawke, Alex (Fictitious character)—Fiction. 2. Intelligence officers—Fiction. 3. Royal houses—Great Britain—Fiction. 4. Attempted assassination—Fiction. I. Title.
PS3602.E6455W37 2010
813'.6—dc22
2010011926

ISBN 978-0-06-201947-9 (international edition)

10 11 12 13 14 OV/RRD 10 9 8 7 6 5 4 3 2 1

For Page Lee, who makes it magic

An eye for an eye only makes the whole world blind.

MAHATMA GANDHI

ONE

BERMUDA, PRESENT DAY

Alex Hawke held the battered gold Dunhill to the tip of his cigarette. First of the day always best, he thought absently, inhaling, padding barefoot across the polished mahogany floor. Expelling a long, thin plume of blue smoke, he sat down, collapsing against the sun-bleached cushions of the upholstered planter's chair.

Pelham, his friend and valet of many years, had all the glass doors of the semi-circular living room at Teakettle Cottage flung open to the terrace. Had Alex Hawke bothered to notice the view, he would have found the riot of purple bougainvillea climbing over the low limestone wall, and, below and beyond that wall, the turquoise sea, ruffled with whitecaps, typically lovely for this time of year in Bermuda.

But he seldom noticed such things anymore.

He'd tried all the usual antidotes for sorrow. Endless walks on endless beaches, the headlong expedition deep into drink, seeking refuge at the bottom of a rum bottle. He'd tried everything, that is, except women. Ambrose Congreve, the retired head of Scotland Yard and Hawke's oldest friend, had unsuccessfully tried no end of schemes to lift Alex's spirits. The latest being women.

"Women?" Alex had said, regretting a dinner party Ambrose

and, his fianceé, Diana, were throwing in honor of Diana's beautiful young niece, a recent divorcée from London. "That part is over for me, Ambrose," Hawke said. "My heart's in the grave."

His life had become a sort of floating dream, as most lives are when the mainspring's left out.

His house was a long-abandoned sugar mill, with a crooked chimney on the domed roof that looked like the spout on a teakettle. The whitewashed stone mill house stood against a green havoc of banana trees overlooking the Atlantic. You could hear the waves crashing against jagged rocks some thirty feet below. Familiar Bermuda seabirds were darting about overhead, *click-click*ing petrels, swooping long-tails and cormorants and frigate birds.

Hawke inhaled deeply, holding the smoke inside his lungs for as long as he could. God, he loved cigarettes. And why not? He rued all those years he'd wasted abstaining from tobacco. That first bite of nicotine afforded life an intense immediacy he seldom felt these days; the whole grey world suddenly awash in colors fresh as wet paint.

Cancer sticks. Yeah, well, nobody lives forever, he said to himself, taking another drag and lazily stretching his long legs.

Alex Hawke, even knee-deep in malaise, was a striking figure of a man. He was tall, well over six feet. He had a full head of thick black hair and a fine, high brow. His nose was long and straight above a sensuous mouth with hints of suppressed cruelty lurking at the edge of every flashing grin. But it was his ice-blue eyes people remembered, eyes that could suddenly widen and send a searing flash across an entire room.

"Up bright and early this morning, m'lord," Pelham Grenville, Hawke's snowy-haired octogenarian butler, said, toddling in from the terrace. He had obviously been out hacking away in the banana groves for he was cradling a fresh-cut bushel of ripe bananas in his arms as he headed for the kitchen.

"Bright and early?" Hawke said, taking a puff and letting his gaze fall on Pelham, irritated despite himself at the man's obvious sarcasm. "What time is it, anyway, you old possum?" He'd stopped wearing his wristwatch long ago. Watches and clocks were an anachronism, he'd informed his friend Ambrose, when Congreve had chided him for his habitual tardiness. The criticism fell on deaf ears. Nine times out of ten, what's the bloody point of knowing the time, anyway? It's not like you're going to miss something worthwhile.

He'd come to a conclusion: *Nothing ever happens.*

Pelham said, "Just going on twelve noon, sir."

Hawke jammed the cigarette into the corner of his mouth and raised his arms above his head, yawning loudly and deeply.

"Ah. The crack of noon. Nothing makes a man feel more in the pink than to be up and about when the blazing sun is fully risen in the azure sky. Wouldn't you agree, young Pelham?"

"Indeed, sir," the old fellow said, turning his face away so Hawke couldn't see the pained look in his eyes. Pelham Grenville, like his father and grandfather before him, had been in service to the Hawke family all his life. He had practically raised young Alex after the tragic murder of his parents at the hands of drug pirates in the Caribbean when the boy was but seven.

"Besides," Hawke said, "I've a doctor's appointment on for this afternoon. There's a treat. Get the eagerly anticipated results of my recent physical. One's health is almost a good enough reason to get out of bed, I suppose. Wouldn't you agree?"

"What time is your appointment, sir?"

"Two o'clock or thereabouts," he said, waving his cigarette in an airily vague manner.

"Your friend former Chief Inspector Congreve will be taking you to the hospital, one hopes."

"Congreve? No, no, don't be ridiculous, Pelham. No need to bother Ambrose. I don't need a Scotland Yard escort. I'm perfectly capable of getting over to King Edward's and back under my own steam. I'll take my motorcycle."

Pelham winced. It had been raining early that morning. The roads were still slippery. The antique Norton motorcycle had become a sore subject between them. His lordship had been arrested at least three times for speeding, somehow charming his way out of being charged with driving under the influence on each occasion.

Pelham said, "I'd be glad to take you round in the Jolly, sir. There's more rain in the forecast. The Jolly might be preferable to a motorcycle jaunt on those slick roads."

"The Jolly? You must be mad."

The bright yellow Jolly was a tiny Fiat 600, no doors, sporting a striped and fringed canvas roof. It was the "circus car" once well beloved by Lord Hawke. It no longer seemed to suit his ever-shifting moods.

"Pelham, please, do try not to be such a fusty old nanny. That motorcycle of mine is one of the very few things I enjoy anymore. I damned well will take my motorcycle and that's the end of it."

"Indeed, sir," Pelham said, turning away. *Fusty old nanny, indeed!* He was wholly unaccustomed to insult, and, although he knew Hawke never really meant to offend, such comments still stung.

"Do you know what I'd especially like on a splendid morning like this?"

"No, sir," Pelham said, not at all sure he wanted to find out. At one time it might have ranged from a simple pitcher of Bombay Sapphire martinis to flying in a chorus line of Las Vegas showgirls for the weekend. One hardly knew what to make of things any longer. But a grey pall of sadness and despair had settled over Teakettle Cottage, and Pelham was not at all sure how much more of it he could withstand.

"A nice, frosty daiquiri, Pelham. Made with those lovely bananas. Gave me the idea, just seeing that splendid bushel of yours, fresh cut from the grove."

"I intended to bake banana bread, sir."

"Well, you've got more than enough there for both, I should think. Throw a couple in the blender will you, and whip up something frothy to get my juices flowing. The old 'eye-opener,' as your famous literary relative's character Bertram Wooster used to say. By the way, what time did I get home last night? Any idea at all?"

"None, sir."

"He strikes again, does he not?"

"Who strikes, sir?"

"The Midnight Kamikaze. Isn't that what you called me the other night? Misplaced my key so I climbed in through the kitchen window as I recall."

"Such colorful phraseology is well beyond the limits of my verbal palette, sir, but perhaps if the shoe fits."

Pelham ducked behind the monkey-wood bar and started making the daiquiri. His lordship, much heartened, smiled at the all-too-familiar whir of the antique Waring blender. Tempted as he was, Pelham knew better than to try to fudge on the silver jigger of Gosling's rum. His lordship would notice, then fall into one of his black moods, thinking everyone, even Pelham, was out to deprive or deceive him in some fashion.

The "black dog," Hawke's euphemism for his periodic bouts of depression, was back, and the once cheerful little bungalow was now the snarling canine's fiercely guarded turf.

Mistrust and paranoia had been the common threads running through Hawke's existence ever since he'd returned to Bermuda from the tragic events in Russia and Stockholm. It had been over a year ago now. Pelham shook his head sadly, switching off the blender. There was nothing he could do for the poor man. Nothing anyone could do, really. Not anymore. And many had tried.

To Pelham's chagrin, Ambrose Congreve, a man who had practically raised Hawke from boyhood, had had no end of heart-to-heart "talks" with his lordship about his self-destructive behavior, all to little or no avail. Congreve's fiancée, Lady Mars, had even taken him to see some kind of "nerve specialist" a few times in Hamilton, but there'd been some kind of a dreadful row at the office and they'd never returned to the doctor.

Hawke said, "Must have been out quite late, then. I suppose I had a marvelous time. I always do. I've an absolute gift for jollity, it seems. Always have had."

He laughed, but it was a hollow laugh and mercifully short-lived.

"Yes, sir. Shall I make luncheon? If your medical appointment is for two, you should leave here by half one, latest. So you won't be rushed."

"Yes, I suppose I should eat something, shouldn't I? I can't seem to recall if I ate anything yesterday or not."

"What would you like, sir?"

"I don't really care, to be honest. Whatever's in the fridge that hasn't turned black should do nicely. I think I'll take that marvelous daiquiri down to the beach. Get a bit of sun. I'm looking dreadfully pale these days, wouldn't you agree? A mere ghost of my former self."

Indeed you are, sir, Pelham thought, but kept his mouth shut. If not a ghost, then soon to be one.

Pelham handed Hawke the frosty rum cocktail. "Sunshine is a splendid idea, sir. Perhaps a swim as well. Do you a world of good, a bit of exercise. Why, I remember when you'd swim six miles every single day, m'lord. All the way up the coast to Bloody Bay and back. Nothing better for one than a good long open ocean swim, you always said."

"Mmm, yes. Well. Perhaps a dip, if I can summon the energy for it. Call me up when luncheon is served, dear fellow. I might be napping down there. Dreadfully tired, lately. Don't know the reason. Perhaps the good doctor can shed some light on it. Middle age creeping up on one, like a thief in the night, stealing one's vim and vigor, I suppose. How old am I, Pelham? Last birthday, I mean."

"You recently turned thirty-three, sir."

"My birthdays are celebrated with ever-diminishing pomp and even less circumstance, have you noticed that, Pelham?"

"You specified cake, no candles, sir."

"Well, there you have it, don't you? The inevitable downhill slide begins! God, let's hope it's short and sweet."

And with that Pelham watched as Alex Hawke rose unsteadily from his chaise longue. He made his way, shuffling at a snail's pace, out onto the terrace, headed for the steps leading down to the beach, the crescent gleam of his daiquiri glass glinting ominously in the noonday sun.

TWO

AT TWO THIRTY THAT SAME FRIDAY afternoon, late for his appointment as usual, Alex Hawke roared into the parking lot of King Edward VII hospital, the old motorcycle going much too fast, and he skidded dangerously on a patch of loose gravel, almost dropping the bike. Almost. He recovered, quite nicely, he thought, dismounted, and leaned the lovely old Norton Commando still unscathed against the trunk of a shady mango tree.

He pulled a packet of Morlands Special Blend from his breast pocket and fired one up with the old gunmetal Zippo he'd carried ever since his navy flying days. One of the great attractions of smoking once again, he thought, was that his old Zippo was back in service again. He even loved the feel of it in his trouser pocket once more, a small comfort perhaps, but still.

His right hand was shaking pretty badly, but he got the damn thing lit and it calmed him considerably while he crossed the car park toward the hospital's main entrance. He was definitely not looking forward to this encounter with Dr. Nigel Prestwicke. The man was an internist recommended to him by his boss at MI6, Sir David Trulove, otherwise known as "C."

Prestwicke, before coming out to Bermuda, had been C's personal physician in London. Hawke had no doubt the results of his recent physical had already been privately forwarded to a disapproving Trulove. It was against the law to share medical information without patient approval, of course, but then, C thought he *was* the law.

Hawke was already twelve months into an extended medical leave from the Service. He'd not been out to his office at Bermuda's Royal Navy Dockyards once. Red Banner, his own covert intelligence unit of MI6, ran agents in Moscow and, now, in Havana and Caracas as well. He'd heard his young staff, Benji Griswold and Symington Fyfe, were chafing under the iron rule of the velvet-handed Miss Pippa Guinness, an old flame, but he had done nothing about it. He'd recently told C he needed a bit more time to pull himself together.

C would not be happy with his notable lack of progress.

"Good afternoon, Alex," Prestwicke said, perhaps a bit too cheery getting to his feet, a formless Colonel Blimp, tall and unevenly bulbous in his long white jacket, with twin shocks of white hair sprouting from his bald pate. He extended a reasonably dry hand and Alex shook it across the desk and took a chair.

"A cup of tea?" the man asked, reaching for a cup. "Fresh brewed."

"No, thank you."

A silence ensued as Prestwicke fussed with his own tea and lemon, glancing at the charts and reports scattered about his desk. He was too shocked at his patient's appearance for words. Lord Alexander Hawke had once been one of the more startlingly good-looking men he'd ever seen in his life. Now, sitting there in the strong sunlight from the window, his face looked as cold as stone and his eyes looked three days dead.

Six feet plus and not an ounce of fat on him, he'd been in remarkable shape for a man in his early thirties. Hunter-killer type, professional, although no one on the island save Ambrose Congreve and a few others knew his real background. Still, Hawke had long been considered a devastating prize, even by women who'd not the slightest clue as to his lordly identity or the size of his fortune.

No more. His speech was slurred and rough. His normally sun-bronzed skin was greyish, his eyes bleary, his dark hair long and unclean; and his strong-boned face was charred with the black of a three-day-old beard that did nothing for him. He'd gone to fat, too, having gained a considerable amount of weight around the middle since his last visit. Obvious, despite the navy blue guayabera, a pleated Cuban shirt, worn outside the waistband of his white linen trousers.

"How are you feeling, Alex?"

"Me? Hell, I feel like a million bucks. Old Confederate bills, buried six feet underground."

"Haven't lost your sense of humor," Prestwicke said with a smile.

"Mind if I smoke?" Hawke asked, his tobacco-cured vocal cords rasping in this small, bleached, sunlit doctor's office. He shook a fresh one from his pack and stuck it in the corner of his mouth.

"Mind? Of course I mind. Those things will kill you, Alex."

"In that case, thanks awfully, don't mind if I do," he said with a smile, lighting up. He had the old hand's ability to talk with a cigarette between his lips. "Lovely. I think of them as a sort of disinfectant, if you know what I mean."

"Any health issues I should know about, Alex?"

"I'm quite sure you, being the expert, would know those things far better than I," Hawke said, taking another puff, throwing his head back and exhaling toward the ceiling. "Otherwise, why in God's holy name would I be here instead of out there? Wherever there is, but certainly preferable to here at any rate."

It was clear the man had been drinking, and it was only two o'clock in the afternoon.

Prestwicke sat back and regarded his patient carefully. He had always known Hawke to be a gentleman, unfailingly polite, in that slightly mannered way of a bygone era that one associated with capes and walking sticks. This, sadly, was an Alex Hawke he had never seen before; he had the eyes of a man trapped in a torture chamber who longs for the tomb.

Hawke knew he was acting every bit the ass, but his mood was black and he'd never had much tolerance for doctors or hospitals anyway. Hospital was where one went to get sick these days, as far as he was concerned. Filthy places inhabited by dunces. Go in with a minor scratch, come out with a major staph infection had been his experience. Absolute bollocks, the lot of them, these bloody doctors and their nasty, disease-ridden hospitals. A nurse had told him once most doctors never washed their hands between patients unless shamed into it by their nurses.

Dr. Prestwicke, ever the gent, smiled and extracted a flimsy sheaf of papers from a blue folder with Hawke's name on it. "Let's get right to it then, shall we? The results of your physical examination? Your blood work?"

Hawke answered yes with an impatient circular wave of his noxiously fuming cigarette.

"How is the drinking, Alex?"

"Fabulous. Never better, in fact."

"Not according to these results. Alex, your triglycerides are through the roof. You've already begun to develop severely impaired liver function. I am telling you now that you simply have to stop. And stop now. Or face very serious consequences."

"I don't want to stop." Alex took another puff and turned his gaze toward the window, transfixed, it seemed, by lightning flashes of iridescent green, a tiny songbird darting about the white bougainvillea branches, brushing against Dr. Prestwicke's windowpane. "And frankly I don't intend to stop."

"Why is that, may I ask?" Prestwicke asked, all the false bonhomie flown from his countenance now. Replaced by God knew what. Concern? Duty? Professional responsibility? Fear of the wrath of Sir David Trulove? All of the above? "Why is that, Alex?"

"You want to know something, Doc? Diana Mars took me to some shrink over in Hamilton. This, this Freudian or whatever had the cheek to ask me what I thought the secret of life was. Care to know my response?"

"Indeed."

"I said, 'Simple, Doc. Learn young about hard work and good manners—and you'll be through the whole bloody mess and nicely dead before you even know it."

Alex stubbed out his cigarette and leaned forward across the desk, looking the man in the eye. Hawke's glacial eyes could still, at such times, assume the steel-blue glint of a loaded gun.

"Listen closely: *I don't want to be here anymore, Dr. Prestwicke.*"

"Now, Alex—"

"Do you understand what I'm saying? I don't like it here. The bloody bottle is the only way out for me. And I do want out. There is something irreparably broken in the works—my will, perhaps. And that's the bloody end of it."

"It will be the end of your life if you don't heed my advice."

"Your point being?"

Prestwicke leaned forward over his desk, made a temple of his fingers, and rested his chin upon it.

"Do you feel suicidal, Alex?"

"I don't feel anything. That's the whole idea, isn't it?"

"Your dear friend Chief Inspector Congreve was in to see me the other day. Terribly concerned. As is his fiancée, Lady Mars. I'll be honest with you. They're going back to London shortly to make preparations for their impending wedding. But they've asked me to organize an intervention."

"Ah, yes, the rubber room. Good luck."

"Meaning?"

"You'll never take me alive. I'm quite serious."

"Alex, please listen a moment. I know you've suffered a shock, a profoundly terrible shock. One that few men could survive intact. The death of your first wife. And now the death of the woman you loved. Carrying your unborn child. I can only imagine how you must be feeling—"

Hawke stopped listening to these platitudes, feeling he'd heard them all somewhere before. When he could stand no more, he interrupted.

"You have no bloody idea how I'm feeling, Prestwicke. Look here. I don't mean to be rude. But the last thing I need right now is your tea and sympathy and more amateur psychiatry. I know damn well what's wrong with me. It's hardly an original story. I've lost everything I've ever loved in my life. My parents were murdered before my eyes when I was seven years old. I met a wonderful woman, the first I'd ever wanted to marry. She died in my arms on the steps of the chapel where we'd just been wed. And then, Dr. Prestwicke, the truly unbelievable happened. I fell in love again. We were to be married. She was carrying my . . . my child—and then—"

Hawke sat back and puffed furiously on his cigarette, struggling for control in the presence of this stranger. He had never once let even his closest friends get this close, and now—this, this what, this bloody doctor—

"Alex, please. Don't do this to yourself. The tragedy in Sweden wasn't your fault, for heaven's sake. Everyone knows that."

"It wasn't my fault? Is that what you said? I *killed* her! Good God, man, I did it myself! Killed the woman I loved and killed my son. My own *son*! She'd had a sonogram just that morning and so we already knew the child's sex—I just can't . . . I just can't stick it any longer . . ."

Hawke, his eyes welling with tears, knew he was dangerously close to losing it. He took a deep breath, willed himself back to composure, and cast his eyes toward the window in a vain search for the little green bird, unable to face the physician.

A long silence ensued as Hawke quietly gathered himself up and Prestwicke allowed him time to do so. Finally, Hawke looked back at the doctor, shrugging his shoulders. He had no more to say. He was empty.

"Alex, please, let me give you something to calm you down. You need sleep. Perhaps you should stay here at King Edward's a few days. Get yourself some bed rest and—"

Hawke leaned forward in his chair and, inhaling deeply, finished his cigarette and stubbed it out in the ashtray Prestwicke had fished out of a drawer for him. Composed now, Alex maintained eye contact with the doctor as he spoke.

"Forgive me. I'm terribly sorry. You've been very kind and patient with me. But I have to leave now. I won't trouble you any further. Thanks for your time. I'm sure you're quite good at what you do. And give my regards to Sir David, will you? That old devil. He's always been like—oh, hell—a father to me. Sorry."

Hawke stood up and turned for the door. He was about to start for it, but he paused a moment and looked back at Prestwicke.

"Whatever happens, please remember this. It was not your fault."

"Alex, please let me try to help you to—"

"The handwriting is already on the wall, Prestwicke. You simply haven't read it yet."

He vanished.

THREE

HAD TO BE THE MIDDLE of the night, but Hawke awoke with no memory of falling asleep. Pelham must have put him to bed again. Given him a blue pill. He cracked a wary eye. Pale blue moonbeams streamed through the seaward windows onto his bedcovers. Odd. There seemed to be a persistent knocking at his door. At this hour? He could hear the sea below, boiling and hissing on the rocks. More knocking. Real knocking, or a dream?

A dream, he decided, but, clawing for the surface, he called out anyway, "Yes? Who is it?"

"Pelham, m'lord. A call for you, sir."

"Call? At this hour of the night? You must be joking. Christ in heaven. Well, then, do come in."

His old friend pushed into the small bedroom and came to stand at Hawke's bedside where he turned on the table lamp. There was a half-empty bottle of Gosling's Black Seal 151 rum standing there, guilty, on the table. No glass, no ice, no water. Just the bottle. No dream, just more awful bloody reality.

Hawke said, blinking up at the Pelham phantasm hovering just beyond the light, "Take a number, please, Pelham. Tell them I'll ring back in the morning. First thing. There's a good fellow." He rolled over and buried his face in his pillow.

Pelham sat on the edge of the bed. He put his hand on Hawke's shoulder and squeezed it gently.

"I really do think you should take this call, sir. I wouldn't dream of disturbing you otherwise."

"I really don't want to talk to anyone. Leave me alone. I'm asleep."

"You want to take this call, sir. I promise you. He's waiting on the line."

"Oh, for heaven's sake, Pelham. Who in God's name is it?"

"The Prince, sir."

"The prince? The prince of bloody what?"

"His Royal Highness, the Prince of Wales, sir."

"Charles?"

"Indeed, sir. His Royal Highness is on the phone right now. Very insistent on speaking with you. I told him you were . . . indisposed."

"I bloody well am indisposed. Waiting, is he? On the phone?"

"I believe I mentioned that," Pelham said, giving it Hawke's exact intonation.

"Well, why didn't you say so? *Charles,* you say? Christ in heaven."

Pelham hurried toward the door, wrapping his thin woolen robe round his frail body, his leather bed slippers slap-slapping the floor. "I'll tell His Royal Highness you'll be with him momentarily, sir. Meanwhile, perhaps a pot of coffee?"

"Yes, yes, black coffee. Where the hell did I put that blasted terry robe of mine?"

"You don't own a terry robe, sir."

"I don't? My rugby shirt, then. The good one with the hole in it."

"Hanging on the bedstead, sir. Here, I'll give you a hand with it."

Hawke shouldered into the crappy old thing and trailed Pelham down the hall and into the main room. Teakettle Cottage had but one ancient telephone, an old black Bakelite model that sat on the monkey-wood bar where Flynn and Niven, Fleming and Hemingway once reigned.

Hawke plunked down on one of the tall wicker bar stools, picked up the receiver, covered the mouthpiece with his hand, coughed once or twice, and then, as cheerfully parched as he could manage, said, "Charles?"

"Alex? Is that you on the line?"

"It is, indeed, sir. Lovely to hear from you."

"Sorry about the dreadful hour."

"I was just turning out the light, sir. Reading Trollope. Heavy sledding."

"Are you quite all right, Alex? I understand you've been not at all well."

"All the better for hearing your voice, sir. Seems an age since we've spoken."

"All my fault, I'm afraid. I'm brutally terrible at keeping up with old friends. I was so completely devastated to hear about your dreadful loss in Stockholm last year. Heartbreaking news. I do hope you got my note."

"I did. Thank you for that."

"Any rate, marvelous to hear your voice again."

"And yours as well, sir."

"Alex, look here, I am so awfully sorry to be disturbing you at this ungodly hour, but I'm afraid I need your help. Need it quite badly in point of fact. You're the only one I can turn to now."

Pelham had handed Hawke a mug of steaming coffee and he'd downed it in one draught and raised the mug for a refill.

"Anything at all, sir. You know that. What can I do for you?"

"I need you back here in England."

"What on earth is the matter, Charles?"

"I'm afraid my boys, perhaps even my mother, are in danger.

Mortal danger, in fact. Of course, Scotland Yard, MI5, MI6, all are ramping up to speed as best they can. But it may not be enough. It's a sense I have. A deep foreboding that someone is brutally determined to murder the entire Royal Family. They simply must be stopped."

"Are the police watching anyone? Any suspects?"

"Of course."

"But it's not enough."

"Precisely."

"Of course I'll be there, Charles. You might have to give me a week or so to pull myself together. I'm a bit of a wreck lately, to be honest."

"You're going through a rough patch, Alex, I know. I've talked to Sir David only this morning. Take whatever time you need to get your strength up, but do come as quickly as possible. Time is not on our side, I fear."

Hawke paused a moment, trying to assemble what was left of his wits. It was a ragtag scattering, and it took every last ounce of his mental energy.

"Charles, one thing. You must have some sense of where this threat is coming from?"

"I do. Some weeks ago, I was here in my library at Highgrove, randomly paging through some old books left me by Uncle Dickie, my godfather, Lord Mountbatten."

"Yes."

"Something fell from the pages of one of the books as I opened it, a book by an Irish author he admired. *A History of the Troubles*. These volumes had been among those in his library at Classiebawn Castle. You remember it, his summer home in Northern Ireland. I think you visited with me more than a few times as a child."

"On Mullaghmore Head. Of course, I remember."

"Where he was assassinated, that IRA operation. After the investigation, two men were arrested, Francis McGirl and Thomas McMahon. Professional bomb makers for the Provisional IRA. McGirl was cleared, reasonable doubt. McMahon was sentenced to life imprisonment. However, at the time of the explosion he was seventy miles away—in police custody, no less. He's out now, by the way, Alex. Early release."

"Obviously a suspect."

"One of many."

"Why in God's name was McGirl freed?"

"Good question. Lack of evidence. We need to find out who was behind that."

"What did you find in Uncle Dickie's book, Charles?"

"A handwritten note, some mad scrawl. I have it in my hand. I'll read it.

"'*Your family bled us white, our blood is eternally on your hands. You cut us to pieces. You will all die. If it takes forever. Revenge is best savoured slowly.*'"

Hawke drew a sharp breath, gathering his wits about him. For the first time in months he could actually feel his blood coursing through the veins again. When he spoke, his voice was surprisingly strong.

"Good Lord, Charles. Was the thing signed?"

"Indeed. Two words. '*THE PAWN.*' Written in a deliberately childish scrawl—or, with the left hand, perhaps."

"So. Pawn. We either have an IRA revenge murder to attract worldwide attention. Or, possibly, a deranged individual acting alone. Someone who perhaps lost his son, or his entire family, fighting against British troops. Made to feel powerless, a mere pawn in the game."

Charles said, "Eye for an eye. Some lone madman threatening, thirty-odd years ago, the commencement of a vendetta against my entire family."

"But, 'bled us white' and 'cut us to pieces.' Both clear political references to the Irish partition, the forced creation of Northern Ireland in 1921. Which points to the original suspects, the IRA. They certainly claimed credit within hours of the murders."

"Yes."

"It's been a very long time since this 'Pawn' has made another move. After all, Lord Mountbatten was murdered in 1979, Charles."

"Alex, consider. How do we know what this man, or some IRA splinter group, has, or has not been, responsible for in the ensuing decades? Our family have had more than our share of tragedy since Uncle Dickie's murder in 1979."

"Point well taken."

"Another thing, Alex, the event that triggered this call. Just last evening I received another anonymous threat. But here's the staggering thing. The note was signed with the identical words '*THE PAWN*.' Same childish scrawl as the first threat."

"Good Lord. What did the note say?"

"*Pawn takes kings.*"

"Pawn takes kings. Small clue, there. Some intelligence, educated, not a mere thug. A chess player, obviously."

"Yes, but 'kings,' Alex. Plural. Meaning me, of course, but all heirs to the throne. My boys, Wills and Harry, as well."

"Signed 'The Pawn'? Handwriting?"

"I'm no expert. But the signature would appear identical to the first one. I've already turned it over to the MI5 cryptology section for handwriting analysis."

"Charles, I will be back in England as quickly as humanly possible. Hell or high water."

"Thank you, Alex. You are the only one on earth I honestly feel I can count on in something this . . . deeply surreptitious. Because I know in my heart you'll take it—personally, if that's not too presumptuous a word . . . considering your feelings for my family, I mean."

"It's exactly the right word, sir. Personally. See you soon then. Try not to worry. We'll find him, and we'll stop him. Please rest assured."

"I've another favor to ask, sorry to say."

"Not at all."

"Your brilliant friend, former Chief Inspector Ambrose Congreve of Scotland Yard. Retired, I hear, to Bermuda. Now back in

London for a while. I know the two of you have worked together with extraordinary success in the past. If you could see your way to asking for his help, he could be invaluable in this case."

"Indeed he would be, sir. And he would certainly be honored to help in any way possible."

"Splendid. Come up to Highgrove for a long weekend, why don't you? Like the good old days. I'll ring up Sir David Trulove first thing tomorrow. Tell him you two are coming. MI6 and MI5 are already involved, of course. But, Alex, you and I will be working closely together. I'll make one thing very clear to Sir David: this is my show."

"Charles, stay safe, you and the boys. Everyone. Sorry I can't be there sooner."

"God only knows this may all be part of some elaborate ruse, I suppose. But I can't afford to take the chance. Not after those two British Army soldiers and a Northern Ireland police officer were murdered by a resurgent IRA paramilitary group in the last month alone. Sinn Fein denies any IRA responsibility, of course."

"No matter who it is, we need to get to the bottom of it at once."

"You're coming. That's what matters now."

"Good-bye, Charles."

"Good-bye, Alex. And God bless you."

Hawke thoughtfully replaced the receiver and looked over at Pelham, who was still pretending to be minding his own business, rearranging the bar glassware, polishing a small silver platter, adjusting a very old picture of a Teakettle houseguest, Howard Hughes, seated tipsily atop a stool at this very bar, hanging askew on the wall.

"Pelham?"

"Sir?" he said, looking up.

"What time is it? I mean right now?"

"Just past four in the morning."

"Set an alarm, will you? Six sharp."

"Yes, sir," Pelham said, unable to keep the smile out of his voice. "Will you be wanting breakfast?"

"Breakfast can wait. I'm swimming up to Bloody Bay and back first thing. Six miles. If I survive that without drowning, I'll have some papaya juice and dry toast. Get it?"

"Got it."

"Good."

THIRTY-FIVE HUNDRED MILES AWAY, the heir to the throne of England quietly replaced the receiver, laying his head back against the deep, worn leather of his favorite chair. He had been bone weary with worry these last weeks, but at last he felt something akin to relief. There was very real danger out there somewhere. But at least he would now have Alex Hawke at his side when he confronted it.

The Hawke family had been close to the Windsor family for generations. Charles had known young Hawke since Alex's schoolboy days, taking pity on him after the tragic loss of his beloved parents at age seven. Young Alex had spent many weekends at Sandringham and Windsor and had always joined the Royal Family at Balmoral Castle in Scotland for the summer holidays in August.

Hawke had always seemed to him a rather strange boy, Charles thought, remote, with no obvious need of other companionship beyond his faithful dog, Scoundrel. He lived in a world apart, wholly self-contained, his nose constantly in some book or newspaper or other.

He was reading at four and read insatiably ever afterward. He had an early fascination with medieval history, castles, architecture, and knights of the realm. He had, too, an abiding affection for the pirates of old, fierce, swashbuckling rogues like his own pirate ancestor, Sir John Black Hawke, or Blackhawke as that old rogue was known along the coast, hell-bent on terrorizing the Spanish Main.

One morning, Alex, about age ten, had appeared in the doorway of Charles's library at Balmoral with the *Financial Times* stock market pages in his hand. He said, "Sir, may I ask you what '*unch*' means?"

Charles had looked up, waved him in, and said, "Unchanged, I believe. Meaning the price of that specific equity remained the same at opening and closing of the market on the trading day."

"I thought that might be it. Thank you, sir."

He had his mother's startling blue eyes, raven black hair, and long thick lashes. His cheekbones were high and wide and he was the sort of beautiful boy who, quite unconscious of his beauty, was much discussed and courted when he arrived at Fettes, his boarding school in Edinburgh.

Pretty boys at school tended to be self-conscious. But Alex seemed wholly unconcerned with appearances, and it lent him a certain charm and distance that made him all the more alluring.

From the first, Charles had noticed, Alex had resisted convention. He had refused, for example, to acquiesce in the inflexible custom of school games: the very notion of winners and losers was anathema to him. Lose? Him? No. The love of play, which had never left him, continually bubbled up, but his joy at winning was far too individual for any organized sport or game, where the notions of "team" and "losing" came to the fore.

Even back then, there was a hint of an almost sinister side to his innate sense of his own power, his singular athletic prowess and mental toughness, a self-reliant feeling that negated any sense of team. Perhaps it was because, in any competitive team sport, he would feel obliged to play at humbly accepting defeat now and then. And that would have seemed false to him. Defeat? No. That would never do.

Hawke simply could not accept the concept of defeat; he would never give in to it. As he grew into young manhood, it was soon apparent that this was not necessarily a bad thing.

Alex Hawke, as it turned out, was naturally good at war. He'd been a decorated Royal Navy airman, flying Harrier jump jets over Baghdad in the first Gulf War, where he was shot down, imprisoned, and brutally tortured before he escaped and carried another gravely wounded man on his shoulders through the burning desert for days before being rescued.

His service record, however, was not unblemished.

Elated upon his escape and safely returned to his old squadron, he'd soon been reprimanded by his commander for "reprehensible conduct ill-befitting an officer." His first official "black mark."

Hawke, overcome with ennui while waiting to return to combat missions, had taken to staging afternoon martini parties with a few close comrades. Of course, there was absolutely no ice in the desert, so Hawke had conceived the notion of flying pitchers of martinis up to extremely high altitudes. The idea was to chill them before putting the aircraft into a nearly vertical dive to the airstrip and deliver them up to the lads before they'd "lost their chill."

Out of natural inclination, the young Hawke had made a deep study of warfare, modern as well as ancient. "C," Sir David Trulove, had said that one of Hawke's more important assets at MI6 was his lifetime of wide reading in military strategy, most recently in counterinsurgency operations and counterterror tactics.

Resourcefulness, knowledge, quick intuition, and an indomitable will, all these coupled with an intense fighting spirit—that was Alex Hawke. And that's what Charles needed most now. He found the thought most comforting, running his hand through his thinning hair and closing his weary eyes.

Under attack from within and without, England needed all the help she could get, and he was grateful there were still men the caliber of his friend Hawke within the realm.

"Thank God for Alex Hawke," the Prince of Wales whispered, mostly in an effort to console himself.

Charles knew Hawke was feeling deeply wounded by the awful event in the skies above Sweden when he lost Anastasia. Perhaps Alex needed Charles's help as badly as Charles needed his. If only he could really help him, somehow get him beyond this great sadness and make him whole again. Maybe this call to action would help. And, God willing, perhaps the two of them could stop the madman who had perhaps murdered his beloved uncle Dickie thirty years ago.

And who now seemed hell-bent on the destruction of the Royal Family.

FOUR

GLOUCESTERSHIRE, ENGLAND

PERHAPS THERE WAS A HAPPIER MAN in all of England that brilliant June morning. There may well have been one or two. But you would be hard-pressed to find someone more joyously alive than one Ambrose Congreve. Bouncing along a sun-dappled country lane, behind the wheel of his Morgan motorcar, a sprightly tartan plaid driving cap on his head, pipe jauntily clenched in his teeth, the sun shining through shimmering spring green leaves, God in his heaven, and, once more, all was right with the world.

His tiny little corner of it at any rate.

Ambrose Congreve, the retired head of Scotland Yard and a brilliant detective, had long been Alex Hawke's best friend in all the world. Ambrose went about life in a fairly straightforward fashion, with few eccentricities or idiosyncrasies, but he was absolutely fanatical about four things. In order of importance, they were: his beloved fiancée, Lady Diana Mars, one. The incandescent Mr. Sherlock Holmes, two. His weekly golf foursome at Sunningdale, three. And his fastidiously acquired wardrobe, four.

Catholic in his tastes, he was basically a tweed man, sometimes given to green velvet smoking jackets from Turnbull's. Or "siren suits" like the ones Churchill had worn during the war. Or bright yellow cable-stitched socks on certain very special occasions. Today, for instance.

A pair of twinkling blue eyes, the eyes of an innocent baby, belied Congreve's gruff voice. This gruff manner, all this cock-of-the-walk huffing and puffing, well, it was all a pose, anyway, and deceived no one. Congreve was brainy, tough, shrewd, and relentless, but he was the kindest hearted of men, a fellow who gazed at the world from behind a remarkable moustache fully six inches long and waxed into magnificent points.

The lane was flat and ran between towering hawthorn hedges. He saw a sharp turning ahead and quickly downshifted, using the heel-and-toe, double-clutch racing method Hawke had taught him when he'd first acquired the car. The lane had now turned upward, climbing the wooded hillside under overarching trees creating deep wells of shadow, shattered by dazzling blades of stark brightness.

Just two weeks earlier, had anyone told you that the famous criminalist would be tootling down a shady Cotswolds lane en route to an early breakfast with Lord Alexander Hawke, you would have thought them mad as a hatter. And you'd have been quite right.

The former chief inspector had sadly given up on Hawke, a sorrowful, lost soul, gone for good. When Congreve and his fiancée, Lady Diana Mars, had recently bade farewell to Bermuda, they hadn't even stopped by Hawke's Teakettle Cottage to say good-bye. Congreve sadly told Diana he simply couldn't face it on the morning of their departure, tears threatening in his baby blue eyes. The sight of Alex in such a wretched state, he told her, the very idea of seeing his old friend for what might very well be—the last time—

No—enough, he scolded himself. That was all behind them now that Alex Hawke was blessedly, miraculously back among the living. The chief inspector sat back and simply enjoyed whipping along the country road in the Yellow Peril, as he'd dubbed his old Morgan roadster. Painted in (what was to him) a most pleasing shade of buttery yellow, this was his dream machine.

The fact that it was the only car he'd ever owned was beside the point. Every time he got behind the wooden steering wheel he cursed himself for a fool, having spent a lifetime oblivious to the joys of motoring, the smell of Castrol, the throaty rumble of the exhaust system. Well, he was making up for lost time now, he thought, grabbing second gear, downshifting for the tight right-hander coming up, accelerating into it, catching the apex perfectly.

He was currently en route to Hawkesmoor, the ancient Hawke family pile in deepest, darkest Gloucestershire. It seemed that Alex Hawke, and here he would pinch himself were he not driving at high speed, had, astoundingly enough, returned home to England! And, the dear fellow was not only home, but he sounded very much his old self again. Full of that old piss and vinegar that made him such splendid company, even in dicey situations sometimes bordering on the extremely perilous.

Hawke's recovery was nothing short of astounding. He fully intended to call Dr. Nigel Prestwicke at Bermuda's King Edward Hospital as soon as possible and offer his unbounded congratulations. The man was clearly one of the medical gods, a healer of the first magnitude. Small wonder that C, the chief of MI6, placed such enormous faith in him.

Purring along, Ambrose relished the moment he'd gotten Hawke's good news, on a Saturday morning just one week earlier.

As his fiancée had other plans that evening, Congreve had been at home, dining alone at Heart's Ease, the cozy Hampshire cottage he'd inherited from his aunt Agatha. His Scottish housekeeper, the positively angelic May Purvis, had just plucked her inimitable gooseberry sampler from the oven when the phone in the kitchen pantry had rung.

"Probably Lady Mars, sir," May said, serving him a generous, steaming portion. "Shall I get it?"

"Hmm," Congreve said, shoveling the stuff in while it was still piping hot. May was gone for a few moments and returned with a great sparkling smile on her pink face. She looked, what was the word, giddy. Giddy as a schoolgirl who's just glimpsed her first film star.

"It's *him,* sir," May said, beaming as if Sexy Rexy Harrison himself were on the line instead of up in heaven.

"Him?"

"His lordship."

"Which lordship, my dear Mrs. Purvis? As it happens, I know several."

"Lord Hawke, sir."

"Alex Hawke? On the telephone? You must be joking," he said, leaping out of his chair and running for the pantry.

"Hullo?" he said, out of breath. "Alex? Is it you? Are you quite all right? Don't do anything foolish now because life is a precious gift that—"

"Sorry to disturb your supper, Constable. It's Alex, yes."

"Alex?"

"I believe I mentioned that."

"How are you, dear boy?"

"Quite well, thank you for asking. Back in the game, I might add."

Clearheaded, Hawke had sounded on the telephone; and completely sound of mind, body, and spirits. Speaking of spirits, he said he'd not had a drop or a cigarette in three weeks, had shed twenty pounds, and was back to his very strict fitness regimen. "Why?" Ambrose had wondered aloud. The man had been so completely submerged in the depths of despair when Congreve had last seen him, there had seemed scant chance of recovery.

It was then that Congreve heard his friend utter those four magic words: "Something has come up." As the cherished phrase came zipping over the wire, the chief inspector had known that, as his idol Sherlock Holmes put it so well, the game, once again, was afoot.

Alex had then invited him for early breakfast at Hawkesmoor. Not only that, he'd told him to pack a bag. Apparently, they would be off for a long country weekend, exactly with whom he would not say. All very mysterious, which suited him just fine. Aside from his rounds of golf at the lovely Mid-Ocean Club course, Congreve had suffered no end of boredom on Bermuda once he and Sir David Trulove had handily dispensed with a murderous gang of Rastafarian thugs on Nonsuch Island.

EARLY NEXT MORNING, CONGREVE, HAVING parked the Yellow Peril safely in the bricked stable yard, rang the front bell of the Hawke family's ancestral home. Hawkesmoor was a lovely old place, originally built in 1150, with additions dating from the fourteenth century to the reign of Elizabeth I. It had frequently been used as a setting in films, most recently in the latest production of *Pride and Prejudice.*

It was set amid vast acres of beech woods, parklands, and gardens designed by Capability Brown, England's most celebrated eighteenth-century gardener. Brown had also created the gardens at Blenheim Palace and Warwick Castle. His true given name was Lancelot, but he was called "Capability" because he nearly always told his landed clients that their estates had great "capability" for landscape improvement. "This particular Lancelot," Hawke had once remarked at a dinner party, "having forsaken a seat at King Arthur's Round Table, would have been an absolute smash in advertising."

When the ancient Pelham finally swung open the great oak door, the look on the old fellow's face was so heartbreakingly happy that Congreve embraced him, the two men hugging each other, both overcome with sheer joy over Alex Hawke's miraculous recovery.

"Where is he, Pelham?" Congreve blurted out. "I've got to see this miracle for myself before I'll truly believe it."

"He just returned from his morning 'run,' sir. He also takes an afternoon 'run.' This morning he ran to the newsstand over at Upper Slaughter and back, just to pick up the morning *Daily Telegraph.* The fact that today's copy was already waiting for him on the entrance hall table didn't seem to matter a whit. You'll find him up in the billiard room, sir. Alone. Shooting a game of what the Americans mysteriously call 'pool.' "

"How does he seem?"

"Risen, sir."

"*Risen*? Well put, Pelham, I must say. One never knows when all those inimitable Wodehousian literary genes of yours are going to kick in."

Pelham Grenville was in fact a distant relative of the brilliant humorist and playwright P. G. Wodehouse.

"Indeed, sir. One only waits in vain for all those royalty checks to start flooding the post."

CONGREVE BOUNDED UP HAWKESMOOR'S GRAND center staircase and turned right at the topmost landing. The billiard room was in the great West Wing, at the far end of this very lengthy corridor. He raced past endless portraits of Hawke ancestry long dead, including the infamous pirate, John Black Hawke, "Blackhawke," who'd taken first crack at establishing the family fortune in the eighteenth century, looting Spanish galleons in the Florida Straits, loaded to the gunwales with gold.

Entering the dark, heavily furnished billiard room, which reeked of centuries of cigar smoke and spilt brandy, he saw Hawke. A hazy silhouette in the brilliant light of the great window behind him, he was at the far end of the great mahogany table, stretched out over the green baize, lining up a difficult shot.

"Alex!" Congreve cried, unable to contain himself at the sight of his friend.

"Shh," Hawke said, not looking up. "This will only take a moment."

He drew the cuestick back slowly, nestled betwixt thumb and forefinger, then tapped the ivory cue ball, which ever so gently grazed the thin edge of the green six ball, sending it neatly into the side pocket with a pleasant and satisfying plop.

"Brilliant shot," Congreve said, honestly. He knew nothing about billiards, of course, but he recognized finesse when he saw it.

"Courtesy of a misspent youth," Hawke said, smiling up at him. "All your fault. You and Pelham needed a tighter leash. Grab a stick and join me for a game of 8-Ball."

"Shoot pool? Me? Do I really look like some kind of barbarian?" Congreve said gruffly. He loathed all sports and athletic activity save one. Golf. Golf, he worshipped and adored, thy staff and thy mashie they comfort me.

Hawke put his stick back in the rack and walked the length of the room toward his friend.

"Hullo, Constable," he said, using the one term of address he knew the former god of all Scotland Yard found most irritating.

"My God, it's true," Ambrose said, taking his friend's measure from head to toe. "You are back."

"I do seem to be in residence, don't I?" Hawke said, extending his hand.

Congreve ignored it and embraced his friend, pounding him on the back out of sheer joy. It was as if Alex Hawke was indeed, as Pelham so aptly put it, "risen." Back from the dead, and though not literally true, it had been a damned close thing indeed.

The world had almost lost him, and there were damn few like him left.

Congreve said, "What on earth happened to you after Diana and I left Bermuda, Alex? We feared we might not ever see you again, frankly. I've never seen such an extraordinary transformation in my entire life!"

"A wake-up call. Literally."

"Sorry?"

"I received a wake-up call in the middle of the night. And I chose to answer it instead of ignoring it, as I would have done most nights. Come along, now, we'll talk about it at breakfast. Pelham's got a small buffet waiting in the Conservatory. Nice and sunny down there, unlike this gloomy den of iniquity."

"Lead on, I am famished. Driving at speed makes a chap ravenous."

"Don't tell me the infamous Yellow Peril is still running."

"Still running? Like a top! I may enter it in the Goodwood Classic Revival race this year. Show Sir Stirling Moss and the lads a thing or two."

The breakfast room was a former conservatory with a domed glass and delicately laced iron ceiling soaring overhead. Potted tropical palms ten feet high stood around the perimeter. Beneath the sparkling glass, Ambrose Congreve and his reborn friend tucked into a hearty breakfast.

The chief inspector's eggs Benedict looked positively voluptuous. Hawke's thin layer of Tiptree's raspberry preserves on a single slice of whole grain bread looked Spartan in the extreme. Both had steaming hot tea, but Hawke's was herbal.

"You're serious about this new regime, aren't you?" Congreve asked, wiping his mouth with his napkin.

Hawke sipped his tea quietly, his eyes focused somewhere in the middle distance. He was present, but he was clearly absorbed with something else.

"Deadly serious."

"Then tell me about this life-changing 'wake-up' call before I go mad. I'm a copper. I can't stand unsolved mysteries."

"Oh, it was a wake-up call, all right," Hawke said, his blue eyes crinkling in the brilliant sunshine of the octagonal room. "Both literally and metaphorically."

"Meaning?"

"Meaning the call actually woke me up in the middle of the night. And it forced me to come to my senses. Such as they are, of course."

"May I ask who was on the other end of the line?"

"You may."

Congreve frowned at this typical childishness. "All right, once more with feeling. Who was on—"

"His Royal Highness, the Prince of Wales."

"HRH himself?"

"Yes."

"What did he want?"

"He called to invite me, and anyone else I cared to bring along, out to his country home at Highgrove for a long weekend. Your oversized brain obviously helped you make the cut."

"So. Not the usual fishing, shooting, and hunting weekend, one assumes?"

"Hardly."

Congreve leaned back in his chair, thinking. It didn't take long to arrive at his conclusion.

"There's been some credible threat to the Royal Family," Ambrose said. "Correct?"

"Hmm. Quite impressive. You should have been a detective."

"Anyone else going to be there?"

"We shall see, but I would imagine so."

"When do we leave for Highgrove?"

"Now would be as good a time as any."

"Alex?"

"Yes?"

"Listen carefully, Alex, because I mean every word I'm about to say. I am deeply glad to have you back. Even if it took something like some, some awful threat against the Royal Family to do it."

"Thank you. Had it been anyone else but Charles, I'm not sure I could have managed to pull myself back from the—"

"But it was Charles, wasn't it? And he called you because he's known you all your life. And he trusts you and you alone. No one else in this country is capable of the kinds of things you do. No one. He knows that."

"Please. Don't be ridiculous."

"Alex?"

"What?"

"It's been a long time. To be perfectly honest, I've missed you terribly, dear boy. I think I may—"

"Oh, Ambrose, for heaven's sake, dry up. Don't go all leaky like a schoolgirl. We're back in action in case you hadn't noticed. Tears are frowned upon both on horseback and under fire."

Congreve smiled.

Alex was back. As Dr. Watson had once said of a rejuvenated Sherlock Holmes, "The man was once again on the foredeck, cutlass in hand, eyes on the far horizon, searching for bad weather or enemy sails."

Hawke had returned indeed, in full measure.

FIVE

GLOUCESTERSHIRE

"YOU DON'T REALLY MEAN TO SAY, Alex, that we are *not* taking the Yellow Peril to Highgrove?" Congreve said, gazing wistfully over his shoulder as they passed right by his lovely Morgan ticking and gleaming in the morning sunlight.

"Sorry, not taking the Yellow Peril to Highgrove," Hawke replied. He was striding quite briskly across the mossy brick, and whistling, Ambrose noticed.

Whistling?

"Why on earth not, Alex?" Ambrose asked, puffing a bit, trying to keep up with Hawke's rapid pace. "You think the Royals might find the old Peril a bit unseemly? A bit of flash? *Outré*? Is that it?"

"*Outré*? Please, try not to use French in my presence," Hawke said, pausing a moment to look over his shoulder. "You should get down on your knees every night and thank God you don't have the world's thinnest vocabulary, a distinction accorded solely to the bloody French."

"A fact, may I remind you, that you learned from me."

Congreve, prior to joining the Metropolitan Police, had been a formidable language scholar at Cambridge and never tired of reminding Hawke of it. Ambrose had the remarkable ability to place a man within twenty miles of his home, wherever in the world it might be, as soon as he heard him speaking. Dialects were recorded permanently in his brain and, by some synaptic perfection of brain machinery, were always on tap for his use.

Slight details of a man's behavior or his dress would have meaning for Congreve that most men would miss: he had an intuitive power of quick deduction that made it extraordinarily difficult for any but the rarest of men to deceive him for long. These powers accounted for his success as a criminalist and the obsessive fondness Ambrose felt for Conan Doyle's transcendent creation, Sherlock Holmes. He and Holmes, Ambrose felt, privately of course, were cut from the same cloth.

Across Hawkesmoor's wide car park stood a large granite stone building with a long row of gleaming dark green garage doors, formerly stables. A steep slate roof sloped down from the high pitch, and there was a dormer window for every room where a stable boy once slept.

As a child of eight, Hawke had decided he liked one of these rooms and the company of the rowdy, fun-loving stable boys far more than his own high-ceilinged corner room in the Hawkesmoor's West Wing. Eventually, he had wheedled and cajoled Pelham into secretly moving him lock, stock, and barrel into one of the tiny stable rooms.

He'd brought with him to the new room exactly half of his books, half his toy soldiers, and half his wooden ship models. The other half of his worldly goods remained in his old room in order to keep up appearances.

Nannies, nurses, and other assorted jailers had been ordered by Pelham to keep mum on the matter of his moving out. Pelham ruled Hawkesmoor with an iron fist in those days and his word was law. Alex took to wearing clothes provided by his new mates, and every day you'd find him mucking out stalls, grooming horses, and repairing tack right along with the lads. Many an afternoon you'd find him, a woolen cap pulled low on his forehead, learning to take fences at a full gallop.

The stable master privately told one of his charges that young Hawke was "as fine a natural rider as ever he'd seen."

So it was that little Alex and Pelham had kept this change of quarters a semi-secret from Alex's grandfather for years. The boy had happily made the stables his residence until he was shipped off to the Fettes School in Edinburgh to begin his education.

"What car are we taking, then?" Congreve asked, a sullen expression on his face.

Behind all those stable doors was a fabulous automotive and motorcycle collection, from the actual British racing green Jaguar "C" type that had, to the Queen's delight, beaten the American Briggs Cunningham to win Le Mans for England in 1953. Among the collection, too, were a lovely midnight blue 1957 Jaguar XK-140 Drophead Coupe and a Corso red Ferrari 250 GT SWB.

"The Locomotive, of course," Hawke said, entering the one opened stable door.

"Morning, sir," said an old fellow in white coveralls. "Just topping the old girl off for you."

"Lovely shine, George. Thanks."

The older man, who had amazingly bushy white eyebrows and muttonchops, was just finishing a wipe-down of Hawke's daily driver whenever he was at Hawkesmoor. Affectionately referred to as the "Locomotive," it was a 1953 battleship-grey Bentley "R"-type Continental.

Modified extensively over the years, he'd upgraded the engine to the Mark IV 4.9 liter and had her fitted with bucket seats reupholstered in dark green Connolly hides. By adding an Arnott "blower," the newly supercharged monstrosity was capable of well over 130 miles per hour.

It had been more than a year since he'd driven her and he'd been looking forward to climbing behind the wheel of his great grey beast all morning.

Once on the road to Prince Charles's Highgrove estate, located at Doughton, near Tetbury, Hawke said, "You've not been to Highgrove before, I take it?"

"No, I've never been to Highgrove, as you know perfectly well, Alex," Ambrose said with some petulance, still pouting about the Yellow Peril being left behind. "But I must say I very much look forward to seeing His Royal Highness's dahlias."

"His dahlias?"

"Yes. Highgrove has one of the most splendid gardens in the country, you know. Seldom open to the public. I'm sure his dahlias are superb. My own 'Bronzed Adonis' came third at the Chelsea Flower Show last spring, did I mention that? I was quite pleased. There was even a rather handsome photo of me in *Country Life*. My dear housekeeper, May, she bought two copies, cut the pictures out, and pasted one into her scrapbook and the other on the door of the fridge."

"Sorry, I must have missed that issue."

"Not a problem. I'll see that you get one."

"Consider my breath held," Hawke said.

"Ah, good, the much longed-for irony is back."

"Ambrose, listen," Hawke said above the engine's muffled roar. "Someone, some organized group, both extraordinarily clever and monstrously determined, is trying to take out the British Monarchy. And has been for years, apparently. I very much doubt we'll have time for leisurely strolls in the garden discussing dahlias."

"Prince Charles is a gardener of the first order, Alex. Highgrove just happens to be the horticultural hot ticket for garden lovers all over the world. I'm sure His Royal Highness will understand my fervent desire to see a bit of his handiwork while I'm there."

Hawke was in no mood to bicker.

"I'm sure you two will have a great deal to talk about. Whether it's prizewinning dahlias or serious threats to the lives of the Queen of England, the heir apparent to the throne, and his two sons, I cannot safely predict."

Congreve said, "Your safe return to poisonous sarcasm is also annoying but gratifying, I must say. More evidence that the real you has returned. Therefore, I shall refrain from any witty rejoinder. Or, *riposte,* as they say *en France.*"

Hawke bit his tongue. "Good."

"Splendid word, *riposte,* don't you think?"

Hawke gave a look but no reply.

Congreve seemed determined to maintain the ensuing silence for the balance of the short journey. Which was fine with Hawke. He was listening quite intently to the exquisitely moving symphony of the Locomotive's 4.9-litre engine and the deep rumble of the custom two-inch twin exhausts.

Music, more melodic than Mozart, to his ears.

His reverie was interrupted by the sudden presence in the rearview mirror of a dark green Jaguar sedan, an older version, on the road behind him. He'd glimpsed its nose on a small lane they'd passed, waiting at a stop sign, perhaps a mile back. Now it was behind him, which was not the problem. The problem was the Locomotive was doing nearly one hundred miles per hour on this straight piece of road, and the Jag was rapidly gaining on them.

"Ambrose?"

"Yes?" he said, still grouchy.

"Do me a favor, would you, and take a look at the car behind us. Tell me what you see."

Congreve craned his head around and looked back through the rear window.

"A dark green sedan, older model. A Jaguar, I think. Four men in the car, two up front, two in the rear."

"Notice anything else?"

"Two things. They all seem to be wearing black ski masks. And they're going nearly as ridiculously fast on this country lane as you are."

"Ah. There you have it. Hold on, will you? There's a grab handle next to the glove box."

"Alex, you're already going quite fast—"

Hawke accelerated up a hill, the great motor roaring as he did so. He put a little distance between him and his pursuers, but as he crested the hill he saw an immediate problem. The road took a sharp right-hand turn at the bottom and then snaked into a section of heavy forest. He waited till the last second to brake for the turn and saw the Jag in the rearview doing the same.

Hawke slowed to the maximum speed at which he could negotiate the narrow and serpentine road. The Jag pounced, got right on his tail, and he knew this was not playtime. The Jag, smaller and more nimble than the big Bentley, was better in corners than the Locomotive. There was no way to lose it as long as they were on these twisting wooded lanes.

"Good Lord!" Congreve exploded.

"What?" Hawke said, keeping his eyes on the road ahead and concentrating on pushing the old girl to her limits. He'd always loved driving at speed, seeing how much he could get away with, looking for his own limits.

"Chap's standing up through the sunroof. Raising a weapon, Alex. I think you'd better—"

The sound of lead plunking against the fastback coachwork of his beloved Locomotive was not a welcome one. Nor were the sudden spiderwebs spattered across his rear window.

Congreve was fumbling with his seat belt, muttering something unintelligible.

"What are you doing, Constable?"

"Doing? I'm diving for the bloody floor! They're out to kill us in case you hadn't noticed."

"Oh, relax, will you?"

"*Relax*? Is that what you said? Are you completely insane? They're shooting at us! Not just from the sunroof, but from both rear windows. Automatic weapons!"

Hawke pressed a small silver button just to the left of the rev counter on the dash. A nearly invisible panel in the burled walnut instrument panel dropped open on a latch and a small, leather-lined drawer slid outward. Inside was a nickel-plated Colt Python .357 Magnum revolver, four-inch barrel. It was held in place by two short quick-release Velcro straps round the barrel and butt of the gun. Hawke popped the straps but left the Python in place.

"We'll be out of these woods and onto another proper straightaway in less than a mile. There's a Walther PPK in the glove box if you feel like shooting back. I don't advise it."

"Shoot back? With that peashooter?"

"Will you please get off the floor? You're far worse off down there if we hit a tree than if you were safely buckled into your seat. As the law requires, may I remind you."

"Safely in my seat? You are mad, aren't you?" Ambrose huffed, and stayed put in the footwell.

"Steady on, Ambrose. The Locomotive is perhaps as heavily armored as any car in England with the possible exception of the Queen's Bentley state limousine. Impenetrable to ballistic artillery. Installed by the same chap who does the work for the Royal Garages. It also has bulletproof glass in every window. Triple-laminated with integrated leaded composites and polycarbonate substrates. That's why you're not dead. Yet, anyway."

"We're impervious, you say?" said Ambrose from his cramped position beneath the dashboard.

"Yes. Glad we didn't take the Yellow Peril? Be honest."

"Who in the world would want to kill us?"

"Let's see," Hawke said, eyeing the Jag now pulling up on the left-hand side in his rearview mirror. "The Russians? KGB? They're probably still a bit peeved with me for having taken out their newly anointed Tsar. The Chinese have never been overly fond of us, ever since we blew up part of the Three Gorges Dam on the Yangtze, among other things. And then there's the North Koreans who—"

Congreve clambered back up into his seat just in time to see the red-and-white-striped barriers of a roadblock a mile or so straight ahead.

"What's that barrier?" he asked, seeing the speed at which they were approaching the barrier. "Security for Highgrove?"

"No. I'd have been warned beforehand. It's part of this ambush. Meant to trap us. Deliver the coup de grâce if need be. Hold on."

The Jag pulled right alongside the Locomotive on Congreve's side. "Get down below the window and stay down!" Hawke ordered, grabbing the Python from the tray with his left hand. Seeing the hefty revolver in Hawke's hand, Congreve slid down, getting his head well below the window frame. The masked thug in the rear seat sprayed the passenger-side windows at point-blank range. None penetrated. When the would-be assassin paused to reload, Hawke lowered the front passenger window electrically. He took a firm grip on the wheel with his right hand. For this to succeed, the Bentley's line would have to be unwavering.

Both cars were traveling at well over one hundred miles per hour, making the shot a bit more interesting. His firm grip on the wheel keeping the big car rock steady, he quickly raised his left hand and sighted down on the shooter. Squeezing the trigger of the Colt twice, he put two shots into the bastard's forehead just as he was bringing the ugly snout of his weapon up to fire again. Put a deadly end to him. Probably made a bloody mess of the Jag's interior as well.

Hawke raised the completely glazed window, replaced the Python, and the drawer disappeared back into the fascia.

"Hold on, I'm going to open her up."

"What? I can't hear a damned thing! You've blown out my eardrums!"

"I said, hold on, I'm going to speed up!"

"Alex, if you say 'hold on' one more time—"

Hawke accelerated, watching the speedometer needle climb toward 120. There was the barricade ahead and it was coming up fast. Two hooded men were standing behind it, automatic weapons at the ready. An older car, maybe an old Rover, was parked halfway on the road beyond them, its doors ajar. The road had straightened, and Hawke floored the accelerator to the firewall for this final bit.

The Locomotive surged ahead and the high whine of the Arnott supercharger kicking in made normal conversation useless. The needle brushed 130 mph and kept climbing.

"You're not going to stop?" Congreve screamed.

"No! We're going right through them," Hawke shouted above the noise. "There is massive security at the entrance to Highgrove. The boys behind us won't come near it."

"You're going to kill those two men!"

"I'm certainly going to try," Alex said with great solemnity, glancing sideways at his friend. And there it was in his stone-hard eyes, if Congreve needed any further proof. Hawke had buried the pain, buried the hurt, buried the bygone days. The world had tried, God knows, but it could not starve the tiger from those eyes.

Congreve, his ears still ringing, closed his own eyes and braced himself.

Hawke accelerated violently, even as his windscreen went opaque in the hail of bullets blazing from behind the barricade. He was now being fired upon from both front and rear. Unswerving, he put the car on the centerline and aimed straight for the two assailants standing in the road, waiting for them to leap aside.

Or not.

At the last second, one shooter dove to the side.

The other stood his ground, boots planted on either side of the centerline, defiantly firing directly into the windscreen of the onrushing Bentley.

The man's life story, ended abruptly by a massive automobile going over 130 miles per hour, was punctuated by two tiny but distinct bumps in rapid succession as the front and then the rear tires steamrolled over what remained of his corpse.

A second later, the left-side front bumper of the speeding Locomotive caught the rear end of the Rover and sent it cartwheeling through the underbrush beside the road like a toy tossed aside. Hawke glanced at his wing mirror and saw the Rover smash into a huge oak and explode into flame.

Hawke pulled out his mobile, speed-dialed a number, and handed it to Congreve, saying, "This is security at the entrance to Highgrove. Tell them exactly what's happened and ask them to alert both the local police and MI5. Say we'll be at the house in less than fifteen minutes. Bit difficult to see, by the way. Hold on."

Congreve gave Highgrove security the details.

And, for dear life, he held on.

SIX

LONDON, ONE YEAR EARLIER

DR. SAHIRA KARIM LOOKED AT HER WATCH. Nearly eight o'clock on a Saturday night. Instead of being where she should be, or, at least, where she dearly longed to be, namely, out at Heathrow putting her fiancé, Anthony, on his night flight to New York, she was sitting at her work-cluttered desk at Thames House. Reams of intercepted cellular transcripts and stacks of neighborhood surveillance reports loomed before her.

It promised to be a long night.

At least her newly acquired corner office came with a spectacular view of the Thames River, flowing beneath the gracefully arched Lambeth Bridge just to her left. Tonight the bridge was aglow with slow-moving traffic, wavering halos of white headlamps, and flashing red taillights crisscrossing in the misty rain.

Completed in 1930, Thames House, the stately buildings where Dr. Karim had worked ever since leaving university, were designed in the "Imperial Neoclassical" tradition of Sir Edward Luytens. Headquarters of MI5, or Five, as it was called, the massive complex was a huge improvement over the Secret Service's former digs on Curzon Street and, later, at 140 Gower Street.

Standing almost directly across the Thames, on the Albert Embankment at 85 Vauxhall, stood the headquarters of MI5's "sister" intelligence agency, MI6. This edifice was an unashamedly modern affair, architecturally controversial, and sometimes referred to as "Legoland" by the wags across the river at Five.

In the British Secret Service, there are two distinct entities: MI6, which deals with international intelligence and security matters; and MI5, which deals strictly with domestic affairs, including Northern Ireland. Both halves of the equation had become increasingly complex since 9/11 and the rise of radical Islam, hence Dr. Karim's preposterous workload on this rainy Saturday evening in June.

Dr. Karim was a striking woman, tall, with olive skin, gleaming black hair that brushed her shoulders, full red lips, and dark, liquid eyes beneath long black lashes. She dressed conservatively, as befitted her position, but there was always a startling flare of color just at her neck, flaming scarlet or shimmering yellow silk. Born an only child some thirty years ago in the grim slums of New Delhi, she emigrated with her family to London, and a tiny flat in Fulham, when she was ten. She'd embraced London on sight and had thrived in it ever since.

She'd moved up a bit in the world since her humble origins in the squalid back alleys of her childhood. Sahira had recently been named MI5's new director of domestic intelligence. Her primary responsibilities included Northern Ireland–related terrorism as well as the domestic Islamic extremist groups active in London and throughout the country. Since the most recent London tube and bus bombings, everyone in the building had been on edge, waiting for the next attack.

MI5's counterterrorism section, under Sahira's direction, had foiled more than a few potentially devastating bombings, but that was not common knowledge outside Thames House, nor would it ever be. One of Sahira's primary qualifications for the job was her scientific background in nuclear and nonnuclear weaponry.

In addition to her international affairs credentials, Dr. Karim had a nuclear physics and engineering background, and she sometimes dabbled in weapons design at MI5. Her proudest achievement was a "warbot," an "unmanned ground vehicle" she had nicknamed "Ugg." A few had been produced and were in use by the British Army in Afghanistan. In addition to guns and cameras, Ugg had sensors capable of detecting poison gas, airborne bacteria, and nuclear radiation.

ONE VERY TROUBLING THING CURRENTLY on her radar was an IRA splinter group, which called itself the "Real IRA" or the "New IRA." Ignoring the long-standing peace since the Good Friday Agreement, the New IRA cell had recently been stirring up a lot of trouble in Northern Ireland. Their strategy was simple: if they killed enough British soldiers, members of the former Royal Ulster Brigade, and civilians, they would surely invite loyalist retaliation, and thus reignite the violent struggle for a unified Ireland.

A year ago, dissident Republicans had murdered two British Army soldiers. More recently, a six-hundred-pound bomb had been discovered, buried just outside the village of Forkhill, in south Armagh, Northern Ireland. Meant to kill a Police Service of Northern Ireland patrol, it had been located and disarmed by Dr. Karim and her MI5 Weapons Disposal team just before it exploded. In addition to the deaths and injuries, it would definitely have generated fierce reprisals, and a tidal wave of renewed violence.

Daily, new and ever-increasing threats from Northern Ireland surfaced, and they whistled over Sahira's head like a scythe.

Closer to home were the radical Islamic terrorists born to immigrant parents right here in Britain. Ever since the horrific London transit bombings in the summer of 2005, Sahira's section had been focused on suspicious activities in the heavily Pakistani inhabited regions of East London. And working-class towns like Leeds and Birmingham.

After years of study, she knew this highly volatile domestic Muslim population demanded constant vigilance and never-ending surveillance. The United Kingdom was now home to the largest immigrant Arab population in Europe, one that was always simmering. And one that could boil over at any given moment.

That's why she was sitting here tonight instead of out at Heathrow kissing Tony, her fiancé, good-bye. They had managed to squeeze in a quick farewell lunch at the Ivy, and he'd given her a lovely string of antique pearls from Asprey's, but still. She already missed him. They were to be married in less than a month.

A high-ranking minister in the P.M.'s cabinet, Anthony Soames-Taylor normally worked at Downing Street. But he would be in Washington for three whole weeks. He was scheduled to attend a series of secret CIA meetings on Anglo-American joint security measures against urban weapons of mass destruction. This emergency session had been called in light of the latest intelligence coming out of Pakistan and Afghanistan.

Number one concern on the Western intel community's list: the radical Islamic takeover of an unstable Pakistan. Besides granting radical Islam a home base, at least one hundred nuclear weapons would fall into the hands of the West's avowed enemies.

The repercussions would obviously be devastating. Not only the nuclear threat posed by the rogue nation, but the encouragement of homegrown terrorists in both America and Britain to engage in more violence.

Sahira was deep into a close inspection of a transcript when one of her two desk phones began blinking red. Shit. It meant the director general of MI5, Lord Malmsey, was calling her. At this time of night on a Saturday, it was most likely not good news.

"Dr. Karim," she said cheerfully, picking up the receiver.

"Sahira, glad I caught you; we've a situation on our hands. Not sure how serious it is yet, but it certainly has that potential. I'll need your immediate involvement. Are you quite busy?"

"No, sir, not at all. How can I help?"

"Well, here it is. A flash emergency signal has just been received from one of the British Air ticket agents out at Terminal Four, Heathrow. But I'm now looking at live feeds from all the T-4 CCTV security cameras out there and I can't see a damn thing out of the ordinary."

"Someone hit a button accidentally?"

"Possibly. Nevertheless, I've already spoken to Heathrow's head of security and ordered our own team out there to Level One readiness, with instructions to stand by until we know what the hell, if anything, is going on. Could be a false alarm, of course. The permanent Heathrow security forces have also gone on alert standby. No one makes a move until we have an accurate threat assessment."

"How can I help, sir?"

"Had a thought. Just occurred to me. I recall that at our breakfast meeting this morning you mentioned your fiancé was flying BA to Washington Dulles tonight on the nine thirty. Correct?"

"Yes, sir. Anthony is probably checking in at Terminal Four as we speak."

"Flying first class, I imagine?"

"No, sir, Tony always flies economy. Says screaming babies are character-building. He'll be in the main hall."

"I'd like you to ring his mobile. Casual chat, good-bye and that sort of thing. But ask him if he's aware of anything at all out of the ordinary out there. Anything we should know about. Don't alarm him, no panic, just say you got an odd call you're running down, probably nothing, you know the drill. Ring me back as soon as you've spoken."

"Will do," she said, hanging up, grabbing her shoulder bag, and tossing her mobile inside as she headed for the door. Her black Mini was parked in the Thames House underground garage. She would call Anthony as soon as she was en route to Heathrow. At this time of night on a weekend, she could be there in less than half an hour. She'd tune in to *BBC World News* radio and monitor the situation on the way.

Tires squealing as she tore around and around the endless parking garage levels, she speed-dialed Anthony on her Bluetooth handsfree.

"Hullo?"

"Anthony, darling, it's me. Missing you already, if that's not inappropriate. You okay?"

"Fine, fine. Just missing you already, too, if that's not too pathetic."

"No, no. It's good. Missing is good. Listen, we got this call a few minutes ago about a possible situation at Terminal Four. Anything weird going on out there that catches your eye?"

"Nope. Nothing but the glamour of modern air travel and those of us lucky enough to be in the queue, so far. I'm snaking along in a human conga line that will ultimately dump me into the bosom of our so-called security checkpoint, whereupon I shall duly remove my shoes and tiptoe through the tulips. I think it would save a good deal of time if everyone went through security naked and then got dressed at the other end, don't you?"

"OK, good, nothing to worry about then. But, darling, if you do see anything even slightly odd, do ring me right back on my mobile straightaway, will you, sweetie?"

"Yes, of course. If you don't hear from me, I'll call you when I land at JFK in the morning. Love you."

"Love you, too."

Sahira downshifted as she exited the garage at a high rate of speed, nearly taking the turn on two wheels.

MR. AND MRS. H. B. BOOTHBY, first-class passengers to New York on BA Flight #44, were next in line to check in. They'd been in London for a week, staying at Claridge's, sightseeing, doing a little shopping, and taking in some theater. They were going home tonight only because Henry had a one o'clock tee time on Long Island, out at Shinnecock tomorrow afternoon.

"Henry," Dottie Boothby whispered to her husband, "do you notice anything odd about the fellow right behind us? Don't look now . . ."

Henry Boothby took a deliberately casual quick peek over his right shoulder and saw a perfectly ordinary-looking young man, late twenties, nicely dressed in a dark suit, white shirt, navy tie. He had one of those Bluetooth devices in his ear and was speaking into a little microphone extending near his mouth. The young man caught him looking and smiled, not in an unfriendly way at all. He carried on speaking quietly with someone on his mobile phone.

Henry said to his wife, "No. Perfectly decent-looking young man."

"He smells."

"What do you mean?"

"I mean he *stinks,* Henry. Like he hasn't bathed in a month, that's what I mean."

Her husband leaned into her and smiled.

"Dottie, I don't smell a thing. Your nose is just too sensitive that's all and—"

"You know what it is? I'll tell you what it is. It's fear sweat, that's what it is."

"Dottie, if I didn't know you better, I'd say you were guilty of racial profiling. And, dear, you know how I feel about that kind of—"

"Next in line, please," the attractive blond BA agent said. Her name tag said "Rosetree." A perfect English rose, Dottie Boothby thought, all that golden hair piled neatly atop her head, the sweet blue eyes, the rosy bloom on her dewy cheeks. She looked for a ring and was amazed some rakish young man about town had not taken this prize.

The Boothbys advanced to the counter and placed their passports in front of her. She was as efficient and friendly as she'd been trained to be and it was only a couple of minutes before they had their boarding passes and were en route to engage the modern nightmare of boarding an airplane.

"I'm going to find Airport Security, right now," Mrs. Boothby said as they moved away from the counter.

"Why?"

"You're supposed to report anyone suspicious, that's why."

"Dottie, don't be ridiculous. You can report someone who acts suspicious. You simply cannot report someone who *smells* suspicious."

"Next in line, please," Agent Allison Rosetree said as the bickering Boothbys disappeared into the crowded main hall.

"Good evening," the young man said, putting his British passport on the counter. She noticed he had a medium-sized aluminum suitcase with wheels and a pull handle. She also noticed strong body odor and a slight sheen of perspiration on his face and filed it away, a fact to remember. Fear of flying was the number one cause, she reminded herself.

Miss Rosetree routinely ran his passport through the scanner, smiled at the result, and said, "Seat 3-A, a window, Mr. Mahmood. You don't start boarding until nine P.M., so please feel free to enjoy our first-class Speedwing Lounge to your right after you pass through security. Everything looks lovely for a smooth flight across the Atlantic, arriving on time at JFK at eight A.M. Eastern Standard. Do you wish to check that luggage or carry on board?"

"It's not luggage," Mr. Mahmood said, the quiet smile suddenly gone from his face.

"Sorry?"

"It's not luggage."

"Looks a lot like luggage to me," she said carefully, professionally, beginning to have serious doubts about this passenger. He leaned into her and spoke barely above a whisper.

"It's a bomb, actually."

"Sorry?"

"You heard me."

"Say again, please. I must have misunderstood."

"I said, listen carefully please, it is a bomb. Fifty pounds of extraordinarily powerful explosives. I'd like you to close this station now. Please inform those waiting behind me that you are no longer checking in passengers."

She looked him in the eye, paused, then called out to the other passengers waiting at the white line, "Sorry, ladies and gentlemen, this station is temporarily closed. My colleagues to the left will be more than happy to take care of you."

There was some mumbling, but like the trained sheep they'd all become, the numb passengers mumbled a bit then moved over to queue up at the rear of various other agent stations.

Rosetree leaned across the counter and whispered very forcefully to her passenger.

"I have to inform you, Mr. Mahmood, that such remarks, while perhaps in jest, subject you to immediate arrest. Have you been drinking? Taking prescription narcotics? Are you completely aware of what you have just said?"

"Miss Rosetree, again, listen very carefully. There are seven of us here in Terminal Four. Two here in the First Class check-in area, and five more out in the main section of the terminal. Each one of my brothers carries an identical explosive device to the one you see here. We are unidentifiable. Our passports are in order. We are in constant communication via the Bluetooth device I am currently using. This entire conversation is being monitored by my six fellow martyrs."

"Well, I—" She lowered her left hand and moved a finger toward the emergency button beneath her computer terminal.

"Both hands on your keyboard. Now. I'm aware that you have the means to signal security with your foot as well. If I or one of my colleagues should detect any aggressive action by any airport security officials or U.K. internal security forces we know are in place, we shall immediately detonate our devices using buttons like the one you see here on my extended luggage handle. Detonators. See it?"

"Yes."

"Good. Now, please, try to remain calm and do exactly as I say. If you comply, no one need die. Understand?"

"Yes."

"I want you to place a call to this number at the BBC Television Center. You will reach Mr. Simon McCoy, executive producer of *BBC World News*. One of my colleagues has just spoken with him and he is expecting your call. Tell him who you are and inform him that you have a passenger who wishes to be patched through immediately to the on-air presenter now broadcasting live, a woman named Betsy Post-Miller. I have a message to deliver to the British people. Unless Mr. McCoy complies immediately, Terminal Four, Heathrow, will cease to exist. Do you understand me?"

She nodded, all of her worst nightmares coming true in this surreal moment.

He passed her a folded piece of paper with a single phone number inscribed. Agent Rosetree picked up the receiver and dialed the number. A man answered immediately.

"This is Simon McCoy."

"Mr. McCoy, you are expecting this call. I am British Airways Agent Rosetree. I have a passenger here who wishes to deliver a message via your on-air presenter, Betsy Post-Miller. You are aware of the consequences should you not comply?"

"I am. Put him on. Miss Post-Miller is in the studio, on air, and expecting this call. She understands the situation."

She handed the receiver to the pale terrorist. He took the phone in his left hand, kept his right hand on the bag handle, his index finger poised above the button.

"Miss Post-Miller, am I on the air with you? Live?"

"You are."

"Do you have a close-up of me on the CCTV cameras?"

"We do."

"What am I wearing?"

"Dark suit, white shirt, dark tie."

"Good. Let's proceed."

"Please don't hurt anyone. We'll give you as much airtime as you wish."

"I would like to address the people of Britain on behalf of my fellow countrymen both here and in our beloved homeland of Pakistan. We came to your shores with high hopes and open hearts. We have found only humiliation and scorn. Our hopes have been dashed and our hearts closed because of your cruel indifference to our dreams of a better life. In our home country, your troops massacre our brothers and sisters, bombing innocent people in Afghanistan and Pakistan daily. Our children are dying daily in the fires of your bombs.

"We will accept nothing less than Taliban rule and Sharia law in our own country of Pakistan. And until the last infidel is dead, until all British forces have left our blood-soaked lands, we, the Sword of Allah, will continue our righteous jihad against our oppressors both here in Britain and in our native land. Consider this as your first warning. It is only the beginning. There is no God but God. We are the Sword of Allah! Allahu Akhbar! Allahu Akhbar! Allahu—"

SAHIRA WAS JUST ACCELERATING UP the curving Departures ramp for Terminal Four when an unearthly blast shook the ground and the sky itself caught fire all around her, a brilliant, blinding orange that scalded her eyes as she swerved the Mini violently to avoid a red London bus that was careening wildly, clearly out of control.

She smashed off a guardrail, hit a parked black taxi broadside, spun out, hit a concrete barrier, and was then flung back across the road, the steering wheel jammed painfully against her chest. She was skidding directly into the path of the bus, which suddenly was airborne, hurtling end over end toward her through the air, completely engulfed in flames. Trapped by the steering wheel, all she could do was stare at it in horror.

Astonishingly, time slowed to a remarkable degree. Slower than the slowest motion, almost coming to a stop. Sahira could distinctly see the passengers inside the bus, many of them on fire—men, women, and children tumbling about inside, flaming rag dolls trapped within the pinwheeling vehicle, hurtling through space. It seemed to be headed directly for the Mini.

She'd never felt more in God's hands than she did at that moment.

SEVEN

GLOUCESTERSHIRE, PRESENT DAY

Highgrove House, the home Prince Charles acquired in 1980, had been purchased for him by the Duchy of Cornwall. This sudden real estate acquisition only added fuel to the nation's feverish speculation that the Prince of Wales was seriously considering marriage to the lovely swan Diana Spencer. The handsome prince and his blushing bride dominated the media in a riot of anticipation. It all seemed predestined, and yet . . .

Perhaps this truly was a union made in heaven, as an enthralled nation had already decided. And, besides. The eyes of the world were on Britain once again, which was only as it should be. Hearts swelled with pride and spirits were lifted as never before, or, at least since Elizabeth II's Coronation in 1953. For England, it was a godsend.

It was a fairy tale.

Highgrove Estate is today a working farm. It consists of rolling parkland fringed by thick forest. A number of farm buildings occupy around nine hundred acres of arable land. The beef herd at Highgrove consists of pedigree Aberdeen-Angus who share the permanent pasture with a flock of Masham and Mule sheep. The gardens, which Chief Inspector Congreve was so especially keen about, consisted of a wild garden, a formal garden, and a walled kitchen garden, all designed by the Prince of Wales.

His goal, Charles had said of the house, was this: "To feed the soil, warm the heart, delight the eye." He'd certainly achieved this and much more, Ambrose thought, eyes everywhere and filled with keen anticipation.

The house, built in 1798, was a classic three-story Regency manor house. Not spectacular by any stretch of the imagination. The rather plain exterior was enhanced by Charles, who had embellished it with a new balustrade, a new pediment, and classical pilasters designed by the Prince himself.

Alex Hawke rolled the Bentley under the porte cochere at the front entrance and got out to survey the damage to his beloved car. Extensive was an understatement. He ran his hand over the still-warm bonnet as if consoling a wounded comrade on the field of battle.

A Special Branch detective, a member of SO14, the Royalty Protection Squad at Scotland Yard, took one look at the severely damaged automobile and approached Hawke on the run.

"Sir! I heard about the attack on the road. Are you and the chief inspector all right?"

"Yes, quite. She's heavily armored, the old girl, thank God. Has MI5 been notified?"

"As it happens, sir, MI5's director of domestic intelligence was five miles behind you on the same road, en route to Highgrove. Sahira Karim. She's at the crime scene now with half the police in Gloucestershire en route as well. Apparently one unidentified man was found dead, the other five have escaped in one automobile, one other automobile burned at the scene. We've used your descriptions and the police are looking for them."

"You're on high alert here, Officer? I doubt there are more of these fellows in the area, but I would not discount it entirely."

"Of course, sir, we went to full alert as soon as we got the chief inspector's call from your car. Any idea at all who attacked you?"

"Yes. Someone who did not want Chief Inspector Congreve and me to arrive here at Highgrove alive."

Hawke turned away and went to help Congreve, who was having trouble opening his door. Hawke tugged at the mangled handle, kicked the door a couple of times, and managed to get it open.

Ambrose Congreve, understandably a bit shaky, climbed out of the battered but unbowed Locomotive in the shade of the porte cochere and gathered his wits about him. He was still alive, after all, and he'd been invited to spend the weekend with the Prince of Wales. He took a deep breath and looked around at the magnificent gardens.

Despite his brush with death and his recently rattled nerves, he still found this entire adventure too marvelous for words.

"Are you quite all right?" Hawke asked, a worried look on his face.

"Yes. But that was very unpleasant."

"More than unpleasant. Disturbing."

"What do you mean, Alex?"

"Whoever planned that attack knew we were meeting in secret at Highgrove today. A private affair with the Prince of Wales. There are two routes in and two roads out. The assassins clearly had advance knowledge of our route."

Congreve nodded his head in agreement. "Indicating they have contacts and allies inside our security forces. A leak. At the top, or somewhere very close to it."

"Not necessarily. Could have been a gardener or a horse groom on someone's payroll. It's happened before."

"True."

"And they didn't want us to attend this meeting. Isn't that interesting?"

"Very," Congreve said.

"Well, we're safely here, so let's just relax and enjoy a weekend in the country, shall we?"

"Couldn't agree more."

Ambrose had never considered himself as one so gauche as to be starstruck by the Royals, but he couldn't control the fluttering of his heart as a liveried servant took his bag and said, "This way, sir, His Royal Highness is expecting you in the Library. You'll find your belongings unpacked in your quarters on the third floor. A footman will show you the way."

Ambrose looked briefly at Hawke and said, under his breath, "HRH is expecting *me*. Did you hear him say that?"

"Of course he's expecting you, Constable. He *invited* us, remember? Do refrain from prostrating yourself at his feet, will you? He's a lovely chap, very bright and very down to earth, and, besides, fawning doesn't suit you at all."

"You can't deny it's still a bit thrilling."

"Oh, please, toddle on. Security will have alerted him to the attack en route. I'm sure he's worried about us. I suggest we not keep him waiting."

They were shown into the Library. The Prince of Wales was seated at his desk, a shock of white tulips in a sparkling vase of cut crystal at his elbow. With his head bowed over a ledger, an ink pen poised in his hand, he was obviously attending to estate business. When he looked up and saw Alex Hawke in the doorway, clearly unharmed, a grin lit up his face, cordially taking in Congreve as well.

"Your Royal Highness," Hawke said with a wide smile, "it was so good of you to invite us to Highgrove. A rare privilege. Exciting journey, as well."

"So I've been told."

Prince Charles put his pen down, pushed his chair back, and stood. Congreve had long known the two men were friendly, but the look on both their faces belied a much deeper, older relationship.

"Alex, this attack is shocking, to say the very least. I hardly know what to say."

"There really isn't too much one can say at this point, sir. Until we find out who was responsible. But let me assure you this is not the first time someone's pointed a loaded gun in my direction. As dear old Winston said, 'There is nothing quite so exhilarating as to be shot at without effect.' "

"Alex, your sangfroid is admirable, but you must understand that one frowns upon the attempted murder of invited houseguests."

Hawke smiled and said, "You're looking well, sir. Happy. Healthy. It's wonderful to see you again."

Charles, looking his old friend up and down, replied, "Well, rumors coming out of Bermuda to the contrary, I must say you, too, look the very picture of health."

"The miracle of St. Sunshine," Hawke said with a smile. "A good tan obscures many sins. Plus a diet so rigid I can't even lick a postage stamp."

The Prince smiled and turned his focus to Congreve.

"And you must be the legendary former Chief Inspector Ambrose Congreve of Scotland Yard? England's own modern-day Sherlock Holmes, according to your friend Hawke. I'm delighted to have you here at Highgrove, alive and well."

"Your Highness," Congreve intoned, visibly stunned by the compliment, "I was deeply honored to be included."

"Well. We'll be getting a report on the incident from MI5 soon. It turns out one of the other invitees is the director of domestic intelligence at Five. She's at the scene now and should be here shortly. Do be seated, won't you?" Prince Charles said, coming around from behind his simple walnut desk. "Some refreshments after your journey? Tea? Coffee? Something stronger? Whatever you'd like."

"Tea! Lovely idea!" Congreve blurted out, the proper form of address not quite ready to trip off the end of his tongue. Charles smiled inwardly. Over the course of his very public life, he'd seen every possible kind of effect that he had on "normal" people. Some of it, like Congreve's, he found rather touching.

The Prince looked over at the footman standing by the door. "We'll have tea, please, William," he said.

"Your Highness," the fellow said, then bowed, retreated backward a few steps, and slipped more quickly than mercury through a door only slightly ajar.

The future King of England crossed the paneled, high-ceilinged, book-lined room and took a well-worn wingback chair by the hearth. A spindly table beside it supported a precariously leaning stack of books. Hawke and Congreve had settled into two occasional chairs facing the fireplace. The tea service arrived within a minute or two, astounding Congreve.

This place operated like a tightly run battleship, Ambrose saw, and he was somehow pleased by the observation. Despite the hoary view most people took of the Royals, doddering around in their palaces, ringing for servants, he'd seen nothing of the like here at Highgrove. It was a spirited, tightly run ship that felt, somehow, lean and mean.

Charles looked carefully at his old friend Hawke, sizing him up for the tasks at hand.

Alex certainly looked fit, well tanned, and, considering recent events, even relaxed, his legs crossed at the knee, looking for all the world like what he was—a man to the manner born—but hard inside, hard as local stone.

Chief Inspector Congreve was another story. A roundish chap, with rather flashy socks, thinning walnut-brown hair, and a well-tended moustache, his hands were shaking too badly to pick up a cup and have his tea poured, so Hawke did it for him. Whether it was from the horror of the recent incident or simply being in the presence of royalty, Charles could not discern.

Hawke poured himself a cup of steaming hot water, plain, no lemon, no sugar.

"A paragon of virtue these days," the Prince of Wales said, smiling. "Abstaining even from tea?"

"Well, I've some serious mending to do and I damn well intend to do it. No caffeine for a while."

Doesn't even drink tea anymore? Congreve thought, staring at the man he thought he knew better than anyone on earth. Clearly not.

Leaning forward in his chair, the Prince of Wales said, "Alex, I made sure you and Chief Inspector Congreve were first to arrive so I might go over a few things with you both privately. After I'm finished with my little spiel, perhaps the three of us will have time for a short stroll in the gardens. There've been a lot of changes since last you were here and I'm most anxious for you to see everything. Does that suit?"

"Certainly, sir," Hawke said, glancing at Congreve at this mention of gardens.

"An honor and a pleasure, Your Highness," Congreve said, giving Hawke a squirrely "I told you so" glance. "I'm an avid gardener myself so it will be a special treat to see what wonders you've created."

"I do love it so," Charles said, getting to his feet and strolling across the room to the tall French windows overlooking his gardens.

Hawke turned toward Prince Charles. "May I ask whom else you've invited, Your Highness?"

"Indeed. I kept it a small group, deliberately. You both know most of them. Head of MI5, Lord Malmsey. Sahira Karim, the woman who was just behind you on the road. Sir David Trulove of MI6, of course, and another chap from MI6. A most delightful Indian fellow who's on my board at the Prince's Trust, one of my oldest, most trusted friends. His name is Montague Thorne, not his real name of course. Monty was orphaned in the Indian partition and adopted at a very early age by Lady Thorne, my neighbor here in the country. He's an absolute fiend for gardening, out there digging away right now. Surely you know Montague, Alex?"

"Just enough to say hello in the lift. Brilliant mind, diligent, and highly regarded. Heir apparent to Sir David, so goes the gossip," Hawke said, and Charles nodded as if he knew that to be true.

"Ah, there's Monty now," Charles said, throwing open the wide double windows and leaning out into the sunshine to wave to his unseen friend below. "Alex, Ambrose, do come say hello to my dear friend, won't you?"

Hawke and Congreve rose and went to the window, standing to

either side of the Prince of Wales. Below, on the gravel pathway, was a tall, good-looking man with a wheelbarrow full of plant cuttings. He had to be close to seventy, but he looked to be in his late fifties.

"Monty, please say hello to Alex Hawke and Ambrose Congreve, won't you? They've just arrived."

"Hullo up there!" Thorne called with a brilliant white smile, doffing his hat. "Welcome to Highgrove, gentlemen." He set down his heavy barrow and strode over so that he was standing just beneath the Library window, rubbing his rough, dirty hands together before placing them on his hips. He wore pleated vanilla trousers and a soaked-through white linen shirt, open at the neck. Removing a white bandanna he wore tied around his neck, he mopped his brow.

"You've been busy, I see, Monty," Charles said, smiling down at him. "Good work."

"Well, those privet hedges round the dahlia beds in the Sundial Garden needed a good trimming so I thought I'd start there."

"Dahlias?" Congreve exclaimed, like a man jolted by five thousand volts via live wire. "What species is Your Royal Highness growing?"

"Hybrids, mostly. Are you familiar with 'Aurora's Kiss'?"

"Indeed I am, sir! Why just last Spring at Chelsea I was . . ."

While Charles, Ambrose, and Thorne standing below chatted happily about gardening, a subject about which Hawke had zero interest, he took the opportunity to study Thorne, who was smiling up into the sun at the three men in the window.

Alex was naturally curious about the fellow who might one day well become his superior at MI6. Although he had, on more than one occasion, overheard Sir David Trulove refer to Monty as "that Thorne in my side," Hawke often wondered what barbs C might utter about him when he was out of earshot.

Thorne was a tall, well-built man, broad shouldered but with a trim waist. His cheeks were sharp planes beneath the eyes. One eye was covered with a black silk eye-patch. The patch, combined with the easy, flashing grin, gave Montague Thorne a rakish, almost piratical air. The actor Errol Flynn came to mind.

His clear, dark honey-toned skin was that of an outdoorsman, rich with a deep, healthy tan. He still had thick black hair, brushed straight back, going to salt and pepper at the temples and close cropped at the sides like a Prussian general. A long aquiline nose and thin lips gave him a somewhat predatory appearance. Hawke decided he liked the fellow on the spot, but why?

The easy smile, the lack of self-consciousness, the twinkle in the one dark brown eye. Both communicated bemusement with the follies of this world, but without the merest trace of self-satisfaction.

Hawke leaned out the window and called down, "Nice to finally meet the legendary Mr. Thorne."

"The honor is all mine, sir," Thorne said, sweeping the sweat-stained white plantation hat from his head and executing a deep bow. "The famous 'Warlord.' What a very great pleasure, indeed."

"Warlord?" Hawke said, baffled.

Thorne laughed. "No offense, Alex. It's what the wags in my section call you. The Warlord."

"I'm afraid I don't get the joke."

Thorne grinned and said, "Why, you're the 'lord,' Alex, the lord who's 'always off to war.' " He put his hands on his waist and threw his head back, laughter bubbling up from deep inside. Quite a jolly fellow, Hawke thought, for all his good looks and polished sophistication.

Smiling, Hawke said, "Ah, I see. I'll have to remember that title when I have new business cards engraved."

"Well, I'd best get cleaned up," Thorne said, "or I shall miss all the fireworks." He grabbed the wooden handles of his wheelbarrow and disappeared around a corner of the main house.

ONCE THE THREE MEN RETURNED to their seats, Charles picked up where he'd left off. "I mentioned the new director of domestic intelligence at MI5, Sahira Karim. Now at the crime scene. She is someone whom, I must say, I don't know anything about. Do either of you know her?"

"She's brilliant," Congreve said. "And apparently quite extraordinarily beautiful. Grew up in the slums of Delhi, family emigrated to England, took a first at Oxford in Far Eastern studies, and went on to take postgraduate degrees in physics and nuclear engineering. She was soon recruited by MI5, for obvious reasons."

"How much does this team know about the situation, Your Highness?" Hawke asked, changing the subject.

"Only that there appears to be a serious threat to the Royal Family, indeed, the Monarchy itself. They know I've asked for your help, Alex, and that of Chief Inspector Congreve. There's one thing I want to make perfectly clear from the outset. You are both working directly for the Crown. I don't want your investigations impeded in any way by Secret Service or HM government red tape. Is that understood?"

He looked at both of them, waiting for an answer.

"Completely, Your Majesty," Hawke said for both. He found himself in a difficult position. C would have his head for this if he found out. But Prince Charles would have *Trulove's* head if MI6 sacked Hawke.

"Any preliminary thoughts as to motive, Your Highness?" Congreve asked.

"Alex and I have discussed this at some length. It was either an IRA publicity stunt, the commonly accepted theory. Or this is a personal vendetta against my entire family. One that began over thirty years ago. The motive is revenge. The first to die was my godfather, dear Uncle Dickie, murdered as you know at his summer home near Sligo, Ireland. Here, please have a look at these."

He passed Hawke a slim red leather portfolio. It bore the heraldic badge of the Prince of Wales, three feathers emerging from a coronet bearing the motto "Ich Dien." German, Hawke knew, for "I serve."

Hawke carefully examined the death threats, then passed the folio to Congreve without comment.

"Ambrose, Prince Charles has already made me aware of these items. I'd like your unbiased reaction first if you don't mind."

Congreve examined the items and returned the portfolio to the Prince.

"Your Highness, you should know that I, personally, was part of the Yard's team investigating your godfather, Lord Mountbatten's, murder. The IRA claimed responsibility in a written statement just hours after the assassination. Two men were charged, but only one, McMahon as I remember, was found guilty and went to prison. Now, he's a free man. Your Highness, may I ask where you found the first handwritten note?"

"Yes. It fell from the pages of a book I was leafing through quite by accident. A book formerly in the library at Lord Mountbatten's castle in Mullaghmore. Uncle Dickie obviously received the threat and thought so little of it, he absentmindedly stuck it in the leaves of a book he was reading at the time and forgot all about it. Never even told his four-man security team, in all likelihood."

"And this recent threat against you and your two sons?" Ambrose continued. "'*Pawn takes kings*?' Where was that note found?"

"Here. I found it here at Highgrove. In this very room, believe it or not."

"Good Lord," Congreve said, astounded.

Hawke asked, "Where, precisely, did Your Highness find it?"

"Taped to the chessboard in that game table over by the window. It revolves, you see, chessboard on one side, checkerboard on the reverse. The boys and I still play checkers occasionally. The last time my wife and I sat down to play after supper, I flipped the board to chess—and there it was, taped to the board."

"The 'Pawn' leaves his calling card taped to a chessboard," Hawke mused to no one in particular.

Congreve said, "So the note was left by someone with direct access to this house. To this very room, in fact."

"That would appear to be the case, Chief Inspector. Troublesome, is it not?"

"Far beyond troublesome, Your Highness," Congreve said solemnly. "I assume your Special Branch detectives have interviewed every member of the household staff? Gardeners, farmers, gillies as well?"

"Of course. Nothing. They're all vetted to a fare-thee-well, naturally, or they would not be in service here."

"Sent by someone who sees himself as a pawn," Hawke said to no one in particular.

Charles stood and went over to the far window, gazing down into his garden, hands clasped behind his back, lost in thought.

Hawke leaned over and whispered to Congreve.

"Play your cards right and there might be a knighthood in this for you, Constable."

Ambrose, who registered exactly the kind of shocked, horrified expression Hawke had been hoping for, whispered a fierce retaliation.

"Your lack of propriety knows no bounds, Alex. You ought to be ashamed. Really."

"I'm simply saying, my dear Ambrose, that if you have charm, by all means ooze it."

EIGHT

MIAMI, PRESENT DAY

HEATHER, YOU ALL RIGHT, BABY GIRL?" she heard her husband say.

Tom was down the hall in his den watching the Saturday afternoon edition of *Live at Five* Metro Miami news. Heather was amazed her husband had even heard her cry of surprise over the surround-sound TV he had going. Some big news event had happened earlier, she wasn't sure what, but he'd been riveted to the big Samsung TV wall monitor since right after lunch.

News-glued, she called the chronic twenty-four-hour bad-news-cycle phenomenon gripping the country. Many Americans suffered from it: Nancy Grace saying, "It's been twenty-two months since little Tracey Childers went missing from a trailer park here in Ocala, Florida. Do local police have new information? We'll be back in a minute."

That sound bite said it all.

And it wasn't healthy, Heather told anyone at the office who'd listen. A steady diet of bad news was bad for your soul. And probably your heart.

"Honey, you okay?" her hubby called out.

"No, not really all that okay, Tom," she shouted from the kitchen, and heard the TV muted a moment later.

"What? What is it, sweetie?" he called from the door of his sanctuary. "Don't tell me it's—you know. The Big One. Time to hit the ground running? Honey?"

"My water just broke so I'd say, yep, time to go, all right."

She heard his heavy linebacker footsteps pounding down the hallway toward the kitchen.

"Omigod, honey, we gotta get a move on! Where's our prepacked emergency bag? I know I put it somewhere. Bedroom closet? Yes! Wait, I'll run upstairs to the bedroom and—"

She'd known it would be exactly like this. No matter how many dry runs they'd made, even putting a clock on the exact time it took from their front door at 2509 Bayshore Boulevard in Coconut Grove to the Emergency entrance at Jackson Memorial, eighteen minutes. On one of the dry runs, Tom had videotaped the whole thing as if it were the real deal. Who's gonna know? he asked her.

And no matter how many times they'd discussed in endless detail exactly what would happen when it was time to go to the hospital, she'd known Tom would forget that they'd placed the packed suitcase in the front hall closet so they could grab it as they went out the door.

Tom and Heather Hendrickson were having their first baby. So she wasn't surprised her husband was a mess approaching a meltdown. She felt amazingly calm, considering. Tom, who was a CPA, a senior vice president with a big Miami accounting firm, was used to having everything under control. Numbers you could control. Nature was something else altogether. Different kettle of fish. What was the old line? If you want to make God laugh, tell him your plans.

Yeah, well, God was having a hissy fit, probably in hysterics right now. She was two weeks early. They'd just finished assembling the crib late last night. Hadn't even painted the nursery yet. Her baby shower was tonight! She whipped out her cell, speed-dialed her sister in Homestead, told her to call everybody and cancel.

"Not up there, honey," her husband said, his voice tinged with panic as he came rushing headlong down the stairs. "Damn it to hell, I was sure we put it—"

"Tom. Listen. It's the red Samsonite in the front hall closet. I'm going upstairs now to change. Why don't you get the bag, take it out to the car, back out of the driveway, and wait with the motor running at the end of the walk. Good idea?"

"Brilliant! You go change. I'll get the bag, I'll be out there in the car, engine running. Hurry up, okay?" He looked at his watch. "We're already six and a half minutes behind schedule."

"TOM, PLEASE SLOW DOWN. IT'S not going to help if we get stopped for speeding."

He was doing eighty, heading north on I-95, weaving in and out of the light weekend traffic. Tom had his head craned over the top of the steering wheel, looking for an exit sign that said South Dixie Highway.

He said, "Yeah. You're right. That would be a disaster."

"Cops deliver babies in cars all the time, honey. It wouldn't be a disaster."

"Have the baby in the *car*? Are you out of your mind? Good Lord, Heather, let's get real here."

"Sweetie, I'm not even that dilated, so would you please try to calm down. Just concentrate on your driving."

"Okay. You're right. Okay, here we go. South Dixie to LeJeune Road. We're almost there."

"So what was so fascinating on the news?"

"You don't know?"

"How could I? I was in the kitchen making casseroles for my lonely bachelor boy all afternoon. You know, for the freezer. So what happened? Wait. I know. The Dolphins are going to play a team they actually have a chance of beating tomorrow. Right?"

"Honey, no, this is serious stuff. You know that maximum security prison out in the Everglades? They call it the 'Glades.' Anyway, seven prisoners escaped this morning. Killed two guards, wounded three more getting out. There's a statewide manhunt going on right now."

"Which way were they headed?"

"No one knows. They disappeared into the sugarcane fields. They've got dogs out, helicopters, the whole deal, and not a trace. The chief of the Belle Glade PD thinks there was an accomplice waiting in a car on one of the dirt roads the cane trucks use to get from the sugar factories to the train depot. It's like a giant maze out there. No wonder they couldn't catch 'em."

"They'll catch them, Tom. Don't worry."

"How do you know?"

"They always catch them. I can't remember a single time where prisoners escaped somewhere and they didn't eventually get caught."

"Right. The ones you hear about. The ones that get away the media don't talk about. Oh, no. These were bad actors, too. At least two of the guys were previously held at Gitmo, before some genius in Washington decided to let them go. Goddamn terrorists on the loose. That's all we need. I'll tell you one thing, I'm glad we're not flying anywhere for a while."

"Why?"

"Why? Because that damn shoe bomber was one of the escapees. That Brit who tried to blow up an American Airlines flight from Paris with a bomb in his shoe. Remember him?"

"Richard Reid was not held at the Glades, Tom. He's currently in a Supermax Detention Facility in Colorado. I'm a federal prosecutor, remember? I know these things."

"Yeah, well, they mentioned him anyway. Terrorists recruiting other terrorists in prison. Jails as terror training camps. Great, huh? Country going to hell in a handbasket. Next thing you know they'll be calling in a Predator air strike on the Miami jailhouse to take out al Qaeda warlords. Here's LeJeune, honey. Two minutes. Hold on."

"I'm already holding on. You hold on."

—

OBSTETRICS IS ON THE SEVENTH floor of Jackson Memorial. Heather was amazed when Tom, who had barely survived three months of Lamaze classes with her, announced upon arrival at the hospital that he would not be going into the delivery room after all. He had made such a big deal about the moment, about being there to help with her breathing, to videotape the climax of the film he already had in the can, as he said, that she was mildly surprised.

But Tom was Tom and sweet, sweet Tom was terrified of the sight of blood and so she gave him a pass. Given his current state of agitation, she was probably better off without him were she brutally frank with herself. He was in no condition to offer comfort or reassurance, much less be a breathing coach to anyone right now.

So he was probably better off out there pacing back and forth or thumbing through old *GQ*s and *Sports Illustrated*s with all the other expectant dads in the ob-gyn waiting room. One could only imagine the karma in that room right now. Wide-eyed panic masked by cheerful male camaraderie. Boy or girl? Who cares, buddy, long as he's got ten fingers and ten toes!

The other good news was she was two weeks early, which might mean a short labor, at least that's what her mom back in Cincinnati had told her anyway, and that was certainly what she was hoping when the contractions started coming hard and fast and suddenly they were wheeling her crazily down the long antiseptically green-tiled corridor toward the delivery room. And then, boom, blasting right through two big swinging doors like a drunken cowpoke.

The gurney seemed to be careening from side to side but maybe that was only the IV Valium drip kicking in or something, because, aside from the really, really bad cramps she was feeling, it was okay, so far, this childbirth thing. But it was incredibly bright in here, like stepping out from behind the curtain onto a blinding stage with every spotlight in the house in your eyes, but that was part of the deal, right?

Really hurting now, and wondering if she'd made a mistake turning down that spinal, that epidural, or whatever, but determined to gut it out just like she'd always done ever since she'd been a little girl. One tough cookie, that's what they'd said about Heather Hintzpeter, and, goddamn it, they were right. Take your spinal and shove it, pal. . . .

She was suddenly surrounded by masked faces. The anesthesiologist was right beside her head, whispering things to her, things that were meant to amuse and relax her, but she had no earthly idea what he was talking about. At the other end of her was her doctor, a young guy just starting out but she had really liked him and trusted him right from the start so everything was going to be okay . . .

"Push!"

"Okay, good . . . push on three . . . and one and two and three—PUSH!"

Heather took another breath—God, it hurt—and got ready to give it another push and then—well, then—

THE WHOLE ROOM SHOOK and there was this loud, horrible noise, like an explosion just outside the delivery room. She saw the doctor's eyes dart up over his mask, looking at his team, silently urging them to be calm at this critical moment . . .

"What the hell was that?" one of the nurses asked, clearly afraid.

"Gas main," another one said. "Or a boiler in the basement. Relax."

A fried electrical noise inside the walls somewhere, *zzzzz-tttt . . . zzzzz-ttttt.*

The lights suddenly went out. There was a deep intake of breath around the table and everyone held it until the lights flickered a few times and finally came on again.

"Generator?" someone asked. "The main power is out?"

"Wait, didn't that explosion sound like it came from *above*?" another nurse asked. And there did seem to be dust falling through new cracks in the ceiling . . . she could see it, feel it on her cheeks.

"*Push!*" Dr. Sabatini said and by God almighty she pushed like she'd never pushed before for what had to be the thirtieth time . . .

The nurse at her right foot screamed.

The baby? Something horribly wrong with her baby?

No. Someone had just come into the delivery room.

She tried to raise her head to see, but the male anesthesiologist put a hand on her forehead and pushed it down. But she'd already seen him—she'd seen a man all in black. Face hidden by some mask with only eyeholes.

He had a large black gun, held at his waist, and he screamed something unintelligible and then opened fire, a horrible staccato sound, and the people surrounding her delivery table were simply shredded, holes spouting blood in every direction, falling away from the table or sprawled across her body.

Then, silence.

She used her elbows, forced her torso upward, straining, wanting to see, see who would do this, who would come into such a sacred place of childbirth and slaughter, who would . . . she looked into the black eyes in the black holes of the ski mask and instantly understood that all of it, everything she cherished, all she knew, was lost.

He saw her now, seemed to react to this single head raised from the table, eyes fixed upon him, and he lifted his weapon, aiming to kill her, she knew that, but she didn't flinch, or defy what fate had decreed; she waited to die. He sighted the gun at her face and now this nightmare would end, and all the while her baby was struggling to be born and so still she pushed, pushed with everything she had, screaming in agony, barely seeing the killer drop his weapon, reach for a cord that dangled from some vaguely recognizable contraption strapped around his waist.

The black figure yanked the cord downward, and the room and all the dead surrounding her, lying across her legs, sprawled upon her belly, inert on the floor, all simply disappeared in one blinding white moment when all was erased and she was hurled backward into a solid wall of pain and then unwanted darkness, even as the bomb's enormous concussion expelled her child into the new world.

> In addition to countless victims and the bodies of the seven recently escaped terrorists, all members of a radical Islamic gang calling themselves the "Sword of Allah," police and rescue dogs also found a lone female survivor amid the twisted rubble of what had been Jackson Memorial Hospital—and, then, only because of her newborn baby's cries.
>
> —*Miami Herald*

NINE

MIAMI

"Seriously, Harry, what in hell does Langley brass think they're doing, wasting a precious resource like me? And hell, you, too?" Stokely Jones said to Harry Brock. "Whole town is blowing up and every damn day they send us out on these dipshit stakeouts? We're overqualified for this kid stuff, man. Must be twenty feds down here from D.C. working the Memorial Hospital case."

"Try forty," Harry said. He knew the president.

America had a new president now, Tom McCloskey, the tall, rugged, former Colorado rancher who had been the vice president in President Jack McAfee's administration. McCloskey had been elected in a squeaker against longtime Senator Larry Reed. Reed, for reasons seemingly unknown to anyone but himself and his head-in-the-sand backers on the Hill, wanted to defang America. To withdraw funding for missile defense systems at home and overseas. To slash military budgets and bring the boys home, wherever they were. To close Gitmo and send all the terrorists back home so they could make more baby terrorists to send back to America.

A major component of the campaign platform of Reed's opponent

Tom McCloskey, and McCloskey's veep candidate, ex–Naval Chief of Staff David Rosow, had been countering the mounting terror threat from within America's borders as well as from without. McCloskey believed homegrown terrorists posed America's biggest threat at the moment. And that only eternal vigilance and military might at home and abroad could save an increasingly fragile Republic.

America, President McCloskey had asserted in his stump speeches, was in the midst of what he called "The Third Wave" of domestic terrorism. The first wave occurred on September 11, 2001, the culmination of years of attacks on America and the west by al Qaeda, a group consisting of Saudi, Yemeni, and other identifiably Arab men. Bin Laden soon realized the United States would guard against such foreigners in the future. Future attacks would have to draw on a new talent pool.

To circumvent added security measures, bin Laden recruited terrorists with French, British, and other passports. Men like "shoe bomber" Richard Reid, traveling on a U.K. passport. And Umar Farouk Abdulmutallab, the infamous "underwear bomber." Or the U.S. Army psychiatrist at Fort Hood who murdered American soldiers, and the "Times Square" bomber who'd been removed from an Emirates airliner just before it pulled back from the gate. This, McCloskey asserted, was the "Second Wave" of terror. The "Third Wave" consisted of U.S. citizens and residents, legal or not, who can fly under the radar of new security measures created to thwart first- and second-wave operatives.

He cited the direct link between 1960s radical H. Rap Brown and the twelve men charged with felonies in connection with the fatal firefight of a Detroit imam with FBI agents. Brown converted to Islam while in Attica prison and was allegedly running a terror network from his prison cell in Colorado. Criminals, McCloskey said, were undergoing Muslim prison conversions at the rate of thirty-five thousand a year. All potential "street operatives" who could and would support the terrorist agenda. Plainly, he said, the fundamentalist ideology has sunk deep roots into American society.

The tight presidential race had ended suddenly on the night of the last nationally televised debate. Responding to yet another sarcastic question about his "cowboy qualifications" from Senator Reed, McCloskey had squared his big shoulders, looked directly into the camera, and said, "Frankly, Senator Reed, I think Americans voting for you are like chickens voting for Colonel Sanders."

Senator Reed never recovered.

And, after what had happened at Jackson Memorial in Miami a couple of weeks ago, it was beginning to look like McCloskey had been right.

"Okay, forty feds, Harry. And are we assigned to that task force? Biggest terror attack on American soil since 9/11? No, not us, we're sitting out here day and night doing frigging stakeouts."

Harry, who'd heard this rap many times in the prior week, couldn't even be bothered to shift his gaze to Stoke from the half-naked blonde currently sashaying across the crosswalk with a teacup dog at the end of a pink leather leash studded with zircons as big as the Ritz.

Brock was wondering how the hell either of them, dog or woman, could walk upright with all that weight up front.

"I could live in that bra," Harry mused. "Very happily. I'm dead serious. I hate my apartment."

"What?" Stoke said.

"The crosswalk, are you blind, the crosswalk."

Stoke, who, according to their mutual pal Alex Hawke, was about the size of your average armoire, was wedged behind the steering wheel. He pressed forward, peering at the woman through the Suburban's grimy windshield as he polished off what remained of his Whopper. One sure way to commit suicide? Put yourself between Stokely Jones Jr. and the pickup counter at a Burger King.

"I mean it, Harry. I got serious shit to do," Stoke said, using his napkin, watching the blonde jiggle by.

"Yeah? Like what?" Harry said.

"Like getting my damn GTO detailed, for starters. Okay? Maintain its high CDI factor."

"CDI? What the hell is CDI?"

" 'Chicks Dig It.' Critical."

"Funny. What else?"

"Hell, who knows? Have a Thai massage. Learn Spanish. Finish reading *Shogun*. Stuff like that."

"*Shogun*? When did you start reading that?"

"Hell, I dunno. When did it come out?"

Harry looked at him and sighed. "You know what? I should have just stayed with the Corps. I don't know why the hell I ever left."

"Once a Marine, always a Marine. Why did you bail?"

"I dunno. I was standing on a street corner one night in Baghdad smoking weed. I thought I had the world by the balls and then I looked down and saw the balls in my hand were my own."

STOKE AND HARRY WERE PARKED on Ocean Drive over in South Beach, with a nice view of the wide sandy beach, swaying palms, and rolling blue ocean to their right. To their left, an unbroken line of art deco hotels, shops, and restaurants. It was pretty early in the day, and most of the local SoBe residents were still sleeping it off.

Miami was definitely not "the city that never sleeps." Hell, it was the city that never woke up, least till round midnight. Unless, of course, you had huge buildings blowing up smack-dab in the middle of town. That was an attention getter.

Jackson Hospital was a real wake-up call, Stoke thought, in a lot more ways than one. According to the latest intel reports, Sword of Allah had combined forces of the Taliban and al Qaeda in Afghanistan and northern Pakistan to become the most powerful terror network on the planet. And now they'd proved beyond a shadow of a doubt that their reach extended deep inside the United States. What was frightening? They were turning American prisons into terrorist training camps.

Stoke had thought he was moving out of the terrorists' crosshairs when he left Manhattan.

Stokely Jones had finally said good-bye to his hometown of New

York City for this beautiful stretch of ocean, and it seemed like he couldn't get enough of it. When his sainted mama had passed, the sale of their old house in Bayside, Queens, and an apartment in LeFrak City had paid for Stoke's penthouse condo in the sky over on Brickell Key. He loved having the Atlantic and Biscayne Bay for his new front yard.

Fancha, his fiancée, a well-known singer and a pretty good songwriter from the Cape Verde Islands, said he loved the ocean because water, *all* water, even the water he drank, was nature's way of "purifying his soul," whatever the hell that meant. He didn't like her equating his soul with tap water. Mess with my mind, he had told her, but don't go disrespecting my soul.

Stoke hadn't been listening, but apparently Harry had been talking awhile because he now heard the CIA man saying, ". . . so, anyway, I can't sleep, I'm channel-surfing, and I get this cable show called *Black Gay Men Speak Out,* which is fine, no problem. God bless 'em. But I'm thinking, why don't they ever, I mean *ever,* have a show called *Straight White Guys Speak Out*? Y'know what I'm sayin', Stoke? Think about it. Hell, maybe I'll get some guys, pals of mine, do a pilot. See what happens."

"Can I be on the show? I ain't white, but I'm straight. That's 50 percent. Just shoot me, you know, from the waist up when I come on the set."

Harry looked over at him, shaking his head.

"Why don't you come up with your own show, Stokely? Huh? Is that an idea?"

"I already came up with my show and believe me, you won't be on it."

"Let me ask you a serious question. If you have sex with a prostitute against her will, is that considered rape or shoplifting?"

Stokely looked over at Brock, thinking: In Nam, in the godforsaken brown-water Delta, back in the day, in or out of combat, Harry would have been just the kind of guy Stoke and the other black dudes in his outfit would have seriously avoided.

A good soldier, just one too many shades too white for the

brothers. Orange County white is how Stoke saw Harry. From some semi-ritzy development called Santa Rosita, if Stoke remembered it right. "The Town That God Forgot," Harry always called it, making some kind of joke about the place.

You just couldn't completely trust a guy who'd grown up in a gated community.

There had been times, over the years they'd worked together, that Stoke thought Harry Brock was just a complete waste of space. But Brock was a true patriot and a badass and he had saved Stoke's best friend Alex Hawke's life one time in the Amazon jungle. That overcame a whole boatload of Harry's negatives.

TEN

I'M SERIOUS, HARRY," STOKE SAID, GETTING back to the topic at hand. "We've had days and nights of this surveillance, and nothing to show for it. What exactly is the program?"

"You asking me?" Harry said, wiping a smidge of mayo from his chin.

"No. That other guy in the car."

Brock, in the passenger seat, looked through the small CIA-issued binoculars to get a sharper image of their target. Big target. A rumpled fat man they had identified as Hamid Kassar, whatever kind of Indo-Pakistani name that was, sitting behind the wheel of a 1958 metallic-blue Bel Air bona fide pussy-magnet convertible. Top down, bald head back on the pleated white leather seat top, Chrome Hearts shades on, catching rays.

Hamid Kassar had been the lawyer for the two Pakistani guys who'd been released from Gitmo and headed straight for Miami. The ones who'd wasted no time getting themselves busted for a crime serious enough to send them out to the Glades. Hook up with the Sword of Allah gang. Six months later, they bust out with five other guys and blow up fucking Jackson Memorial Hospital.

Harry cursed the genius brigade on the Hill who'd voted to release Guantanamo prisoners. All you did was put hardened terrorists on the street. Or, almost worse yet, put 'em back into American prisons where they could recruit naive gangbangers with no education into believing in all this radical Islam "Hate America" crap.

It was like Washington believed we couldn't import, or, worse, *let in* enough effing terrorists slipping across our unprotected borders, so that now, *now,* we had decided to start growing our own! And when they kill us, we get them lawyered up like they were American citizens!

Insanity? Ya think?

In the Bel Air's passenger seat was this older, more refined lounge-lizard type, blue blazer, Bing Crosby straw hat with a madras hatband, and, if the chunky gold Rolex was real, maybe even affluent, but still unidentified. Looked druggy. Country Club druggy maybe, but definitely druggy. In his notes, Stoke had written WM instead of a name. White male was the best he could do right now.

Still looking through the field glasses, Brock said, "Contrary to what you may think, the *quesos grandes* in Washington don't consult me on these sensitive matters, Stoke. Hard to believe, I know. But, see, somebody at the Pentagon, or the White House, or on the Seventh Floor at Langley, they order me to do things. And I go do 'em. Or I pay you, or other people like you, to do 'em for me. Get it?"

"I get it," Stoke muttered, letting Harry get under his skin, which was stupid.

"Good. I would think you were old enough and experienced enough in this line of work to understand that fairly basic concept by now."

Harry Brock, handsome in a square-jawed Bruce Willis kind of way, was a ripped, hard-bitten CIA paramilitary officer, now a field agent. He played his assignments pretty close to the vest, but Stoke had always figured Harry for a guy who'd killed more people than most battalions.

Brock and the human mountain known as Stokely Jones, formerly of the U.S. Navy SEALs, the New York Jets, and the New York City Police Department, had enjoyed a lengthy and mostly rewarding working relationship over the years. First working directly with Stoke's closest friend, British MI6 intelligence officer Alex Hawke, and, more recently, Harry'd been hiring Stoke's small intel company, Tactics International, based here in Miami, to work cases in Florida and the Caribbean.

Tactics, jointly owned and operated by Stokely Jones and Alex Hawke, was now operating under government contract to do special ops in south Florida, working for the CIA. Since the federal agency was Tactics's largest client by far, Stoke made nice to Harry even though his wiseass California sense of humor sometimes got on his nerves. Bit of a piss-artist, that's what Alex Hawke had called Harry Brock one time. Right on the money.

"My eyes hurt," Brock said. "Take these glasses for a while, all right?" Stoke shot out a hand the size of a Smithfield ham and palmed the tiny binos. Brock flicked open the glove compartment and pulled out a large pair of Zeiss high-powers. Less discreet, maybe, but easier on the eyeballs.

The supersized Pakistani, suddenly magnified, was instantly more interesting. The guy kept his dark eyes moving constantly, in the rearview, side to side. Looking, or waiting, for someone? Harry felt himself go from simmer to low boil. The Pakistanis, with their unstable government, loose nukes, and Taliban–al Qaeda connections, were giving Iran a run for its money at the very top of the CIA's shit list over the last couple of years.

And a lot of Pakistani émigrés like the chubby legal eagle up there, in the United States either legally or illegally, still officially TBD, were kept under close surveillance these days. Especially since the tragedy at Jackson Memorial Hospital, spearheaded by this puke's two Sword of Allah clients, sprung from Gitmo, who'd escaped prison and killed hundreds of innocent civilians.

What you were seeing were immigrant terrorist gangbangers doing hard time in the prison system, joining or starting Muslim Brotherhood gangs, and then recruiting non-Muslims in the joint and getting the brothers radicalized before they were released into the community.

At this very moment, Stoke's sole employee, Luis Gonzales-Gonzales, a one-armed Cuban he called Sharkey, was one of many who had been sent undercover inside Florida and other state prisons like the Glades, aka the Florida Correctional Institution, trying to penetrate the Sword of Allah.

S.O.A. was one of the newer Muslim gangs to take power within the American prison system, after only two, maybe three years of existence in the United States. It was a group that had already proven itself extraordinarily capable of any atrocity. Scary thing? Harry told him CIA estimated the total American S.O.A. prison membership *already* at over five thousand and climbing. That's five thousand suicidal terrorists sitting around in the slam every day thinking up new ways to kill Americans.

When Stoke told Shark it was a crappy job but somebody had to do it, he meant it. American prisons had quickly become America's own little madrassa hothouses, taxpayer-funded terror training schools where budding Islamic fanatics learned little tricks of the trade like how to blow up major hospitals.

See, you didn't need a 767 full of jet fuel to be a terrorist anymore, he'd told Sharkey right after Jackson Memorial blew sky-high. All you needed was enough suicidal gangbangers wearing backpack bombs and whacked out on meth and religion to take out a whole damn hospital. All you needed was a small sleeper cell school-bus driver in Poughkeepsie bringing his AK-47 to work one day in a pillowcase. And on and on.

What was your run-of-the-mill prison con learning in the joint these days? Not the finer points of vanity license plate production. No. It was how to embrace a hijacked religion, learn how to hate America and kill civilians, that's what, and it wasn't good. You couldn't even trust an ex-con to be patriotic anymore.

"Whaddya see up there, Stoke? Anything unusual? Any action between these two dickwads?"

Stoke shook his head slightly while still looking through the small binoculars. Nothing. But something weird was going on. He couldn't shake the odd feeling that there was more to this than they were seeing.

Yeah.

Definitely feeling jumpy, all of a sudden.

But why?

ELEVEN

The bad hunch made Stokely Jones scan the beach area away from the blue Chevy several times but, aside from a skinny Jamaican Rasta guy, wearing nothing but his jockey tighty-whiteys and matted dreadlocks, doing a one-handed handstand on his skateboard, he saw nothing remotely out of the ordinary.

He shook off the jitters, grabbed a little handheld radio off the dash, and called the CIA Miami field agent sitting two blocks north.

"Armando, you see anyone or anything out of place around here, hombre?"

A raw, tobacco-cured voice came back. "Nope. I gotta say, guys, this is one weird neighborhood for arms deals. What, are those two getting ready to move, you think?"

"No, just checking." Stoke knew Armando Hernandez, the older Hispanic agent, alone in a low-key Jeep Cherokee, was probably happy just to have some time to sit and do that Sudoku stuff he loved so much. Filling in little squares with numbers for hours at a time? What was up with that? Stoke couldn't understand the attraction, but what the hell, the whole damn planet was suddenly flooded with stuff he didn't understand.

Hell, he couldn't even think of a single TV show he'd liked since Redd Foxx died and *Sanford and Son* went off the air.

One thing he had come to realize was just how many freaking third worlders had invaded the Miami metro area. As a New York City Police detective, he'd been assigned to the Bed-Stuy section of Brooklyn, which was a great town if you were a bullet. He had spent so much time on gangs that were either Hispanic or black that he never paid much attention to groups like these radical Muslims. One reason you had that first attack on the World Trade Center in '93?

Nobody gave a damn.

Now, seemed like the whole intel community had Pakistan under a microscope. That pissant, dicked-up country of mass confusion was up to its ass in radicals who wanted to kill Americans. Up in the Northern Territories, the Taliban and al Qaeda were taking turns, blowing shit up every other day. Plus, the fifth-largest country in the world population-wise had a dangerously unstable government, run by a crooked president who got in on a sympathy vote when his beautiful wife was assassinated.

On top of that, there was a whole shitload of loose nukes just sitting there about a mile from the Islamabad airport. Just imagine, Harry said, what would happen if the Taliban/al Qaeda axis of weasels managed to start a war between Pakistan and India. A war that took down the already shaky Pakistani government and put it in the hands of the radical Islamists in the Pak military? Now you've got the world's first Islamic rogue country with nuclear weapons, that's what.

That by itself had gotten Stoke's attention.

So, given all that, the racial profiling part of this current assignment he could understand. Maybe this Hassan guy was a Paki loose-nuke specialist, who knew? Maybe he was doing a drugs-for-weapons deal with Mr. Country Club. But, without more information, it was hard to get excited about stalking the guy's fat ass every damn day.

Brock, borderline bored to tears himself, said to his partner, "How's Fancha doing these days?"

"Been in a bad mood ever since her first solo CD album went out."

"Why?"

"Well, it didn't exactly go platinum."

"Yeah? What did it go?"

"It went plastic."

"Not good."

"No. And now she wants me to give up my beautiful penthouse over on Brickell Key. Move in with her on Key Biscayne. Get married or something."

"So?"

Stoke hated this subject. The whole marriage thing was beginning to spook him a little. Normally, he'd call his pal Hawke about it. But Hawke wasn't giving advice these days. He was still hurting big time over the loss of his fiancée and their baby. Stoke, at one point, had been so worried he'd flown over to Bermuda to surprise him. See if he couldn't get him to snap out of it. But Hawke had already snapped. And he was already completely out of it. After a few heartbreaking days, Stoke left Bermuda fairly sure he'd never see his old friend alive again.

Stoke hefted his binoculars. After a few seconds of holding them aloft, he rested them on the steering wheel and looked at Harry.

"Whoa, do you see that?"

Brock was still watching the two men yakking in the old blue Chevy. "What is it?"

"Chick on Alton now walking straight toward us. More hookers looked like her they'd change the Constitution and make prostitution mandatory."

Brock allowed his larger, high-powered binoculars to veer just far enough to see who his partner was talking about.

She had tight white jeans and long blond hair, but dark features. Her low-rider top exposed plenty of cleavage and her body had the movement and musculature of an athlete. For some reason she didn't really strike Harry as a prostitute. Dead wrong area of town for working girls in the middle of the day. She obviously had no bearing on whatever deal they were watching go down in any case, but he couldn't take his eyes off her.

Stoke refocused his binoculars on the two guys in the Chevy. They were speaking with a whole lot more animation and intensity now. Lots of hand gestures from the Pakistani *Maltese Falcon*–looking guy. The bosomy babe was still half a block away as he started to wonder why she would be dodging cars, walking down the middle of the damn street instead of over on the sidewalk.

Brock, eyes glued to his binoculars, said, "If hookers were horses, this chick would be frickin' Secretariat."

"Yeah, and if all the women in Texas are as ugly as your mama, the Lone Ranger's gonna be alone for a long, long time."

Predictably, Harry fired off a single-digit salute.

Just as Stoke raised his tiny binoculars, Harry flinched in the front seat and shouted, "Jesus F. Christ."

Then Stoke heard the shots. He saw the image a split second later in the lenses of his binoculars. The long-legged prostitute had a small machine pistol pointed at the blue Bel Air and was spraying the two cats they had under surveillance.

She fired in short bursts, controlling the weapon, and keeping the barrel of the small automatic right on target. Knew what she was doing.

Stoke had the passenger door to the Suburban open and was sliding out as he told Harry to call in their position and situation to Armando up the street. Then added, "Call 911, too."

He drew his Glock .40-caliber pistol out of the holster on his hip and had it in his hand as he raced toward the Chevy. The shooting had stopped and he could see blood on the driver's-side door.

The blonde looked up, scanning the area. Her eyes fell on Stoke and she automatically raised the machine pistol toward him.

He darted to one side and crouched behind a parked Volvo

wagon. He heard the rattle as she fired off eight quick rounds. The tire closest to his head popped and hissed as it lost all pressure.

Stoke sprang up, looking to acquire his target, and sighted in where the woman had been standing. He saw nothing except the newly perforated Chevy and two newly dead men in the front seat. His eyes searching across the street with his pistol, he low-crawled up to the next car.

The street was empty.

He stood and moved quickly until the woman stopped at the corner of a run-down motel office.

Stoke had just started toward the motel when she turned and fired again in his direction, forcing him behind the Chevy and its silent occupants.

Then Harry rolled down the street in the blue Suburban. The brakes screeched and the big SUV came to a sudden stop right next to Stoke.

Harry yelled, "Jump in, she's headed west."

Stoke hesitated then decided his foot pursuit had not accomplished much. He kept low as he darted around the front of the Suburban and hopped up into the cab. They were west on the next block, Tenth, he thought, in a couple of seconds.

Harry, panting, said, "What the hell is goin' on?"

"No idea, but that was no simple business deal."

Stoke could hear sirens in the distance as they squealed around the corner and saw a new black Dodge Charger roll away.

Harry punched the gas and the lumbering Suburban closed the distance. When they were directly behind the smaller car, a heavily muscled arm popped out the passenger-side window with a machine pistol that Stoke could see was an old MAC-10. Without exposing his head, the man sprayed a dozen rounds. About half of them pinged off the big Suburban, causing Harry to jerk the wheel violently in every conceivable direction.

Stoke groped for the seat belt, hoping to secure himself as the truck swayed, hesitated, then flipped off the street, rolled once, and struck a utility pole. The Suburban came to rest on the passenger side, wheels spinning uselessly in the air. Worse than not wearing his own seat belt, his partner Harry was also unsecured and Stoke saw him become unwedged from the steering wheel and seem to float through the air for a moment before landing directly on top of him.

Not only was everything dark, it was pit-smelly as hell. Don't you wish Harry used Dial? Don't you wish everybody did?

"Harry?"

"Yeah?"

"Could you please remove your left elbow from my right eyeball?"

"Oh. Sorry."

"Hate to disturb you, my brother. But I have to leave now."

TWELVE

MIAMI

STOKE SOMEHOW SQUIRMED HIS MASSIVE BULK out from under Harry Brock, who wasn't exactly fighting featherweight division himself, and squeezed delicately out through the shattered windshield. He turned and tried to help Brock exit the vehicle, taking both of Harry's wrists in his hands and pulling. Something was stuck. Seat belt wrapped around his leg?

"Are you hurt?" Stoke asked. Harry had a major gash above both eyes that gave him that bloody horror-movie look, only now the blood looked real.

"Naw, just a little embarrassed about that utility pole, thanks," Brock said, using both hands to scoop the fresh blood from his eye sockets.

"Yeah, I thought they taught high-speed pursuit where you went to junior college."

They both turned their heads as Armando in the white Jeep Cherokee screeched to a stop next to the Suburban currently wrapped around the utility pole. The beefy older agent popped out, fear etched on his face, a dead cigar jammed in one corner of his mouth.

"Jesus, are you guys okay?"

Stoke was already running for the idling Jeep. "Armando, help Brock climb out of that mess and tell someone I'm in pursuit of a late-model black Dodge Charger westbound over the MacArthur Causeway. They gotta be headed that way."

He didn't wait for a response and was in the Jeep pushing the sketchy 3.7 liter V-6 to its absolute limits right from the start. He felt the top-heavy vehicle tilt as he took a right turn hard. The CIA had bought the car for surveillance, not speed. Stoke felt the Cherokee shudder and tilt again as he took the turn onto the causeway, ignoring traffic signals and other vehicles just like he was racing down the final furlong at Hialeah.

Horns blared and he was aware of hostility from other drivers, but at least he was where he wanted to be.

He leaned forward and searched far ahead, hoping to catch a glimpse of the black Charger with the deadly blonde inside. Star Island whipped by on his right, then Palm Island. The bay was just another detail he had to ignore as he weaved in and out of traffic, almost clipping a lawn service truck packed most likely with illegal Guatemalans.

Laying on the horn to get people's attention, he finally started getting a clear view of the road ahead, the causeway rolling onto the little key that was home to Parrot Jungle. His heart raced as he took the long curve flat out. He saw the Charger. In addition to the blonde, there were three or four guys. They were cool, driving calmly, right at the speed limit.

Stoke gathered enough presence of mind to calm down, blend in behind them, and call in his position to Miami-Dade PD. He reached into his pocket. Empty. He patted his pants, then realized his phone was in the wreckage of the Suburban they'd wasted back at the beach.

His hand slapped his hip, and he was relieved to feel the weight of his pistol still in its holster. He tried to figure out how many rounds he had left and decided he was ready with the extra magazine he had clipped to the other side of his belt, hidden by a loose, unbuttoned Aloha shirt. The Miami Dolphins T-shirt he wore underneath was soaked through with sweat.

He waited as the black car rolled toward the mainland and the city of Miami. This was a good thing. If they got into a chase over there no one knew the streets better than he did. Not after three years of on-and-off patrols and dead-end stakeouts all over this tropical paradise.

Then things changed for the worse.

The driver of the Charger spotted him. Stoke saw the passengers inside all turn around at once, then the car swerved violently across a lane, cutting off a taxi, to take the exit onto Biscayne as the Charger rapidly picked up speed.

He yanked the steering wheel and fell in behind them as they blew through the light at the base of the ramp and swerved south on Biscayne, causing two oncoming cars to squeal to a stop, fishtailing at the green light. Stoke took advantage of the traffic stoppage and rolled through the same light, jerking to one side on Biscayne to avoid a utility worker still yelling and giving the single-finger salute to the Charger speeding south.

As the Charger fast approached a railroad crossing, the big red lights started flashing and the gates started coming down. The driver accelerated, beating the gates and getting airborne as he crossed the elevated tracks. Stoke, who could see the Atlantic Coastline freight train speeding toward him out of the corner of his eye, had no choice. He floored it, crashed through the gates, caught air, and made it across the tracks just before the roaring train could clip his rear bumper.

At Bicentennial Park, the Charger suddenly took a sharp right to head west. Stoke now knew the driver definitely wasn't local because he was headed into the hood and if you'd ever been there, you knew there weren't a lot of ways out. Plus, I-95 would keep him from going farther west. Stoke was closing the gap, the guy behind the wheel unsure of himself now.

Then the Charger clipped a parked car when it took the next corner too sharply, and the guy spun out, tires smoking, careening into the parking lot of an abandoned office complex.

Keeping his tactical sense about him, Stoke pulled across the exit to the lot, blocking it, and stopped the Cherokee. Throwing the door open, he rolled out to one side, keeping an eye on the Charger's occupants, especially the killer blonde.

The first burst of fire told him one of the others in the car had something much heavier than a MAC-10. The assault rifle rattled the tin can Jeep and forced Stoke to fall back to a delivery van parked out on the street.

The gunfire followed him and he moved farther back, sensing instantly that this was a stupid idea. Like the doggie who finally caught the car, now he'd caught it he didn't know what the hell to do with it. He was facing at least four heavily armed assailants who had a huge advantage in this confrontation. The police jargon for this kind of thing was an asymmetrical situation. Basically, it meant you were fucked. This day wasn't going at all like he'd planned.

He crouched and waited, slammed a fresh mag into the Glock, hoping to God the Miami-Dade cops would respond soon. He needed help and needed it right that second. Anybody listening out there? Or, God help me, up there? He crossed himself, using his Glock hand.

Then a shot came from the side of the parked truck on his left and he knew he'd been flanked. He whirled around to see a young, muscular man in jeans and a T-shirt point a pistol and fire another three rounds at him.

This was a tight spot and he obviously had no backup. He was dicked and re-dicked. He knew it, they knew it. Advantage, assholes. He fired two rounds back at the man, mainly to keep the guy's head down and then looked for any other position that might be safer.

The blond Amazon queen had stayed by the Charger and had a MAC-10 sighted down on him. The other two men were moving in a fast crouch to his right.

Was this how his career was going to end?

Maybe, but not without a fight.

Stokely strained to hear any hint of approaching sirens but with all the guns going off, every damn one of them pointing at him, it tended to drown out any chance he had of hearing help on the way. The only reason he was still alive today was that he was really good in situations exactly like this one. He took comfort in that, stopped feeling sorry for himself, and put his damn brain and instincts to work.

Time to man the hell up, Stoke.

He decided to make them come to him and use his handgun in the smartest way possible, up close and personal.

Then he got his wish as this muscle-bound dirtbag popped up right next to him. Where the hell had he come from?

Stoke turned, raised his pistol, and fired before it was all the way up. The first round hit the man in the knee, stunning him for a second. The next round blew out his hip, sending him sprawling onto the rough asphalt, his pistol loose at his side.

Stoke kicked the unfamiliar semiautomatic away from the wounded man, now twisting and moaning in pain on the ground. Before he could even assess the guy's injuries, more rounds bounced off the truck near his head, making him duck. He was still seriously outgunned and outnumbered.

He quick-peeked around the rear of the truck and saw the long-haired man with the heavy assault rifle start to advance on him, moving fast. Shit. Then it got weird. Without any action from Stoke, more shots rang out and suddenly the advancing ponytail dropped straight to the ground in the parking lot, his big black rifle clattering to the asphalt and blood pooling under him.

What the hell?

More shots came from a car somewhere behind and to the right of Stoke. Then this bloody-faced guy pops up, firing at the blonde with the MAC-10 as he advanced. He was good, sent her scrambling for cover. Satisfied, he dove behind the truck right next to Stoke.

Harry Brock said calmly, "You doing okay, little buddy?"

Stoke stared at him silently and nodded his head at his partner. "How the hell—?"

"I requisitioned a civilian vehicle, got your position from Miami-Dade. A brand-new Corvette convertible, actually. Scared that poor sumbitch to death when I reached in and pulled his keys. Sorry I'm late but I got stuck at that railroad crossing where you almost bought it. Longest goddamn train I've ever seen. You're lucky you made it, partner."

"Jesus, Harry."

"Stay cool, all right?"

Without another word, Brock scrambled away, reached down, grabbed the badly injured man on the ground, hoisted him onto his shoulders, and then ran flat out across the parking lot, using the man as a makeshift shield, firing steadily at the others as he crossed the lot.

Stoke naturally thought Harry was crazy because no one in his right mind would pull a stunt like that. But Harry could shoot, no one disputed that. Stoke snuck another peek and saw the bearded Charger guy aiming where Brock had already dumped the guy and disappeared behind a pimped-up Ford 150 truck with chrome dubs glinting in the sun.

The blond chick, too, was shielding her eyes, lining up on the position where Harry was crouching.

Stoke took a second to carefully line up the long shot with a handgun and fired three times at the blond woman. She dove for cover, yelled something to the remaining accomplice, and stayed low, starting to move toward the Charger. First the bearded asshole ran out to drag back his lifeless comrade.

Stoke scrambled to the other side of the truck and saw Harry Brock stand up behind the truck bed and take dead aim at the Charger as its engine roared to life. He fired twice, two long bursts, then ducked to avoid a spray from the MAC-10. Seconds later he popped up again, looked over at Stoke, smiled, shot him a thumbs-up, then ducked down again behind the 150.

The black Charger left a lot of rubber behind peeling out of the lot and screeched to a halt on the far side of the street. Stoke saw them load the other injured man into the backseat and then speed off.

Then he heard sirens.

Finally.

Just the end of another perfect day in paradise, baby.

And how was your day, darling?

THIRTEEN

HIGHGROVE

TWO SPECIAL BRANCH DETECTIVES WERE STATIONED on either side of the closed dining room doors. Officers of SO14, or the Royalty Protection Squad, were charged with providing high-level security for at least twenty members of the Royal Family. Two more were stationed outside, working in the shrubbery beneath the windows, disguised as gardeners. All were discreetly but heavily armed.

Security was always tight at Highgrove, but after what had happened to Lord Hawke this morning, Special Branch had gone to another level entirely. Nearly half the people on the estate at this moment were Special Branch, many of them disguised as farmers in the fields, gardeners, gillies, and horse trainers.

"I should like to begin this afternoon's meeting by once again welcoming everyone to Highgrove," Prince Charles began.

They were all comfortably seated at a round dining table in a large windowed bay. This was the small dining room that overlooked the kitchen gardens. Luncheon had been efficiently served and was being cleared. A few luncheon plates remained on the carved mahogany table, but they were quickly being replaced with pads and pens at each place, crystal pitchers full of iced water, tumblers for seven, and the red leather portfolio containing the two death threats discovered by the Prince of Wales.

Seated at a small desk located at a discreet distance behind the Prince was his private secretary, Sir Hugh Raleigh, a thin, balding fellow in a shapeless tweed jacket, quietly taking notes. Hawke watched him, realizing that this unremarkable amanuensis was in reality the true keeper of the gate. And, thus, the source of enormous power.

Conversation during luncheon had naturally consisted of events surrounding the ambush of Hawke and Congreve on the road earlier. Next to nil had been said about the topic that had brought them all together. The room went silent as the door was opened by a footman and a beautiful black-haired woman in a severely tailored pink Chanel suit appeared, striding purposefully toward the table.

"Sorry to be late, sir," she said with a shy smile and a little bob of a curtsy to the Prince of Wales.

Charles got to his feet and walked across the room to greet her.

"Sahira Karim," he said. "We're so glad you're here, Doctor Karim. Welcome to Highgrove."

She bowed her head slightly and said, "A great honor to meet you, Your Royal Highness."

"Come sit down and have a bite to eat. You're not too late and you must be starving. You know most everyone here, I assume. Have you met my dear friend Lord Hawke and Chief Inspector Ambrose Congreve?"

"Lord Hawke and I are old friends," Sahira said, going over and shaking his hand. "But I've not had the pleasure of meeting the famous Chief Inspector Congreve. It's a great honor, sir," she said extending her hand and smiling warmly.

Without being asked, a liveried steward put a fresh place setting on the table for the new arrival. Hawke suddenly found himself seated next to Lord Malmsey's MI5 assistant, this youngish, extraordinarily attractive Indian woman who had been engaged to one of Hawke's closest friends.

Anthony Soames-Taylor had been at Fettes with Hawke and

they'd shared a common love of shooting and foxhunting while at school and then later in life. Tony had been tragically killed in the terror holocaust at Heathrow the year prior and Hawke had not seen his fiancée since.

He'd forgotten what an extraordinarily good-looking woman she was. He'd always been slightly mesmerized by her lambent beauty.

"Miss Karim," Prince Charles said, "I wonder if you could update us on your findings at the scene of the ambush this morning?"

"Yes, sir. Five of the six attackers escaped in the Jaguar sedan. We've got police checkpoints on all roads leading out of Gloucestershire, but we imagine they've ditched their clothing and the original car and are now driving a stolen vehicle, possibly two. I think they may have slipped the noose, unfortunately, otherwise we'd almost certainly have them by now."

"Sorry to interrupt," Hawke said, "but you should reduce the number you're looking for from five to four. I shot one in the Jaguar during the chase."

"Dead?"

"Very."

"Thank you, makes our job a bit easier. On the other hand, there is some very good news. We managed to get the vehicle ident number off the burned Rover. We've already run it against MI5's national terror database. Belongs to a man named Sean Fahey, one of the assassins involved in the recent murder of the two British Army soldiers in Northern Ireland.

"We now know for certain that the attack on Lord Hawke and Chief Inspector Congreve was an IRA operation. We've no idea how they learned of this meeting, but clearly the attack was meant as a warning shot across our bow. We know who the attackers were, and our investigation is thus off to a flying start, I'm happy to report."

Hawke and Congreve looked at each other across the table. Hawke, astounded, mouthed the letters *IRA?* and Congreve nodded. If the IRA knew about this most secret of meetings, one had to wonder just how far up the political ladder this treachery went. Still, he reminded himself, there could easily be a horse groom or trainer here at Highgrove who was an IRA sympathizer and paid informant. Anything was possible at this point.

"Excellent, Sahira," Charles said. "Good work! Now please don't let good manners spoil good food. The lamb is marvelous, I think you'll find."

The table fell back into general conversation and, after Hawke whispered his thanks to the beautiful Indian MI5 officer, they began discussing the ambush in great detail. It was the first real conversation he'd had with an attractive woman in over a year, and he found himself oddly ill at ease.

"Alex," she said softly, "I've never thanked you for the incredibly kind phone call you made after Tony's death that night at Heathrow. Your funny stories and memories of your school days together touched me deeply."

"I'm still sorry for your loss, Sahira. One never gets over these things, I'm afraid."

She looked at him and placed her hand over his. "Alex, I never wrote to you after your own devastating loss. I couldn't find words to express my sympathy, I'm afraid. I do hope you'll forgive me someday."

Alex had no reply.

Always difficult, talking to a beautiful woman, to be sure, but he noticed her eyes still lingering on him, a few seconds too long, and it was disquieting. Luckily, the conversation was soon cut short.

Judging by the set of Prince Charles's jaw, Hawke knew they would clearly be getting down to business. Charles rose to his feet.

"Time to attend to matters at hand, I'm afraid. I would ask one thing. Please let's do keep this discussion informal. As of this moment we are all simply colleagues, not Royals and subjects. Consider me one of the team and do not hesitate to pose any question to me at all. I will do the same. Do we all agree?"

Everyone nodded heads, answering in the affirmative.

"Obviously," Charles continued, "my family have borne threats of greater magnitude before. In September 1940, a German Dornier bomber was moments from destroying Buckingham Palace. But RAF Fighter Command pilot Ray Holmes, whose Hurricane's eight guns had just run out of ammo, had other ideas.

"He deliberately rammed the German bomber in mid-air at 400 mph, taking off its tail section. Holmes parachuted to safety. The stricken Nazi bomber missed the palace entirely and slammed into the ground near Victoria Station with such force that it was embedded in the soil."

Charles paused a beat, looked around the table, and added, "My stalwart grandmother, who remained in London throughout the Blitz, was, needless to say, stirred, but not shaken."

There were polite chuckles and smiles all round and the Prince continued.

"However, I can assure you that my family find this present circumstance most unpleasant. The Queen herself is sanguine. I am not. I am convinced that these past and recent threats to the Monarchy are real. And that the IRA killers behind them are keen, determined, and fully capable of achieving their ends. Witness this morning's atrocity on the road to Tetbury. We are extraordinarily lucky to have Chief Inspector Congreve and Lord Alex Hawke here with us today."

There were quiet murmurs of approval around the table.

"The first question I have is for you, Chief Inspector Congreve. You were part of the on-site team that investigated Lord Mountbatten's murder in Ireland, were you not?"

"I was, sir."

"And were you satisfied with the outcome of that investigation? An IRA operation?"

"At the time, in the main, I would have to say yes, sir. We all were. However, subsequent events, the note you found in Lord Mountbatten's book, for instance, might lead me to rethink our conclusions."

Charles said, "The two men charged with the murder were both IRA Provisionals, of course."

"Yes, sir."

"But only one went to prison. McMahon. Odd, isn't it?"

"Thomas McMahon, yes, sir."

"And the other suspect?"

"The prosecution was unable to build a strong enough case against the second suspect, a man named McGirl, Your Highness."

Charles smiled at the inadvertent use of his title. He was accustomed to it. "But, still and all, your team were ultimately convinced that McMahon was guilty, am I correct, Chief Inspector Congreve?"

"I certainly was at the time, sir. My Irish colleague, Constable Drummond, had learned that McMahon had trained as a bomb maker in Libya. And there were traces of nitroglycerine on his clothing when he was arrested. His fingerprints were all over that bomb. Molded gelignite was his signature explosive."

"Still, Chief Inspector, I have examined the record carefully. It clearly shows McMahon was some seventy miles away when the bomb that killed Uncle Dickie exploded. It's certainly possible that a third party was involved?"

"Yes, sir. We were forced to conclude that the bomb was detonated by a remote radio-controlled device. Operated by someone other than McMahon, watching from the shore. Hidden in the woods above the bay, but able to visually confirm Lord Mountbatten's presence aboard *Shadow V.*"

"In other words, it is entirely possible that the man who made the bomb was IRA, but the man who pushed the button was not even IRA?"

"Entirely possible, sir. But I must say with the evidence we had, no one doubted this was an IRA operation. The IRA claimed sole credit for the assassination within hours of the explosion. And that was the end of it."

"Sir David, your point of view?"

"I'd have to agree with your line of thought, sir. The death threat you found is reason enough to speculate that someone else, perhaps not even affiliated with the IRA, may have been involved in the murder. Sympathetic to their cause, perhaps, but not directly connected. A third party. Someone deeply aggrieved, and waging a personal vendetta against Mountbatten."

"So, a third suspect. Involved in the assassination, but perfectly willing to let IRA Provos take all the credit, Sir David?" Hawke asked his MI6 superior.

"Something like that, yes. Deflect suspicion in order to carry out a personal agenda."

"But, why? Why commit the murder of the century, at that point, and not take the credit?"

The Prince of Wales thought for a few moments and said, "Indeed, Alex. Someone with an altogether different, nonpolitical motive is a distinct possibility. Someone with an apolitical, deep-seated, personal grievance against Lord Mountbatten. A disgruntled employee, a stable groom, for instance. It happens all the time. Of course, all of this speculation certainly doesn't preclude the fact that the perpetrator was simply a third IRA conspirator."

"It certainly does not, sir," Congreve said quietly. "With all due respect, sometimes a cigar is just a cigar."

Charles said to Thorne, "Monty, you've made a private study of Uncle Dickie's murder. Your thoughts?"

Hawke looked over at Thorne. He'd arrived at the luncheon in a startling three-piece white suit, beautifully tailored, a sky blue silk tie, and a pair of shoes to make even Congreve seethe with envy. Traditional wingtips, but made of snow-white suede. In the grey world that was MI6, here was a strutting peacock of the first order.

Thorne gently cleared his throat, looking around the table until he was sure all eyes were upon him before speaking.

"I'm sure you're all aware that, despite his heinous crime, Mr. McMahon is today a free man, having been released in the Good Friday Agreement. Outrageous, but there you have it. And, shortly after his release, Prince Charles receives a second death threat with an identical signature to the Mountbatten threat. Mere coincidence? Perhaps. But, as Chief Inspector Congreve so eloquently put it, 'Sometimes a cigar is just a cigar.' Therefore, we are looking at him again, hard. It is my position that Thomas McMahon is the most plausible suspect in this new threat."

"Anyone know of Mr. McMahon's last known whereabouts?" Congreve asked.

"Last known address after prison was a council flat in Belfast," Thorne said.

"I think I might pop over and have a chat with his neighbors about his present whereabouts," Ambrose said. "Sooner rather than later."

"Good idea." Thorne leaned forward and said, "Look here, despite the fact that this case was closed over thirty years ago, I'm quite happy to discuss other possible suspects. But, I beg you, let's not dispute known facts. We know the motive, of course, do we not? Whoever penned the first death threat obviously blamed Mountbatten and the Royals personally for the horrific tragedy that befell his mother country."

"Ireland?" Sir David said. "Or perhaps India?"

Montague Thorne unsuccessfully suppressed a weary sigh. "Yes, of course, Ireland, Sir David. *Split in two*? Bled us white? Pawns in the game? This has been the quintessential Irish mantra for centuries. Still, the record clearly shows that no stone was left unturned in the investigation. MI6 looked at the Soviets for it, primarily the KGB. And also at the Libyans, where the bomber McMahon had trained. He was IRA, no doubt about it, and this was clearly an IRA operation."

Sir David, agitated, persisted with the line of questioning. "But why didn't the killer simply act alone? Suppose he wasn't even IRA? A lone killer with motives of his own? Certainly possible. Then why does he involve the IRA at all? Sympathy for the cause? Or simply to divert suspicion away from himself and his true motives?"

Hawke looked up, stroking his chin. "Possibly both, Sir David. But the murderer also needed a bomb, and Lord knows there were plenty being built around Belfast at the time. More bomb factories than pubs. Ideally, he would have to find a bomb maker reasonably nearby Mountbatten's residence in Northern Ireland."

Congreve said, "Precisely. Someone exactly like Tom McMahon, the resident IRA bomb expert of County Sligo. And, let it be said, a fellow who would have enormous incentive to lend the real murderer a hand. Possible, isn't it?"

"All quite possible, wouldn't you admit, Lord Malmsey," Hawke said, looking at the MI5 man whose responsibility it was to keep his eye on the restive immigrant populations of England and Northern Ireland.

Malmsey, flustered, shifted uncomfortably in his chair. "Of course anything is possible. I'm not at all sure where this line of thought is headed."

Hawke, smiling, said, "Lord Malmsey, a hypothetical question. Based upon the language contained in the first note Prince Charles discovered, our killer had an abiding, visceral, personal hatred of his victim, Mountbatten. Wouldn't you agree? And supposing, for the time being, perhaps, being less politically motivated than the IRA, this hypothetical murderer had far less need of taking credit for his death. Yes?"

"I suppose," Malmsey replied, unconvinced.

Hawke continued. "Then we come to the new threat His Royal Highness has received, carrying the identical signature. Surely you'll agree it would lead one to believe this personal vendetta is still ongoing, thirty years after the fact. Yes, or no?"

"Yes, I suppose it's possible."

"So, what is the current threat level aimed at the Royal Family? Any recent uptick we should all be aware of? And, if so, where is it coming from?"

"Uptick is putting it mildly," Lord Malmsey said.

FOURTEEN

LORD MALMSEY NARROWED HIS EYES. Threats had risen dramatically in recent years, as a new generation of young Royals traveled the dangerous world, leading very active social lives. It had put enormous budget and manpower pressure on resources at both Scotland Yard and MI5, and there were no easy answers.

Plus, Britain had an increasingly restive, percolating immigrant Muslim population and was ill-equipped to deal with them effectively. Common knowledge. He was doing the best he could with limited resources, stretched thin. But, were he to be honest, Malmsey feared for his job lately.

He'd recently been pressured by the Home Secretary to promote Miss Karim to her new position even though he'd made it plain he believed such advancement was premature if not wholly unwarranted. The woman was glamorous, intelligent, and, he thought, far too interested in seeing her name in the newspapers. But he was an old hand. And he wasn't through yet.

He looked at her and thought, *What sharp little eyes you have, my dear. Wait until you get to my teeth.*

Lord Malmsey said, "I'd like to let Miss Karim answer that question. She spends every waking moment dealing with the domestic radical Muslim situation. Miss Karim?"

"The reality of the situation is this," Sahira said, rising to her feet, and Hawke found himself gazing at her with unfeigned interest. She was perhaps not beautiful in the classic sense of the word, but she was an extraordinarily handsome woman, had a remarkable figure, and was clearly brilliant. He now remembered why he'd considered his late friend Tony Soames-Taylor such a lucky man.

She said, "Yes, we have certainly picked up a rising number of threats to the Family. And I can state unequivocally that the vast majority of them originate in the Muslim community. And we run down every single one. We've yet to find many truly credible threats to the Royals. Mostly hoaxsters, cranks, poseurs, that sort."

"Can you be more specific about the threat level, Miss Karim?" Hawke asked.

"I would say we now average five to six threats against Her Royal Majesty alone every week, two or three for the heir to the throne. Most come to naught when we run them down, thank God. The ones who appear serious are arrested and investigated."

"And what's the profile of your targets?" Trulove asked Sahira Karim.

"The youth, Sir David. The disenfranchised young Muslim residents of the Indian and Pakistani barrios of the East End in London. The truth is, London has become an incubator for violent Islamic extremism, a rage fueled by disenchantment at home and growing anger about the wars in Iraq, northern Pakistan, and Afghanistan."

Sahira Karim continued. "Our long tradition of tolerance has made us an oasis for immigrants and political outcasts from around the world. The large influx of Pakistanis and other Muslims in the '70s and '80s led to the nickname Londonistan. Britain currently houses Europe's largest Muslim communities."

"Who keeps you awake at night, Miss Karim?" Prince Charles suddenly asked.

"Other than my neighbors in the flat upstairs? The Pakistanis, sir. All of my attention is focused on them at the moment. Recent Internet chatter is most disturbing. And, as in America, our prisons have become recruiting and training centers for militants and suicide bombers. I am certain more homegrown domestic terror attacks are coming."

"Pakistan," Hawke said. "Now there's a country that scares the living daylights out of me."

"As well it should, Alex," C said. "Mr. Thorne here is flying out to Afghanistan and Pakistan tomorrow for one of his regular visits with our sympathetic commanders and warlords in the Northern Provinces. You and I will discuss the Pakistan situation with him when he returns next week."

"May we get back to the specific threats against the Crown?" Ambrose asked C.

"Of course."

Congreve coughed discreetly into his closed fist and said, "I'm obviously very disturbed that His Royal Highness found the latest threat in this very room. Taped to the underside of a revolving chessboard. Outrageous. I'm going to need a look at the Highgrove guest book going back at least a month. See who had access to this room. And I think every employee on the estate should be exhaustively interviewed by Special Branch."

"Agreed," Charles said. "It's certainly nervous-making. I've been advised to return with my family to Clarence House in London, but I'd much rather stay here, to be perfectly honest."

"We've already trebled security on the estate," the Prince's private secretary said, looking up from his notes. "Perhaps we should quadruple it for the time being? Until this matter is resolved?"

"Yes, I fully intend to do that at all the Royal residences and palaces until we get to the bottom of this," Lord Malmsey said, "effective immediately."

Prince Charles was suddenly getting to his feet, looking around the table at each of them. The meeting was coming to an end.

He had very kind eyes, Hawke thought, watching him. A gentle, thoughtful man who tried very hard to do his duty to his beloved England. This was the man who would be King, and a damn fine one, Hawke thought, one day. He suddenly remembered why the two of them had grown so close over the years. A common sense of duty. And a lack of any sense of privilege.

"Thank you all very much indeed for being here," Charles said. "After this extraordinarily thorough and extremely helpful discussion, I suggest we all have an extra glass or two of claret at dinner this evening, or none of us shall sleep a wink all night. Dinner will be served promptly at eight. I look forward to seeing you there. We are adjourned."

Hawke picked up his pen and scrawled a note to Ambrose, folding it carefully and passing it to him as discreetly as he could. The detective, keeping the note out of sight, opened it and read these words:

Mountbatten, Ambrose. That's where this all begins.
Find out who really killed him, and we find our villain.
H.

HAWKE WAS DRESSING FOR DINNER that evening when he heard a soft tapping on his bedchamber door.

Opening it, and still fussing with his ill-behaved black tie, he saw Ambrose Congreve standing there in the wide hall, firing up his pipe.

"Oh, hullo, Alex. Not dressed yet? I wonder if I might have a word?"

"Good timing, old dragon. Can you help me with this damnable bow tie? I hate these things, don't know how Churchill had the patience for them every day, especially when Hitler was breathing fire down his neck."

"Go over to the mirror. I have to stand behind you and tie it the way I normally do. And look at your pocket handkerchief. It's all wrong."

As Congreve got him properly adorned, Hawke said, "You've something on your mind. I can smell it on you. Or perhaps it's just your cologne."

"It's about the old Mountbatten case."

"Speak, memory."

"I didn't want to mention this in front of His Royal Highness, or anyone else in that room. Might raise false expectations. Might start a wild-goose chase."

"I'll chase any goose you've got at this point. Spill it."

"There was a third suspect in our original investigation. We called him the 'third man.' "

"Really?"

"We kept his name out of the press. You could do that in those days. We couldn't find him. We tried for years. The man was a ghost. Cold case."

"You're talking about him being the button pusher? The Mountbatten bomb?"

"Hmm. Possibly. We were looking at him for something entirely different, but yes, he might well have been this 'Pawn' as he styles himself."

"An Irishman?"

"Most likely, yes. We got on to him through a paid informant inside Sinn Fein. This fellow was spending a lot of time in Northern Ireland. We had hearsay evidence that he met secretly with McGirl and McMahon the bomb builder a few times prior to Mountbatten's murder."

"What were you originally looking at him for, then?"

"A series of murders that occurred over that summer, in Northern Ireland. A brutal serial killer. With a signature. All victims were young women. Pretty. Fair skinned, blond, blue eyes. The women were just random girls abducted from the forests and seashore around Belfast and Sligo, hikers, picnic types. That was the only element in common. The whole north of Ireland was terrified that summer. They'd even given our third man a moniker. They called him the Maniac in those days."

"And?"

"The murders stopped with the death of Lord Mountbatten. He never struck again. At least to my knowledge. My colleagues and I continued our search for him long after the trial had ended. We even offered a huge reward for information leading to his arrest. Nothing. I believe to this day he was Mountbatten's killer. Long dead now. Or just very good at hiding. There is no 'Serial Killers Anonymous,' you know. Serial killers don't stop. They either get caught or they die. So suicide or some kind of accidental death would be the likely scenario."

"Fascinating. Did you ever have a name?"

"We did. Smith."

"Just Smith?"

"Yes, Alex."

"I think our next stop is Northern Ireland. This Smith needs finding. Serial killers suffer from overwhelming feelings of inadequacy, as you well know, Constable. They crave publicity, notoriety. But they don't care whether they're famous or infamous. Our man Smith may well be the 'pawn' who murdered Lord Mountbatten as well as all those poor girls. Although God only knows why."

"Find him and we'll know why," Congreve said. "If he's still alive."

"What about Miss Karim's concern about increasing Muslim extremist threats to Charles and his family?"

"I can't really say at this point. I don't discount threats from any quarter. Smith's crimes could easily be simply coincident with the political assassination of a Royal in Mullaghmore. However, Alex, I still believe what you said in the note you passed to me. It all begins with Mountbatten."

"I pray I'm right. We don't have a lot of time."

"I'm afraid you're closer to the truth than you know, Alex."

"Why?"

"The name 'Pawn' was never made public. It was a very long time ago, you know, 1979."

"And, Smith? Did that name go public?"

"No, it did not."

"One thing occurred to me while dressing," Hawke said. "I don't want to alarm you."

"Yes?"

"I was driving in the center of the road when the Jaguar pulled alongside the Locomotive."

"Yes?"

"He could have easily gone to the driver's side, but he didn't. He went to your side."

"I was the target?"

"Possibly. And now that we know it was an IRA hit, well . . ."

"Smith is after me, too. He's aware of my role in the Mountbatten investigation. He knows I was on to him. And he doesn't want me prying into this matter again."

"My thoughts exactly. And he has someone on the inside. Either here at Highgrove, or Buckingham Palace. An equerry, a secretary, anyone who is privy to HRH's personal schedule. How are you getting along with the new regime at Scotland Yard, Constable?"

"I'm a god there. Always will be."

"Very funny. I've arranged for a driver to get us back to London immediately following lunch on Sunday. So tell Diana you'll be returning early enough to take her to your regular supper at the Connaught Grill."

"Will you join us? She'd adore to see you."

"Thanks, no. I've an early meeting with C Monday morning, so I plan to have a quiet evening at home and get some sleep. But perhaps you could have a word with the Royalty Protection Squad at the Yard first thing Monday morning? Explain the whole situation to SO14 and also my suspicions about an IRA death squad perhaps stalking you, as well as Charles. We could use a little help."

"Consider it done."

"I've spoken to my pilots. We're taking my plane to Sligo airport in Northern Ireland Monday afternoon. Wheels up at three. Not a long drive to Mullaghmore from there. We'll hire a car."

FIFTEEN

LONDON

THERE WERE FEW THINGS IN LIFE Alex Hawke treasured more than being alone at home on a rainy Sunday night. His large house in Belgravia had many nooks and crannies where he could curl up with a good book. But it was the small window seat in the third-story sitting room overlooking Belgrave Square that he loved most. A hard, slashing rain beat against the windowpanes as he turned the yellowed pages of the book given him by Prince Charles at Highgrove.

He'd wandered into Charles's library after dinner the first night, looking for something to read himself to sleep. Charles had entered the room looking for some documents on his desk and had recommended *Our Man in Havana* by Graham Greene.

The book was the tale of an Englishman named Wormold, a divorced vacuum cleaner salesman in Havana. Wormold is, for various obscure reasons, recruited by the British Secret Service as a spy. Hawke found himself laughing aloud in parts and soon realized that Charles had not chosen the book at random. He'd meant it as an inside joke, but he had also known Hawke would love it. Wormold's biggest seller was a vacuum called the "Atomic Pile."

An inspired choice. And, even though the book was quite good fun, he found himself drifting off periodically, only to wake and gaze across the room at the dimly lit painting hung above the mantel. His mother, seated, was lovely in a long white satin dress; and his father, standing beside her in his dress navy uniform, ramrod straight, looked every bit the modest hero Hawke knew him to be. The portrait had been painted just weeks after their wedding.

They looked so very happy, he thought, and so very much in love. And so blissfully unaware of the unspeakably cruel fate the future had lying in wait for them in the short decade they would have together.

From downstairs came the faint echo of the front door bell. He looked at his watch. After eleven. Who in the world? He put the book aside and stood up. You could see the front entrance from this window if you tried hard enough.

He peered down, but all he saw was the top of a large and glistening black umbrella at his door. Pelham was no doubt making his way to the door at this very second, and a few moments later he watched the umbrella pass between the four great fluted pillars of white marble and make its way inside his house on Belgrave Square.

He glanced at the telephone on his writing desk, waiting for the intercom button to start flashing.

It accommodated him and he picked up the receiver.

"Someone to see you, m'lord," Pelham said, calling from his private pantry.

"I was afraid of that. Perhaps they could see you instead."

"You yourself were specifically requested, sir. I'm sorry to disturb your solitude."

"Who is it?"

"A Miss Sahira Karim, sir. On her way home from a party at the Indian ambassador's residence and thought she'd pop in and say hello."

"Well, I suppose it could be worse."

"Indeed, sir. Quite a lovely woman. But I suspect perhaps madam was overserved at the soiree and thus the lateness of the hour."

"Where is she now?"

"At the drinks table in the drawing room, sir. Pouring herself a rather large scotch if I may be indiscreet."

"I'm in my pajamas and a robe. Do you think that will suffice?"

"I would strongly advise against it, sir."

"Oh, all right, I'll throw something on and be down in five minutes."

"I shall inform her of your intentions, sir. Shall I light the fire? There's a bit of a chill in that room and she's soaked to the bone."

"Yes, yes, of course. Thank you, Pelham."

"My pleasure, sir."

Hawke found Sahira sitting cross-legged, Buddha-like, on the floor in front of the roaring fire. She had her back to him, but he could see she was sipping whiskey from a crystal tumbler. He regarded her in silence for a moment, taking in the long black hair, still wet and gleaming in the firelight. She was wearing an elegant silk sari. The folds of fabric were silver-gold with veils of aquamarine. It held its sheen, even soaking wet. Hawke guessed she was wearing something very bright and colorful, perhaps a ruby brooch, at her neck.

"Sahira," Hawke said softly from the doorway, so as not to alarm her.

She turned fully around and said as she smiled, "Dear Alex, you must think me quite mad."

"Not at all. I'm delighted to see you again."

He'd been right about the brooch. And the rubies.

She said, "As the old cliché would have it, I was in the neighborhood. I decided to walk home from a dinner party just over in Eaton Place. It was threatening rain, but then I love storms."

Hawke knew how she felt. Bad weather always cheered him more than blue skies. Storms enchanted him, always had.

"Good thing you had an umbrella," Hawke said, crossing the room and sitting in a well-worn leather club chair by the hearth. He was wearing a faded flannel shirt the color of smoke and grey pleated trousers. On his feet were a pair of scuffed leather boat moccasins he'd bought at some ship chandlery in Key West.

"Yes, isn't it?" She giggled, tugging at her wet sari.

"You look as if you barely escaped drowning in the street."

"Ah. Well, I did actually have an umbrella, you see, but I neglected to employ it until I suddenly found myself standing at your front door, pushing your bell."

"That would explain it," Hawke said, smiling, though of course it didn't.

"Please forgive me for intruding, Alex. I can't really explain it, but I had this overwhelming urge to see you tonight."

"Name a man who would not be flattered."

"Join me in a drink?"

"No, thank you. I quit."

"Good for you. I wish to God I could."

"You can."

"Well, not tonight obviously . . . I've been thinking about you, you know. That's silly, of course you *don't* know. But I have. Ever since seeing you again at Highgrove." She gazed into the fire for a few long moments and then said, "I felt drawn to you. The moment I saw you and then when I heard your voice again."

"Well, we have something very much in common, don't we?"

She sighed, looking back into the crackling fire.

"We do, Alex."

"A sad coincidence of loss."

"Do you believe what they say? That time heals all wounds?"

"No. My mother and father were murdered before my eyes when I was seven. That event is seared into me. It feels like a steel ball in the center of my chest. Sometimes it glows red hot."

Hawke saw a single gleaming tear roll down her cheek. She didn't bother to brush it away.

"I'm just so lost without Tony. Nothing makes much sense anymore. All my plans, my dreams. Children. A little house somewhere. Do you feel that way about her, about—"

"Anastasia."

"Anastasia, yes, I'm sorry, such a lovely name."

"I did for a long time. Just getting up and living through another day seemed like sheer folly. But, now, I think losing my mother, both my parents the way I did . . . it hardened me. Inside. Made me stronger somehow. I never felt the same way about life after they died. I looked at other boys who had their mothers, their families. I had no one. No one but me. I put my trust only in myself."

"A lack of trust in anyone else. Or anything else."

"Yes. That, too. And a smoldering anger at God."

"Oh, yes."

"You're shivering, Sahira. How rude of me. Would you like a blanket?"

"That would be lovely, thanks."

"Splash of scotch as well?"

"Good Lord, no. I'm rarely this tipsy, you'll be relieved to learn."

"I'll be right back."

WHEN HAWKE RETURNED WITH THE BLANKET, Sahira hadn't moved. She was leaning toward the fire with her bare arms wrapped around her knees.

"This should do the trick," he said, draping the woolen blanket around her shoulders. He collapsed back into his chair looking at her profile in the flickering firelight. "Better?" he said.

"Hmm. Thanks. Much."

"We'll find them, you know, these bloody bastards who killed

Tony. Sword of Allah, for God's sake. We'll run them to ground sooner or later and put the sword to them. I promise you."

"Yes. It helps to hear you say that. We now have a common enemy, don't we?"

"Another awful thing we have in common," Hawke said.

"Alex, may I ask a favor?"

"Anything."

"May I spend the night here?"

"Here?"

"Yes."

"Are you worried about the storm? I could easily drive you home."

"No. It's not that. I don't—don't want to be alone tonight."

"We've certainly no shortage of guest rooms. I'll ring Pelham. He'll make sure that we—"

Hawke reached for the telephone, but Sahira reached up and stayed his hand.

"Not a guest room, Alex. I want to sleep with you, in your bed. I want to wake up in your arms. Don't worry. We don't have to do anything. I just have this overwhelming need to be close."

"Any port in a storm, so to speak."

"No, Alex, don't misunderstand me. I want to be close to you. I've wanted it for a long time. Ever since that first afternoon we all met, when you and Tony gloriously had your shirts off, playing rugby in Hyde Park. I never told you, of course, because of Tony."

"Told me what, Sahira?"

"That I always wanted to be with you instead. From that first day. It's awful, I know. Don't look at me that way. I did love him very much. Adored him. He had a marvelous mind and the kindest heart. And he made me laugh, thank God, after all the bloody twits from the City. Forgive me, but this is something I had to tell you. You don't have to say anything, I wish you wouldn't, so please don't feel uncomfortable."

"Well, Sahira, I don't—"

"And now that I've unburdened myself and told you the truth, you can drive me home if you wish. Perfectly understandable were I in your place. But I would give the earth to hold you for one night. Just one night. Easy question, yes or no."

Hawke stared into those dark brown eyes for what seemed an eternity. He could come up with a thousand reasons why this was idiocy. But the simple and uncomplicated truth was, sitting here, looking at this beautiful woman, he discovered he wanted someone to hold too. He smiled down at her and gave his answer.

"Yes."

She reached up and put her hand on his knee, whispering the words, "I was praying you would say that."

They sat like that for a long time, her hand on his knee, both staring into the fire, neither feeling the need to speak. Hawke put his hand over hers and squeezed it gently. *Even this,* Hawke thought, *even this small comfort is something I still need. Moments like this. Anastasia would want this for me. I know she would.*

"Would you mind if I shed this soaking sari?" she said suddenly. "Even with the blanket, it's miserable."

"What's the old joke, 'you need to get out of that wet dress and into a dry martini'?"

She got to her feet and handed him the blanket. "Will you hold this for me a moment?"

"Of course. You'll find the loo is right—"

She put a finger to her lips and said, "Shhh. This will only take a minute."

And then, standing before the fire and smiling down at Hawke all the while, she began to disrobe, unwinding yards of glistening silk from her wondrous body.

"Sahira, do you really think this is a good idea?"

"I really do."

When she was naked, standing in the shadows of the dying fire, the beautiful sari puddled at her feet, she leaned forward and put out her hand to him. The movement made her large dark-nippled breasts sway dangerously close to his lips and Hawke felt faint memory stir, as something inside him was rekindled for the first time in an eternity.

"Will you please take me to bed, Lord Hawke? It's past my bed-time."

THE RAIN BEAT STEADILY AGAINST his bedroom windowpanes, the storm unabated, now accompanied by tumultuous thunder and sudden lightning strikes nearby that filled the high-ceilinged room with white fire. The storm awakened him a few times during the night and he was always startled to find Sahira by his side, her head on his left shoulder, her hair spilling across his chest, her hand cradled in his, snoring softly.

He'd drift off after a while, content, even happy for her presence.

Sometime later, toward dawn, he awoke to find her hand had found its way to his belly. She was rubbing it lightly, making little circles around his stomach that got wider and wider. Her fingertips brushed his semi-aroused penis, and quickly withdrew.

"Sorry," she whispered in his ear.

"Don't be."

She slid her fingers down over his belly and took him into her hand. She began stroking him, slowly at first, and then, as he grew harder, more quickly.

"Is this all right?" she said, as lightning struck a nearby tree and ignited the room for the briefest instant.

"Yes."

A few moments later, she shifted in the bed and rested her head on his stomach. She brushed the very tip of him across her lips, lightly grazing them a few times, and said, "And this?"

"Yes."

She took him deeply into her mouth and closed her lips around him and the sensation caused Hawke to arch his back and moan involuntarily. Any doubts about how deeply he had missed this part of his natural life fell away like a shedding of old skin. He would mourn his beloved Anastasia until the day he died. But were the living served by a lifetime of abstinence in honor of the dead?

This is not a betrayal.

"Alex," she said, lifting her head, her breathing heavy and somewhat hoarse, "I know all this is strictly against our rules."

"It is."

"But I need you inside me. I have waited a lifetime."

"And life is so short."

"Are you going to make me beg?"

"No."

"Please," she said. "Please. Now."

Hawke stared at her face, those large dark eyes luminous even in the waning blackness of the room, and said the first words that came into his head.

"I would be honored."

He entered her slowly and gently and the two brokenhearted people made love until exhaustion drove them to sleep.

In the early morning he woke to find her lying on her side staring at him.

"Top of the morning," he said sleepily.

"Top of the morning."

"Staying for breakfast?"

"Can't. England and Lord Malmsey await me. Desperately."

"Know the feeling."

"Alex?"

"Yes?"

"Before I go, I need to ask you one last question. All right?"

"Fire at will."

"Have you any possible idea of why we were both made to suffer such cruel losses? Anastasia, Tony, your dear parents?"

"Yes, I think I do."

"Tell me."

"Quite simple, really."

"Please tell me."

"God sinned."

SIXTEEN

NORTHERN IRELAND, JULY 1979

"LOVELY SPOT, MR. SMITH," FAITH MCGUIRE allowed, rolling onto her side and propping her pert little chin into the palm of her tiny little hand. It was chilly in the dappled shade of the overhanging trees, the late afternoon sunlight filtering down to the green grass but not providing much in the way of warmth. Smith was gazing out to sea, giving her his best side, and she gazed unashamedly at his profile. He was a handsome one, all right, just like she vaguely remembered from the pub the night before.

They sat on a small shady bluff overlooking the ponderously heaving blue Atlantic, gazing at a small island just offshore. He'd brought a blanket and a jug of wine. Tools of his trade, Smith thought, smiling to himself. A jug of wine, a loaf of bread, and thou. Isn't that what the poet said? And don't forget the knife. He had not forgotten the knife. . . .

"Whatever was it the Bard said about a summer day?" he asked.

"Silly boy. I've no earthly idea what he said or didn't say. Never even heard of him. And, move your hand, please, sir."

"The Bard was a poet, my pet," he said, stroking her rounded thigh through the thin cotton of her white skirt with the pink polka dots. She hadn't dressed for the day. She had dressed for him.

"A poet, eh? Do you know one of 'em, then? You being such a fancy schoolteacher and all. One of his poems, I mean."

"I know them all, of course. The sonnets, at least. Would you care to hear one?" He moved his hand up and cupped one of her heavy breasts.

"I'd blooming adore it, I would. No one's ever told me a poem before."

"I'll tell you one in a bit, but first, lean back and let me look at you."

A swath of dark gold hair fell across her forehead, hiding one eye. He pushed it gently away. He looked deep into her pale blue eyes. Had she known what he was looking for, she would have run for her life.

He stared at her as he slipped his hand inside her blouse and began to fondle her breasts.

"Do you see what I see?"

"I see some of me very most private buttons being unbuttoned is what I see, sir. And I ain't that kind of lass so I will thank you very kindly to—"

"But you said you loved me."

"Right. Love, he says. A pint or three after we was introduced last evening, you'll remember."

"I remember everything, dear girl. It's my private hell."

"How you do go on. Still. I'm saving meself, I'll have you know. So don't get any fancy ideas. I'm Catholic, y'know. We wed 'em afore we bed 'em, as me sainted mum says."

"I know that. But I love you, Faith McGuire. In my way."

"Now, who said anythin' a'tall about love?"

"You did. Last night in Belfast, at Bittles Bar."

"That was just Arthur talking."

"Arthur?"

"Arthur Guinness." She giggled. "Do you get it? Guinness? Talking? It's a common enough pub joke."

"Bit of a wit then, are you, darling?"

"Oh, go on."

"I mean it."

"You'll take your hands off me if you know what's good for you. You heard of Billy McGuire? That's me older brother. A right knee-capper he is, too. You dinna want to be on the wrong side of 'im, I'll tell you."

"How many men has he killed? In Londonderry? I think you said his garrison was in Londonderry last night? Yes?"

"Billy doesn't say much about the regiment. Against rules and regs, he says."

"His regiment. That's the Prince of Wales's Own Regiment of Yorkshire? Infantry, isn't that right?"

"Like I say, he don't say much."

"Too bad about that eighteen-year-old British soldier shot by a sniper last week. On foot patrol in the Creggan housing estate. Your brother tell you about that, did he?"

"You ask a lot of questions for a man taking a girl for a picnic. How do I know you ain't IRA? A bloody Provo, right? Is that what you are?"

"Don't be a silly girl. I'm just naturally curious, I suppose. I happened to be present when the soldier was shot. I was the only eyewitness to the shooting in point of fact. I know precisely who killed him. Know him quite well, in fact, watch him shave every morning."

"Listen. We don't talk about such things in my family. It's dangerous. And we especially don't talk about such things to strangers."

"I want to ask you a very serious question."

"Then ask."

"Would you marry me?"

"Me? Marry you? Barmy."

"Would you?"

"Never."

"Why not?"

"We're from two different worlds. We got nothing in common."

"Two different worlds," he said, a brief glint of bright red anger flashing in his dark eyes. He'd looked away just in time. She hadn't seen it.

"As different as two can get. Look, I don't want you to think I've anythin' against yer kind. But, really, it's just not thinkable. I think you're as handsome a bloke as ever there was, but—"

"But what?"

"A bit old for me, I'd say, Mr. Smith. Unless you were very, very rich of course. But you're only a poor schoolteacher. Or so you say, anyway."

"Would you like to row out there to Mutton Island? It's not that far."

"I told you I would. Going with a big strong fella such as you, aren't I? It's a haunt, y'know, that island is. Sure it is. Beasties. Goblins and banshees. When I was a wee one, I heard stories of people going out there. And never coming back."

"I'll take care of you, don't worry."

"It's what you promised. Show me the ruins, you said. The old Norman watchtower and the abandoned schoolhouse. And the graveyard."

"Of course. I'll get the wine, you button yourself up and wrap this blanket round, it's getting quite cold. Storm front coming. My boat is the pretty little blue one down there on the beach."

"Are you sure it isn't too rough, the water? I can't swim a stroke."

"It's only half a kilometer across the strait. I think I can handle it. Let's go."

MUTTON ISLAND ROSE FROM THE SEA to a height of 110 feet. It was covered in wind-whipped grasslands and surmounted by the ruins of an ancient settlement that still stood at the western end. It had been periodically inhabited since prehistory, and the legendary "Children of Lir" had spent their last three hundred years on the island. They were now spending eternity in the island's ancient graveyard.

Myths about the place were common, most generated by the presence of a Pagan tombstone, six feet high, with hieroglyphic inscriptions. It stood in the center of the graveyard in absolutely pristine condition, despite countless centuries of horrific Atlantic weather conditions.

Pulling hard against the fierce rip of the narrow strait, Smith recalled the first day he'd seen this desolate, uninhabited place. He'd been drawn to it for any number of reasons. Not the least of which were many outings like this one, a beautiful fair-skinned lass seated in the bow of his rowboat, looking for adventure with the handsome stranger.

He timed and caught a wave that carried them high up onto the smooth rocky beach. He shipped oars and waited for the wave to recede, leaving them high and dry, so to speak. Once they'd climbed out, he fastened the long painter round a large boulder. Then he took her hand and led her across the slippery rocks to a pathway he often used. It led to the graveyard. Climbing it, he began to perspire.

They reached the top.

"It's lovely out here. Makes you wonder why no one ever comes. Lived here all me life and never been."

"Mind your step," he said. The weather-worn stone tablets of ancient graves had been heaved up topsy-turvy, as if the soil itself was rejecting them. Thick tendrils of fog had wreathed themselves into the ruins, and the graveyard had suddenly become an altogether more haunting place. She was shivering. She hadn't dressed for the cold sea wind.

"Who is buried here? So many graves."

"Children. Centuries ago."

"Sad."

"Yes. Death comes and we go."

"And what might that be?" she asked, pointing at the six-foot obelisk and wrapping his worn woolen blanket more tightly about her. "The grave of some great laird, I wonder?"

"A Pagan tombstone, certainly. The grave of an infidel. A kafir."

"What's a kafir?"

"Someone who doesn't believe in God."

"Who doesn't believe in God?"

"You'd be surprised."

"There's writing on it."

"The hieroglyphs are proving much harder to decipher than I first imagined. But I'm working on it."

"You're some kind of . . . archaeologist . . . then, are you?"

"Yes, something like that," he said, walking toward the old stone building. "I make a study of graves."

"And that building there? It seems to be the only one still standing, if you can call it that."

"I call it the schoolhouse. It was probably a church since it's adjacent to the cemetery. But I like to think of it as the place where I do my work. Teaching. And learning, of course. Oh, the things I do learn."

"Oh. You seem to know an awful lot about this frightful place for someone who ain't local."

Thunder rumbled overhead and there was a searing crack of nearby lightning. The air was suddenly charged with electricity. Fat drops of cold rain began to spatter on the upended stone markers of death. The temperature had dropped at least twenty degrees in the last fifteen minutes.

"You'll catch your death out here," he said. "Come inside the schoolhouse. Quickly. I want you to see something. In fact, I want to teach you a lesson. About life and—"

"Teach me a lesson, eh? Cor, the way you do go on!"

"It's my sense of humor. I simply can't help myself."

She looked at him quizzically but went through the low opening, peering into the gloom.

He followed her into the one-room stone structure. The floor was covered with small white pebbles. There were no windows and only the single heavy wooden door. Faith thought it odd that the door looked so new, and had a bolt, but said nothing. She was staring at the strong shaft of light that came through a crack in the roof.

There was a rough-hewn stone table directly in the center of a jagged beam of sunlight slanting between the rain clouds. Beneath the table she saw a large wooden hatch, as if it covered a set of stairs leading below to . . . what? A cellar?"

"Look at the lovely light in here," she said, turning to smile at him over her shoulder. He had his back to her, fussing with something about the door. He turned to her and smiled. An odd smile, rather queer, nothing like the easy smiles on the cliff overlooking the sea. It made her uneasy, like a small cold ache in the pit of her stomach.

"Why did you close the door?" she said as he approached her. Out of the corner of her eye, she saw it all. The cot. The books scattered on the floor. The rotting food and empty wine bottles on the ancient stone floor. Lightning struck close by, filling the room with white light.

This was where he lived.

Horror began to steal its way into her mind, hot blood racing upward, flooding her skull.

He smiled. "If you were granted one wish, Faith McGuire, what would you wish for?"

She tried for a laugh. "To stop drinking with strangers."

"I promise you, Faith, today will be the day you stop drinking with strangers."

She edged toward the door, blindly reaching out for the handle.

"Don't bother, Faith. I locked it."

"Locked it! Why on earth would you lock this door?"

"So you can't get out. Not until you've answered every last one of my questions about your brother's regiment. I need this information, you see. It's my trade. I'm rather a spy. I trade information for favors. Simple, isn't it."

"Ah, yer full of it, ain't you? Trying to scare a poor young girl like that? I know your kind. Open that door and I'll give you a kiss, but only one. You don't scare me a lick."

"You should be scared, my dear girl," he said, moving toward her. He pulled something from his jacket pocket and held it up into the light.

"Oh, my God."

"If you have a god, my dear, now would be a good time to have a quick word."

"What is it? What are you going to do? Have your way with me? It ain't necessary, mister. I'm no virgin. I like it, y'see, can't get enough. I'll do whatever you want. Just don't hurt me."

"Oh, I've no doubt you'll do as I say. But now it's time for the Q & A, my darling."

He pressed the tip of the carving knife against her cheek.

She screamed once, found herself backing away and hit the edge of the table, hit it hard with her hip. She put a hand down on the table to steady herself. It was covered with a crusty dried substance that flaked off onto her hand. In some dim recess of her brain she knew instantly that it was old blood.

"It's covered with—"

"A sacrificial altar," he said quietly. "A Pagan ritual. Centuries old."

"Please. Don't hurt me. I know how to make men happy. I'll do it for you. Anything. I swear it! On my knees, I'll swear it, only don't—"

"Oh, don't worry about all that nasty business. I'm not that kind of man. I find all that rubbish rather messy and disgusting, to be honest."

He moved closer. She opened her mouth to scream as he raised the knife.

He jammed his fingers into her mouth, hooking his left thumb under her jaw, and pushed her back onto the table. Her large breasts were heaving beneath the low-cut white cotton peasant's blouse, and he yanked it down at the neckline, ripping the cloth away from her shoulders with his knife hand.

"Will you talk now, Faith? Will you tell me everything I need to know?"

He missed the hand coming for his eyes. She screamed as she went for them, intent on gouging, and he'd time enough to turn the other cheek, as they say, and all she managed was to rake three shallow wounds down the side of his face.

He slashed her with the knife. She was moving frantically now and the wound was only superficial.

"Faith. Your brother's unit is charged with the protection of Lord Mountbatten. I want to know how many men are assigned to his unit, and I want to know what their rotation schedule is!"

"No!"

He slashed again and the blade struck bone, a rib, but the blood was spurting and he gripped her jaw harder, slamming her head against the table with a hollow thud.

She quieted down a bit, dazed.

"Now talk," he said, but he was convinced he wasn't going to get anything out of this one.

He took a moment to compose himself and regarded her calmly. She was still wriggling too much for his taste, and he cracked her skull once more against his altar.

"Do you or do you not intend to answer my questions about your brother's regiment?"

"Yes! Yes I do! Just stop. Don't—"

The bloodlust was up now. He'd never get anything but lies out of this simple girl. And he certainly could not allow her to go free, not now.

Pity.

He raised the knife above his head, bringing it down in a wide ripping arc. The vicious blow tore away most of her throat.

He took a step back to avoid that awful spouting gout of blood and said, "I'm sorry, Faith. That was mean. You should never have trusted me. No one ever should. They all learn that lesson too late, I'm afraid."

She was silent now.

He went over to his miserable cot and lay down, sick to his stomach over what he had just done, swallowing the vomit. The rage blooming inside him, the hot red need to kill finally extinguished, he lay there, disgusted, panting, hating himself, drenched in the hot blood of Faith McGuire. He seemed to have a half-empty wine bottle in his hand and he drank it down in a single draught.

In the morning, Faith would join all the others down in the catacombs. But for now, at last, he could get some sleep. He stared at the old magazine cover of Mountbatten taped to his wall. Scrawled across his face were Roman numerals, scribbled there every night as Smith marked off the remaining days until he struck. A grease pencil hung by a string, and he used it to mark off one more day, one more week.

Now, to sleep.

Perchance, if he was lucky, to dream of his unsuspecting nemesis.

SEVENTEEN

NORTHOLT AIRFIELD, ENGLAND, 1947

LORD LOUIS MOUNTBATTEN STOOD on the glistening tarmac in the dewy light of dawn. He was gazing up with nostalgia at the silver fuselage of the familiar Lancaster heavy bomber. This particular aircraft, a York MW-102, with its four Rolls-Royce Merlin V-12 engines, had flown Mountbatten on countless missions during his days as Supreme Commander, Southeast Asia. Early in the war, he'd converted the Lancaster to his own specifications. Mountbatten had just refitted her yet again with bunks for a relief crew to shorten the flight time required for his upcoming journey.

Lord Mountbatten was a man on a mission, an extremely vital mission, and he literally had not a moment to spare. Millions of lives were literally hanging in the balance and he'd been chosen by his King and the prime minister to be the reluctant savior of these teeming masses.

The Hero of Burma had no burning desire to be remembered by history as a savior. He was a lifelong warrior, moreover, a victor, not some bloody diplomat or politico. One need only look at the legions of decorations now festooned so proudly upon his chest to know him for what he was. His idea of negotiation was a fight to the death. Far more importantly, did he want his name forever engraved in the history books as the man who'd begun this lamentable unraveling of the British Empire? Churchill thought the whole idea of giving up empire was blasphemy. For once, Mountbatten was completely in agreement with his bullheaded nemesis.

If this was not the end of empire, then certainly it was the beginning of the end. He had argued tirelessly with the monarch over his decision to send him to India. He neither wanted the Crown to give up this bastion of empire, nor did he have any wish to preside over this debacle. A religious struggle between two warring religions, Hinduism and Islam, for which there was clearly no solution.

But such was his fate.

His valet had already stowed Lord and Lady Mountbatten's personal luggage on board, all sixty-six pieces of it, so complete it included a set of silver ashtrays that bore the family crest. Also on board, in an old cardboard shoebox stowed in an overhead bin, was a family heirloom. It was the diamond-studded tiara Edwina would wear when her husband was proclaimed the new Viceroy of India.

In the reddish glow of the cockpit, the pilot and copilot of the York MW-102 went through their final preflight checks. Mountbatten and two of his old wartime comrades completed one final walk around the aircraft. With him were Colonel Ronald Brockman, head of his personal staff, and Lieutenant Commander Peter Howes, his senior aide-de-camp. How many trips had they taken on the old girl, Lord Louis was thinking, good Lord, how many, from the frontline posts in the jungles of Burma to every great conference of the war.

His two friends noticed that the normally ebullient Mountbatten seemed gloomy and introspective, his mood matching the weather perfectly. It was not at all, they privately thought, remotely like him. A bit full of himself, but normally a cheery sort.

The copilot leaned out of the cockpit window and announced loudly that the flight was ready for takeoff.

"Well," Mountbatten said to his friends with a shrug and a sigh, "we're off to India. The world's largest powder keg. I don't want to go. They don't want me out there. We'll all probably come home with bloody bullets in our backs."

THE VICEROY'S HOUSE IN NEW DELHI was a palace of such gargantuan dimensions that it could only be rivaled by Versailles or the Peterhof Palace of the tsars. Behind the endless parade of grand white marble columns lining the exterior façade were floors and walls of white, yellow, green, and black marble quarried from the same veins that furnished the astonishing mosaics inside the Taj Mahal.

So long were the palace corridors that, in the basement, servants rode from one end of the building to the other on bicycles. On this particularly historic morning, five thousand of those servants were giving one last polish to the marble, glass, woodwork, and brass of its thirty-seven grand salons and its three hundred and forty rooms. Gold and scarlet turbans flaring atop their heads, armies of servants whose white tunics had already been embroidered with the new Viceroy's coat of arms scurried down corridors on some final errand.

Outside, in the manicured Mogul gardens, more than four hundred gardeners toiled in the sun, perfecting the intricate maze of grass squares, rectangular flower beds, and splashing vaulted waterways. Fifty of those gardeners were mere boys whose sole job it was to shoo away unwanted birds.

And over in the stables, the five hundred horsemen of the Viceroy's personal mounted bodyguard adjusted their scarlet and gold tunics before mounting their superb black horses. The entire household was a frenzy of activity. And all of them—horsemen, chamberlains, cooks, stewards, and gardeners—were preparing for the enthronement of one of that select company of men for whom this splendid palace had been erected, the man who now approached this very moment—the last Viceroy of India.

THE STUNNING BLACK HORSES of the Viceregal Bodyguard suddenly hove into the view of countless thousands jamming the streets of Delhi, colors flying, drums beating, buglers trumpeting. The new viscount turned to his wife, Edwina, and managed a smile. *Here we are at last, darling,* the smile said.

Home, God help us.

He looked, people later said, like some brilliant film star in his immaculate white naval uniform. Serene, smiling, his adoring wife beside him, Louis Mountbatten rode up to the foot of the grand palace steps to lay his claim to Viceroy's House. He arrived in a gilded landau built half a century earlier for the royal progress through Delhi of his cousin George V.

As the landau pulled to a stop, the bagpipes of the Royal Scots Fusiliers began a plaintive welcome. Stepping down from the carriage, Mountbatten turned and held out his hand for the beauteous Lady Mountbatten. The roar of the crowd was literally deafening. Here was the man who had come to preserve the peace and to preserve this sad, lost country. To somehow prevent the outbreak of an unimaginable religious war that would soak the ground of India with the blood of countless millions.

FIVE LONG MONTHS PASSED, and Mountbatten had grown weary of the struggle. The endless meetings with Gandhi, Nehru, and Jinnah. While they argued and schemed, the political situation grew worse almost daily. The death toll among warring Moslems, Hindus, and Sikhs was mounting. Provocations on both sides abounded. A sacred cow, wandering inside a tiny Moslem village in the Punjab, was slaughtered, its bloody carcass delivered in a cart to the Hindu village across the valley. The resulting violence of that blasphemy left hundreds, perhaps thousands, dead.

India was now a powder keg with a very short fuse.

Mountbatten knew then that he could only stave off the inevitable for a very short time. He could only present a front of supreme confidence until that wretched hour when England would have little choice but to abandon her responsibilities and slip away.

It had come to this, he told his wife one night in bed: he could watch the Indian pot boil but he could not, ever, extinguish the flame beneath it.

Delhi was already gasping in the first searing blasts of the hot season. In the mornings, beyond the opened windows of his study, scorching breezes fried the dhak trees in the Mogul garden, the branches seeming to emit sparks in the sun's phosphorescent white glare.

With each passing day, there was fresh evidence of increasing violence and bloodshed. Just five days after Mountbatten's arrival, an incident between Moslems and Hindus took ninety-nine lives in Calcutta. More recently, a conflict in Bombay left forty-one mutilated bodies on the pavement. And, now, the violence flared unabated throughout the land.

Mountbatten, at his wit's end, summoned India's senior police officer to his study and asked a simple question.

"Tell me the truth, Chief Inspector. Are the Indian police capable of maintaining law and order in India or are they not?"

"No, Your Excellency, we can no longer maintain law and order."

That night Lord Mountbatten put in a call to Buckingham Palace.

He told his King the time had come.

England must prepare at once to abandon India.

The cost in blood and treasure would be incalculable. The once great land that had been England's shining pride of empire would be ripped asunder for all time. For the glorious British Empire that had been, this was the beginning of the end.

EIGHTEEN

COUNTY SLIGO, NORTHERN IRELAND, JUNE 1979

FIVE INVISIBLE MEN SAT AROUND the battered kitchen table staring at each other through eye slits in their black balaclavas. It was a bit odd, Smith thought, all of them including himself wearing these bloody ski masks, sharing a bottle of Irish whiskey. There was no heat in the house but for what was in that bottle, so unseasonably cold on this rainy June night that they all wore leather gloves.

The two gentlemen who had transported him from the IRA pub in Belfast out to the safe house in the County Sligo countryside had been sent outdoors with a bottle of Tullamore Dew and a pair of automatic rifles. Sentry duty. He doubted they'd be disturbed.

The safe house was an old place, long abandoned. There was a crooked sign over the door, faded and peeling. The Barking Dog Inn. The old building sat deep within a thick wood at a bend in the river. Despite the shutters, there was heavy black paper taped to all the windows in the small, plain kitchen and also in the parlor filled with musty-smelling furniture, the only two rooms he'd seen. A flight of stairs led up into total darkness.

"And yer name would be?" the largest of the four heavily armed men finally asked.

"Smith," he said automatically. It was the only name he ever used now.

"Smith?"

"Yes. Just Smith."

"Awright, Smith. And what might yer first name be, then?"

"Mister."

"Mister, is it? He's funny, ain't he, lads? I need your full fuckin' name, Mister Smith. We're bleeding sticklers on that kind of detail, ye can well understand."

"John," he said, using the first name that popped into his mind. Red rage was blooming inside him and he wanted to kill this filthy, sarcastic bastard. But he needed him too badly. Hell, he needed all of them too badly.

"Bloody hell, John Smith. Where are you from, then?"

"Mutton Island. I doubt you've heard of it."

"Desolate place, ain't it? Hainted by banshees."

"I need my privacy."

"You'd better have a right good reason for being here," one of the anonymous black woolen heads said, looking at him over the rim of his mug. "You ain't leavin' alive if ye don't."

He was mildly unnerved. Odd. Nothing unnerved him, ever. But finding oneself alone in an abandoned old house with four heavily armed killers seemed to have adverse effects. He found it quite interesting from a psychological point of view. He spoke, keeping his voice calm and deliberate.

"You kill people quite easily. So do I. Kindred spirits, that's what we are."

A silence ensued, in which his fate was clearly being privately debated by the four Provos. Finally, the big IRA soldier spoke.

"You have something for me?"

Smith withdrew a manila envelope, slid it across the table, and the IRA officer eagerly rifled through the contents. He studied a few pages very carefully and then, seemingly satisfied, looked up at the man with a hard eye.

"This is good intelligence, Mr. Smith, the genuine article it would seem. How did you happen to come by all this information?"

"I find people who have information and force them to tell me things by whatever means necessary."

"British soldiers?"

"Certainly not. That would be suicide. My informants are those who are *close* to British soldiers. People with whom they share sometimes valuable information."

"And how do you make these people tell you things?"

"Unbearable pain."

"Cold bastard, ain't he?"

"Are you Billy McKee, sir?" Smith asked.

"Might be. Might not. There's many a Billy McKee in this godforsaken land of ours."

"Let us assume you are. Then, Mr. McKee, I should think your colleague in Dublin would have explained the reasons behind my desire for this meeting. This British military intelligence of mine, an endless supply of it, is yours for the asking."

"How much?"

"I don't want your money, Mr. McKee. I want your help."

"Why don't you tell me and my colleagues here exactly what you've got in mind, Smith."

Smith cleared his throat and placed his gloved hands palm down on the rough wooden table.

"I wonder if I might first have a taste of that whiskey. It's been rather a long journey. I'm parched."

McKee filled a cracked glass with whiskey.

Smith drank it down and it blistered his throat.

"Another, if you don't mind?"

"Pour him another crapper, Sean."

"Crapper?" Smith said, worriedly.

"Don't worry, mate. Irish for a half-glass of whiskey."

"Thanks," Smith said, and downed the second tumbler. He looked round the table into the eyes of the four rather fearsome-looking IRA Provos. The moment had finally arrived.

"Well, Mr. Smith?" Billy McKee said. "Sometime tonight, I hope?"

"Sorry," he croaked. The whiskey burned his throat, and he was trying to suppress a cough with a fist to his mouth, "I want to do much more than provide military intelligence to the IRA. I want to—to assassinate someone."

"Who doesn't?" one of the anonymous men said, to general laughter.

"Point taken," Smith said. "You fellows have perfected the art of political murder. I admire your skills, your tactics. I can't do this killing alone, you see. The chance of failure is too high. I've come because I need to ask for your help."

"I wouldn't think an island hermit would make that many serious enemies, Smith. Besides, why the hell should we help you assassinate anyone?"

"Quite simple. I will assume all the risk. You gentlemen will get all the credit."

"Look. Let me cut past the chase to the outcome. I don't want to waste time here, Mr. Smith. Anyone who you'd be interested in killing would likely not be anyone of interest to us. So, any notion of us helping you, or—"

"Oh, I think you'll consider my intended victim someone of enormous personal interest. I would not be here were that not true."

"Who is it then, for the love of God?" Billy said, draining his whiskey. The Provo commander was beginning to believe his Dublin colleague had found someone who could be genuinely useful. What the man said next confirmed that belief.

"I intend to murder Lord Louis Mountbatten."

There was a moment of astonished silence, and then Billy and three other IRA soldiers broke into laughter, long and loud. Pushing back from the table, Billy said, "You? You're going to kill Mountbatten? Yer a bloody fool. You must be insane. No one can get within a thousand miles of that imperial toff. We've looked into it, believe me."

"It can be done."

"You seem pretty sure of that."

"For some months now I've been spending a good deal of time here in Northern Ireland gathering intelligence on the British Army and, at the same time, deciding how best to assassinate that pompous bastard. In point of fact, I know precisely how to do it."

"Why in God's holy name do you want to kill him?"

The Provos couldn't see it, but deep red anger flushed Smith's face beneath his balaclava. His breathing became shallow. His temples were throbbing and his heart was thudding with an abiding anger and hatred, seeded in his boyhood, that over the years had grown into a now uncontrollable passion.

But Smith managed to keep his emotions in check as he spoke. It would not do to have these men realize the depths of his madness, nor his willingness to kill anyone who thwarted him or got in his way. He needed them too much.

"Personal reasons," Smith said quietly. "Suffice it to say, I hate these English Royals as much as you do, if not more."

"Listen to me, Mr. Smith, traveling IRA sympathizer with yer fluty toff accent. You think we wouldn't have taken out Lord Louis long before this if we thought it was possible? It ain't, believe me. There's no way to get close enough to a member of the Royal Family to even spit on 'em."

"That's not a good enough reason not to try, if one wants something badly enough. I, for one, want it more than badly enough, believe me."

"Shall we just kill this crazy bugger and have a drink? Or let him speak his piece, mates? We've already got his information," Billy McKee said.

"Let the bugger speak his mind if he's a mind to," Sean, the man next to Smith, said. "We come all this way out here t'night, why not? Worth a laugh."

The others nodded, and McKee leaned forward over the table, shoving the whiskey bottle out of his way with his beefy forearm.

"So let me make sure I've got this straight," Billy said, smiling. "You yourself intend to do the dirty deed. Alone."

"Correct."

"But we get all the credit. The Irish Republican Army claims sole responsibility for the execution? In the unlikely event you're successful."

"Correct."

"Why kill him, in particular? Aside from the fact that he's an arrogant, preening, aristocratic bastard who made a mess of your bloody country and now bedevils our own?"

Smith looked down into his lap, his shoulders heaving.

For the first time, the Provos could sense the burning hatred and powerful passion for revenge that had driven this man to them. It was in his body language. Murderous hatred poured off him in hot waves.

"*Vengeance will be mine!*" he cried, looking up and slamming his fist down on the table with enough force to upset their liquor glasses. "Do you people understand me? Listen closely, Mr. McKee. I want to murder *all* these Royal bastards. Every fucking one of them. Why, if I could, I would roam the graveyards of England digging up British monarchs long dead and crushing their bones to dust beneath my heels. And smash every last one of their bloody skulls against their own tombstones!"

The four men stared at him in stunned silence.

"Good enough for me," McKee said, astounded at the depths of the man's feelings. "What say the lads?"

"Aye," they murmured, nodding their heads as Smith had expected. They now knew they had little to lose, and the world to gain, after all.

"What'll you be needing then, from me?" McKee asked.

"Explosives, for starters," Smith said, getting his emotions once more under control.

"What kind of explosives?"

"Untraceable. Compact. Easily transportable. Waterproof. Completely reliable. What do you recommend?"

"How close you think you can get to the fella?"

"Very close."

"Within five hundred yards?"

"Closer. But I'd err on the side of more is more. Leave nothing to chance."

"Fifty pounds of gelignite ought to do it, mate."

"Familiar with gelignite. Never used it, however."

"We use it all the bloody time. A kind of blasting gelatin, easily moldable, dissolved in nitroglycerine and mixed with wood pulp and potassium nitrate. Very stable. And very cheap. And very fuckin' serious."

"I'll need a remote detonator."

"You bloody well will unless you plan to join his bleeding lordship in hell," the Provo said, earning a few guffaws and bottoms up around the table.

Smith said, "It's done, then? That's it? You'll help me?"

"When I'm completely satisfied you are who you say you are, yes. That envelope of yours looks pretty good to me. But we're all still alive because we are extremely thorough in our investigations. Until then you'll be ensconced in a little locked room upstairs. Pip and Scottie McBain standing outside will rotate. Feed you and make sure you don't stray from yer quarters. Understood?"

"Completely. I'd do the same myself."

"All right, then."

Smith took a breath, then said, "All right, then. Good. Thank you."

"We're done here, looks like, mates. You'll be hearing from us, one way or the other, Mr. Smith. Let's hope, for your sake, you're an honest man. Or you'll not leave this house alive."

"I never claimed honesty, sir, only truthfulness."

"Sounds like ruddy Mahatma Gandhi himself, don't he, boys?"

"Mahatma never killed a flea," one of the Provos said as they all rose from the table. "Much less the last Viceroy of India. But here's a queer bloke seeming determined to do just that!"

"Bloody unlikely, ain't it, Pad?"

"Dunno. This one's got a look in his eye like I've never seen. He just might do it. He could bloody well pull off the impossible."

NINETEEN

MULLAGHMORE, NORTHERN IRELAND, AUGUST 1979

THE MONTHS PASSED QUICKLY. NOT SURPRISING, Smith thought, what with his normal responsibilities coupled with all the travel, meticulous planning, and intelligence gathering he had done, plus certain "extracurricular" activities he had been conducting out on the island. Weekend jaunts from his remote digs off the coast, slipping into Mullaghmore harbor of an evening for a quick look round before fading away, returning by boat to his perfect hideaway on Mutton Island.

The fishing village of Mullaghmore overlooked a small harbor. A few commercial boats and pleasure boats bobbed at their moorings on warm summer days. Only twelve miles away lay the border with Northern Ireland, so the town was a popular vacation spot for terrorist IRA volunteers.

It was also the vacation home of one of the Royal Family's most venerated and public figures, Lord Louis Mountbatten. A powerful member of the family, it was Lord Louis who had arranged the courtship of his nephew Prince Philip and then Princess Elizabeth, now the reigning monarch.

If Mountbatten was sanguine about his security, it was with good reason. There had never been a single attempt on his life. The only terrorist attack in Mullaghmore had come one night courtesy of some lads at the pub. They'd sneaked down to the harbor and drilled holes in the bottom of *Shadow V,* Mountbatten's beloved fishing boat, hoping she'd sink with the morning tide.

She didn't.

A mile or so away from town, atop a hill known as "Fairy Rock," which overlooked the bay, stood Classiebawn Castle, the summer home of Lord Mountbatten. It had been the site of many jolly family holidays for over thirty years. It was not a castle, really, just a large Victorian mansion. But it had a turret, and it was the home of a Royal, so historically, it had been called a castle. Built in 1874, it overlooked the forbidding rock-faced cliffs and the tide-washed strands of Donegal Bay, with the windswept island of Inishmurray visible in the near distance, and the open sea in the far.

IT HAD RAINED LIKE MAD every day all summer long. But tonight, stars appeared and the clouds seemed to be scudding away; a slice of yellow moon glimmered on the dark bay. The forecast for tomorrow was sunny. *Good boating weather, with any luck at all,* Mountbatten thought, closing the seaward bedroom windows before retiring, *and about time, too.*

Smith, standing in the stern of the small fishing boat, was reassured by the sound of her motor chugging steadily. The *Rose of Tralee,* she was called. The two IRA men, Tom McMahon and Francie McGirl, had provided her, no questions asked.

Smith, his balaclava pulled down over his face, put a pair of high-powered binoculars to the eyeholes. He raised the glasses to the great manse atop Fairy Rock. Though it was quite late, lights still shone in a few of the upper windows, and he could make out Mountbatten's flag fluttering from its standard atop the turret. The banner only flew when the lord of the manor was in residence.

Smith's most recent intelligence indicated a number of family members in residence in addition to Mountbatten himself. His grandson, Nicholas; Lady Brabourne; Lady Patricia, her husband and son; and Timothy Knatchbull. There were others, but their names were not known to him.

It didn't matter. Only one of them mattered.

McMahon, at the helm, was running just above idle speed. They had kept their navigation lights on, after some debate, as it was felt the chances of anyone taking notice of *Rose of Tralee* were slimmer. Still, they'd taken precautions. The rucksack filled with fifty pounds of high-powered explosives was weighted with lead. It sat tethered to the transom where it could easily be lowered silently and sunk should they be approached by the local Gardaí patrol boat, whose schedule was famously unpredictable.

None of the three men were armed.

The two IRA Provos were attired as if returning from a long day of offshore drift fishing for salmon, and they had taken the trouble to fill the live well with fresh fish. The nets were piled on the deck aft of the small pilothouse. On the boat's stern, she bore Sligo as her hailing port. Their story was, should they need one, that they'd been offshore fishing, had engine trouble, and were pulling into Mullaghmore for the night, hoping to make repairs next morning, and to return to Sligo Harbor by noon.

McGirl, with a professional touch Smith admired, periodically squirted oil onto the hot manifold, and the engine was smoking nicely, believably, should anyone official approach and start asking questions.

"There she is," Smith said quietly, pointing at a green runabout moored at one end of the town dock. It was well past midnight and no one was about. The little houses dotted on the hillside seemed fast asleep, not a light in a single window. Only the pub at the other end of the town dock showed any signs of life. But this was, Smith reflected, Ireland after all.

There was a dim, flickering lamp on a post at the far end of the dock, casting yellow light on the *Shadow V*. She was no gentlemen's yacht, just a simple twenty-seven-footer, completely open at the stern, with a rounded cuddy cabin forward. She looked good for family outings and lobstering, which is exactly how Mountbatten used her.

"Tom," Smith said softly, eyeing the closing distances and the speed of his boat, full knowing this precise moment posed the highest risk of failure. "Circle round and come up from behind her at idle speed. We'll take *Shadow* dead slow on our starboard side. Gently, please, Tom, ever so gently."

"Done," Tom said over his shoulder.

McMahon throttled back to dead slow and did as the assassin had asked. He ghosted to a stop just as they came dead abeam of Mountbatten's boat, rubbing up against her wooden hull soundlessly. Smith reached across the narrow distance and grabbed the gunwale of Mountbatten's boat, bringing them to a stop.

"Good enough, then, gentlemen," Smith said, quickly and quietly, lifting and deftly placing the fifty-pound rucksack on the teak deck of the open cockpit of the *Shadow V*. The two IRA men looked at each other. This Smith was surprisingly strong. He was tall and slender, a bookish bloke, they'd imagined. But he clearly took care of himself.

McMahon stepped out of the pilothouse, shook his hand, and said, "Well, then. Good luck, Mr. Smith. Succeed, and we'll build a bloody statue of you in Belfast Square someday maybe. Won't look anything like you, of course, so no worries there."

"Or have my name on it, I should hope," Smith said as he smiled.

McGirl squeezed Smith's shoulder and said, "Best of the best, mate. Be dog wide, sir, and don't get yerself caught. Pray for sunshine tomorrow, ye can be certain they'll not be leaving this dock if it's bucketing rain again in the morn."

"Oh, I've been praying for sunshine tomorrow all my life," Smith said, pulling the two boats, which had drifted apart, a bit closer together for boarding.

"Aye. Prayin's one thing."

"There'll be blood in the water tomorrow, no matter which side God is on, McGirl," Smith said, easily stepping over the *Rose of Tralee*'s gunwale and climbing into *Shadow V*'s cockpit, staying low.

The whole exchange had taken less than a minute. He heard McMahon engage the throttle, and the *Rose* slipped off into the dead quiet harbor, not a Gardaí patrol in sight. As he'd hoped, the IRA had been both willing and helpful. They'd played their part to perfection. Now the fate of the devils who had destroyed his world was in his hands alone.

TWENTY

THERE WAS A DEEP LIVE BAIT well in *Shadow V*'s transom. This was where lobster pots were stowed when not in use. The hatch cover provided for a seat for whoever was steering the boat. The assassin crawled toward it on his hands and knees, dragging the heavy rucksack along with him. He knew every inch of this boat, having obtained and studied the original plans from which she was built.

He even knew why she was painted emerald green; it had been Lady Mountbatten's favorite color.

So, when he lifted the hatch cover and placed the lid carefully on the deck, he knew the precise interior dimensions of the bait well. Here the bomb would go. He had designed it to fit snugly down inside the well, once all the lobster pots were removed.

This he did patiently and quietly, one at a time, on his knees, stacking them neatly on the deck. There was a pub at the shoreside end of the town dock and you never knew when some chap might step outside to stagger home to the wife, so it was best to stay low. The pile of briny-smelling pots grew beside him, and finally he saw there was room enough in the well for the rucksack.

Carefully, he lifted the bomb and fitted it into the now open space. Perfect. He opened the flap on the rucksack and inserted the detonator, just the way the bomb maker McMahon had shown him. He noticed his hands were shaking a bit, but it was understandable. He hadn't done a lot of this sort of thing.

He flicked a drop of nervous perspiration from the tip of his nose and then thumbed the toggle switch that armed the bomb. The small radio detonator carefully sewn inside the seam of his black foul-weather jacket was now a very lethal weapon.

A little red eye had begun blinking down there in the dark bait well and his heart beat faster.

About four cubic feet of open space remained above the bomb. He filled it with lobster pots and used most of them to do so. The remainder he heaved over the side, knowing the ebb tide would carry them out before morning. He closed the hatch cover upon which Lord Mountbatten always sat when the boat was under way. He loved his little boat, and Smith knew it.

It was only a matter of time before—

He heard two men, mumbling drunkenly, emerge from the pub. They got louder, strolling out to the end of the dock. They were close and there was no time to duck under the cuddy cabin. He flattened himself on the deck, as near to the dockside bulkhead of the boat as he could get. Damn it, he silently cursed. This was no time to be discovered aboard Lord Mountbatten's boat. He'd kill these two unfortunates if he had to, slit their throats with his fish knife, but that would cause no end of complications. He'd no choice but to lie there, dead still, and hope they were too inebriated to notice him.

"Ye know what they say about beer, Paddy O'Reilly?"

"You don't buy it, ye only rent it."

"Exactly," the first man said.

"I'd say the day's rent's long overdue, wouldn't you?"

"Time to bleed the lizards awright, Bucko . . ."

He knew exactly what was going to happen. He heard two zippers being yanked down and the shuffling feet of the two men on the dock now standing directly over his head. Two streams of urine spattered on the *Shadow V*'s deck not a foot from his face. He caught some of it, of course, but he'd his foul-weather gear on and as a child he'd suffered far worse indignities.

Lying there in the dark, still as stone, watching that black pool of piss spreading across the deck, he smiled. He liked the idea of these two blokes strolling down the dock of an evening, just to relieve themselves on Mountbatten's pride and joy. "Piss on you, oh mighty Lord Mountbottom," one of them said as they zipped up, had a wee chuckle, and returned to the pub.

Lord Mountbottom they call him, Smith said to himself with a smile. The locals' moniker was a fitting enough tag for the old bastard.

HE SAW A FEW FLASHLIGHT beams darting among the trees in the forest as he made his way up the hill. Special Protection guards. He'd shed his black foul-weather gear and the balaclava. He was now dressed in a black turtleneck jumper and black trousers, with the black watch cap pulled down over the tops of his ears. He kept just inside the woods at the side of the lane.

Reaching the hilltop, he skirted the well-guarded Classiebawn estate and moved quickly and silently toward his refuge without incident. It was the end of the summer, and he assumed, correctly, that the Irish Gardaí and the Special Branch men assigned to protect Queen Victoria's grandson would be more interested in a final pint of Guinness or a wee dram of Tullamore than some interloper with murder on his mind.

He slept that night, fitfully, inside the damp and crumbling ruin of a Norman watchtower. Water seeped from the mossy old stones like tears. The thousand-year-old tower stood amid a copse of green wood overlooking a moonlit Donegal Bay. He tried to sleep, but all night long he was beset by frightful dreams. In one, he was but a small boy, sent out to slay a great fire-breathing dragon, alone, in order to protect his family.

Unlike St. George, a great knight, he'd only been a defenseless boy, and the dragon had easily engulfed him and his family with great licks of fire. After the dragon slithered away, he saw them all, his father, mother, and sister, as from above, twisted and charred like sticks, strewn about the marble steps leading to the flaming ruins of what had been their home.

In another dream, one he had frequently, a fire-breathing locomotive pulled into a huge and darkened station pulling a long train of boxcars. When the doors to all the cars were pulled open, gallons of viscous red blood gushed out, flooding the platform. Every single cattle car was full to overflowing with the bloody, horribly mutilated corpses of murdered Moslem women.

THE NORMAN WATCHTOWER MADE a decent enough shelter. He'd discovered it a few years ago, on one of his earliest surveillance trips to Mullaghmore, and had known immediately that one fine day it would suit his purposes perfectly. At last, a few hours before daybreak, he slept. When he opened his eyes, looking up through the ragged holes of missing stone in the tower, he knew he'd been right about his timing.

God was with him.

The morning dawned blue and clear, an almost supernaturally lovely day after all the weeks of drenching rain. There was virtually no wind at all. He was stiff from sleeping on the bare, damp ground, but ten minutes of vigorous stretching and breathing exercises brought him fully awake, his blood coursing through his veins with anticipation of what was to come.

There was just enough of a spiral stone staircase remaining inside the tower for him to climb to the top. From this splendid vantage point he had a view that included all of Classiebawn Castle and its grounds, the green hills beyond, the narrow lane that led down the hill to Mullaghmore, the harbor, and the placid blue bay sparkling in the morning sun.

He pulled a fish knife he'd stolen from the Sligo boat from his trouser pocket and quickly slit the seam of his jacket. There, in a waterproof packet, was the detonator. He slid it out of its waxed pouch, unwrapped it, and gazed upon it almost lovingly.

It was a simple aluminum box, no bigger than a pack of cigarettes. It had a dial that showed battery strength (full), a warning light, and a toggle switch, currently in the "off" position.

He set the detonator on the wide stone balustrade of the curved wall and raised his binoculars to his eyes. For a few hours, the house was quiet and it was difficult to be patient. Then, around eleven, there was a bustle of activity in and around the castle. Children and dogs racing in and out of the house, slamming doors, nannies pushing strollers to and fro, gardeners cutting fresh flowers in the gardens.

It looked like the first day of summer, not the last.

Half an hour later he saw Mountbatten emerge from the front entrance of the castle. He was surrounded by family, by laughing and skipping children, all delighted to see the sun shining at last. The old man was dressed in faded corduroys and a rough pullover. All the members of his family, young and old, were carrying something, a picnic basket, a thermos, a jug of wine.

He watched Lord Mountbatten march his little army along the drive leading away from the house. They turned, as he knew, hoped, prayed they would, to the right and began descending the hill toward Mullaghmore harbor.

SHADOW V, A BRILLIANT GREEN in the noonday sun, was waiting at the end of the dock. In no time at all, they'd all boarded, children and adults both clearly excited at the prospect of a day on the water. A young boy, fifteen perhaps and clearly a local, cast off the lines. There was a puff of blue smoke as Mountbatten reached down and started the little three-cylinder diesel engine.

Then Lord Louis took his normal seat, on the portside hatch

cover above the well where the unused lobster pots were normally stowed.

He bent forward and engaged the throttle and the little boat moved away from the dock. Proceeding at a stately pace, *Shadow V* slowly eased beyond the harbor's protecting stone walls until she'd cleared the long jetty. The happy party proceeded along the coast, still barely a stone's throw from shore, for a few hundred yards. Then they came to a stop so Mountbatten could inspect his lobster pots.

It was time. Smith whispered a silent prayer to heaven and thumbed the detonator switch. For a moment, nothing happened and he stared in disbelief at the little green boat bobbing there among the lobster pots.

The sudden explosion shattered the summer stillness into a thousand pieces. A great geyser of splintered wood, blood, oil, and broken bodies shot high into the air. The shock of the blast shook the Norman watchtower to its ancient foundations; indeed, the force of the detonation was felt miles from the fishing village of Mullaghmore. In the roiling bay, nothing remained of *Shadow V* but countless green splinters of wood, bobbing about everywhere you looked. And then there were the bodies, floating facedown.

The deed was done.

The man who had just murdered one of England's greatest heroes remained steadfastly at his post, moving his glasses back and forth from body to body, desperate to see Mountbatten's mutilated corpse pulled from the water. Townspeople in small boats instantly sped to the rescue. A huge debris field spread across the water, slick with fuel oil, and here and there the small bodies of children floated in the water.

He didn't care about the incidental dead; they didn't trouble him in the slightest. The amount of blood on this English bastard's hands would never be equaled in ten thousand lifetimes. A small blue fishing vessel came to a stop beside one of the larger of the floating corpses.

He held his breath, focusing on the face of the corpse. Yes. It was him. Two men pulled what was left of Lord Mountbatten into the boat. Despite grievous injuries, he appeared to be alive, if only just. Smith waited atop the tower just long enough to watch Lord Louis Mountbatten expire. It didn't take long.

The man who had betrayed his nation died almost immediately, there on the deck of the small blue boat, both of his legs almost completely severed from his upper body.

God be praised.

The great Mountbatten, partitioned at last.

Now Smith could begin to sound the fathoms of his vengeance against the British Monarchy in earnest. As he made his way down the spiral staircase inside the watchtower, he suddenly realized that he was in no hurry to wreak his terrible havoc. He had a lifetime to plan each exquisite act to perfection and then execute it flawlessly. He would be the very soul of patience. He would strike only when the circumstances were perfect.

Each and every wound he inflicted would be a moment and a memory to *savor.*

And he believed, he *knew*, in every fiber of his being, that he would never be caught.

Never.

In the most solemn and uncharted depths of his dark soul, Smith conceived he had been put upon this earth for one reason: he was born a battle mace to crush a corrupt and rusting crown.

HOURS AFTER THE HORROR at Mullaghmore shook England and the civilized world to the core, the following statement was issued by the Provisional Wing of the Irish Republican Army in Belfast:

> THE I.R.A. CLAIM RESPONSIBILITY FOR THE EXECUTION OF LORD LOUIS MOUNTBATTEN. THIS OPERATION IS ONE OF THE DISCRIMINATE WAYS WE CAN BRING THE ATTENTION OF THE ENGLISH PEOPLE TO THE CONTINUING OCCUPATION OF OUR COUNTRY.

TWENTY-ONE

MIAMI BEACH, PRESENT DAY

CHANDRA FELT AN ALMOST OVERWHELMING URGE to trigger her automatic stiletto and jam the razor-sharp blade straight up through her boss's jaw. Through his tongue and into the soft tissue of the palate at the roof of his mouth. She knew the sharpened tip would come to rest at the base of his brain, just behind the nasal cavity. This was one of the exact thrusts the weapon was made for. The kidneys, heart, and behind the ear were the other targets she went for with a great deal of regularity and success.

She'd been late. That's why she was being quote-unquote "punished" by this asshole. She'd been sent to Miami International with the van to pick up four new "students" arriving from Islamabad, Pakistan, via Jihad, Dubai, Caracas. Planes out of Venezuela were *always* late, but he blamed her anyway.

She took the "students" to the safe house they kept for new arrivals, a run-down two-story bungalow off Calle Ocho in Little Havana. Student housing for terrorists, the IED frat house she called it. They were moving a hundred kids a month through that dump. And Bashi got a big cut out of each and every one he delivered safely into the system.

Tomorrow, the students would disperse and begin their own personal crime waves. Crimes sufficiently serious to warrant the attention of the police, the courts, and finally the prison system. Then their real mission began. Preaching the hijacked gospel of the Prophet inside whatever joint they landed in.

Along with the daily religious instruction came bomb building, terror tactics; all this in preparation for the Caliphate, the "Big Day." It couldn't come soon enough for her. She hated her job, Miami, and the loathsome pig who often treated her like a bad dog. But he was a rich bastard, and he was exceedingly generous. The gorgeous new Bentley Arnage in her town-house garage was all the reminder she needed of that.

Tonight, he had kept her waiting for at least a half hour, standing before his desk, not being allowed to speak, while he made endless phone calls to various mullahs and warlords on Afghan mountaintops using his encrypted sat phone.

The only thing that kept her homicidal desires in check was the fact that he still owed her money, a *lot* of money. Enough to live like a princess for the rest of her life. If she killed the fat bastard, she'd never see a penny of it. She just had to roll with it for a little longer, that's all.

The burly, unshaven man in his fifties finally put his phone down, shook his head, and said in his guttural Afghan-accented Urdu, "I understand that you accomplished your goal, my darling child. My concern is the considerable amount of media attention you have brought upon yourself. Look at me."

Her eyes drifted from him to the big plasma screen on the wall above the fake fireplace . . . LIVE AT FIVE BREAKING NEWS. . . . Bashi's latest problem was scrawling across the bottom, MURDER ON THE BEACH!

"Bitch! You see what I am saying?"

"Following orders. Sir."

"Yes. But, still."

"Excuse me. Sir. You wanted these two dead. The last two alive who could tie us to Jackson Memorial. You didn't think a double homicide in broad daylight was going to attract a media story?"

"Two men gunned down in a car is one thing, but a running gun battle with government agents is quite another. How many casualties did you suffer?"

She was silent, looking across the large room full of gilded furniture. A newly redecorated penthouse suite at the recently rejuvenated Fontainebleau Hotel, overlooking the Atlantic. Rented by the month. Twenty grand a month.

The awful blond wig she'd worn on the job was on a sideboard with the liquor, sitting atop one of the artfully arranged Styrofoam heads. Four colors. Another of his many fetishes, she thought. Wigs. Why else keep them so neatly arranged in his living room? And in the top drawer of the sideboard, the rest of his—

She looked him in the eye.

"Two casualties. Abdullah was wounded severely by the black agent who chased us, and I had to put him out of his misery. And the other man, Caucasian, arriving at the end, whoever he was, killed Machmud with a couple of extraordinarily well-placed head shots. On the run."

"And this other shooter, the late arrival, he was also you believe with the CIA? Not local gendarmerie?"

She shook her head, her dark eyes glued on the fat man in front of her. Disgusted with herself that this pig was her lover. The things she had done. Willingly and unwillingly. She knew his background and the extraordinarily perverse evil he was capable of.

Until 1999, when he was quietly removed from the Khan nuclear lab in Islamabad, Bashi was one of the scientists who worked on the gas centrifuge program that Dr. Khan stole from the Netherlands and brought home to Pakistan. Then he'd designed the reactor at Khushab that produced fuel to move to the next level—a plutonium bomb. He was hailed as a genius, the hero of all Pakistan.

Over time, people started wondering if he was playing with a full deck. He was always talking about sunspots. He even wrote an extensive treatise in Urdu about the role sunspots played in triggering the French Revolution, World War II, and uprisings against colonial masters around the world. Sunspots. He still couldn't shut up about them. They finally sent him north to forge alliances with the Taliban.

His name was Bashir al Mahmoud Bashi, because he was tight as a tick with the new prez, and still had access to the entire Pakistani nuclear program. The Sword of Allah sleeper agents who had penetrated the nuclear weapon storage facilities were under Bashi's control. And the fat bastard was completely out of his fucking mind. No one knew that better than she.

She looked him in the eye.

"I told you I don't know who the white guy was. He moved so blindingly fast and shot so well that none of us got a good look at him. He didn't even show up until we were over in the city of Miami. I thought we had the big black man dead and done with. Then—well, you know the rest."

Now the fat man made a show of tidying up his fingernails with his small solid gold nail clipper. Tiny little clips here and there. Delicate, like brain surgery. He purposefully didn't look at her. This was the time of the biggest threat. Was he trying to lull her into a false sense of security? That was the way of the old-style Taliban commanders. Before they flayed you alive, they lulled you to sleep.

She knew Bashi had made his reputation long ago in Islamabad and later providing sophisticated nuclear weapons for Iran and North Korea. He would still be in a powerful position today had his mind not stripped a few gears over the ensuing years. And he would surely be dead, long ago, had the Soviets invading Afghanistan not turned his backbone to steel. And had he not come under the powerful protection of the Sword of Allah.

Now he looked up at her. His cold grey eyes were still powerful enough to send a slight shiver down her back.

"Are you ready to handle this other matter?"

She nodded.

"When?" he asked.

"Soon."

"Are you planning to make it a message or do it quietly?"

She looked up and leveled her eyes at him. "It is a fluid situation. Missing two of my best men, I may decide to do it quietly. Do you have a preference?"

"People have been asking far too many other people far too many questions. I don't know exactly how much they know about Pakistani ISI operations, but in the interest of caution he must be eliminated. I don't care how."

"What about the two CIA men who chased us? Should we handle them as well?"

"Did either get a good look at you?"

"The black one saw me in my wig with plenty of cleavage. Usually that's all American men notice. But we did face off over our gun sights. He looked into my eyes."

"Then you might want to spend a little time finding out more about these inquisitive federal agents. You have names?"

"The giant black man only. It shouldn't be too difficult to learn the other."

"Good girl. I will talk to you after this fucking traitor general has been eliminated. Do you know the American agent's full name? This black man who saw you?"

"Yes."

"How did you learn it?"

"He runs a company called Tactics International. Over in the Grove. He questioned me a few months ago about my visa. He had a list and thought my visa was illegal. When he found out it wasn't, he scratched me off the list, apologized, and went away. It was before my facial surgery. He won't remember."

"Who is he?"

"Stokely Jones is his name. Pity you're not handling this one yourself, Bashi. You could hit him. He's a very, very big target."

TWENTY-TWO

MIAMI

STOKELY JONES DOWNSHIFTED, GRABBING third, accelerating up and over the humpbacked bridge. It crossed over from downtown Miami to his magical island hideaway, Brickell Key. *Is this living, or what?* he asked himself, hearing the satisfying blip of the black-raspberry metallic GTO convertible's race-tuned engine, feeling the deep rumble of the tuned twin exhausts in his bones. Sex? Something like that, maybe.

Sometimes he actually had to wonder: Does sex with Fancha, his gorgeous fiancée, even hold a candle to this completely badass Pontiac?

The answer was always, unequivocally, yes. Nothing could ever hold a candle to his love for Fancha. Period. Still, Stoke curled his hand around the ivory shift knob of the Hurst four-speed shift lever as he downshifted again. If they had cars up there in heaven, he had no doubt, all those angels up there in paradise, they cruised GTOs down those streets of gold.

Passing the entrance to the ridiculously expensive and beautiful Mandarin Hotel on his right, top down, salt air breezes blowing, speakers blaring "Let's Stay Together," one of Al Green's greatest hits, Stoke got that old feeling again: complete disbelief at his current tropical luxury lifestyle. Former Harlem homeboy gangsta makes good? Oh, yes indeedy, life was good.

God was good. America was good. And, God, please bless America. We could sure use it right now.

Damn, I must be in a really *good mood,* he thought, approaching the tall glass and steel Brickell Towers on his right. He slowed for the turn, singing a song:

Yeah, we're movin' on up, movin' on up, to a dee-luxe apartment in the sky . . . and I feeeeel good, da-da-da-dum . . .

Keeping time to the lyrics and rhythms in his head, palm beating on the steering wheel, and, man, here he was, home again at last.

He hooked a right and swung into the gently curving palm-lined driveway leading to his own personal paradise, his condo in the sky, the light-filled penthouse overlooking Biscayne Bay that he called home. Paid for with the sole proceeds of his sainted mama's six-story apartment house in Bayside, Queens. He'd only lived in Miami a couple of years. Now he couldn't imagine living anywhere else. New York?

Fuggedaboutit.

He kept an eye peeled for the building's aging security man, Fast Eddie Falco, normally scouring the premises in his custom Rolls-Royce grilled golf cart at this hour. Stoke had stopped by Books & Books in the Grove, picked up a couple of paperback copies of the selection his two-man book club would be reading this week. The John D. MacDonald's Men's Reading Society would soon be digging into *The Dreadful Lemon Sky.*

Eddie, a former jockey, had spent his entire life as a railbird over at Hialeah before retiring. Never read word one not related to his beloved ponies and the jocks. Then one day Stoke introduced him to Travis McGee and his houseboat, the *Busted Flush.* Boom! Just like that, Eddie Falco found a whole new reason for living besides horses and football.

Just before turning into the ground-floor garage, he thought he caught a glimpse of Eddie's heavily customized fire-engine-red cart. Seemed to be parked beneath a palm tree. Actually, shit, it looked like he'd rammed the damn tree head-on. Stoke, thinking heart attack, screeched to a stop, leaped out over the closed passenger door, and ran across the thick green grass. Eddie was slumped forward over the wheel. Damn it! Unless a coconut had landed on his head, he'd probably blown an artery.

"Eddie! You okay?" he cried, racing toward his friend.

Eddie was definitely not okay. But it wasn't a coconut head bop or a heart attack. Looked like he had a deep wound in his right leg, just above the kneecap. The blood had soaked one whole leg of his khaki pants and pooled around his shoes. What the hell? He'd let a palm tree run into him, yeah, but not hard enough for even a minor injury.

Stoke leaned under the fringed white canopy, examining the hole in his pal's knee.

"Eddie, what the hell, man? What'd you do to your leg?"

"Ouch!"

"Sorry." Stoke probed the wound with his index finger. Narrow, but deep, down to the bone.

"The grille. How's it look?" Eddie said through clenched teeth.

"The what?"

"The grille!"

"What grille?"

"The goddamn Rolls-Royce grille! Did I dent it? Scratch it? Tell me, Stoke. I can take it."

"Eddie, f'crissakes, forget the grille. What the hell happened to your leg?"

"Aw, shit, Stoke. Somebody stabbed me."

"Stabbed you?"

"Yeah. I'm bleedin' to death, here, f'crissakes," Eddie croaked, and he looked like he might croak for real, too. Old man was in shock, his face white as a sheet, eyes dilated. And blood was seeping out of him, out of the cart, onto the grass.

Stoke pulled out his cell, punched in 911, and whipped off his belt, cradling the phone between his shoulder and his ear, waiting for an answer as he wrapped the belt tightly around Eddie's thigh just above the wound. "C'mon, answer me, damn it . . ."

"Nine-one-one. What is your emergency?"

"Listen carefully. My name is—"

Eddie eyed him with a watery eye. "Don't you hate it when they say, '*Por Español,* press one'?"

"My name is Stokely Jones Jr., resident at Icon Brickell Towers, 495 Brickell Avenue, Brickell Key, downtown Miami. I have a stabbing victim here, deep puncture wound to the thigh, lost a lot of blood. I need both EMS and Miami-Dade Police assistance immediately."

"Yes, sir. Could you repeat—"

"You heard me. This man needs help now. Make it happen." He snapped his phone closed and cinched the belt tighter. The flow eased up a lot.

"Stoke, am I gonna die here?" Eddie moaned, looking up at him.

"Die? Shit, no, you ain't even about to die. I got this belt cinched above your knee. Cut off the bleeding. Ambulance on the way. You're going to be good as new. What the hell happened here, Ed? Take a deep breath and talk to me."

"Some wacky broad, man. Trespassing on private property. I spotted her ass over there in the garden, trying to hide behind the birds-of-paradise, looking up at the building with a pair of binoculars. Asked what she wanted, she says the master key card, crazy bitch. Ow! Fuck!"

"Sorry, it has to be real tight. Hurts like a bitch, I know. Can't help it."

"Yeah, but Jesus, Stokely."

"What happened next?"

"I drive over here, tell her to leave. She tells me go fuck myself. Then she pulls this goddamn diamond stiletto out of her handbag, jams it in my damn knee, that's how I rammed this tree. She says gimme the key card or I make it an even pair. My fuckin' knees! What am I gonna do? I hand it over. She takes the key card and splits and—hell, I dunno, I must have passed out."

"Diamond stiletto?"

"Yeah, the whole handle was gold, encrusted with diamonds."

"What did she look like, Eddie?"

"She was fuckin' beautiful, that's what. Some blond babe with tits out to here, that's what she looked like. Shit! This hurts!"

Stoke heard sirens screaming in the distance. He looked at Eddie hard. The bleeding had stopped. His color was coming back. He'd live.

"Hold on, Ed."

He ran for the entrance to his deluxe apartment in the sky.

"Stoke! Wait!" he heard Eddie screech behind him.

He stopped short and turned around. "What?"

"Did ya get the books? *Dreadful Lemon Sky*?"

"Jesus, Ed. Yeah, I got the books, okay?"

Eddie smiled and grimaced at the same time, and Stoke ran for the elevators.

TWENTY-THREE

FLASHY BLONDE WITH A HUGE RACK was gunning for him, huh? Great. He'd been thinking about her, the chick with the MAC-10 at the beach and in the black Charger, wondering if she'd come calling. She knew he'd seen her face and she seemed like a woman not out to meet new friends. He'd given Miami-Dade and the feds her description. And he'd been keeping his eye out for her, ever since the little shoot-out over on South Beach four days earlier.

Now he wished he'd said something to Eddie about keeping an eye out for her too. But he hadn't been that smart, and now Eddie had paid for Stoke's own stupidity and he cursed himself for it.

The beach bimbo was right now waiting for him up in his apartment. Had to be. Why else would a woman stab an old security guy and demand his master key? He hit PH and leaned back against the elevator's marble wall, trying to see how this was all going to go down. Picture the thing in his mind.

There was a big black leather chair in the living room. His personal chair. An Eames chair, the wispy decorator had called it. Chair faced south, out toward Biscayne Bay and the Keys; it had a matching leather footstool. His "watch the Dolphins get their asses kicked again" chair, he called it. It also swiveled.

It would be the most likely place for her to wait. Sit in that chair, swiveled around, directly facing the front door, cradling your nasty little black machine gun in your lap, your finger on the trigger, the lever set on three-shot bursts. Yeah. Maybe make it fun. Pour yourself a nice glass of wine from the jug of Almaden in the fridge, sit there all afternoon and wait for the big black dude to come home. That's the way he saw it going down anyway, and he was pretty good at visualizing this shit.

The elevator stopped on 60 and the doors slid open.

To the left was the corridor leading to his apartment. To the right was a door with a stairway leading to the roof. Stoke knew it wasn't locked because painters had been up there for the last couple of days, painting all the air-conditioning and heating equipment with some kind of rust-proofing paint. Shit got rusty fast in Miami, he'd learned from Eddie.

He quickly climbed the steps to the roof, trying to remember if he'd left the main sliding glass doors to his terrace open or shut. Open, he thought. But today was hot as hell, so he may have closed them and let the AC cool the place down while he was out. If they were open, he had an idea.

The entire rooftop, big as a football field, was covered with tiny white stones and the glare of the sun was painful. He crossed over to the eastern side of the building and calculated exactly where his terrace would be, right below the southeastern edge of the roof. He knelt down, looking below, suddenly very conscious of the amazing height sixty stories high in the sky.

He dropped to his knees and placed his hands carefully, shoulder width apart, gripping the raised four-inch steel rim sheathed in aluminum that went all the way around the four-sided building, took a deep breath.

Then he stretched out flat on the roof, digging the toes of his shoes into the stone, edging his body out into midair till his belt was almost to the edge. He could now lean out and down, take a quick peek at his terrace doors.

Please be open.

Closed.

And locked, he remembered. Shit. He always locked those sliding glass doors, even though it was ridiculous up here in the sky. Old habits die hard. He pushed back, heaved himself up, and got to his feet, thinking. Can't go in the front door and the terrace is locked up tight.

Es un grande problema, hombre, as Fancha would say. But big men solve big problems. He lifted his shirt, pulled the SIG 9mm out of the holster in the small of his back, checked his weapon. One round in the chamber and a full mag.

Now what?

The terrace. Yeah. The terrace was the only way. She'd have her back to it, eyes focused on the doorknob of the front door. The good news: the terrace behind her was just about the last place on earth anyone would be expecting company to drop in unexpectedly.

But once you drop in, then what? How the hell do you get through the sliding glass doors? Knock twice and smile? Mouth the word *Domino's* with your hands behind your back? Pizza man?

He looked around the rooftop, pulling down on his right earlobe. Old habit. Back in the day, thinking of some damn way or other to get his SEAL platoon out of a fucking VC ambush without anybody else getting killed, he'd started the ear-pulling thing. Nervous tic.

The doors were the problem. Glass too thick, terrace too narrow to get any force behind a surprise kick. So you're out there, she hears a thud and spins the chair, sees your ass, fires a short burst, and you're punched back over the railing, lost in space, already deader than the deadest damn doornail in the history of doors.

He looked around the rooftop for inspiration.

Paint cans. There were a shitload of Rust-Oleum paint cans everywhere, some used, some full, all scattered about a big spattered canvas tarp the painters had laid down around the perimeter of the

HVAC shit. Brushes in old cans full of paint thinner. So, the cans, Stoke. Something with the cans, okay? What?

He picked up a long piece of rope, one end tied to some unused scaffolding, the other end coiled up, about fifty feet of it. Good strong half-inch nylon. Rope. And a full gallon of paint tied to one end. That could work.

He smiled at the whole damn thing. Funny how your mind worked sometimes. Came up with some crazy shit you'd never even dream of. Over the years, he'd learned to just go with it, go with the flow, see where it would lead. Instinct. Why he was alive today. Snap decisions on the fly, right or wrong. Bet on yourself, like his mama always told him.

You jes bet on your own self, Stokely Jones. You hear me? Your own self. That's all you got.

Secret of life.

He tied one end of the rope to a standpipe near the southeast side of the roof, a double bowline. Tied the other end to the big can of Rust-Oleum. Heavy as shit, as paint goes, most probably full of lead.

He swung it in a gradually increasing arc a few times, just to get the heft of the can. Felt good out there, the Rust-Oleum, at the end of his rope, so to speak. Like it might actually work.

So.

How does this go down?

Girl down there in his apartment, patient, even sipping chilled vino maybe, waiting for him in that comfy black leather Eames chair, fingering the trigger of the MAC-10 in her lap, eye on the door, thinking, Come to mama, Mr. Jones.

Meanwhile, the potential victim is standing up here on the damn roof right over her head, sixty stories up in the sky, half-blind and scared shitless by the acrobatic feat he was about to attempt, contemplating a surprise appearance without falling sixty stories to the ground or getting his crazy ass shot all to pieces.

He swung the heavy can in a tight circle, really hard a few times in ever increasing arcs, finally flinging the can way out into the sky and bringing it back toward the terrace to complete the arc, can coming back hard, right up under the eave of the roof, right into the glass of his doors, hearing it smash through, making a huge noise, and then grabbing the rim of the roof and just doing a Tarzan flip over the edge, hoping to Jesus he'd land on his feet inside the railing of his terrace, not outside.

He heard the *phut-phut-phut* of an automatic weapon equipped with a noise suppressor just after his feet hit the terrace. Rounds taking out what was left of the glass. He ducked, grabbed the SIG, and dove through the nearest jagged glass door, rolling behind the heavily upholstered leather sofa to his right. Silent rounds thudded repeatedly into the sofa as he crouched behind it, struggling to come to grips with what he'd seen in those few seconds before he went for the floor.

It wasn't the blonde sitting in the chair.

No, it was some bald-headed fat guy, stark naked from the waist down, shooting at him. And the blond chick? She was on the floor, topless, kneeling between the guy's legs. As Stoke dove, he'd seen her crabbing bare ass toward his front door, reaching up for the knob. It didn't take much imagination to figure out this cozy little scenario. Chick gives guy head while they're waiting for the shooting to start.

What the hell is it with these people?

He heard the door slam and knew she was gone.

He crawled around the edge of the sofa and quick-peeked. Chair was empty. The guy was backing toward the door, difficult because his pants were still down around his ankles, swinging the gun side to side at waist level. This wasn't turning out right, his look said. He saw Stoke's face appear for a split second and put another burst into the sofa, shredding Stoke's beautiful leather furniture to pieces.

You can mess with me, Stoke thought, *but not with my furniture. That really pisses me off.* He shouted at the guy from behind the sofa.

"Pull your damn pants up, asshole, and tell me why you were getting a blow job in my favorite chair without even being invited in."

Another burst, high and into the ceiling. Stoke peeked around the side. Saw the sweaty three-hundred-pound guy frantically reaching around behind him for the doorknob still at least five feet behind his fat ass, waddling backward like a goddamn duck with his pants down. Wasn't pretty.

Stoke called out, "Here I come, chubby, ready or not."

He popped up at the opposite end of the couch and put two rounds in the guy, one in each knee. Fat Boy screamed and collapsed to the floor. Hearing the MAC-10 clattering on his beautiful parquet floor, Stoke, seriously angry now, yanked his ruined sofa backward toward him and leaped right over the thing. He was squatting on top of the fat man with his gun in his face in less than two seconds.

At that moment two cops in black Kevlar outfits took the door down, putting their guns on Stoke, saying, "Police! Freeze, asshole! Drop the gun! Now!"

Stoke accidentally dropped his SIG on the fat guy's face and backed away. The cops looked at the half-naked limp-dick white man on the floor, then up at the huge black guy in the New York Jets sweatshirt.

"This ain't exactly what it looks like, Officers," Stoke said, putting his hands up.

"This is Miami, asshole," the older cop said. "It's always exactly what it looks like."

TWENTY-FOUR

MULLAGHMORE, NORTHERN IRELAND

ALEX HAWKE AND AMBROSE CONGREVE HAD flown Hawke's plane across the Irish Sea, arriving in Northern Ireland at the tiny airport at Sligo. Very tiny. Only two flights a day, one to Dublin, one from Dublin. They had driven by hired car almost due north to the tiny fishing village of Mullaghmore, stopping briefly at a small inn for a Plowman's lunch and a chance for Ambrose to get on the telephone and arrange for tonight's meeting.

They now walked through the heavy rain past The Pennywhistle pub to the end of the Mullaghmore town's wooden dock.

There they paused, looking down at the choppy black water. It was a dark, blustery night, and the scattered lights of the little fishing village shone like halos through the mist on the surrounding hillside. At the top of the hill behind them, Lord Mountbatten's Classiebawn Castle was a looming, dark presence.

"This is it, then," Congreve said, shining his flashlight into the dark water. "*Shadow V* was moored right here, the night before the murder. Usually she was moored to one of those buoys over there near the shore, but Mountbatten had ordered her moved right here to the dock that afternoon."

"So they could get an early start pulling pots next morning," Hawke mused.

"Precisely."

Hawke looked over his shoulder, down the glistening length of the dock to the noisy Pennywhistle. "So the bomber carried a fifty-pound bomb the length of this dock? Past the pub? Even on a dark night that would carry considerable risk of discovery."

"True. That is why we surmised he arrived at the crime scene via hired boat. From Sligo most likely, as it's the nearest harbor. Much less conspicuous, a boat, especially at night. Simply come alongside the *Shadow V*, his confederates drop him off, he climbs right aboard Mountbatten's vessel with his package. The hired boat, an anonymous fishing vessel, steams away, never to be seen again. The killer plants the bomb in the bait well with the lobster pots and disappears down the dock and up into the woods."

"Makes sense."

"There's an old Norman watchtower up there. Splendid view of the entire bay. I'll show it to you in the morning. We found reason to believe he slept there. Bits of day-old food, cigarette stubs, a book of matches. Sleeps on the ground, wakes up at dawn, and climbs to the top. Follows Mountbatten's movements with binoculars all next morning from atop the tower. That's where the killer, whoever he was, detonated the bomb, in my opinion."

"That was in your official report?"

"It was indeed. Seen enough?" Ambrose said, rain streaming down his face.

"Yes. Let's go have a pint and see if your old friend has decided in our favor."

Ambrose, upon entering the pub and shedding his macintosh, saw his man standing at the far end of the long bar, staring into the smoky mirror, raising a glass of whiskey to his lips.

"There he is," Congreve said to Hawke. "End of the bar. White-haired fellow."

Hawke nodded, staring at the man. He'd never expected him to come.

"You never cease to amaze me, Constable."

"I have hidden powers of persuasion. I keep them folded in my breast pocket. Get them from the Bank of England. May I suggest you take that table in the corner by the window? I think it best I have a word with him alone. Complete our financial transaction without causing him any embarrassment. Then we'll join you."

Hawke sat, staring at the raindrops running down the window and the hazy harbor lights beyond, letting his friend conduct his business in privacy. A pretty barmaid agreed to bring him a pint of Guinness and he sipped it slowly, not knowing how long this evening might last.

Ten minutes later, Congreve appeared with a gaunt, white-haired man, tall and stooped, with very sad eyes.

"Alex, this is Thomas McMahon."

Hawke got to his feet and shook the man's gnarled hand, looking him in the eye. "Mr. McMahon, thank you for coming. I'm sure this can't be pleasant for you. Won't you sit down? Another whiskey?"

The man convicted of the murder of Lord Mountbatten nodded his assent and sat down, staring in stony silence at the scarred and battered tabletop. He was in his eighties and looked every day of it. Broken blood vessels made a map of his cheeks and long thin nose. His eyes were pale blue and watery. His hands trembled. A man who had traveled a hard road and seen more than enough of it.

Ambrose took the other chair and signaled the barmaid over.

"Three whiskeys, please," he said, pushing his chair back to accommodate his rather expansive midriff. Then he said to McMahon, "Tom, Alex and I are old friends. He bears you no ill will for events in the past. We've come to Ireland to find answers to some old questions, that's all. We'd be extremely grateful for any help you can give us."

"I'll say what I know. No more. I ain't a tout."

"That is all we ask," Hawke said gently.

"I went to bloody prison for a crime I dinna commit."

"The jury thought otherwise, Tom," Ambrose said, putting a

quieting hand on the old fellow's trembling forearm. "Based on the evidence presented."

"The jury was wrong. And so were you, damn you!" he said, raising his voice and peering fiercely into Congreve's eyes.

Clearly the man had started drinking much earlier in the day.

Congreve kept his tone under control. "That is entirely possible. I did the best I could. It's all any man can do."

"Ah! You admit you may have been wrong, then, Detective Inspector?"

"I admit mistakes may have been made during the investigation and the trial. That's all I will say."

"I was seventy miles from the scene of the crime when the bloody bomb went off! You knew that. That was stated in court!"

"You were the bomb builder, Tom. The bomb was gelignite, your signature explosive. There were traces of it on your clothing when you were arrested."

"I built bombs, f'crissakes. I had traces of gelignite in me clothes every day of the week. What does it prove? That my bomb killed Mountbatten? No. It proves nothing."

"Tom, listen to me," Congreve said quietly. "Mr. Hawke and I have come to Ireland to look at another suspect. Someone I was interested in at the time but was unable to build a case against. If we can find that man, and connect him to the murder, well, no guarantees, but it is very possible that your name could be cleared. At worst, your charge would be reduced to accessory to murder."

"Would me sentence be reduced as well, then? Would I get me thirty years back? D'ya think so, sir?"

Hawke signaled the barmaid for another round and she delivered it promptly.

Hawke eyed the IRA terrorist, waiting until he had his undivided attention.

"Mr. McMahon. Chief Inspector Congreve is here because he thinks there is a possibility you may be innocent of some of the charges against you. Were I you, sir, I would treat him with a bit more respect. He is the only man on this planet in a position to right any wrongs that may or may not have been done to you. If you continue to address my friend in this abusive manner, we shall simply get up and leave you to your fate. Do you understand me?"

McMahon glared at Hawke for a second, saw the red glint of anger in the Englishman's eye that many had seen before, and said, "Aye."

"Good. In the summer before Lord Mountbatten was murdered, there were a series of brutal murders of young women in the north of Ireland. Were you aware of these murders?"

"Who wasn't? There was a maniac on the loose."

"Did you know any of the victims?"

"No. They was all pretty young girls. I was a happily married man and didn't dabble. I didn't drink then, never set foot in a pub."

"Why do you say that word? Pub?"

"He met them in pubs, didn't he?"

"Did he?"

"What everyone said. What do I know? I wasn't there, was I?"

"Did you ever hear anyone call the murderer by name?"

"Not that I recall, no."

"A stranger. Any other strangers you can recall that summer?"

"Aye, there was one. Another feller. Right crazy, that lot."

"Crazy in what way?"

"Told me mates he wanted to kill Mountbatten."

Hawke looked at Congreve. "Did this come out in the trial, Chief Inspector?"

"Yes. It was all hearsay, of course, just like this. The existence of this 'stranger' was never proved by the defense. No substantiation at all."

"This crazy fellow, Mr. McMahon, exactly what did he want from your mates?" Hawke said.

"He wanted a bomb."

"That's all?"

"No. He said he needed a boat as well."

"A boat? Why?"

"Why? So he could slip inside this harbor in the dark of night and plant a bomb on the *Shadow V*, that's why. And that's just what he bloody well did, too. Have a look at the testimony, you'll see."

"Where did he get the bomb?"

"From me mates. The bomb squad, we called ourselves back then. So we provided him with a bomb. That was the end of it."

"Was it one of your bombs, Mr. McMahon?"

"Now, Mr. Hawke, how the devil would I know that? I wasn't the only IRA man building explosive devices in them days, as I told you. We practically had a bomb factory going full steam. Are ye going to drink that whiskey there or let her evaporate?"

Hawke slid the untouched glass across the table. McMahon lifted it and threw it back.

"You have any idea what this so-called stranger looked like?"

"How could I? Never saw his face, did I. Even at our meetings. No one did."

"Why not?"

"Always wore a balaclava, didn't he? Secretive bastard, so they all said. No address. Rumor had it he lived all alone on some bloody island."

"Irish?"

"English."

"How do you know he was English if, as you claim, you never saw his face?"

"His bleedin' accent, that's how. Spoke just like you, Mr. Hawke. A fuckin' toff if ever I heard one."

Irish whiskey was beginning to get in the way of this interview and Hawke looked across at Ambrose. They both knew it was time to end it.

"Did this particular toff bastard have a name, Mr. McMahon?" Hawke asked, his tone flat and devoid of inflection.

"Doesn't everybody?"

"What was his, just out of curiosity?"

"Smith."

"Smith. You're sure of that?"

"I said Smith and I meant Smith."

"Thank you for your time, Mr. McMahon. If we have any further questions, we'll be in contact with you again. If you should remember anything you believe might help this investigation, here is my mobile number and Chief Inspector Congreve's. And, now, you'll excuse us."

"Another whiskey afore you go?"

"You got your money. Have as many as you like."

Hawke pushed back from the table and stood, wrapping his woolen scarf round his neck. "Ambrose?" he said.

Congreve ignored him, staring at McMahon. "Mr. McMahon, one more question if you don't mind. A moment ago you mentioned an island."

"Did I then?"

"Yes, you did. You said 'rumor had it he lived all alone on some bloody island.' "

"Ah, I did say that, didn't I? What about it?"

"Do you by any chance remember the name of that island?"

McMahon grinned, showing a mouth stuffed with large yellowed teeth. "It was a long time ago, Detective Inspector. Nigh on thirty years now. Memories fade."

"Think harder."

"It would cost you a bottle of Mr. Jameson's finest."

Congreve signaled to the barmaid, ordered another bottle of whiskey.

TWENTY-FIVE

"THE NAME OF THE ISLAND, THOMAS McMahon, if you please."

"Right. Lamb Island, I think. Or, maybe Sheep Island it was. Hell, man, I dunno. Something like that."

"Think, Mr. McMahon. I need to know the exact name of that island," Congreve pressed.

"Mutton Island. That was it, all right. Mutton Island. Off Sligo."

Congreve stood and paid the barmaid, taking the bottle of Irish whiskey from the tray and placing it before the old IRA man.

"As Mr. Hawke said, if you think of anything else, please call. I will make it well worth your while. Good night, Mr. McMahon."

"You two figuring on going out there any time soon? Mutton Island, I mean."

"We're determined to locate Mr. Smith, dead or alive. If, as you say, he lived on Mutton Island around the time of the murders, I suspect it will be the first place we look. I bid you good evening, sir." Ambrose started to get to his feet. The Irishman shot him a look.

"Wait," McMahon said. "Sit down."

Ambrose did. "What is it?"

"I wasn't going to say anything about this. But I figure this is me only chance. If you gents are willing to pay me some serious money, I'd be willing to part with some very serious information."

"We're all ears, Mr. McMahon," Hawke said. "This is your one chance."

"You fellas heard of something called 'the Real IRA'?"

"Don't be ridiculous," Ambrose said. "They ambushed and killed two British policemen in an attack on the Massereene Barracks last March. They don't acknowledge the Good Friday Agreement of 1998 and the long-standing peace. I'm afraid these people are determined to provoke more bloodshed and I think it is abominable."

"Yer afraid with good reason," McMahon said, downing his whiskey and pouring another. "They've got something in the works, y'see. In the late planning stages. And—"

"Mr. McMahon, with all due respect," Hawke said, "how are you in a position to know what these people are planning? Ever since their Omagh bombing killed twenty-nine people and injured two hundred twenty others, they've been considered a credible terrorist organization both in the United Kingdom and the United States. Believe me, we watch their every move very carefully."

"But you ain't on the inside, are ye, Mr. Hawke?"

"And you are?"

"Aye. I'm up to me old tricks. Building fireworks for them. Old habits die hard, y'see. They're using land mines, homemade mortars, and car bombs now, and I'm privy to a lot of stuff I shouldn't know about because I keep me ears open."

"And now you offer to betray their trust for money, Mr. McMahon. One naturally wonders how reliable such information might be, seeing as how selling legitimate information will place you in a very dangerous position. You know what the IRA does to traitors as well as I do. Why are you doing this, one wonders."

"I'll tell ye why! These bastards betrayed me, they did. Betrayed all of us! They use my skills but there is no respect anymore. They let me take the fall for Lord Louis, spend half me bleeding life in prison.

Now they look at me as if I ain't there. Besides, they're bringing in weapons from foreigners now, and I'm sure me days are numbered."

"Foreigners? Collaborating with the IRA?" Hawke said, leaning forward. "Foreigners from where?"

"I forget."

"Look, here, McMahon. How much money do you want?" Hawke asked, up to here with the man.

"Enough to leave Ireland for good and start a new life for meself. What's left of it, anyway. I want to die in a nice warm bed, with the cool hand of a fair colleen on my brow if not elsewhere." He downed his drink, licking his lips, pouring himself another.

"Tell us what you know. We'll bicker later. But if we think your information is valuable and believable, we will provide you with sufficient funds to resettle outside Ireland. Agreed?"

"Aye."

"Well, then?"

"There's a safe house. I go there now and then to make product deliveries, if you take my meaning. There's a huge cache of weapons in that basement. Their arsenal, if you take my meaning. Enough to blow up half of Ireland. For the last month or so, it's been a bloody frenzy there. People coming and going all hours, day and night, most of 'em masked. Lot of high-level boys talking late into the night. Planning."

"Planning what?"

"I ain't privy. You'd have to ask the man himself. Smith is in charge."

Smith?

Hawke and Congreve, stunned, looked at each other in shock.

"Smith?" Hawke said, keeping his voice steady.

"That's what I said, didn't I. Maybe I just signed me own death warrant, but there, I've said it, and fuck all."

Congreve said, carefully, "Smith is still involved with the IRA? We were under the impression his involvement ceased thirty years ago, after the Mountbatten murder."

"Ceased? Why do you say that? Why, they practically anointed him the bloody King of Eire after he pulled that killing off. Mountbatten was just the beginning for our Mr. Smith. He was always in for the long haul."

Hawke said, "The long haul?"

"That's what I said."

Hawke leaned forward, making sure he had the man's attention. "Mr. McMahon, this is a very serious matter. Please try to concentrate. What other acts of terrorism against Britain and the Crown was Mr. Smith involved with?"

"Too many to recall, to be honest. But I can name a few for certain."

"Please."

"That Christmas bombing at Harrods in London that killed five and injured almost a hundred. 1983 it was, I believe. That was Smith. The next year, he almost got Lady Thatcher and her entire Cabinet down at that hotel in Brighton. So many others. The mortar round fired into Downing Street back in '91 . . ."

"Good Lord," Congreve said, leaning back in his chair, trying to digest what he'd just heard. Smith, still out there? Still attacking Britain? It was almost inconceivable he could have gone this long without attracting the attention of the Secret Service or Scotland Yard.

Hawke said, "You say he's in the midst of planning another operation. What do you know about it?"

"Only that it's big, like I said earlier."

"A bomb, you said."

"Aye. But a bomb like nothing seen in these parts. A Big Bertha of a bomb that will wreak more havoc and kill more people than in all the years since 'The Troubles' began is what I hear."

"A conventional weapon?" Hawke asked, glaring at the man.

"I can't say. I'd tell ye if I knew. Honest I would. Maybe brought in by Smith himself. He's traveling all the time, and I don't mean down to Brighton for the sea air."

"When is this operation?"

"Soon. I hear a month or two, but it could be sooner."

Congreve said, "This safe house. In order to get your money, you must tell us its exact location. Once we have confirmed that, you'll be paid. How much do you want?"

"I was thinking twenty thousand pounds sterling would do me quite nicely."

"Think fifteen thousand pounds sterling and you have a deal."

"Done," McMahon said with a smile that revealed stained and crooked teeth. He then poured himself another drink.

"Where, exactly, is the house located?"

"Heard of the Dog, a small river in County Sligo?"

"No."

"Not really a river, more like a stream. A tributary that runs off the River Mourne. Follow the Dog to a town called Plumbridge. The house is three miles due north of the town center. It's an old place called the Barking Dog Inn. A farmer's sheepdog drowned in that river one night. Some say you can still hear him barking when the moon's full, under that old wooden bridge. The house stands in a wood, not too far from the bend in the river. It's due east of the only bridge over the Dog for miles. A wooden bridge."

"We'll be in touch, Mr. McMahon," Congreve said, ending the meeting.

The famous criminalist stood up and followed his friend Hawke through the crowd gathered at the smoke-filled bar and out into the wet night. Ambrose could not possibly have been more excited than he was at this moment. McMahon was a thoroughly reprehensible character, but, possibly, he had just provided them with unbelievably valuable information.

Nothing less than confirmation that there had indeed been a "third man" as he and Constable Drummond had insisted from the start right up to the very end. Not only did he exist, he was still very much alive. Active, if one could believe McMahon, in this dangerous New IRA uprising. And he was apparently operating within a few miles of where they stood at this very moment.

STANDING OUTSIDE, CONGREVE SAID, "WE'VE got our 'pawn,' Alex. Smith! It has to be. Still alive after all these years? Astounding. Still functioning? It beggars belief."

"We don't have him yet, but by heaven we may have just gotten a whole lot closer. McMahon's evidence is all hearsay, of course. No proof of any of it. But if we could prove murder out on Mutton Island, and tie Smith to it, well, then—"

"Yes, my thoughts exactly. I'm not quite sure where to begin. What do you think, Alex. Mutton Island first? Or confirm the presence of this IRA safe house? The Barking Dog Inn."

They started walking through the misty rain to the hired car. An ungainly little beast called a Ford Mondeo. It certainly wasn't the Locomotive. In fact, Hawke had taken to calling it "the caboose." Once inside, Hawke pulled a map from the car's glove box.

Hawke said, "Mutton Island is only one hour's drive from here. And not far offshore. Let's get out there as quickly as possible. Hire a fishing boat. See what's to be seen, if indeed anything is. After that, we'll turn our efforts toward an investigation of this bloody Barking Dog Inn. We'll need time, men, and weapons to set that operation up properly. I'll have to make all the necessary arrangements with British Army forces in the event it's determined a full-scale raid on the safe house is warranted."

"Quite right. But, still, you must admit it's a breakthrough. Smith still at it, Alex? In Northern Ireland?" Congreve said.

"We'll find out, I suppose, when we check in at the Barking Dog Inn. If Smith is among the plotters there when we take it, and we manage to take him alive, I'll have some extremely good news for the Prince of Wales."

"You're not going to call him now? With what we've just heard?"

"I think not."

"Why? He'll be jubilant."

"I simply don't trust this fellow McMahon. Throw enough money and booze at him and he'll say what he thinks you want to hear. This could still be the wildest of goose chases."

"I don't think so, Alex. You know that feeling, when you've finally got the bone in your teeth?"

"Not really."

"Well, I do. And I've got it now."

"Good feeling or bad feeling?"

"For a copper? Best feeling there is."

"Can you hold that thought until we get to Mutton Island?"

"Can and will."

TWENTY-SIX

MUTTON ISLAND, IRELAND

I REALLY THINK I AM GOING to be sick, Alex," Congreve said. It was later on the night of their unpleasant but highly intriguing meeting with the bomber McMahon. "And if you think I'm joking, you're about to see highly visible proof to the contrary."

His friend Hawke was at the helm of the ridiculously small and wildly pitching fishing boat. Sheer insanity. A night crossing to Mutton Island in a vessel less than twenty feet in length. Barmy, of course, but then Alex Hawke never gave a damn about weather when it came to boats. Sheeting rain, massive rollers, howling wind. Ideal for night crossing to some godforsaken island, was his view.

Surely this could have waited until morning?

Hawke. Just the name was a clue. The man was possessed of a keen sense of every small thing about him, above it all, often seeing what others didn't, missed opportunity and lurking death. He owned an icy courage that bordered on the bizarre, especially at moments like this. Hawke often reminded Ambrose of Winston Churchill, during the war, going out for his morning battlefield stroll, nonchalantly smoking his signature cigar in no-man's-land, blissfully ignoring the German bullets whistling by his head.

Both men mortal, to be sure, but they didn't act like they were. Not at all.

"Just don't get any on my shoes!" Hawke said loudly. You had to shout to be heard over the keening sounds of wind and wave. Remaining on your feet was no small feat, Congreve thought miserably, no pun intended.

Hawke eyed his friend. In the dim overhead light of the tiny wheelhouse, Congreve's normally cherubic pink face looked the ugly, varicolored shades of a nasty bruise. He was seasick all right, but he'd be on solid ground soon. Hawke imagined his old friend could likely manage three solo circumnavigations of the earth without ever acquiring his sea legs.

Ambrose said, "Don't be crude. Makes no sense to come out on a night like this, Alex. In this disgusting vessel. Every inch smells of fish guts and worse."

"It's a fishing boat."

"Well. Don't they, at bare minimum, these fishing blokes, at least hose them down every other decade or so?"

"Not usually. No need, really. The stench is part of the charm. Hold on, brave landsman, here comes a fairly sizable roller. Hard a'lee, me lads!"

They plowed through the huge wave just before it crested, black and white water roaring over the bow, smashing the wheelhouse, the whole damn boat awash. A miracle the window glass didn't blow out and slash them both to ribbons. Congreve spit seawater out of his mouth and shouted into Hawke's ear.

"Can't you slow down? Or just pull over?"

"Constable, you cannot just 'pull over' in a boat."

"Oh, for God's sake, you know what I mean. Just stop the damn thing until this storm blows over."

"That is called 'heaving to.' It would be much worse to do so, I assure you. Instead of slamming through these waves, we'd be getting slammed by them."

"And we're not now? Why on earth couldn't we have waited till morning, then?" Congreve asked, staggering on the heaving deck, trying to keep his feet under him and the contents of his stomach out of sight where they properly belonged.

"Going to get much worse around midnight. This is just the leading edge of the low pressure front. You'll be seeing Force 8 gales out here tomorrow."

"How much farther to the damned island?"

"Island of the damned, from what I've read."

"Alex, please. You are not amusing."

"Mutton Island is just now coming up on our port bow, actually. Wait for the next lightning strike and you'll see the cliffs off to our left. I've checked the map and found a protected spot to beach the boat. Luckily, it's in the lee of this wind."

"Thank God."

"No, thank me. God had absolutely nothing to do with it. Experience has taught me he really doesn't care for me much. Has it in for me, actually."

Ambrose was wise enough to remain silent.

Finally, Hawke said, "I've been thinking about something McMahon said. Odd."

"Yes?"

"He said Smith had an accent. To be precise, he said he 'spoke like a bloody toff, just like you.' Meaning me, of course."

"An Englishman. Good Lord, that went right by me. More drunken raving, I was probably thinking."

"Yes. But what if it wasn't?"

"Smith, an Englishman? I suppose he could be sympathetic to the Irish Cause, there's no shortage of those about."

TWENTY MINUTES LATER, HAWKE HAD run the boat's bow high up on to the shale beach and secured a line to a formation of rock that seemed to have survived for aeons. Ambrose immediately scrambled ashore, never so happy to plant his feet on solid ground in his life.

Once Hawke was satisfied the boat was properly secured, he joined Congreve at the top of a rocky ridge.

"Let me have a look at the map," Hawke said, snapping on his yellow rubber-coated flashlight. It cast a wispy white beam on the rocks and grassy banks beyond. Both men were wearing black macintoshes and old-fashioned sou'westers on their heads. Still, the cold wind and icy rain were cause for misery.

Congreve pulled the map from inside his foul-weather gear.

"All right," Hawke said, pointing, "here is the Norman watchtower. There are a cluster of old stone cottages just west of the tower. The ruins include an old church and an oratory."

"Not to mention a graveyard," Congreve said, studying the map.

"Off we go, then!" Hawke said cheerily and marched off in the direction of the tower with the air of a man leading a troop of young sea scouts on an exciting expedition. He soon disappeared through a veil of rain and Ambrose, his stomach at last becalmed, thumbed on his own flashlight, following the wavering beam of the torch up ahead. The ground was quite rocky and you had to mind your step. He had bought a pair of knee-high Wellies for this trip and was damn glad he'd done so.

It took twenty minutes over rough ground for the two men to locate the ruins of the ancient settlement. The rain had slacked off considerably and visibility was much enhanced. They examined the crumbling tower and the hieroglyphs on the strange obelisk in the middle of the graveyard. They worked in silence, each looking for any hint or trace of human habitation or activity.

Congreve, who had begun his career at Scotland Yard walking the streets of London before quickly rising to the rank of detective inspector, had long ago hewn to Locard's Principle, the foundation of all forensic science laid down by Edmund Locard, a man known as the "Sherlock Holmes of France." Since Congreve was a fanatic Sherlockian, this doubly endeared the Frenchman to him.

Monsieur Locard's principle simply stated that "every contact leaves a trace." Even though the last contact this Mr. Smith may have had with Mutton Island was perhaps thirty years prior, there was the possibility of concrete evidence of his presence to be found here. And Ambrose Congreve meant to find it.

He pointed his finger and said, "That building there, at the far edge of the graveyard, seems to be the only one remaining with a fairly intact roof. And thus suitable for habitation. I suggest we start our search for evidence there, Alex."

The white stone building had no windows. There was only a single wooden door, narrow and low. People were much smaller when this structure had been built centuries earlier. Bad diets. Hawke went through first to save Ambrose the embarrassment of being seen to squeeze his rather substantial girth through the narrow opening.

Both men played their lights around the four walls and the floor. The dirt ground was covered with small white pebbles as had been some of the pathways throughout the cemetery. In the center of the room, directly beneath a dripping crack in the roof, stood a large, slablike stone table. It looked more like an altar than a place to eat, and Ambrose, looking around, decided that is exactly what it had been. This had been a Pagan house of worship.

Thunder was still rumbling overhead and periodic flashes of lightning turned the inside of the tiny church a blinding white every few minutes. There was a continuous *drip-drip-drip* of rain spattering on the stone altar from a ceiling crack above.

"Look over here, old stick," Hawke said, his light shining on bits of rotten wood and pieces of decayed fabric cast randomly into a corner.

Congreve leaned down to inspect it. He had donned a pair of surgical gloves and was using a pair of tweezers to lift the fabric and poke at the thin strips of wood.

"A cot," he said, standing up with a rusty metal hinge in his hand. "Bedding. Someone slept here for a time. And ate meals. There are some very rusty cans of Heinz beans over there. Of course, it could have been anyone at all. Campers, birders, and the like."

"But it could just as well have been our friend Smith, Ambrose. This debris is at least three or four decades old. If this sanctuary really was a haven for campers or naturalists, there would be far more evidence of recent presence. There is none."

"I wholly agree. All we need now is evidence of a crime."

"Right. I'll get the Yard to analyze what's here. DNA from the bedding perhaps. Prints from the cans."

Hawke went on to say, "I think Smith could have lured his victims out to this island and murdered them in this very room. Remote, isolated, uninhabited. Perfect, in fact. And a graveyard conveniently located just outside his front door."

Congreve was now inspecting the surface of the stone slab carefully with his flashlight and a magnifying glass. It was remarkably clean, he thought. Dusty maybe, but with very little accumulation of the dirt one would expect. Almost as if it had been scrubbed clean at some point.

"Alex, there are faint markings on this stone. No pattern. Random slash marks, some quite deep that could well have been made by a knife—hold on—what's this?" Stepping forward, the toe of his boot had stubbed on something hard beneath the small stones.

He bent to his knees and swept away some of the tiny white pebbles beneath the slab. There was nothing but the hard-packed earthen floor. But upon closer inspection he found what he'd accidentally hit with his foot. There was a half circle of rusted iron protruding from the soil.

"Alex, could you step over here for a second? I think I've literally stumbled upon something under the altar. I need you to put a light on it while I do some digging."

Hawke held the light while Congreve used a small spade to carefully dig the soil away. He quickly uncovered an intact iron ring about four inches in diameter.

"A catacomb below, do you suppose?" Ambrose said with excitement, and he began to spade away the damp black dirt surrounding the iron ring. He struck wood about three inches down.

"Or a coffin?" Hawke asked.

Suddenly both men whipped their heads around at the sound of a low, ugly growl coming from the doorway.

A black dog, lean and muscular, was peering inside. A feral dog by the looks of him, fangs bared, milk white tusks that could crush through a man's wrist or calf bone like so much soft clay. The animal stood staring at the two men with a total absence of fear. Alex did not like the stiffened front legs or the ridge of raised hair along the animal's spine, both signals of an attack. Nor did he like the look in the animal's black eyes. It was raw hunger. Stringy loops of saliva hung from the long lower jaw full of teeth.

The animal started slowly moving toward them through the doorway, languid, unafraid.

TWENTY-SEVEN

"No sudden movement," Alex said to his friend Congreve, barely above a whisper. "Sign of weakness. He'll attack instantly if he sees it."

As Hawke said this he slowly slipped his hand inside his mac and gripped the butt of the SIG Sauer P230 holstered beneath his arm, inserting his finger inside the guard. Because of its relatively small size there was never a telltale bulge. But its magazine capacity was only seven rounds of .380 ammunition.

On an uninhabited island, this lack of firepower was highly unlikely to be a problem. Now, it had all the makings of one.

"Shoot him, Alex; look, he's getting ready to lunge for us!"

"I will only if I have to," Hawke said, his gunsight now leveled between the dog's eyes. "Raise your flashlight slowly above your head and fling it right at him. If it doesn't scare him off, I will shoot him."

"Good Lord," Congreve said, raising the heavy flashlight with a trembling hand and flinging it at the wild dog. He missed by mere inches, yet the dog didn't even flinch. He snarled viciously and suddenly leaped forward. Alex Hawke shot him in midair, a quick round to the head. The dog dropped to the ground without a sound, quite dead, barely inside the church door.

"Back to work," Hawke said, holstering his weapon.

"Good Lord," Congreve said again, staring at the dead animal as he bent to retrieve his flashlight. A dog built like this monster could rip a man to shreds in a matter of seconds. The rough seas he'd crossed were beginning to have a certain charm.

TEN MINUTES LATER, USING TWO small hand spades, they had cleared away all the soil. A wooden door, old, but hardly ancient, had been buried beneath the altar and hidden beneath a few inches of carefully tamped-down black earth. Hawke grasped the iron ring and pulled.

The door squealed loudly on its rusted iron hinges but swung open with surprising ease after all these years of disuse. The poisonous air that instantly wafted out of that centuries-old hole in the ground made both men choke and gag.

Congreve staggered back, eyes watering, kicking dirt and pebbles into the yawning black opening. Hawke leaned forward and played his light about the space below.

"What's down there?" Congreve croaked.

"No idea. But whatever it is, it's what we came here to find."

Hawke leaned deeper into the hole with his light. The only object of note was an ancient stone staircase descending darkly into God only knows what fresh hell lay below.

"I'm going down there," he said to Ambrose. "Care to join me?"

Congreve pulled a white linen handkerchief from somewhere inside his mac and clamped it over his nose and mouth. Seemingly unable to speak, he nodded his head in the affirmative. He crouched by the foul-smelling hole in the earth as Hawke descended; his nose was running and his eyes were tearing so badly he could barely see.

"You'd better come down and see this, Constable," Hawke's voice called seconds later.

Congreve, despite all his wanton misgivings, went down the worn stone staircase only to find that Hawke had not moved a foot away from the steps.

"Look at that," he said.

Congreve, who'd been busily watching his feet descend the treacherous staircase, raised his eyes and followed the beam of Hawke's light.

"Ah," he said.

The room was one large square, with an opening at the far side. It looked to be a tunnel leading off into more darkness.

"Ah, what?" Hawke said.

"A crypt." Ambrose played his light over the four walls, each completely decorated from floor to ceiling with yellowed human skulls jammed together to form a nightmare decor.

"I know it's a crypt, Ambrose. What I'm talking about is that tunnel leading off to God knows where."

"Tunnels intrigue me," Congreve said. "Always have."

"And me as well."

"This room is either Pagan or Early Christian, I'm not sure. We may find out at the end of that tunnel."

"Then let's proceed with all due haste," Hawke said, leading the way.

The tunnel was fairly wide but less than five feet in height, so both men had to stoop to pass through it.

Hawke figured they'd traveled about a hundred feet when they came into the next room.

It was round, with a domed ceiling, the entire space decorated like the first, with human skulls crammed together, floor to ceiling. In the very center of the room, directly beneath the dome, was a large circular structure.

"And what might that be?" Hawke asked, shining his light on the thing. It was a circle of stone, perhaps eight feet in diameter, and it rose about four feet from the earthen floor, which was covered with the small white pebbles. From Ambrose's vantage point, the structure looked to be empty.

"Well, it's definitely not a child's wading pool," Congreve said, advancing slowly toward the thing. It was very, very old stone, and the exterior was decorated with carvings and hieroglyphs similar to those on the obelisk in the graveyard above. Ambrose dropped to one knee and began examining the symbols carefully with his omnipresent magnifying glass.

"Have you been inside the catacombs beneath Rome?" he asked Hawke.

"No."

"You'll find similar structures there. This is a fountain, oddly enough. At one point, the room surrounding this fountain was filled with hundreds, perhaps thousands of human bones."

"That fountain is where the smell is coming from."

"I noticed that," Congreve said. "Look inside, please."

Hawke held his breath, put one hand on the rim, and looked into the fountain or whatever it was. The stink was coming from the stuff at the bottom, a foul grey sludge that stank to high heaven. Clearly the source of the foul underground air.

"Disgusting," Hawke said. "Have a peek."

Congreve rose and peered inside.

"Yes, just as I thought."

Saying nothing more, he again donned his latex gloves. Then he leaned over the edge and dipped his right index finger into the pungent muck. Quickly withdrawing it, he held it for the briefest moment under his nose.

"Hmm."

"I hate it when you say that. What the hell is that god-awful stuff?"

"Sulfuric acid. At one point this fountain was filled to the brim with it."

"But who—?"

"Our mysterious Mr. Smith. This is where he disposed of his victims. He rid himself of the bodies in this Pagan fountain. Submerged his victims in acid, hopefully postmortem. Completely destroyed the physical evidence. Bad luck."

"No remains at all?"

"No. I'm afraid we've come all this way for nothing, Alex. Every trace of those poor women's bodies is gone. I know of cases where someone is tried in the absence of any trace of a body. But they are extremely rare. Only a tiny fraction of them ever come to trial."

"Let's get out of here, then, Ambrose. The stench is unbearable."

"I agree. I think we might— Ouch! Damn it!"

Congreve stood up, rubbing his right knee.

"What happened?" Hawke said.

"One of those damned pebbles. Dug right into my knee."

He bent to brush it from his trouser leg, hesitated, then plucked it off his flannel trousers and held it to the light.

"We may be in luck after all," he said, flicking open his small gold magnifying glass and holding the thing up to his eye for closer inspection.

"Because of that damn pebble?"

"It's not a pebble, Alex; it's a gallstone. Not animal, either. A human gallstone, in fact."

"Is that proof of anything?"

"Indeed it is. Under a molecular microscope, we might determine the presence of something called *Helicobacter.*"

"And what might that be?"

"DNA. Human DNA."

He withdrew a small Ziploc baggie from his rain gear and dropped the precious nugget of evidence inside. Hawke was already halfway through the tunnel, and Congreve quickly followed in his wake.

Considering the horrific stench underground, he was surprised to find Alex Hawke waiting patiently for him at the bottom of the stone staircase.

"What is it, Alex?" he said, joining him.

"Up there." Hawke pointed with his flashlight. "At the top of the steps."

Another feral dog, this one bigger and blacker than the first, stared down at the two men below. Its eyes shone bright red in the gleam of Hawke's light. The animal's sharp snout was smeared with red blood. The blood was dripping down, spattering the stone steps below.

"Cain has been having a go at Abel," Hawke said.

"What?" Congreve said, his focus riveted on the gleaming red eyes above.

"This one's been munching on his dead brother in the doorway," Hawke said. "The scent of blood must have drawn him in."

"Alex, consider. Would you imagine there are many more of these wild dogs on the island?"

"Yes. They breed in the wild and they tend to run in packs."

"How many more might be out there, would you suppose?"

"No idea," Hawke said, pulling out his gun.

"How many rounds do you have left in your weapon?"

"One for this major bastard above. Five more for the rest."

"I think it's high time we bid farewell to Mutton Island."

"I agree," Hawke said, raising his gun and shooting the menace at the top of the steps.

THEY WERE CROSSING ROCKY GROUND, nearing the boat when the wild dog pack began to appear. The first one came slinking out from behind the ruins of a small stone cottage. It followed them, loping along at a distance. Moments later it was joined by two more, racing up from behind. Hawke held the SIG Sauer, a round in the chamber, in his right hand. An expert marksman, he wasn't worried about hitting his targets. He was worried about having more targets than bullets.

"Alex?"

"I know. I saw them. Bummer. Walk faster but do it gradually. We're almost there."

"Bummer?"

"Slang. Harry Brock talk for bad luck. He says it all the time. California, you know."

"Ah, our old chum, Mr. Brock."

Alex was conscious of movement on both sides, shadowy figures moving ever closer, stalking them.

"Slow down," he said to Congreve. "If they see you running, they'll attack."

"You slow down if you want. I don't think we can outrun them."

"I don't need to outrun them. I just need to outrun you."

"Alex, if you think that is remotely humorous—"

A dog leaped out of the mist, directly in front of them. He launched himself at Ambrose going for his throat. Hawke fired instantly, and the dog dropped heavily to the ground, mewling in pain, literally a mere foot from Congreve's Wellies.

"Run hard for the boat," he told Ambrose. "Do it now. I'll lag behind. Dogs will go for the easy meat first, but it won't take them long to devour this one. Use this knife to slice the mooring line, then shove the boat into the surf. If another dog comes at you, go for his throat with the knife. Stab first, then rip with the saw blade, that's what it's for. But for God's sake, strike to kill. Shout when you're safely aboard."

Congreve looked at the knife and said, "I'm uncomfortable with knives, Alex. Always have been."

"You have another choice. When the dog lunges at you, simply grab each of his forelegs in midair, grip them tightly, and rip his chest apart. It works; I've done it a few times with Chinese police dogs."

"I'll take the knife."

"I thought so. Now, go!"

Congreve didn't need encouragement. He raced ahead, the saw-toothed assault knife in his hand, soon disappearing into the heavy ground fog. He quickly reached the rocky beach and made his way carefully down the slippery boulders to the shaly beach below. The boat was right where they'd left it, although the flood tide was in a bit and she was almost afloat. That would make it much easier to shove her offshore to wait for Hawke.

He was about to use Hawke's assault knife to sever the mooring line when he heard a low growl from above. He whirled round just as the beast leaped from the rocks above, snarling like some demon out of hell. Congreve braced himself, instinctively raising the knife to protect himself, and, seeing that the animal's throat was exposed as it lunged, he thrust upward with the blade as the dog came down. Instead of withdrawing the knife, he did exactly as Hawke had instructed, almost decapitating the rabid beast in the process.

It fell to the ground at his feet, dead.

Ambrose, breathing heavily, simply stood and stared down at the corpse, hardly able to believe what he'd just done, with a knife of all things. It never failed to amaze him what human beings were capable of when they found themselves in extreme circumstances. Sheer instinct, and the will to live, had made even an overweight, middle-aged detective who smoked and drank too much a very formidable foe against a rabid dog.

HAWKE, PRAYING THAT WHAT LITTLE he remembered of canine behavior was correct, ran forward a hundred yards, turned, and dropped to one knee. He held his pistol in both hands, swinging it in a smooth arc from side to side, the adrenaline rush bringing all of his senses to the fore.

The dogs converged on the wounded animal, snarling, growling furiously, snapping at one another, all of them fighting for a piece of fresh meat and the taste of warm blood. Couldn't even count how many. Ten? Fifteen? More maybe.

It took about a minute for the first one to turn his attention away from the shredded animal on the ground and focus on Hawke. It approached cautiously at first, then broke into a lightning-fast run. Hawke waited until the beast got within twenty yards before he killed it.

He got to his feet and ran another hundred or so yards, before turning and dropping to his knee again, gun in both hands, becoming his enemy like he'd been trained to do: all eyes, all ears, all nose. Waiting. Half of the pack soon broke off and came for the freshly dead. Ignoring the man in the mist beyond, they went in for the quick feed.

Hawke made an instant decision. He had four rounds left in his weapon. He no longer had his knife, the one thing that could keep him alive. No matter what happened, he would kill three dogs as soon as they turned away and started for him. Keep that one last round in the chamber. Just in case. Run like hell for the boat as soon as he heard Ambrose's summons.

He didn't have to wait long.

Having devoured the last dead dog, the pack turned, sniffed the air, and started coming for Alex Hawke. They were cautious now, having learned something about their human prey from previous experience. They also fanned out, which made things far more difficult. The ground mist didn't help either. He flicked on his flashlight. It picked out all the red eyes.

Something about them, those terrible bobbing eyes and what they represented, death, made him feel more alive than he had felt since—since Stockholm. Since Anastasia Korsakova. Since he'd lost her. Since he'd lost his lust for life. Since he'd lost everything.

"Come on, you miserable bastards," Hawke said through his gritted teeth. "Come closer. I've got something for you."

The dogs went from hazy apparitions in the fog, to stark black silhouettes with bouncing red rubies in their heads, to ferocious snarling animals who wanted desperately to kill and eat him. He sighted in on three. One in the middle of the pack, two on either side. He aimed and shot, one, two, three rounds cooked off, and three dogs went down.

The pack hesitated, saw what had happened, and went into a renewed feeding frenzy that reminded him of shark behavior. Brutal and fascinating, a wild dance of life and death that was almost hypnotic. He tore his attention away from the blood feast at the sound of Congreve's muffled voice in the mist.

"I'm aboard the boat! Do you hear me?"

Hawke jumped to his feet and surely ran as fast as he'd ever run in his life. One of the damn dogs elected to pester him, nipping at his bloody heels until he wheeled and shot the beast dead, expending his last bullet just as he reached the beach, splashing into the surf and diving over the gunwale of the little boat, bruising his shoulder when he hit the deck.

He got to his feet, wiped the stinging saltwater from his eyes, and smiled at Ambrose.

"Ahoy, Captain. Ensign Hawke reporting for duty."

"Thank God. Start the engines and get us away from this accursed place."

"Any problems along the way, Constable?" Hawke asked, firing the engines.

"None at all, thank you."

"What about the corpse of that dog lying on the beach?"

"Oh, that? Wasn't a problem at all. Slit his throat from ear to ear."

"Shall we be off, then, do you suppose?"

"Indeed. I fancy a rather large whiskey at the Pennywhistle before turning in. Would you care to join me?"

"I should be delighted."

"Done and done."

"On our merry way, then, Constable," Hawke said, and, firing the engines, he shoved the throttle full forward and powered away from Mutton Island, glad he and his companion seemed to have all of their body parts intact.

Mutton Island had been relatively easy.

Something told him the Barking Dog Inn was going to be an entirely different matter.

Congreve, pulling his collar up against the cold, wet wind, said, "Alex, have I ever mentioned an old acquaintance of mine? Chap by the name of Bulldog Drummond?"

"No. I've heard the name, of course. He was a character in a series of mystery novels I read as a boy. By an author who called himself 'Sapper.' "

"This character is quite real, I assure you. And I think he would be of enormous help to us in this next mission. We worked the Mountbatten assassination together. Retired now."

"Fine. Where do we find him?"

"He lives in the little town of Glin on the River Shannon."

TWENTY-EIGHT

WINDSOR, ENGLAND, NOVEMBER 1992

THE QUEUE WAS TRUDGING FORWARD at last. Smith pulled his battered fedora down around his ears and pushed his thick "national health" eyeglasses up on the bridge of his nose. He'd considered a beard for the occasion but decided a lush moustache would suffice. He looked down at his long, baggy overcoat, making sure too much of his trouser legs didn't show.

That wouldn't do at all, he smiled to himself.

Shuffling along, looking bored, he pulled a well-thumbed brochure out of his pocket and studied it for the hundredth time. He was actually looking forward to this expedition in more ways than one.

This massive complex had been in continuous use since William the Conqueror had selected it as the site of a fortress after his conquest of England in 1066. Smith had frequently read how much the Queen adored the place. How she frequently spent her weekends at Windsor Castle, using it for both state and private entertaining as well as riding her horses on the vast parklands and estates.

She certainly had room to stretch her legs out here, he chuckled to himself, noting the statistic that claimed there were an astounding five hundred thousand square feet of floor area under this mélange of centuries-old rooftops.

"Ah, these Royals, they do like to live like kings and queens," he said over his shoulder to an irritating, noisy American woman behind him. A mistake, he knew, but he was antsy, and he'd taken pity on the husband. She'd been blathering nonstop to her silent and clearly long-suffering spouse ever since they'd formed up the queue, loudly lecturing the poor soul in excruciating detail exactly what he was going to see once he got inside these hallowed walls.

"Don't they just?" the frowzy woman said, whirling on him, a tigress hungry to pounce upon fresh meat.

"Hmm," he said, wanting to take a knife to her wagging tongue.

"Well, they deserve it, I suppose. After all, the Royals *are* kings and queens," she said.

"Quite right, madam. I hadn't thought of it quite that way before."

She was surprisingly small for her voice, a beaky, birdlike creature, someone who looked as if she'd like nothing more than to pop up, perch on his shoulder, and start screeching into his ear. Had he not more important things to do, he might actually have taken the time to pursue this cheeky little monster. Follow her home into her cave and fillet her avian corpus.

"And where are you from?" she asked, thinking him exotic.

"Ah. A penetrating question. I am a Londoner, madam."

"London? Really?" she said, speaking as if it were some undiscovered, faraway destination instead of a thirty-minute train ride to Paddington Station. "We've just come from there."

"Fascinating."

"And what do you do?"

"Arson."

"How interesting. And what are you most excited about seeing today, if you don't mind my being such an old nosy parker?" she chirped. To his astonishment, she actually winked at him!

"Well, the Royal Private Apartments, of course. You know, the furnishings, the priceless works of antiquity. That sort of thing. How about you?"

"Oh, well, Queen Mary's Dolls' House, of course! I collect dolls and miniatures back home and I've never been so thrilled in all my life. We're the Harveys, by the way, Herman and Marva Harvey. From Celebration? No? Disney World? No? Well, you're obviously not much of a world traveler, are you? It's near Orlando, Florida. And you are?"

"Next in line, I'm afraid, madam."

"Oh." She looked devastated at this snide dismissal.

"Well. Lovely meeting you both," he said, moving forward and sliding his prepaid ticket beneath one of the half windows to one of the many pink-faced young English roses with their starched white collars. She smiled up at him after taking his ticket.

"If you'll step to your right as soon as you're inside, you'll find your tour group is just leaving, sir. You're the last one, so I shouldn't dillydally."

Which meant he'd be at the group's rear, just as he'd planned, counting off groups of twenty before joining the queue.

"Beg pardon, miss. The Queen's Private Chapel," he said, smiling at the pretty young thing with his brilliant white teeth. "Is it open today?"

"So sorry, sir. Closed. Restoration work."

"Ah, too bad. Maybe next time."

He moved inside and joined his group.

"Let's begin, shall we?" the reed-thin male guide said in a properly fluty voice. "Our first stop, the State Apartments. If you could all manage to stay together it will make your visit far more pleasant, as you don't want me scurrying off in search of a lost duckling in midsentence, do you? If you have any questions at all, my name is Colin."

There was a brief moment of appreciative twittering and then they were off like the obedient little flock they were expected to be.

Smith paid no mind to the pontifications of their fearless leader, he just shuffled along at the rear, sometimes falling back to inspect a painting by Van Dyck or Rubens he'd always admired. Then he'd quickly catch up, making sure the palace guide noticed that he was a dutiful soldier, trying his best to stay with the squadron. He'd need a favor from this chap, and soon.

Fifteen minutes later, they were about to go to the right and enter the Private Apartments overlooking the East Terrace. It was at this point that he began making his way to the front of the group. He sidled up to the skinny guide and whispered, "I say, Colin, bit of an emergency here. I saw a loo back there on the left and I'm terribly afraid I need to use it very badly."

There was a distinct sniff of disgust, and then the man, clearly displeased with this glitch, peered down his long thin nose and said, "We shan't be able to wait. You'll just have to catch up."

"Won't be long. Thanks so much," he said and made his way through the group and back along the corridor to the Gents they'd passed a few minutes earlier.

Entering the loo, he quickly ducked into one of the four stalls. He shed his overcoat, rolled it up tight as any City man's umbrella, and shoved it into one of the large painter's pockets. Beneath the innocuous overcoat he wore paint-spattered coveralls. Inside the coveralls, under his armpits, hung two plastic containers. He had secreted them in two large curved aerosol flasks, strapped to his ribs, invisible.

He hung his fedora on the hook provided, flushed the apparatus, and stepped outside the stall.

The green-tiled room was empty, as he'd expected. He'd taken this tour enough times to know how much the guides loathed letting anyone use this particular facility, holding everyone up. Returning to the corridor, he only had a few feet to walk before he came to a door opening outside onto the Upper Ward, or Quadrangle as it was popularly called.

Walking quickly across the manicured grass, he was able to make his way to another door that led to the Queen's Private Chapel just as his group was trooping by. No one, of course, took any notice at all of him, especially the snooty guide who wouldn't be caught dead acknowledging the existence of one of the many painters currently doing restoration work in the Chapel.

He looked at his watch. Eleven twenty. Plenty of time until the painting crew came back from their "elevenses" tea break. He stepped over the red velvet rope and pushed through the carved oak doors with the sign NO ENTRY! CLOSED FOR RESTORATION. Once inside, he quickly took his bearings.

It was a small room, this private chapel. Most beautiful, he thought, was the ornate wooden ceiling decor of blue Romanesque arches edged in gold. The eight red silk upholstered chairs that were normally arranged before the altar had been placed in a corner and draped with a protective cover of thick canvas. The floor as well was covered with canvas and scattered about were paint buckets, solvents, ladders of various heights, and tall, tripod-mounted spotlights with powerful thousand-watt halogen lightbulbs.

His eye alit on one of the spotlights. It had been left on. Quite hot already. Perfect. It was standing atop its sturdy tripod, dangerously close to a lovely blue satin curtain that extended down from the ceiling. *Close,* he thought, smiling to himself, *but not quite close enough.*

He quickly moved a tall ladder next to the spotlight and climbed to the very top. Then he reached inside his overalls for the flexible plastic spray tube attached to the aerosol canister under his arm.

He pushed down on the button that controlled the nozzle and a strong stream of powerful accelerant jetted out, soaking the curtain. He moved the nozzle up and down, saturating the material. When the first canister was empty he began to use the second, soaking a second curtain only a few feet away. Then he descended to the floor and admired his work. The curtains were ideal. He picked up the tall illuminated spotlight and placed it so that its scorching bulb was nearly touching the first curtain.

It only took a second.

The lovely blue silk draperies literally exploded into violent scorching flames, reaching up instantly to lick the beautiful wooden ceiling above. Then the second curtain ignited, spreading the fire rapidly to another part of the ceiling.

The alarms wailed.

Earsplitting warnings blared throughout the state apartments as he slipped out of the Chapel and headed back across the grassy Quadrangle to the loo. Inside the stall, he once more donned the long overcoat and fedora. That done, he stepped back out into a corridor in chaos. Above the shouting, he could hear the sounds of sirens, fire companies already racing up narrow winding streets from the town of Windsor. He quickly made his way outside onto the Quadrangle again, walking at a steady pace away from the conflagration.

He'd spent months preparing for this day. At first, the mere notion of what he had done had seemed unthinkable. No one could do what he dreamed of doing. The barriers were insurmountable, the chance of success nil. No amount of ingenuity was sufficient, no derring-do could do it.

And yet . . . Smith had done it again, plunged yet another stake into the rotten innards of his nemesis, nothing fatal, mind you, but still a devastating psychological blow to the Monarch. He would not stop until he dealt the last, deadly blow, but in the meantime he would savor these small triumphs, rejoicing in each as they came.

Now, making his way hurriedly but inconspicuously out of the castle grounds, he saw that the fire was now burning completely out of control, fire teams pissing water everywhere he looked. It was beginning to look to Smith as if he'd managed to burn down a good portion of one of the most potent and enduring symbols of British imperialism.

Yes. He had practically burned down the Queen's favorite castle. Poor old dear would be heartbroken, he imagined. He could not know it, of course, but his success today would be one of monumental proportions:

More than a hundred rooms would go up in flames that day. It would take more than 250 firefighters over fifteen hours and one and a half million gallons of water to put out the blaze he'd started. It would take five long years to restore it at the staggering cost of thirty-seven million pounds from the Queen's coffers.

Not bad for a single day's work, Smith thought, descending on the endless moving stairs down to the tube. *Not bad at all.* Standing on the grimy platform waiting for the train, he found himself literally shivering with pleasure.

Another day of retribution to salve for a moment his aggrieved heart, his tortured soul, his fevered brain.

TWENTY-NINE

GLIN, COUNTY LIMERICK, IRELAND

JOHN BULLINGTON DRUMMOND WAS KNOWN throughout England, Scotland, and Wales as the author of one of the most beloved books ever published between two covers. It was called *The Care and Feeding of the Proper English Rose Garden.* Jack Drummond had spent most of his life writing his somewhat flowery masterpiece, although he was neither a writer nor a gardener by trade. He was, until recently, a policeman.

Drummond had retired, after a long, honorable career of dedicated service, to the bonnie banks of a fabled river. Retired in style, you might say; he lived in a right fairy-tale castle now, one of the loveliest in all Ireland. Glin Castle, a gleaming white edifice, had a charming toy-fortress quality about it. It was built in the late eighteenth century and overlooked the wide and gently flowing Shannon, now black dotted with coots and tufted ducks.

Well, Drummond lived *near* the castle to be honest, in the Gardener's Cottage, which rubbed shoulders with the stables. Still, it was a lovely little stone house, covered to the rooftop with roses. It was one of three battlemented Gothic folly lodges set about the five-hundred-acre wooded demesne, fiercely defended by the FitzGerald family for more than seven hundred years.

Jack found he awoke each morning filled with the simple love of life. The much-heralded golden years finally had meaning for him.

Prior to retirement, his home had been in the battle-scarred north of Ireland, a tiny council flat in a small town called Sligo. He'd been chief constable in Sligo Town for nearly four decades and had helped solve many crimes, including one of Ireland's most horrific assassinations, that of Lord Louis Mountbatten.

Drummond, having had his fill of enforcing the laws by day, then scribbling his masterpiece madly by night, had now retired to more or less permanent obscurity. He had become head gardener for the Knight of Glin. Which, he thought, had quite a nice ring to it.

The Knight, a most amiable fellow widely known by his proper name, Desmond FitzGerald, had hired Drummond based on the strong recommendation of his wife, a passionate gardener herself. Like everyone else, she'd read *Care and Feeding*, and immediately joined the countless legions of gardeners who proclaimed Jack Drummond a genius. She'd invited him for tea and a book signing at Glin Castle one afternoon and offered him the job on the spot.

For his part, he was delighted to now find himself in the employ of one of Ireland's oldest and most distinguished families. The current Knight was the twenty-ninth to hold that noble title, a fact that Drummond found quite remarkable.

The Knights of Glin were a branch of the great Norman family the FitzGeralds, Earls of Desmond. The family had been granted vast lands in County Limerick in the early fourteenth century by their Desmond overlords. The whole family were from the Norman Maurice FitzGerald, a companion-in-arms to the legendary warrior Strongbow, who'd acquired his fierce moniker in the twelfth century or thereabouts for his skill and use of the long bow.

Drummond was busy whacking away at floribunda and surgically pruning "Double Delights" in one of the Knight's countless hybrid tea rose beds that morning when he heard a familiar voice calling his name.

"Bulldog! I say, Bulldog, where the dickens are you? I can't see a thing for all these bloody roses!"

Ambrose Congreve, and someone named Hawke, were expected, of course; Congreve had called ahead. He'd never arrive unannounced, too proper for that by half. And he was the only man on earth Drummond allowed to call him "Bulldog."

There was a story behind that. There was always a story. One rather late and liquorish pub evening, Congreve had gotten to his feet, pulled a black spiral notebook from the inside of his stylish Norfolk jacket, and opened it with a flourish and a clearing of the throat. He then started in to reading aloud a "tribute" to his new colleague in the Mountbatten murder investigation.

"Ahem . . . 'Drummond . . . has the appearance of an English gentleman: a man who fights hard, plays hard, and lives clean . . . His best friend would not call him good looking but he possesses that cheerful type of ugliness which inspires immediate confidence . . . Only his eyes redeem his face. Deep-set and steady, with eyelashes that many women envy, they show him to be a sportsman and an adventurer. Drummond goes outside the law only when he feels the ends justify the means.' "

"Rubbish," Drummond said.

"Sound like anyone we know?" Congreve had asked, when Drummond stared at him in stony silence.

"Where the hell'd you find that nonsense?"

"I copied it. From a book. By Sapper. I'm rereading it now, having none of my beloved Sherlockian volumes at my disposal."

"Pulp fiction."

"Pulp truth, Bulldog," Congreve had replied. And he'd called him by that name ever since. Drummond, snipping away at his roses, was snapped out of this reverie by a loud wail, once again calling his name.

"Bulldog! I say, where the hell are you, you little leprechaun? Have you fallen down a rabbit hole?"

"Over here!"

"Over where?"

"Here, you damn fool," he said, and flung an empty wicker basket high into the air so the world's most brilliant detective might accurately deduce his whereabouts.

"Oh. Over there. Why didn't you say so?"

A moment later Drummond could hear his old friend's heavy footsteps approaching on the gravel walkway. He was not alone. Someone with a more athletic gait was following in his wake. This man Hawke, or whomever.

"Oh. Hullo, Bulldog."

"Hullo, Congreve. Who's this?"

"May I present my dear friend Lord Alexander Hawke?"

Hawke shook the man's rough red hand. "Alex will do, Mr. Drummond." But Drummond wasn't listening to him. He was eyeing Congreve through narrowed eyes. Ambrose had told Hawke the man was difficult and the less he said, the better. Alex was happy to let Congreve do the talking.

They stared at each other in stony silence.

"Haven't changed much, have you?" Ambrose finally allowed.

"Nor you."

"Ugly as ever."

"Still fat as a Yorkshire pig."

"Drink?"

"Not too early?"

"Never too early."

And so they all three traipsed along winding garden pathways through endless acres of multicolored roses to Drummond's cottage. Entering the tiny kitchen, they sat opposite each other at the round wooden table. Drummond put a decanter of Irish whiskey on the table, the strong sunlight gleaming on the facets of the carved Waterford glass, a retirement gift.

"Help yourself, gentlemen," Drummond said, and slid two small glasses across the table. After they'd both downed one and replenished supplies, Congreve plastered his most serious expression on his face and looked at his old colleague.

"This is police business."

"I'm retired. I'm in the rose business."

"Involves the Mountbatten case."

"Case closed."

"Case reopened."

"What the blazes are ye talkin' about?"

"I think our 'third man' has surfaced."

"And what makes ye think so?"

"The Prince of Wales found a death threat in one of Mountbatten's books. It was signed 'The Pawn.' "

"So?"

"Prince Charles recently received yet another threat from the Pawn. 'Death to Kings.' Clearly a reference to His Royal Highness and his two boys."

"Same signature? Same hand?"

"Identical."

"Fresh?"

"As a hen's egg."

"Anythin' else?"

"Alex and I spoke to McMahon the other evening. He's out of prison, I'm sure you know. Freed by some lunatic in the Good Friday pardons. Two days ago, over in Mullaghmore, we had a nice little chat with him."

"Say anything new, did he?"

"I asked him about the missing girls. Did he know anything about that."

"Did he?"

"More than he was telling, I think."

"He have a name for the third man?"

"Same name we've always had. Smith."

"And how, pray tell, is any of this new information?"

"Be patient, will you? He said he'd heard rumors this Smith was living on an island just off the coast. Place called Mutton Island. I went out there with Alex. Amid the ruins of an ancient settlement, we found evidence of this mysterious Mr. Smith. We also found evidence of murder, by God. And we found human remains."

"Jesus Lord."

"We've got fresh DNA evidence, Bulldog. We're back in the game. We'll finally get to the truth of this thirty-year-old crime!"

"We? What is it you want from me?"

"Help. Despite your many unpleasant qualities, you're still the best copper I ever worked with. You were the one who first quoted Sherlock Holmes to me, and I shall be eternally grateful for that alone."

"Did I? What was the quote?"

" 'When you have eliminated the impossible, whatever remains, *however improbable,* must be the truth.' "

"Ah, *The Sign of the Four.* One of my favorites. What exactly do you want of me? I'm quite busy as you can see."

"I want a look at your old files, first of all. Get the names and addresses of all the female victims. Get the M.E. to run a cross-check of their samples with the new DNA we found. If we get a match, everything else opens up. With this fresh evidence in hand, we're bound to turn something over. With your help, we just might crack it, Bulldog. Only if you're willing, of course. All these gorgeous roses."

Drummond cast his eyes out the window at the sun beaming down on his beautiful roses. Was any place on earth lovelier than this castle and its gardens? Could he bear to be away, even for a short time? He looked at Congreve, remembering what a great team they'd made, each complementing the other's strengths, and weaknesses. Their failure to find and prosecute the "third man" had been the one blemish on an otherwise sterling career of some forty years.

He looked at Ambrose and said, "We find this bloody Smith, we solve both cases. For good. Forever."

"That's correct. The murderer of the girls. And Lord Mountbatten."

Drummond turned his eyes on Alex.

"You met our McMahon, Mr. Hawke, did ye trust him? I never did. A drunken, lyin' cur, my estimation."

Hawke, startled out of his reverie, said, "We don't need him anymore, Mr. Drummond. We've got physical evidence of murder. Serial murder, in fact."

"Hmm. I do have a week's holiday coming up. But I've already told my employer I wouldn't be taking it."

"We need a cover story. Tell me. Is your dear mother still alive?" Congreve asked.

"Ah, no, she's not. She passed in Dublin, just last year she did, bless her sainted soul. Ninety-seven years old. She's at her final resting place in St. Stephen's cemetery."

"She's back, Bulldog."

"She's back?"

"Yes, back. But, sad to say, she's not doing all that well, I'm afraid. Fading fast, in fact. We could lose her any day now."

"You're talking about me blessed mother."

"I am indeed."

"You're a right bastard, aren't you?"

"In matters like this I am."

"Life and death."

"Precisely."

"Unfinished business."

"Quite."

"I'm in, damn you," Bulldog barked.

THIRTY

MIAMI

So she's giving the fat guy a BJ while he's sitting in your favorite chair waiting for you to come waltzing through your own front door?" Harry Brock asked Stokely.

"Correct."

"But you got inside locked sliding glass doors by swinging down from the roof on a rope?"

"You got it."

"Same blond broad who whacked the two guys we were staking out on the beach?"

"Yep."

"But she got away. From your apartment, I mean."

"She did."

"And the fat guy tried to whack you with a MAC-10?"

"He did."

"Your leather couch looks like shit."

"Tell me about it."

"You think they can stitch that up? Patch it, maybe?"

"What do you think, Harry? Patch it up? All that rich Corinthian leather?"

"Sucks. Can you put in for something like that, I wonder?"

"That's a very good question, Harry."

"You pissed at me about something? I went to the Bahamas for a couple of days, okay? I had some time coming. I met somebody. Jesus."

"No, I am not pissed. I'm just trying to concentrate on this goddamn Dolphin game. Third and goal. We could score here. Okay? I told you most of this shit already."

"It's only preseason."

"That's the only kind we win."

"They figure out who the fat guy is yet?"

"Bashi? Yeah. Bashir al Mahmoud. Pakistani. Formerly called Gitmo home, now a legal resident of the United States of America, courtesy of our all new and improved Homeland Security immigration policies."

"Bashi. Shit. The guy we were trying to get to."

"Right."

"So, instead of us having to sit out in the blistering sun all day looking for this asshole, he just comes over to your apartment. Sits in your favorite chair."

"That's about it. Shit! Interception."

"So, now what?"

"We go for the fumble."

"I mean the *case,* asswipe."

"Oh, that. We take a room at the Fontainebleau."

"Who does?"

"You and me."

"Together?"

"Of course. We're partners, partner."

"Listen, Stoke. You wanna come out of the fuckin' closet, do it with somebody else, okay, stud? I ain't interested."

"Funny. Wait. Holy shit, another interception! D'you see that? Damn! We're still in it, baby. Stick their dicks in dirt, Dolphins. Let's see some bad sportsmanship out there for a change."

"So, the Fontainebleau."

Stoke spoke, his eyes never leaving the TV.

"Bashi had leased the presidential penthouse there on a long-term basis. We swept it clean. Computers full of incriminating shit. White slavery, pornography, possible terrorist activity, money laundering of massive cash coming in from Pakistan and Afghanistan poppy fields."

"Cash used for what?"

"Services rendered here in the U S of A."

"What kind of services?"

"That's what we need to find out, Harry."

"Probably not out there rehabbing houses for Jimmy Carter's Habitat for Humanity, I don't guess."

"Probably not. Now, shut up. Third and long. And . . . another pick. Can you believe this damn team?" Stoke pointed the remote at the TV and it went mute.

"You did good, Stoke. I got to hand it to you. Served this fat pig up on a sterling silver platter. They gotta be loving your ass up at Langley."

"Made your white ass look good, anyway. For hiring me."

"What about the b-i-m-b-o, b-i-m-b-o, and Bimbo was her name-o."

"She's coming back to Bashi's penthouse. Sooner or later."

"Why would she do that?"

"Because there's a wall safe there, behind a fake wall in the back of the closet that hides another fake wall. It's got twenty mil and change in small, unmarked bills inside it."

"Twenty million fucking dollars?"

"Right around there, yeah."

"You guys just left it there?"

"Yep."

"Why?"

"Why do you think?"

"Because the b-i-m-b-o knows about all that hidden jack and hopes, no, *believes* you couldn't possibly find it. So she's abso-fuckin-lutely positively going nuts, got to come back to that suite and crack that safe no matter how incredibly dangerous such a stupid idea is or may well be."

"Incredibly stupid move on her part."

"But she'll do it."

"She'll do it."

"Hotel in on this? If she tries to check in?"

"No. We'd have to keep someone on the front desk all the time. Better just let them be natural, somebody shows up and wants to spend ten grand a night on a room."

"You ever hand somebody who works in a hotel a fifty and ask for a better room? They take it?"

"Good point, Harry. We get the hotel manager in on this, use your CIA creds."

"Exactly. Forty-eight hours. She'll show up. Guaranteed."

"You're good, Harry. Turn pro someday, keep your shit together. Ah, shit, Pennington, don't throw the damn ball, run it, you dick-head, run left, you're wide open, man!"

"Stoke?"

"What?"

"Our new stakeout, if I have this straight, is not a shitty Suburban or a rusted-out Ford Taurus with chicken bones under the seats."

"No. Not."

"It is a palatial penthouse suite at the Fontainebleau Hotel on Miami Beach."

"It is, Harry. Our suite is right across the hall from Bashi's former residence. Only two suites on the top floor. We'll get management to put a security camera on Bashi's front door. We'll be able to monitor it twenty-four seven. And give the manager instructions to have the front desk call our room immediately should anybody try to check in or gain access."

"This could be good, Stoke. A stakeout in a penthouse at the Fontainebleau? I like it."

"I thought you might. An upgrade from cold coffee and stale Krispy Kremes in a piece of crap SUV anyway."

"You been inside our rooms?"

"Yep."

"Ocean view?"

"Pool."

"Still. We'll have government-issue high-powered optics. Keep up to date with the latest in ladies' swimwear fashion."

"Bet on it."

"And room service. Adult movies twenty-four hours a day."

"Uh-huh."

"I like this."

"I knew you would, Harry."

"When do we check in, Stoke? I can hardly wait. We can order up a pitcher of extra dry martinis and an extra cheese pizza with pepperoni, mushrooms, and onions. Curl up under the covers and watch *Brokeback Mountain* together if you want."

Harry Brock, ladies and gentlemen, Stoke thought to himself. *What a card.*

FORTY-EIGHT HOURS LATER, STOKE and Harry had pretty much exhausted the room service menu, the minibar popcorn and candy and scotch, the soft porn movies on the adult channel, the telescopic chicks by the pool, the Weather Channel, not to mention their patience with CNN, MSNBC, and each other.

It was midnight and finally Stoke's turn to go catch some Zs. Stoke had put them on a watch system. Four watches, six hours on the security monitor, six blissful hours in the rack while the other guy sat out in the living room and popped reds to stay awake looking at a crappy black-and-white movie about a goddamn hotel door for six entire hours without blinking.

Harry Brock was standing in the doorway in his T-shirt and boxers, drinking a mug of steaming coffee while wolfing down a really disgusting-looking slice of cold pizza.

"Morning," Brock said groggily, not too happy about it either.

"Yep. *Bedtime for Bonzo,* Harry," Stoke yawned, getting up out of the armchair they'd stationed in front of the security monitor and stretching his aching back. Getting old, Stoke. Aches and pains. He was beginning to understand why they said old age wasn't for sissies. Time to start hitting Gold's Gym over at the beach three or four times a week, work out on the speed bag, get his rhythm back, put in some serious ring time.

"Yeah? Who's Bonzo?"

"It's a goddamn movie, Harry. Ronald Reagan and some chimp named Bonzo. Jesus. Don't you know anything?"

"What's on the TV today? Anything good?"

"Yeah. This movie called *The Door.* Really, really long and nothing ever happens."

"Sounds good. Who's in it?"

"Nobody. But it's a laugh riot. You will laugh your damn ass off, Harry, I swear to God. Grab a seat while it's still warm."

"Funny."

"G'night, Harry, don't forget your little red pills."

"Fuck me," Harry said disconsolately. The graveyard shift, 12:00 midnight to 6:00 A.M., was the most grueling of all.

THIRTY-ONE

HARRY PLOPPED DOWN IN THE CHAIR, settled in, and stared up at the monitor with a look of abject misery. He had not the faintest idea why he had ever thought this stakeout was going to be a wild and crazy few days in the lap of luxury on the beach. It sucked. Big time.

Stoke padded off to his bedroom, one of four down a long hallway, hit the pillow on his fabulous king-size bed, and was instantly sound asleep. Two seconds later his bedside phone rang. He looked at the fuzzy green numbers on the digital clock. Somehow, it was almost six o'clock in the morning.

"Yeah?" he said.

"Stoke, it's me. Sharkey."

"Shark, tell me how you got this number."

"I called Fancha. She gave it to me."

"I don't believe you."

"I tole her, man, this is an emergency. She gave it to me."

"What kind of emergency?"

"Life and death. I gotta come out of the joint, man. Right now. I'm dead serious."

"Tell me."

"I don't know where to begin is the problem. See, there's this crazy con on my cell block in the Glades. Seminole Indian guy. Calls himself Chief Johnny Two Guns. Former championship prizefighter who murdered his own mother with a fucking tourist-shop tomahawk he bought in Alligator Alley. Know what he tells me yesterday?"

"No."

"He says 'Got some good news and bad news for you, Nurse Shark-boy. Nurse shark, get it? Funny, huh? The good news is, he says, I'm getting married tomorrow. Bad news is you the squaw."

Stoke said, "That's bad."

"Tell me about it. Anyway, he's out in the yard every day sayin' I'm his bitch. I got to wear Revlon Love Dew lipstick during lockdown. And a blond wig, Stoke; man calls me his little 'Cuban Firecracker'; I'm telling you, man, it's just a matter of time before I get my butt fucked. Flipping out in here, I'm saying, I mean what the hell, man? I didn't put in for this shit."

Luis Gonzales-Gonzales sounding all wound up like he was about to come unsprung.

"You juiced right now, Shark? You jacked up on shit?"

"Ah, hell, no. Clean and mean. Ask me a question."

"Capital of Idaho?" said Stoke. Shark, for God knows what reason, had decided long ago it would be a good idea to memorize all the U.S. state capitals.

"Boise."

"Alaska."

"Juneau. Okay? Satisfied? I ain't wrecked. Now get my ass the fuck out, boss."

"Anybody else troubling you?"

"Lemme see. Aryan Brotherhood? Yeah, they're troublesome. Big white asshole skinhead with a swastika on his forehead. Calls himself 'The Bonecrusher.' And there's this other guy see, in that Islam cell you want me to penetrate. He's this Black Muslim cat, calls himself Ishtar, big sonofabitch, three hundred pounds at least. Eyes bulging out his head like hard-boiled eggs. He says he catches me doing the nasty with the Chief he's going to cut my dick off with a razor, one inch at a time."

"That shouldn't take too long."

"Don't mess with me right now, Stoke. Serious. I can't take this place a second longer. And when I get out, I'm taking early retirement. Spend more time with my remaining limbs."

"Sharkey, you know how to protect yourself against this kind of shit. You got your shank."

"Shit, that's the thing. They did a shakedown of my cell and found my shiv inside my mattress. I got nothing, man, nothing. You know what it's like to be a one-armed Cuban cat doesn't weigh much more than a hundred pounds in a bug-house full of homicidal maniacs like the Glades?"

"Did you penetrate that radical Islam cell yet? Get me some names besides this Ishtar cat? Say yes and you can come out."

"Penetrate the cell? Fuck, that's the problem. I penetrated the damn cell and now they trying to penetrate me! That's what I'm talking about, Stoke. Penetrate my ass! And if I don't pick up the soap, they whack me. I gotta come out, Stoke. Please get me out. I'm beggin' you. I can't do another day in stir."

"Look, Sharkey, I understand. But we need to get inside these bad boys' heads and find out what the hell kind of bad shit they got in mind once they get out."

"I found out some stuff today, peeking at the Wizard's laptop when nobody was looking."

"Wizard?"

"Little old Pakistani guy who seems in charge. Looks like Yoda in *Star Wars*. Has this long pointed white beard. Wears a robe all the time, some kinda Arab writing all over it. Talks like Yoda too. I think he does it on purpose, you know, give himself a little personality."

"He's got a computer? You can't have a computer in the slam, man."

"He does, Stoke, all I can tell you. Smuggled in by a guard at Admin who's on the little guy's payroll, how do I know? Got one of those little plug-in aerials that gives you Internet access."

"Where's he hide it?"

"I dunno. I heard about it and paid some guard named Figg a grand to let me get a quick look at it when everybody was out in the Yard."

"Can you get back at that computer? Steal it? Then you can come out."

"I got to come out now, man, I'm serious. Ishtar catches me poking around trying to steal the Wizard's shit, I'm dead on arrival."

"Calm down, Sharkey. I got an idea. I don't like it, but I guess I got no choice but to do it."

"Tell me."

"I'm coming inside with you."

"What?"

"I can get myself incarcerated at the Glades with you. Have us put in a cell together so I can take care of your skinny ass. Keep you from getting married to somebody you're not totally in love with. Steal the Wizard's computer."

"Okay, okay, that's really sounding good, man, but when?"

"Tell me where the Wizard keeps his laptop and how the hell they let a con have one in the joint."

"Smuggled in. He's got a battery charger and some kind of antenna he plugs into it that picks up cell-phone towers, I think. What do I know. No idea where he hides it but someplace good because the hacks toss his cell all the damn time and they can't find it. So, when? Like, tomorrow?"

"As soon as I put away the bitch tried to kill me and almost killed my good friend Fast Eddie Falco."

"How long will that take, you figure?"

"Not long. I'm sitting on her twenty million bucks but she has to go through me to get it."

"Why can't Harry do that? He's goddamn CIA."

"Harry sucks at surveillance. No patience. He's got severe attention deficit syndrome."

"What?"

"Don't worry about it. Just hang in there, okay? Stop taking showers for a few days. Maybe the stink'll keep 'em away from you too. I'll come take care of you, Sharkey, I promise."

"Okay. But what do I do until you get here?"

"Eat a lightbulb and get yourself sent to the prison hospital."

"Eat a lightbulb?"

"Nobody said it would be easy, Shark."

Stoke hung up. He would have killed to go back to sleep but it was 6:00 A.M. and he had to go relieve his partner.

He grabbed some coffee in the kitchen and went out into the living room. Harry was on the floor doing push-ups, which was okay as long as he kept one eye on the monitor.

"Beddy-bye time, little buddy," Stoke said to Brock, sitting down in the armchair and sipping his hot java. "The hell are you doing down there?"

"I'm trying to wear myself out so I go to sleep instantly," Harry said, the words coming out funny because of the push-ups. "Think I ate too many reds."

"Clock is ticking, partner."

"Twenty more."

"Anything interesting happen on TV?"

"Yeah, I guess. Somebody checked in."

"What?"

"Yeah. The night manager called me from the front desk about three in the morning. Some sheik and his family. Just flew in from Dubai. You know what they charge for that suite across the hall? Ten grand a night."

"Harry. Tell me you checked this guy out."

"Of course. That's why we're in this fucking dump."

"And?"

"And it was a sheik and his family, like the guy said. Wife, dog, five little rug rats all under the age of ten. And luggage. Two bellmen with carts stacked with those big steamer trunks, the luggage with the brown LVs all over, you know what I mean?"

"Louis Vuitton."

"Yeah, those. Okay, that's it. I'm hitting the sack, pards. Keep your eyes open."

"Harry. Stop."

"What?"

"Come back here. Describe the wife. Tell me exactly what she looked like."

"The wife? Hell, Stoke, it was a whole family. Seven of them, like I told you. Oh, and a little white dog on a diamond-studded leash."

"What did the wife look like, Harry?"

"Shit, Stoke, I didn't get that good a look at her."

"Why not?"

"Well, for starters she was wearing one of those black burkas. A fancy one. The one all the rich Arab women wear."

"So you're saying you didn't see her?"

"Of course I saw her. I saw her fucking husband. I saw her fucking children. And I saw her luggage and her fucking dog. Gimme a break, man. I've been eating reds all night and I'm a little ragged here."

"Ragged? I'm not in a real good mood, Harry. Seriously. I just got off the phone with Sharkey. I'm going to prison soon, Harry, a very bad prison."

"What? Why?"

"Later. Now, you tell me all those people are still inside that suite across the hall. That they did not come out. Not one of them. Not ever."

"Not one of them came out. I swear. I was watching that door, man. I been all over it."

"They order any room service? Maid service? Bellmen? Plumbers? Electricians?"

"No. Not a soul. I swear."

"You think about maybe waking me up, Harry?"

"It didn't seem like that big a—"

"Did you think about telling the manager to bring their passports up to our suite? So you could, you know, sorta check them out?"

"No. I mean, yes, of course I thought about it. But—"

"Did you think about what a good disguise a burka would make for a woman who didn't want to be recognized?"

"I—"

"Get your weapon, Harry. We're going across the hall to pay the sheik a visit. We're hotel detectives checking on the sheik's security arrangements in case they give us any trouble. Okay?"

"Good idea."

"They better be in there, Harry."

"They're in there, dude. Unless they can fly off balconies, they are most definitely fucking in there."

THE PRESIDENTIAL SUITE WAS EMPTY. Stoke examined every square inch of it. You'd never know anyone had set foot in it. Only by going into the master bedroom walk-in closet, where there were chunks of plaster and plaster dust all over the goddamned floor where a fake wall had been taken down, and a big damn hole punched in the real wall behind it, would you know somebody had been there. There was a very substantial wall safe with the door hanging ajar. It was empty too. Imagine that.

"Shit," Harry Brock said. "Shit, shit, shit."

"Yeah," Stoke said, too angry with his partner to say more.

"So how did they get out, Stoke? Jesus."

"It seems there is a small service elevator in the suite's kitchen pantry. It's behind a china cabinet that swings out from the wall. So room service can bring meals and hors d'oeuvres up directly and heat them for cocktail parties and shit."

"Oh."

"Yeah."

"Our guys didn't know about the service elevator?"

"No, Harry, they did not. I did not. I should have. My bad. You feel better now?"

"How the hell you get twenty million in hundreds out of the damn suite? Out of the hotel?"

"I dunno. Steamer trunks with little brown LVs all over them, maybe? Huh? You think?"

"Right."

"But all those kids. The dog. The sheik."

"Relatives. Cousins, nephews, who the hell knows."

"Yeah, relatives. Except for the dog."

"Harry, I'm going to kill you."

"You know what? I don't blame you. Give me five minutes alone in that bathroom and I'll kill myself."

"I can't wait five minutes. Besides, I'd really rather do it myself, Harry," Stoke said.

THIRTY-TWO

PALM BEACH, FLORIDA

DRIVE EXACTLY 39.7 MILES DUE WEST of Palm Beach, Florida, and you will soon find yourself on another planet. There you'll find the miniburg strip called Belle Glade sweltering amid vast cane fields. BeeGee, as Stoke called it, was about as far removed from the money, tropical splendors, and glamour of Palm Beach as the earth is from the sun.

In addition to a smattering of smoke-belching Big Sugar factories out in the fields, a gas station, and a grotty Burger King, BeeGee is also the home of an infamous hellhole penal colony called the Glades Correctional Institution.

The Glades, for short. Think *Cool Hand Luke* meets *Devil's Island* and you've got yourself a pretty good mental picture. Established in 1932 as Florida Prison Farm 2, inmates were originally sent there to grow vegetables for other state institutions. Now it's just GCI, or as the medium-to-close custody population calls it, the Glades.

Stoke, who would be incarcerated inside the razor-barbed wire boundaries of the Glades in a few short hours, at three o'clock that very afternoon, had told Harry Brock he wanted to have his "last meal" in Palm Beach. Palm Beach? Brock had said. Wasn't that where Bernie Madoff had lived? That's how much Harry knew about Palm Beach.

Stoke was starving. He knew exactly what he wanted, too. Cup of black bean soup followed by a rare bacon cheeseburger, mushrooms, fried onions, lettuce, extra mayo, at a restaurant called Taboo on Worth Avenue. Maybe even two bacon cheeseburgers. What the hell. God only knew how long he'd be inside the joint.

They were blasting up I-95 from Miami in Stoke's GTO, top down, Barry White CD pulsing, pushing the bass envelope on the Bose system. It was Stoke's particular fave, *Staying Power,* the one Barry White album that had the six-minute duet with Lisa Stansfield, the one called "The Longer We Make Love," on it. Stoke, behind the wheel, was singing along with Barry.

The blacker the berry, the sweeter the juice,
The longer we do it, the more we get down to it . . .

When they reached the I-95 exits for Southern Boulevard, Stoke took the one going east toward the Atlantic Ocean. Moments later, they were rumbling over what the Palm Beach locals called the South Bridge, brothers standing on both sides of the bridge, fishing in the hot sunshine, little Styrofoam coolers with ice and beer at their feet, not a care in the whole damn world. And that lucky old sun, he just rolls around heaven all day.

"You really look depressed," Harry said, looking over at him.

"Me? Nah. Hell, I got it all, baby. See that big pinkish house over on the left? Big green lawn rolling down to the water. Know what that is?"

"Yeah. A big pink house."

"That just happens to be Mar-a-Lago, Harry. Home of none other than the Donald himself. Donald and me, hell, we practically neighbors now. Glades is only about forty miles from here, y'know.

Turn this car around, it's a straight shot west out Southern Boulevard. Way I see it, me and the Donald live on the same damn street. 'Course, I don't have a pool and a nine-hole golf course, but still."

"You are depressed."

Stoke, still pissed at Harry over the Fontainebleau debacle, reached over and turned Barry up, now on another CD backed by a full orchestra and Love Unlimited doing "Love's Theme," and concentrated on the music and just cruising Ocean Boulevard, breathing the salt air, the wide blue Atlantic sparkling on his right, gorgeous flowery mansions flashing by on his left. Beautiful. He had a lot of sins, but envy had never been one of them. He appreciated every damn thing he had.

When they got to Worth Avenue, he hung a left, crossed County Road, and pulled up right in front of Taboo.

The unpretentious restaurant was smack-dab in the middle of some of the most expensive shopping real estate this side of Fifth Avenue or Rodeo. The only thing Stoke ever shopped for here was the very expensive bacon cheeseburgers at Taboo. He had bought a couple of pairs of white boxers when Brooks Brothers, a couple of doors down the avenue, was having a sale. But he didn't think that really counted as legitimate Palm Beach shopping.

The valet parking guy came over to the GTO, his mouth hanging open. The rumble of the straight pipes was pretty strong here on the narrow street. Stoke could feel eyes on him as he climbed out of the car. Good. Let 'em burn their eyes on me moving, as the old song said. He climbed out, handed the kid the keys.

"What color is this?" the kid said, caressing the mirrorlike fender.

"Black raspberry. Metallic."

"Custom?"

"Bet your ass."

"How many horses?"

"You can't count that high, son. Now you take care of it and I'll take care of you."

"Yes, sir. I'll just put it right here in front where I can keep an eye on it."

"There you go. Class up the avenue a little bit, right? All these tacky-ass Rolls-Royce Phantoms and Ferraris and Lambos and shit. Now you got some serious Dee-troit iron parked right here, you watch business pick up. Guaranteed."

They went inside, immediately confronting a wall of ice-cold air. A shortish, sophisticated-looking man in a suit and tie, half-glasses perched on the tip of his nose, rushed up and shook Stoke's hand. "Mr. Jones, long time no see. What brings you back to Palm Beach?"

"Doing a little shopping. Actually I'm meeting Detective Garcia here for lunch. Oh. Franklin, please say hello to my driver, Harry Brock."

"Franklin De Marco, Harry," he said, shaking his hand but looking over Brock's shoulder at two spangled and suntanned blondes in stacked heels just sliding in right through the front door. Cougar Cruisers headed for the bar, but God bless 'em, they pulled in the gents. Short, most of them, Franklin joked privately, until they stood on their wallets.

Franklin tore his eyes away from these two human commercials, flicking them briefly at Harry, and said, "I am the owner of Taboo. Mr. Jones here is one of my favorite customers. Never orders just one of anything. Detective Garcia has already arrived, Mr. Jones. I gave her one of our very best banquette tables in the Jungle Room. Follow me, won't you?"

"Driver?" Harry hissed at Stoke as they trailed Franklin past the long bar, every stool occupied by beautiful human females with a wide variety of breasts and with large frothy cocktails on the bar in front of them.

"What?"

"You just introduce me to the owner as your driver?"

Stoke said, "Yeah, well, whatever."

"Wait, is that a fireplace?"

"Yep."

"In July? What the—?"

"Hey, Michelle," Stoke said, kissing her cheek as he slid in next to her on the banquette. Harry took the chair facing the two of them. He couldn't quite get over the surprise of Detective Garcia. She was a total babe. Silky black hair that fell to her shoulders, beautiful face, and a body that—

"Harry, this person you're staring at is my old friend Detective Michelle Garcia, Palm Beach PD. Michelle, Harry Brock, CIA spook, Washington."

She extended her hand across the table and shook Harry's hand, giving him a friendly smile. *And, wait, she's nice,* Harry thought, already moving into a rose-covered cottage and having plump pink babies with her. You never knew. Stranger things have happened.

The waitress came over, smiled knowingly at Stoke, and took their drink and food orders. "Be right back," she said.

Harry said, "So, Detective. Nice to meet you."

"Call me Michelle, okay? Nice to meet you, too, Harry."

"Palm Beach PD. Tough gig, huh? So, how do you and Stokely know each other?"

Stoke glanced at Michelle, rolling his eyes—*This guy is not my fault.*

"Well. We worked a few cases together over the years. I started out with DEA down in Key West after Quantico, before I came up here to paradise. I'm the one who arranged to find Stokely a nice room out at the Glades Motel. I'll be driving him out Southern to Belle Glade and officially turning him over at three."

"Nice, really nice," Harry said for no apparent reason.

She looked at Stoke, who was no help at all, and said, "Well, you know, we're old friends, and—"

High society. Everybody in the place chatting up a damn storm while Stoke, thinking only about Sharkey and the danger he'd put him in, sat and watched the clock over the bar. He looked across the table at Brock, saw all his sunny charm and California surfer sunshine beamed at Michelle.

"Harry, listen up. You know that fat dickhead tried to kill me in my own damn condo? Bashir al Mahmoud or whatever? Turns out Bashi used to own one of the largest houses on the beach here in PB. Billionaire's Row, they call it. Rod Stewart was his next-door neighbor. I ran his name, saw the former address, ran it by Michelle, and it turns out she busted him once. Few years ago. It didn't stick, but she learned a whole lot about him."

"What'd you bust him for, Michelle?" Harry asked, big smile, trying really hard to be a swell handsome guy who, at the very same time, was just, darn it all, naturally curious about law enforcement matters.

"Drugs. White slavery, child prostitution. And soliciting minors. Bashi, that's what he called himself, had some woman recruiting little girls for him. She'd cruise some of the poorer neighborhoods over in West Palm, parks, playgrounds, chat up pretty young girls on the sidewalk, tell them how easily they could make a few hundred dollars. In one hour. Just go with her over to Palm Beach to this really rich guy's mansion on the beach and give him a massage. No sex, just a straight massage. Of course it was always more than that."

"What a dick."

"Tell him the rest, Michelle."

"Well, Mike, that's when Mike Reiter, our former chief, now FBI director, had us put a surveil on the woman who worked for Bashi. Every week she'd drive over to PBI airport in West Palm, sometimes even Orlando or Lauderdale, and meet planes coming in from Morocco, Saudi Arabia, or Caracas via New York.

"We'd check them out, alert Immigration. Young guys, all clean-cut, clean visas, no Interpol red flags, nothing. She'd take them to the Marriott up in Jupiter, check them in, then she'd head back to Bashi's beach blanket bingo party pad over on South Ocean till the next batch flew in."

Harry said, "This woman, what'd she look like?"

"Oh, you know the type. Blond, Victoria's-Secret-model type. Tall."

"We know the type all right," Stoke said to Michelle. "She's working South Beach now. Or, at least she *was*. Right, Harry?"

"We've got Bashi in custody, Michelle," Harry said, a teeny bit defensive. "Illegal entry, attempted murder."

"Who the hell he try to off?" Michelle asked.

"Me," Stoke said.

"Why?"

"I know what his girlfriend looks like."

"And now?"

"Not talking. He's all clammed up."

Brock said, "Waterboard the fat piece of shit, then."

"Can't. Now illegal to get prisoners wet. Might catch a case of the sniffles. End up in their jammies in sick bay. Do you know how much that would cost the government in Cold Care Plus alone?"

"God save America," Brock said. "I think we've lost it."

"Airboard him," Stoke suddenly said, "is what I'd do."

"What?"

"Nothing. These guys Bashi's been bringing in from the Middle East," Stoke said. "They come here, scatter, disappear after a month or so. Maine to California. But one thing. Know where they all end up? Same damn place. Stir. Commit some crime, armed robbery, assault, anything sufficient to land them in the joint. So you gotta ask yourself why?"

"Missionaries," Michelle Garcia said. "That's what we call 'em anyway."

"What's that?" Harry asked.

"It's what they are in prison for," Detective Garcia said. "Spread the word of radical Islamism throughout this country. And tell the newly converted what they are supposed to do with that new knowledge. Primarily, what these young men are brought to America for is to spread the gospel. It is ridiculously obvious. But you think anyone in D.C. is concerned about this? Masses of immigrants here to recruit naive U.S. prisoners, in effect, captive audiences, to earn the Islamic Gangbanger Ph.D. degree? Doctorates in hating the American infidels? No one is even looking at this problem, much less talking about it. It is, or will be, a huge problem for this country when these guys start hitting the street and spreading the word. Believe me."

"I believe you, Michelle," Stoke said.

"Great. I got one guy who thinks this is serious."

Harry said, "So this is the deal. They do the crime to do the time, get released, hit the Greyhound stations, get anonymous jobs all over the country, and then—"

Stoke sighed and rubbed his reddened eyes with his knuckles and said, "Blow us up. Scare the living shit out of all of us. From the inside out. Cheapest damn form of warfare in history. Get enough of these assholes operating around the country, raising hell in every town, sooner or later they shut us down, the whole damn country. Nazis couldn't do it. Japanese couldn't do it. Russians couldn't do it. But these guys? Shit."

Harry said, "I'm with you, Stoke. I'm down with everything you just said. I really respect what you're doing today. Going inside, I mean." Stoke just stared at him until he turned away.

Garcia said, "Big Black Muslim gang operating inside the Glades. Recruiting migrant workers, hardened cons, and anyone else they can get their hands on. It's one of the first fully franchised gangs we saw in the system. Now they number in the thousands. Sword of Allah. Get cane workers, local black and white farm kids, in for minor offenses, kids who don't know any better, talk about how America enslaves them all, always has, how to do something about it. Strike back at the Great Satan."

The food came and Stoke was happy to see it. He shut up, just thinking about not this gorgeous cheeseburger, or the next one after that, but the one after that. When he was out. When he'd learned whatever he had to learn inside the Glades, got his friend Sharkey out alive, his virginity intact. But first he'd figure out who was behind the radical gang culture growing in the prison system.

Not just Florida, either, or California; these gangs were everywhere, ultimately threatening everybody in his whole damn country.

It was just a matter of time until they started running around like those ragheads in Kabul, blowing shit up. These guys really pissed him off, threatening Americans on their home turf, still the home of the brave and the land of the free.

He hadn't spent the best years of his life in Nam for this. Lost all those brave boys, his buddies, the SEAL platoon he commanded and loved with all his heart, all those young kids calling out to their mamas when they died, ripped to shreds by Charlie, guts spilling out of their stomachs, Stoke trying to hold their insides inside them with his hands.

This new enemy would pay, all right, just like he'd made the VC pay, one way or another. You could listen to the media. Or you could listen to your heart. This was the greatest country the world had ever produced. And anyone who wanted to try and bring it down was going to pay dearly for the privilege.

He knew a whole shitload of people who felt exactly the same way he did. Take the fight to them. Wherever you found them, get right up in their face. And keep fighting until every last one of the bastards bit the dust.

He stuck an onion ring inside his burger and took a big bite, feeling a whole lot better about what he was about to do inside the Glades. He was doing his duty and that was the only thing he knew that was really worth doing. One thing for damn sure. He was going to penetrate these radical Islamic sons of bitches, learn their plans, and break their goddamn backs on the wheel of American justice.

And if he couldn't waterboard 'em, he'd airboard their asses. At night. That's right. Threaten to throw them the fuck out of Black Hawk choppers deep into the Everglades. Talk, or you're gator bait, pal. Congress hadn't outlawed that yet, had they? Airboarding? You always had to stay one step ahead of these criminal-coddling nannies up in Washington, else they'd put an end to America soon as they could.

"Stoke?" Michelle said. "Sorry. Time to go."

"Yeah," Stoke said, looking at his watch. "Listen up, Harry."

"Yeah?"

"You take the turnpike back to Miami. Not 95, OK? Safer. No trucks allowed. You keep your speed at 55. Not 56, 55. You don't talk on your cell, you don't text anybody, you don't even turn on the radio. All you do is drive. Okay? Eyes on the road, hands on the wheel. Thing is, I don't want anything bad to happen to you, see? You're my bud, right? We partners, right? Got each other's backs?"

"And all this has got absolutely nothing to do with the GTO, right, Stoke?"

"The GTO? Damn, you insult me. That GTO sitting out there? Stopping traffic on Worth Avenue even as we speak? That's just metal, my brother. Metal and rubber and plastic. You? You're a human being, Harry. You are a gift from God."

"Gee, thanks, Stoke. I love you, too, man."

"But I swear to God, Harry, you put one scratch on that car and I will rip your tiny testicles off and feed them to you one at a time. I will then stick cotton so far down your throat it will come out your ass, make you look like a goddamn Playboy Bunny. Are we clear?"

"You two boys having a problem or something?" Michelle asked innocently.

"Problem? Nah, we cool," Stoke said. "Cool Hand Brock here is driving my GTO back to Miami. Most likely with the top down. While I'm going straight to goddamn jail. You see a problem?"

THIRTY-THREE

LONDON

C'S OFFICE ON THE TOP FLOOR of MI6 Headquarters, an odd architectural mix of the new, the newer, and the newest, was located at 85 Albert Embankment in Vauxhall on the banks of the Thames. It was a far cry from the Service's rather grotty old digs near Regent's Park, but then Hawke usually preferred the old rather than the new when it came to architecture.

Sir David Trulove's private sanctuary, however, was pleasantly reminiscent of a captain's cabin dating from Admiral Lord Nelson's era. Varnished wood paneling, electrified oil lamps on gimbals, period mahogany furniture, valuable marine art on the walls, a brass chronometer and barometer standing to either side of the model of Admiral Lord Nelson's *Victory* atop the carved mantelpiece.

The only things missing in C's lovely office, Hawke observed once to Congreve, were portholes.

It was Monday morning, a few days following the harrowing but profitable visit he and Congreve had paid to Mutton Island. After Hawke had a series of meetings with British Army intelligence officers for Northern Ireland, Ambrose had remained in Ireland, he and

Drummond returning to the island with the Yard's Scene of Crime lads for a thorough forensic examination of the entire scene. Lab results from the human gallstone found at the scene had not yet been released.

Hawke, who loathed meetings of any type, now found himself in the middle of yet another one, no matter how congenial he found the surroundings. In addition to Hawke, C had invited his protégé Montague Thorne to this command performance. Thorne, the reigning expert on all matters Pakistani, Indian, and Afghani, and an American fellow, CIA, who introduced himself to Hawke as Abdul Dakkon.

Dakkon was tall and lean with black eyes, swarthy good looks, and a neatly trimmed black beard. Hawke put him in his late thirties. He was Moroccan, he said, born in Tangier. Despite his navy suit, white shirt, and red tie, he had the unmistakable look of an agent who'd spent most of his life out in the field. An unremittingly harsh field, Hawke surmised from the looks of him. Somehow, he'd lost his right arm. The empty sleeve of his jacket was sewn across his chest, in the same fashion that Admiral Lord Nelson had dealt with the issue.

Also present, his old friend and new lover, the nuclear physicist and counterterror expert from MI5. Sahira seemed to have dressed knowing Hawke would be present. A short blue skirt and a tight-fitting white silk blouse that left little to the imagination. She was wearing glasses, perusing an impossibly thick binder, presumably filled with schematics of fission-fusion thermonuclear weapons. Fascinating stuff, Hawke imagined, from the intensity with which she studied each page. He could hardly wait to read it himself.

Anything to keep him from staring at Sahira.

Genius, Hawke had read somewhere, was the ability to hold two completely discrete thoughts in your mind at the same time. Miss Karim, in addition to studying her binder, was simultaneously carrying on a very involved conversation with Montague Thorne regarding the resurgence of the Taliban in Helmand Province, Afghanistan.

The only one missing at the moment was Sir David himself, running late apparently, and Hawke contented himself with sipping the horrid company coffee and gazing surreptitiously at Miss Karim while she and Thorne now chatted about the very real possibility of war breaking out between Pakistan and India.

The Allies were tiring of this seemingly unwinnable war even though the consequences of losing it could be apocalyptic.

C burst in suddenly, apologized in his typically perfunctory manner, and eased himself into his leather chair just to the right of the fireplace. He looked frightfully cheerful for this ungodly hour on a Monday morning, and Hawke's guard went up involuntarily.

Sir David got his pipe going, smiled at Hawke, and said, "How was your abbreviated island holiday in Northern Ireland, Alex?"

"Adrenaline fueled, I would say, sir."

"So I gather. You made good progress, however?"

"We did indeed."

"If you could possibly spare a few minutes after this meeting, I'd like to hear about it in some detail. Are you available?"

One was always available.

"Of course, sir," Hawke said.

"Well, then, let's get down to the matters at hand, shall we? In light of the current events in his specific region of interest, Mr. Thorne has agreed to provide a brief overview of the current political situation vis-à-vis Pakistan. Monty?"

Thorne stood and began passing around thin MI6 binders marked "MOST SECRET" on the red covers. Even his physical movements, Hawke noticed, were polished, at once economic and elegant. He glanced at Sahira to see if she was watching him too. She wasn't.

Thorne sat down and said, "Thank you, sir. Inside those binders you'll find a summary of what we in my section have taken to calling the 'Second Nuclear Age.' To say what we've learned is 'disturbing' would be a grave understatement. We estimate that Pakistan has at least one hundred nuclear warhead-tipped missiles hidden inside the country. Some of them are known to be located just beyond the perimeter of the Islamabad airport. The infamous Dr. Khan has reestablished a facility for creating nuclear weapons there as well.

"We have no idea where, of course, and their government refuses to tell us despite our expressed concerns about the security of those weapons. To make matters worse, they are building more all the time in laboratory compounds on the edge of the Islamabad airport. You will find sat recon photos of the referenced area in Section Two.

"What happens or fails to happen at those two compounds is far more likely to save or lose a British or American city than are the billions our two countries spend each year maintaining our nuclear arsenals. Designed for a different age, America and Britain's combined nuclear arsenals are, in my opinion, the new Maginot Line in the age of terror: huge, scary, and, I'm afraid, fundamentally useless.

"Most states have an army. Pakistan's army has a state. The country's leaders operate at the army's pleasure. And their ability to control their own nuclear arsenal is the most frightening nuclear challenge facing the West today.

"Pakistan is the only nuclear state on earth with a powerful military insurgency in its very midst. We know for a fact that the combined forces of the Taliban and al Qaeda, now grown immensely strong under a single command and known as the 'Sword of Allah,' definitely have aims to take over the country by force or intimidation, and the insurgents most assuredly want to acquire the bomb."

Thorne paused a moment and turned his gaze toward each person in the room to ensure he had their undivided attention.

"It is hardly reassuring that the Pakistani government has veered between a dictatorship that has supported both the United States and the Taliban simultaneously, and now has a democratic leadership known chiefly for its corruption and ineptitude.

"An urgent new wave of intelligence has recently been flowing through MI6, MI5, CIA, and the Pentagon. Taliban and al Qaeda forces along the northern Pakistan-Afghanistan border are focusing anew on the Holy Grail of terrorism that eluded them before 9/11. They are unswerving in their determination to acquire either the secrets to the Pakistani bomb . . . or the bombs themselves."

Hawke held up a hand.

"It's been over a year since Sword of Allah struck Heathrow. Perhaps American Predators have beheaded the leadership, Monty?" Hawke asked.

Thorne paused a moment before replying. "It's true we've succeeded wildly with the drones. Many key leaders have been killed. But I think they're stronger than ever. I think their influence is growing around the world. They have Iranian funds, Russian funds, cells around the world, and now, someone at the very top who has considerably more brainpower than Osama bin Laden. Sheik Abu al-Rashad."

"Nevertheless, Monty, Alex is right," C said. "At least we, I mean Five and Six, seem to have driven this Sword of Allah underground here in the United Kingdom."

"Perhaps that is true," Thorne said, but Hawke got the distinct feeling Monty didn't mean it.

"So. Where are we?" C said.

"I must tell you. Two things keep me awake at night. One, recent intelligence concerning the steadfast efforts to infiltrate the labs and put sleepers inside the nuclear arsenal storage facilities at Islamabad."

"And the second?" C said, patience wearing thin.

"And, two, the rising internal threat levels against our own population and infrastructure. And, finally, this new 'Real IRA' rising up in Northern Ireland and their recent threats to the Prince of Wales and the Royal Family itself."

"Good Lord," Trulove muttered. "A plateful."

"Yes. When the world's biggest threat looks more like loose nukes escaping Pakistan rather than *launched* nukes out of Russia, all of our old Armageddon avoidance tricks go out the window. The world has suddenly become a far more dangerous place, I'm afraid."

There was no disagreement.

THIRTY-FOUR

SIR DAVID SAID, "I BELIEVE ALEX Hawke has a question."

"Monty," a thoughtful Hawke said, interlacing his fingers and resting his chin on it, "it might be helpful to describe explicitly a 'day after' scenario for us. To be clear, could you tell us exactly what, precisely, happens the day after a nuclear weapon goes off in a major British or American city?"

"Good question, Alex. There is a 90 percent probability the weapon will have come out of either North Korea, the old Soviet arsenal, or Pakistan's arsenal. If I had to guess, I'd definitely say Pakistan. But, once you figure out the guilty party, then what? Launch a nuclear strike against a quasi ally for something that country's president probably didn't even know was missing? When he's still sitting on a ton of nukes? Not happening, Alex. Which leaves us only one option: find a way to lock down Pakistan's nuclear storage facilities. Find out where the holes are and close them. And do it now, before it's too late."

C turned those crafty blue eyes on Alex. "And that, my Lord Hawke, is your next mission."

"And when do I depart?"

"As soon as humanly possible. I'll need time to organize logistics at the other end. A week at the outside. I know you wish to continue with your investigation in Northern Ireland. You've got a week, maybe less if I can speed things up in Islamabad."

Hawke sat back and silently regarded his boss, deeply conflicted by what he'd just heard. He craved this new mission, literally hungered for the great game now going on in Pakistan and Afghanistan.

Still. He had sworn a solemn oath to Charles, and he believed he was on the right track after Mutton Island. Not to mention the conversation with McMahon. To abandon all that now would be tantamount to—

"Alex? Did you hear what I just said? You've got perhaps a week before you depart."

"Yes, sir. I know. It's just that I'm still concerned about my efforts on behalf of the Prince of Wales, sir. Congreve and I are, well, we are quite confident we have made significant progress—but a week may not be sufficient."

"Alex, with all due respect, you do not work for the Prince of Wales. You work for MI6. And that means me. And it means investigating and stopping internal and external threats to our entire country such as those presented by this 'Sword of Allah' that Montague is so rightfully concerned about. There are literally hundreds of men and women whose sole responsibility is the safety and security of the Royal Family. They've rather proven themselves fully up to the task over the centuries. Wouldn't you agree?"

"Yes, sir. I understand all that. But I promised His Royal Highness that—"

"Alex. If you don't mind. I think we should save this discussion for a private meeting, don't you?"

"Sorry, sir."

"You've met Mr. Dakkon, Alex?"

"I have. We chatted briefly while we were all waiting for you. Sir."

C shot him a look for that one, but continued, "Mr. Dakkon is a veteran CIA Arabic linguist and field agent on loan to us from Washington. He has served for the last ten years, operating undercover both in Pakistan and the Hindu Kush mountains of Afghanistan. He will be your assist on this assignment. If you have any questions about Mr. Dakkon's intel qualifications, you are free to call your friend Director Kelly at Langley."

"Thank you. I will."

"You are probably wondering about the loss of his right arm. He will not tell you what happened but I will. He was captured by al Qaeda fighters in Kabul. He was subjected to severe torture. The enemy demanded to know the location of an American forward operating base in Helmand Province. He refused to give it up and some bloody butcher took his arm off at the shoulder with a sword. They left him for dead in the desert. They've come to regret it."

"I admire your courage, sir," Hawke said, looking the man in the eye.

"Alex, Mr. Dakkon has spent the last five years of his life infiltrating the army under control of the most powerful Taliban commander in northern Pakistan. Sheik Abu al-Rashad. Al-Rashad, a longtime enemy of al Qaeda, is widely believed to be the mastermind behind the Sword of Allah's terror operations worldwide. Abdul here has risen very high in Sheik al-Rashad's estimation and has gained his complete confidence. Isn't that correct, Abdul?"

"He looks upon me as the son he never had, sir," Dakkon said, proudly, but with modesty.

"That relationship has recently produced a good deal of very critical intelligence, all of which is included in your briefing books. It concerns Sheik al-Rashad's ultimate plan to overwhelm the security forces surrounding the nuclear facilities at Islamabad airport and secure Pakistan's weapons of mass destruction for his own use. Thus, taking over the country. That's the bad news."

"And the good news?" Hawke asked, suddenly energized by the

prospects of this new mission. He'd been simmering. Now he was on full boil.

Dakkon said, "The Sheik has many rivals in this race to acquire Pakistan's nuclear arsenal. Both within opposing factions of the Taliban, al Qaeda, and ISI, Pakistan's intelligence service. There have been numerous attempts on his life by the opposition. He is somewhat constrained by this array of enemies."

"America's new president, Tom McCloskey, and the Pentagon are very anxious to ensure that Sheik al-Rashad not win this race, Alex," C said.

"Why is that?" Hawke asked.

"Because we know the Sheik is a very smart man, with enormous economic resources," Trulove said. "He is for sale, as are many of those government officials responsible for the security of the arsenal. Dakkon has just informed me that rumor has it, many of the guards who control access to the warheads and trigger devices may be receiving massive sums from al-Rashad. Or he may be holding the guards' family members hostage. Presumably under threat of death unless they comply with his wishes.

"We cannot rule out the possibility that he has, or will have, access to nuclear devices. These weapons would simply disappear as guards on the Sheik's payroll look the other way. We can't control what happens politically in that country. But we can put a lot of heat on Sheik al-Rashad."

"Is this hard evidence, Mr. Dakkon?" Hawke asked.

"Only rumor, but rumor is the political currency of Pakistan. We are not aware that any weapons have fallen into his hands. Nor are we sure that they haven't. We need to find out."

Thorne added, "If you and your team discover the Sheik is secretly looting the nuclear arsenal, both the British and American governments are prepared to step in and take control away from the corrupt Pakistani government."

"Hence a slightly safer planet, Alex," C added, taking a leisurely puff.

Montague Thorne said, "Which is where Miss Karim's expertise with nuclear weapons comes in, Alex. She will be joining you and Mr. Dakkon on your visit to Islamabad to inspect the storage facilities for Pakistan's nukes. And she will be with you on your trek up into the Hindu Kush to confront Sheik al-Rashad. It will fall to her to ensure that any stolen weapons end up safely in our hands. Once we've decided what to do with them, she will oversee that process."

"Question, Mr. Dakkon," Hawke said.

"Abdul, please."

"Abdul, where is the Sheik located?"

"He moves around. He's constantly fighting skirmishes both with Pakistan's anti-Taliban militia and with rival factions both within the Taliban and al Qaeda. But he has a heavily fortified central base of operations deep inside an anonymous mountain high in the Hindu Kush. That's where we're headed, after Islamabad."

"How do we get up into the mountains?" Hawke asked.

"I know what you're thinking, Alex," Sahira said. "Camels, right?"

"How did you guess?"

"No one likes camels. Especially you. It was written all over your face."

"I like camels," Abdul Dakkon said, a big white smile suddenly appearing.

"Why?" Hawke asked, unable to comprehend how anyone could stand the foul-tempered, noisy beasts.

"I like the way they smell," Abdul said.

Hawke laughed.

"Well, I suppose I'll have to give them another go, Mr. Dakkon."

Dakkon said, "The trails we'll be taking in the mountains are about two feet wide in places. One misstep and you're looking at a few thousand feet of air before you hit the ground. Camels and horses don't make missteps. That's why I like them. And we'll be using a great many mules to transport food, water, and weapons."

C stood up, indicating that the meeting was over. "Thank you all for coming. We'll be seeing a lot of each other in the coming days. Alex? Let's have a nice cup of tea and talk about Ireland, shall we?"

"Lovely," Hawke said, his mind already somewhere else.

"Have a look at this first," C said, handing him a folded piece of paper. "Delivered anonymously to the Ambassador to the Court of St. James at Winfield House last evening. The American ambassador personally brought it over to me this morning. It's why I was a bit late."

Hawke opened it, his heart skipping a beat when he saw the familiar scrawled signature beneath the single sentence:

THE CHILDREN WILL DIE FIRST.
THE PAWN

"Good Lord. Wills and Harry. Has the Prince of Wales been informed?"

"Of course. Look here, Alex, I appreciate your feelings in this matter of threats to Prince Charles. But I have spoken to him at length about the necessity of your leaving as soon as possible for Pakistan. Your mission is to counter a very real threat to our entire nation. He understands completely. I assured him Ambrose Congreve would remain on the 'Pawn' case until your safe return. At which point you could, if necessary, resume your involvement. Do I make myself crystal clear?"

"Indeed."

"Very good. Now tell me about Northern Ireland. I understand there's progress."

"We found human remains. Possibly from the girls who went missing that summer, presumably victims of Smith. Ambrose is still there with his former partner on the Mountbatten case, a man named Drummond. The two of them are quite determined to put this case to rest. Should they succeed, we will have taken the first step toward identifying the killer. We also have startling new information about a third suspect in Lord Mountbatten's murder, a man named 'Smith,' which may or may not prove out. Either way, we've got the scent. The bone in our teeth. And, possibly, the Pawn himself."

"Well done," C said thoughtfully.

"Thank you, sir," Hawke said, stunned at perhaps the first and only time the man had ever paid him a compliment.

THIRTY-FIVE

PARIS, AUGUST 1997

SMITH SAT STOCK-STILL IN THE SEMI-GLOOM, transfixed by the flickering black-and-white image of the famous woman on the monitor. It had been years since his triumph at Windsor Castle. Oh, he'd had some minor opportunities to plunge yet another stake into the Royal heart of Britain, and he had even taken advantage of a few.

But tonight?

Tonight would be the result of patience and incredibly meticulous planning. And it would be cataclysmic, a world-shaking event that would rock the Royal Family back on its heels like nothing he'd done since Mountbatten's murder. It would shake them, and their bloody nation, to the very foundation.

And, best of all, it would be the perfect opening act leading to his grand finale. His final day of reckoning with his implacable enemy. The epic culmination of his life's work, the realization of his childhood dreams of total vengeance. The penultimate penalty to be paid.

An eye for an eye.

He saw that she was just finished dressing, suitably chic for a late-night Paris rendezvous. Now, leaning into the gilt mirror above the bureau, applying her lipstick, she smacked her lips together a few times and essayed a smile. Happy with the result, she picked up a crystal flute of champagne.

Eyes shining, she raised the glass to herself.

She had not looked better than at this moment, he thought, not in years. But that pained, haunted look he'd seen in her eyes during the bad times remained. She looked like what she was, a woman on the run, in search of peace.

Four flatscreens stood atop his room's faux Louis XIV desk, bathing the tiny bedroom in cool, phosphorescent blue. An hour earlier, he had tapped into the hotel's CCTV security camera system: three of his monitors were broadcasting alternating live feeds directly from various areas inside the building. The hotel's front and rear entrances, the guest and service elevators, the employee entrance, and the foyer directly outside the white and gold double doors of the hotel owner's suite on the floor above.

It was not called the Imperial Suite for nothing. An exact replica of Louis XIV's rooms at Versailles, it was the single-most expensive hotel room in all of Paris.

This fourth screen had a real-time feed, but the feed emanated from inside the doors of the Imperial Suite. He could toggle views from either of two hidden cameras. His engineer had done well. One downward-view camera inside the ceiling-mounted living room fire sensor, the other a rotating lens, swiveling 360 degrees inside a lightbulb in the master bedroom's chandelier. Images from the opulent bedroom now captured his rapturous attention.

He wore a headset with a lip mike so he could communicate quietly and instantly with a colleague currently waiting in the Place Vendôme outside the ridiculously expensive hotel.

"Any time now," Smith said softly into the mike. "She just finished dressing."

"That's too bad. How much longer?" the man on the motorcycle said. "The natives are getting restless out here."

"Ten, fifteen minutes maximum. I see Dodi's cars are already waiting outside the hotel's front entrance."

"Just arrived. His black Range Rover HSE and his father's black hotel Mercedes."

"That could change. Keep your eyes open."

"Say the word, sir."

"Stand by."

The voyeur returned his attention to matters at hand. He had to smile at his all too predictable reaction to the partially dressed woman on the screen: damp brow, pulsing heart, the hint of an erection announcing itself.

Highly trained in the key indicators of human behavior, he should have expected his own involuntary reactions to the subject, of course. She'd always had this effect on him. She had this effect on everyone; the whole damn world was at her feet, so why should he be exempt from her charms? Still, such feelings were a bit disconcerting at this moment in time, all things considered.

The woman, still a fresh-scrubbed, dewy-eyed beauty at thirty-six, was sporting a healthy tan from a week's yachting off Sardinia. She stood peering at her body in the gilt mirror over the bureau. Satisfied, she slipped her slim tanned arms inside a short black frock coat. Smoothing it down over hips hugged by tight white Versace jeans, she leaned again into the mirror inspecting her makeup, puckering her lips, a new string of pearls swinging from her neck—

Smith slid the zoom button forward, going in for a tight close-up of that famous face.

Her face aglow after two or three glasses of champagne in the beautiful Ritz Hotel suite with her new lover, the princess looked like a woman who had found a momentary escape from the wreckage of her life. She looked like a survivor, wearied by the fray but determined to find a way out of her well-publicized maze of constant sorrow. An exit from all that, a port in the storm, that's how she saw her newest lover.

This new man provided that and more. And, in a fortuitous twist of fate, she'd managed to insert a razor-sharp political dagger into the hearts of those who had caused her enormous suffering. She could only imagine their horror at the notion of a divorced Egyptian playboy as the stepfather of the future King of England. How utterly delicious, even though it would never happen.

Smith had seen her many moods, of course, both in the flesh and in the media. But tonight he thought she looked extraordinarily relaxed and beautiful. Was it real? he wondered, or just that highly developed art of seduction she'd practiced so assiduously, made manifest?

Enter the lover. Smith blinked and leaned forward. He found himself gazing curiously at the rather callow male who now entered the frame with an unattractive swagger. The arriviste had acquired the aura of worldwide fame now, but it was only the reflected glory of the shining princess that afforded him this paltry notoriety.

Her lover came up from behind her, placed his hands on her waist, and nuzzled her neck, kissing her ear, staring at the reflection of the two of them in the mirror.

"Happy, my darling?" he purred.

"I miss the boys. But yes."

"I got along with them quite well, didn't you think?"

She leaned in again to apply more lip gloss. "Wills will be King of England one day. Poor thing. All those dodgy relatives kissing his royal arse."

The divorced Egyptian playboy laughed at the exquisite irony of it all. Since he'd met this fabulous woman his life had suddenly, miraculously, taken a serious turn for the better. Imagine. Stepfather to the King of England. That would show the old man what kind of son he had.

His father owned this hotel. The most famous and expensive hotel in the world. He had stolen it from some Saudi prince whom he well knew never bothered to read the fine print. The Ritz Paris was one more jewel in his father's crown, one that included Harrods department store in London, among other priceless treasures.

His father had suffered, however. He was a man who had, to his eternal chagrin, tried to buy his way into London society without success. Expecting a knighthood, instead he had been shunned and humiliated by British Royals and aristocrats for years. But now, finally, he stood at the brink of miraculous revenge.

His son was about to wed the mother of the future King of England.

Dodi could almost hear Papa licking his chops somewhere offstage, flipping through *Hello* magazine, page after page of his son and the Princess frolicking on the glamorous Riviera. Revenge, on a platter. A dish best savored slowly. Perhaps now his father would take him a bit more seriously. Perhaps even now the tables were turning in favor of the son. Certainly the limelight was his and his alone and he gloried in its glow.

"I have a little something for you tonight, you know," Dodi said, nuzzling her neck.

"Hmm. Not something that comes in a small black velvet box, one hopes?"

"It might just," he said, ignoring the small gibe. Was she teasing him? Leading him on? He could never tell with women, especially this one. After all his dead-end romances, here was a woman who defined "high maintenance." But, God, she was worth it. When first he'd set his sights on her, he'd felt adrift, never knowing what to say or how to react to anything she said or did. But it was different now.

Now he was beginning in his small way to understand his much wiser father's counsel during this courtship, his father's perception of what made her tick: Listen, my son. Her thoughts travel no straight rational line, he had said. She has an active but reckless and whimsical mind that rushes to sudden violent conclusions; a mind that is touched by a certain kind of brilliance, but a brilliance that zigzagged as haphazardly and uselessly as lightning.

He had not understood at the time of the lesson. Now, as he was beginning to see, he felt his confidence growing.

She pulled away from him, picking up her handbag and giving

him that shy smile from beneath her lashes. "No baubles now. Perhaps later. At your apartment. I want to get out of here. Away from all these horrible people."

He said nothing, just quietly grasped the small velvet box in the pocket of his leather jacket. A half hour earlier, he'd crossed the Place Vendôme to see his friend the famous jeweler, Alberto Repossi. Alberto had a star-shaped ring with five diamonds for sale, a quarter of a million dollars. It was from the *Dis-Moi Oui* collection: "Tell me yes."

Dodi bought it on the spot, knowing his father would gladly pick up the tab.

ON THE SCREEN, SMITH COULD see that the false knight in his faux shining armor was clearly agitated. His cell phone chimed, and he turned away from the Princess, scowling angrily. He began pacing back and forth rapidly, a hungry tiger in a gilded cage. He had his mobile pressed tight to his ear, and he was berating one or the other of his two personal bodyguards, Trevor and Kez. He was speaking in a whisper, but the powerful microphone above his head picked up every word.

Grabbing his champagne glass, Dodi now moved over to the nearest bedroom window, peering down into the twinkling darkness of the Place Vendôme, angrily shaking his head at the snarling packs of paparazzi, waiting like hungry wolves for a bit of fresh meat.

Smith leaned forward, eyes on the monitor, adjusting the volume in his earphones, concentrating on the young man's every word. This operatic fantasy was unfolding rapidly now, and it had all the elements of high drama. The fat lady was finally stepping out of the shadows, ready to sing for the lovely swan peering once more into her beloved mirror.

"Listen up, Trevor," Dodi said angrily to his primary bodyguard. "I don't give a good fucking damn about your security protocols right now, right? We're out of here and Henri's driving. Okay? Back to my apartment in the Rue Arsene Houssaye, understand me? It's a bloody madhouse out front. A hundred paparazzi and tourists at least! I'm looking at this bedlam right now, for God's sake, and I'm not putting the Princess through it again. We'll use the caravan already out front as decoys. Call Henri immediately and lay on another Mercedes at the rear. Tell Ritz Security I want a car down there now! Rue Cambon entrance, *tout de suite!*"

He listened a few moments more, made a disgusted face at the phone, and said, "My father has already approved this move, so don't give me any more of your shit. If either you or Kez want to ride up front with Henri, fine. But one of you only, understand me? And no second car following us. It's only a mile and a half to my bloody apartment, for God's sake. It is not a problem. Got it? Good."

Dodi slammed the phone off on his thigh and dropped it into a pocket of his suede jacket. Catching Diana's eye in the mirror, he smiled easily at her and said, "All taken care of, darling. Whenever you're ready."

"Two seconds," Diana said.

He raised the glass of wine to her and downed it in a single draught. Pulling the bottle of vintage Roederer Cristal from the silver ice bucket, he saw that it was empty. Time for another? No. It was getting late. There was chilled white wine and caviar waiting for them at his apartment. Time to go.

Dodi turned back to the window and smiled at the thought of how this magical evening would end. They'd had a wonderful few days together aboard his father's yacht, *Jonikal,* cruising off the French and Italian Riviera. Diana seemed truly happy now, despite the fact that Trevor and Kez had made a dog's breakfast of their earlier arrival at the Ritz. Cameras jammed in her face, besieged by rude questions, Diana had fled inside the hotel in tears.

And she'd clearly been unimpressed with the Villa Windsor. A lovely mansion in Paris, formerly the home of the Duke and Duchess of Windsor, a house his father had strongly hinted would be his, should he and Diana wed. For the first time in his life, Dodi sensed his powerful father's approval at the direction his life was taking.

You, my handsome son, will be stepfather to the two heirs to the throne of England . . . then we shall reign.

Those were the exact words his father had whispered to him as they had stood at the stern rail of the yacht *Jonikal,* watching Diana and her two sons speeding around and around the yacht on Kawasaki wave riders.

Dodi patted his pocket. He wanted to give her the ring tonight. But she was right. Not here in this hotel suite owned like everything else by his father, but in the private luxury of his own Paris apartment. He was his own man now, or would be soon, anyway.

Smith saw Dodi look at his watch and then looked at his own.

It was exactly 11:37 P.M.

THIRTY-SIX

SMITH HAD ONLY THIS MORNING TAKEN the tiny bedroom on the fifth-floor rear at the Ritz. Siberia under normal circumstances, but perfect for his needs. Earlier that day, upon learning of Dodi's plans from his own agents on the ground at Le Bourget airfield in Paris, he'd had his engineer, Amir, set up this surveillance equipment. First he tapped into the hotel's closed-circuit TV system, forty-three cameras in all, which provided views both inside the hotel and at the front and rear entrances.

He had then powered up the carefully hidden minicams and microphones his man had installed in the hotel's Imperial Suite. He had a very expensive Ritz engineer on his private payroll and the man had done an excellent job of providing total coverage inside the suite and throughout the hotel.

He reached out and toggled a switch, quickly clicking through various camera viewpoints until he found what he wanted. He now saw what Dodi had been so upset about: the front entrance to the hotel. A frantic pack of paparazzi lay in wait, at least a hundred or more, even now jostling one another for position.

Since the rumors of a Dodi-Diana romance had surfaced days earlier, journalists and photographers had descended on Paris from all over Europe. Each one hoped to get the "money shot," a photograph that could fetch over a million pounds. He could see their riotous mood, rabid dogs going in for the kill.

Yes, he could see this turning very ugly the moment the famous face appeared at the entrance.

There were rumors Diana was pregnant. If only one of these thugs could get a shot of a small bulge in that sleek figure—the baby bump was worth millions.

Two cars were parked out front, a Ritz black Mercedes stretch limousine and Dodi's personal black Range Rover, drivers already behind the wheels. Henri Paul, the Ritz's chief of security, kept emerging from the lobby, shouting to the paparazzi, "Won't be long now, boys! She'll be out in a minute or two, so, gentlemen, start your shutters!"

Eyes flashing like shining marbles in the flickering blue video light, Smith adjusted his lip mike. He was looking at the pack of snarling motorbikes, photographers clambering onto the pillion seats behind the drivers. On the periphery of the crowd, in the shadow of Napoleon's Column, was a blue-and-white BMW K1300S motorcycle.

It was essential equipment tonight, the most powerful and fastest production bike in the world. "Omar," he said into his lip mike and saw the man astride the BMW turn his head instinctively toward the top floor of the hotel.

"Sir?"

"Change of plans."

"Yes, sir?"

"They're going to use the rear entrance. Rue Cambon."

"When?"

"Now. Hotel Mercedes, standard. That means non–armor plated, no blackout windows."

"Perfect. I'm on my way."

He saw the BMW accelerate away, slowly so as not to attract too much attention, leaving the square.

Smith toggled back to the Imperial Suite. Dodi, now dressed in jeans, a leather shirt that hung outside, and cowboy boots, was waiting for Diana at the bedroom door.

"You look so beautiful tonight. I am so lucky."

"Don't be ridiculous." Diana laughed. "I look beautiful every night. Everyone says so, or hadn't you heard?"

She giggled and took his hand, following him out into the living room beyond with a toss of her short blond hair, leaving her cares behind her in the mirror, determined to have fun.

Smith switched off his video equipment and removed his headset. Standing, he grabbed a black nylon camera bag and slung it over his shoulder. He donned a motorcycle helmet and pulled the goggles down over his eyes. The invisible man once more. Then he headed for the door. He deliberately left it unlocked because his engineer would be here momentarily to remove everything, erasing every trace of his presence.

His room, being one of the least expensive in the hotel, was conveniently located next to the service stairway. It was the work of a moment to descend to the ground floor and exit the hotel at the rear.

DIANA AND DODI LEFT THE IMPERIAL SUITE at 12:14 A.M. They descended the stairs to the back entrance of the Ritz, waiting for the Mercedes just inside a narrow service corridor. Dodi ordered Trevor outside to watch for the hotel limousine and chatted with his acting head of security, Henri Paul, who would be driving them to the apartment.

"Car's here," Trevor said five minutes later, sticking his head inside the door.

The bodyguard clearly wasn't happy. This bloody backup car, a

Mercedes S280, had no bulletproof armor. Worst of all, it did not have darkened windows. On top of that, Dodi's designated driver, the Ritz head of security, Henri Paul, seemed to have spent a little extra time in the bar.

The whole bleeding thing was totally unprofessional. A cock-up of major proportions just waiting to happen, and there was precious little he could do about it. For not the first time, he decided he'd soon tell Mr. Dodi Fayed to kiss his bloody arse good-bye. He'd never been a generous boss, never offered a kind word or a congratulatory smile. And now that she'd come into his life, well—

Dodi placed his hand gently at the small of Diana's back and ushered her outside to the waiting sedan. Henri took the keys from the hotel driver and slid behind the wheel. A few suspicious paparazzi who had sniffed out the ruse now stepped out of the shadows and flashbulbs pierced the darkness. Diana lowered her eyes and shielded her face with her right hand as Trevor quickly ushered his two charges into the backseat, then climbed into the front next to Henri Paul.

Before starting the car, Henri turned and smiled at Dodi. "Managed to give most of those rotten buggers the slip this time, eh, boss?"

Boss? Dodi simply stared at him, trying to suppress his anger. This was not the way an employee addressed him, not in front of the Princess of Wales, certainly. For the first time, it occurred to him that Henri seemed a bit off. He looked over at Trevor and mimed swigging a bottle, nodding his head toward Henri.

Trevor nodded his head yes, but he certainly didn't seem decisive about it. He was angry, though, angry at everybody. Dodi was breaking all the rules, and his security team was not happy about it. For the first time in weeks, Dodi felt a ripple of apprehension wash over him.

"You're quite sure you're all right to drive, Henri?" he demanded of the driver.

"Certainly, sir. No problem at all. Have you home in five."

Dodi slumped back in his seat, taking Diana's hand and pulling her toward him. He was surrounded by idiots, but now was not the time to let another staff row spoil what he desperately hoped would be the most important evening of his life.

Trevor immediately got on his radio and gave Kez, in the originally booked hotel Mercedes at the front entrance, the heads-up that they were about to move. Two minutes later, the Mercedes and the Range Rover sped away from the front entrance on the Place Vendôme. Dodi's ruse had quickly unraveled. At that point, most of the paparazzi were already en route around back to the Rue Cambon entrance where, at 12:20, Henri Paul left the flashbulbs popping and pulled away from the back entrance, accelerating rapidly up to speed.

"Seat belts, please," Trevor said over his shoulder. Neither of them paid him any mind. *Sod it all,* he said to himself, not even bothering to fasten his own. It was only a mile-and-a-half journey. Five minutes, tops.

Protocols had long ago gone out the window, he fumed privately. His professionalism had been compromised through no fault of his own, and he'd bloody well had it with this lot.

Neither Trevor nor anyone else noticed a large, blue-and-white BMW motorcycle following them a few hundred yards back.

Trevor heard Dodi talking to Diana in the dark backseat of the Mercedes. "Only a few minutes, darling, and we'll be home," he said, kissing the top of her head.

HENRI PAUL SPED UP THE ONE-WAY Rue Cambon, then swung the big car right onto the Rue de Rivoli, headed for the Place de la Concorde. He continued south along the west side of the square past Cleopatra's Needle, almost all the way to the Seine. Ignoring red lights, he swung the car right onto the dual freeway called the Cours la Reine, on a heading parallel to the Seine. Almost immediately, they entered a series of tunnels, and Henri increased his speed, the needle moving past one hundred on the speedometer.

"Why the hell are you going this way?" Trevor demanded of the driver, annoyed. This route was much longer than the direct route up the Champs-Elysées, and he didn't want his party to spend one second longer in this bleeding car than was absolutely necessary.

"Give the bastards the slip, that's why," Henri muttered, eyes on the rearview mirror. "None of them will be expecting us to take this route."

"Christ," Trevor said under his breath, thinking, *Right, now we've really gone off the bloody charts. And if nobody gives a shit anymore, then neither do I.*

He suddenly caught sight of a big motorcycle gaining ground in the rearview mirror. Henri Paul had seen it, too, and he was speeding up. At least the bastard on their tail wouldn't get any good photos, Trevor thought. It was dark inside the tunnels and the unlighted interior of the car would cause exterior reflections on the clear windows, too many to get any kind of a decent shot of the occupants, now giggling over something in the backseat.

The car was plunged into semidarkness as they entered the Pont de l'Alma Tunnel at very high speed.

"Jesus Christ, man! Watch out!" Trevor shouted, grabbing the dashboard with both hands.

Diana clutched the rear of the front seat and lurched forward to see what was happening. Then she screamed.

"My God, we're going to hit him!"

They were coming up far too fast on a white Fiat Uno. And the car was swerving right into their lane. Henri swerved hard left in order to avoid a collision. He managed to miss it, but not completely. They clipped the left side of the Fiat with their right mirror and front door.

"Dodi!" Diana cried, swinging her fist at him. "Do something!" The huge concrete pillars supporting the tunnel roof sped by in a blur, and dangerously close.

"What the hell is going on, Henri?" Dodi bellowed, leaning forward from the rear. "Are you out of your fucking mind? Slow down, for God's sake!"

Henri Paul downshifted and braked in an effort to get the speeding car under control.

At that moment, Diana, terrified that Henri was out of control and driving dangerously, peered over Trevor's shoulder, fearing for her life.

Something caught her eye just to the right of the Mercedes.

She saw a large blue-and-white motorcycle with two men, a squat driver and a taller man behind him on the pillion seat. As the big bike pulled abreast of them, she saw the man on the rear seat reach into the camera bag slung across his shoulders.

"I'll lose this fucking bastard, just you watch," Henri Paul said, accelerating once more.

"No!" Trevor shouted. "Slow down, Henri, damn you! One more stupid picture doesn't matter. And the rest of the pack is at least a bloody mile behind us."

Henri Paul ignored the bodyguard and downshifted, depressing the accelerator, determined not to let these mongrels overtake him and his precious cargo. He was shocked to see the motorcycle effortlessly rocket ahead of him, despite his efforts.

Suddenly the motorcycle swerved directly in front of the Mercedes, red brake lights flashing.

What the hell?

"Seat belts!" Trevor shouted again, desperately snatching his own across his chest. Diana strained forward between the two front seats, looking at the motorcycle now directly in their path, red taillights flashing, obviously braking to get a shot of their terrified faces through the windshield.

"God damn these people!" she cried out, tears coursing down her cheeks, bringing her fist down in frustration on Trevor's massive shoulder.

Would there ever be peace for her? Ever?

She saw the man on the cycle's rear turn around and face them, raising his camera—no, not a camera—some other kind of thing, like a strange gun, and—

A blinding flash of light exploded into Henri Paul's and Trevor's eyes. Inside the Mercedes, the awesome power of the Northrop ten-thousand-watt military laser gun was devastating.

Instantly blinded by the catastrophic glare, stunned, and completely disoriented, driver Henri Paul took both hands off the wheel and covered his scalded eyes. Dodi and Diana froze. They were skidding and swerving directly toward the tunnel's massive center pillars.

"Oh, God!" Diana screamed, blinded, and fully cognizant of certain death exploding in her brain.

"Oh, dear God, we're going to—"

In a split second the heavy Mercedes slammed headlong into the thirteenth concrete pillar at full speed. Henri never even had the chance to apply the brakes. The airbags all deployed on impact, but since none of the occupants were wearing seat belts, they afforded scant protection.

Dodi and Henri Paul died instantly. Trevor, hurled facefirst into the windshield, was knocked unconscious, the entire front of his face ripped away.

The Princess of Wales was alive.

But she had sustained a massive internal injury when the car's arrested momentum flung her violently against the front seat. She was bleeding from the nose and ears, lodged between the backseat and Trevor's seat. Her heart was still beating strongly.

It was pumping blood slowly but surely through the small tear in her aorta, the red tide rising steadily inside her thoracic cavity. As time passed, the invisible wound was slowly bleeding what precious little was left of her life out of her.

Horn wailing, water, steam, and smoke rising from the shattered engine of the unrecognizable Mercedes, Diana, Princess of Wales, lay in the darkened, crumpled vehicle, moaning softly, "Oh my God, oh my dear God."

In a heavily wooded area of the Bois de Boulogne, on a dark and empty street, Smith ordered his driver, Omar, to stop the motorcycle.

He needed to stretch his legs, he said, climbing off the pillion seat and walking around to the front of the BMW.

"Dead men tell no tales," Smith said, and, turning, plunged his stiletto straight into the man's heart. Then he lowered the kickstand and pulled Omar's body back to the pillion seat. After attaching Velcro straps to each of his wrists, he climbed aboard the BMW. He pulled the straps forward, fastening them around his waist.

And then he disappeared into the summer night.

THIRTY-SEVEN

COUNTY SLIGO, IRELAND

IN THE GREY DUSK OF A LATE summer evening, three men stood on a hillside in the shadows of a thick wood, gazing at a house standing at the bottom of the hill. The wind was howling dismally, with only the harsh, discordant cry of an occasional seagull rising above the wind. The tide was in and with it came a dank, iodine-tinged mist. There was an occasional rumble of thunder to the west, perhaps a storm rolling in from the sea.

The old three-story house was called the Barking Dog Inn. It seemed deserted and gave off an almost sinister appearance. All the windows were shuttered. The uncared-for gardens were a mass of unkempt weeds and desolate, overgrown flower beds. The unpainted garden gate opening onto the dirt road, a former cart track, was in need of a top hinge and swung drunkenly in the wind from the unpainted fence. A few tired trees surrounded the inn, swaying dismally in the wet wind.

Through his binoculars, Hawke saw that it was a property gradually falling to pieces through lack of attention. So far off the beaten track, it was unlikely it would ever receive any. In short, it was perfect in every way, the very ideal of an IRA safe house. Perhaps, though he doubted it, McMahon had been telling the truth after all.

"Admirable," Ambrose Congreve remarked. "A safe house so situated is a godsend to anyone who covets his privacy."

"Aye," Drummond said. "I've lived in these parts for nigh on sixty years and I've never even heard of this infernal place. No one has used this place, much less this road, for years."

"McMahon vouches for it," Congreve said, like a man still less than convinced the house was anything it was purported to be.

"Not exactly the beehive of terrorist activity our highly paid informant described," Alex Hawke commented. "Let's go down and have a closer look, shall we?"

As the men started down the steep and muddy hillside, branches dripping with moisture brushed across their faces and they all turned their collars up against the evening chill. It was slippery going and they had to step carefully to avoid a sudden fall.

Hawke took the lead and was slightly annoyed at his comrades' lack of progress. It would soon be nightfall, he thought, pausing to give Congreve and Drummond a chance to catch up. He'd no intention of an all-night stakeout in this forbidding place—especially with rain threatening at any second. Foolishly, they'd not prepared for this at all.

"What was that?" Ambrose said suddenly, gripping Drummond's shoulder and looking round at something or other.

"Nothing," Hawke said irritably. "What do you think it was?"

Congreve, peering fearfully into the gloom, said, "Thought I heard a creaking sound over there—as if something, or someone, were moving through the bushes. Must have been the wind, I suppose."

"Of course it was the wind," Drummond said. "What are you so damn jumpy about?"

"Jumpy? I'll damn well tell you what I'm jumpy about. And frankly, I'm surprised the notion hasn't occurred to you as well."

"What are you talking about?"

"A trap, Bulldog. I don't trust this bloke McMahon a tinker's damn. A duplicitous drunkard. Suppose he had second thoughts? Woke up in a panic? Told his IRA mates about his conversation with Hawke and me at the Pennywhistle the other night."

Hawke said, "He's certainly capable of that. Panic, I mean."

Ambrose said, "Or it was premeditated. He gives us the 'secret' location of this Barking Dog Inn. Claims it's an IRA safe house. And they bloody well lay a trap for us. Here. Tonight."

"Why forfeit the money? A big sum. He hasn't collected it yet."

"Bulldog, we sent him to prison for twenty years. Innocent, he says. He wants revenge. And this place seems too—undisturbed—it doesn't feel right."

Hawke surprised Congreve by readily agreeing with him. He reached into his rucksack and pulled out a lightweight 9mm Heckler & Koch machine gun with a folding stock. He also retrieved a pair of night-vision goggles and hung them by the strap around his neck.

"I think you make a strong point, Constable. This is an ideal setup for an ambush. Isolated. Rigged with IEDs for all we know. I say we take cover in the underbrush on that ledge overlooking the house. It's going to be spitting rain shortly and we'll have good protection under those trees overhead. We'll sit tight, give it an hour or so. If nothing happens, we'll climb back up the hill to the Land Rover."

"And if something happens?" Drummond said.

"No action. We'll take note of it. Assess the situation. Then come back with a good deal more firepower and manpower. I can arrange for a British Army tactical unit to accompany us."

"Excellent idea," Congreve said, much relieved, wrapping his waxed Barbour jacket tight around his body. "Rain's coming. Let's get moving."

Nearly an hour later, wet and hungry, they heard the rattle of a laboring engine. They saw a misty pair of doused headlights spiking through the trees lining the old cart track. A few moments later an ancient truck came to a halt at the front gate of the Barking Dog Inn. The engine was switched off, then the headlamps.

Two men, one thickset, both armed with short, stubby machine guns, climbed out of the cab and did a quick surveillance of the road and the immediate area around the house. They were dressed in black with balaclavas over their heads. Satisfied they were unobserved, one of them went to the rear of the truck and unlocked and lifted the canvas flap.

The other entered the house, and soon lights could be seen through cracks in the shutters, upstairs and down.

Six men emerged from beneath the tarp at the rear. All armed and wearing camo from head to foot, they dropped to the muddy ground. Men still inside the truck began offloading wooden crates, heavy enough to require two men to carry. The rain was pouring now, and they slogged their way up the front walk, getting whatever equipment they had out of the weather as quickly as possible.

When the job was completed, the two men in black left the six others behind inside the house and climbed back up into the cab. The old truck started up and rumbled away, back toward the river and the bridge. It was clearly an important delivery, Hawke saw, but a delivery of what?

"Seen enough, gents?" Hawke asked, pushing the NVG goggles up on his forehead.

"Indeed," Congreve said. "Let's get back up to the road as quickly as possible. They may well send sentries out. I would."

At that moment, two men emerged from the shadows at the rear of the house, both obviously carrying automatic weapons. They separated instantly, one heading toward the river, the other heading for the hillside where the three spies crouched in the undergrowth a hundred feet above.

"Move out," Hawke whispered.

Half an hour later, all three were safe and warm inside a late-model black Range Rover, Drummond at the wheel. He had "requisitioned" the vehicle from the Knight of Glin. They were speeding down a twisting snake of narrow road, hemmed in by tall hedgerows, headed back to the town and the small establishment where they were boarding.

"Nice car," Congreve said as they sped along through the thick countryside. "How long have we got the use of it?"

"The Knight's got a bloody fleet of them," Drummond told Ambrose. "He'd hardly miss just one for a few days."

Hawke said, "Bulldog, when we get to town, if you don't mind dropping me at the British Army HQ, I'll have a word with my contact there, after speaking with Sahira Karim at MI5. Tell them about what we've seen. Prepare a plan of action. I should be back in the pub for a pint and a bite to eat at nine."

THE BRITISH ARMY SENT THREE scouts and a sniper out to the safe house that very evening. After a wet, sleepless night, they'd been lying concealed in the woods all day long. IRA soldiers in camo and balaclavas had been coming and going since daybreak. More trucks had arrived, delivering what looked to be heavy weapons.

At the army HQ, an assault unit spent the day arming and preparing plans for an attack on the safe house. It would occur in the predawn hours of the following morning. The Regiment had conducted six tours in Northern Ireland over the years, taking heavy casualties in Derry and in the terrorist-plagued countryside of South Armagh.

Then came the Good Friday peace accords and the violence was finally and mercifully quelled.

But this new enemy had tired of peace recently and wanted war. These battle-tested army soldiers were more than prepared to give it to them. Their mission was to take out the leadership of the New IRA before they were able to ignite a new cycle of violence.

IT WAS NOW NEARLY THREE o'clock in the morning. Pitch-black, no moon, no stars. The house, which was dark, was completely surrounded by a team of elite British Army soldiers. When Hawke first arrived, he learned that mortars had been placed on the hillside above the house. Hawke, with the backing of MI5, had convinced the commanding officer not to use them. He argued that there might well be valuable intelligence, laptops, maps, and so on, located inside and to risk destroying such cache was unwise.

One hour before daybreak, at 0457, the British commando attack would commence. The troops would storm the house. It was estimated that there were at least twenty heavily armed men inside. Some of the crates off-loaded from the trucks had been identified as containing Russian-made RPGs, rocket-propelled grenades, and mortar rounds.

HAWKE HAD A DIFFICULT TIME with Congreve and Drummond. Both men had to be persuaded to remain up on the same bluff overlooking the house where they'd spent a cold damp hour the evening before. They wanted front-row seats and were determined to get them.

"I knew I should have left you two in town," Hawke finally said in frustration. "Damn it, you're both being completely unreasonable. And, frankly, unprofessional."

"This is our fight too," Congreve said, slipping his hand into the pocket of his tweed jacket and feeling the butt of his small Walther .380. "We don't want to be stuck up here on the hill in the cheap seats. Especially since you're going to be down there in the thick of it."

"This is not even remotely your fight, Ambrose," Hawke said. "And, frankly, I can't even believe we're having this discussion. This is a fight for a commando team. Highly trained professionals. Men who actually do this for a living. They wear Kevlar, not tweeds, to a firefight. They are using weapons you wouldn't know how to load, much less aim and fire. A lot of those boys down there are battle-tested veterans of Iraq, men who've done house-to-house fighting in places like Basra and Fallujah, under the worst possible conditions."

Congreve was silent, chewing on the stem of his pipe, keeping his own counsel. Finally, he looked at Hawke and spoke.

"And yet you yourself are going to participate."

"No, I am most likely not. Not at this point, at any rate."

"You're certainly dressed and armed for it."

"I'm simply prepared should I get the chance. I am trained to do this. If I can be of help, I will. You will recall my solemn promise to the Prince of Wales about finding his godfather's murderer. He may well be inside that very house."

"My apologies, Alex. Silly idea of mine. No one is any better than you at this type of warfare. You certainly should not be wasted sitting up here and watching the whole shooting match with Bulldog and me."

"No, I should not. But unless someone thinks I can help, I'm unfortunately going to be in the armored personnel carrier with the commanding officer. A fate worse than death from what little I know of the man."

"Who is he?" Drummond asked. "I've dealt with most of 'em over the years."

"Masterman," Hawke said.

"Major Milo Masterman?"

"The very same."

"God save you, Alex. You're better off walking into a barrage of live fire than sitting it out with that nasty bastard. They should have put him in front of a firing squad years ago, simply for being a flaming arsehole."

"Yes. At any rate, wish me luck."

With that, Hawke was up and away into the darkness, moving swiftly down through the woods toward the cart track on the far side of the hill. This is where Masterman had ordered his APC command post positioned, camouflaged heavily with brush.

As Hawke ran, he was thinking of every possible argument he could give to the assault team leader as to why he should be allowed into this fight. His blood was up. And when it was, there was scant use trying to stop him. But stepping on toes when someone else's men's lives were at stake was something he'd always tried to avoid. He wouldn't want it done to him, so he never did it to anyone else.

There was possibly priceless intelligence to be had inside the Barking Dog Inn. Of that he was now convinced. Weapons from foreign foes, but which weapons and which foes?

And, he felt, this was all tied to the Pawn. To Smith. A man Congreve had been convinced was guilty of a heinous murder thirty years ago. A man who even now might be inside that house. He could not explain his conviction, even to himself, since it was based on the ravings of that drunken madman, McMahon.

But the feeling was there and it was strong.

He had always trusted his gut.

And it had made all the difference.

He'd keep a solemn promise to Charles. And that was the end of it. He'd think of something, some way to get into this damn fight. He whipped out his mobile phone and punched in a number.

THIRTY-EIGHT

BELLE GLADE, FLORIDA

Good afternoon, Sergeant. I'm Detective Michelle Garcia, Palm Beach PD."

"Afternoon, Detective Garcia," the short, doughy-looking corrections guy said, making a big show of looking at his watch. "Three fifteen. 'Specting you a little earlier, Detective. This your prisoner, here, John T. Smoke?"

"Yes, this is Mr. Smoke. I am putting him in your custody."

"My friends call me 'Smokehouse,'" Stoke said to the corrections officer in the voice he dredged up from the bottom. "I better not ever hear you say that name."

"All this boy's paperwork in order?" the guy said, ignoring Stoke. Like he got shit from cons all the time, rolled off his back like swamp water off an iguana.

The corrections officer had a khaki gut pouring over his black leather utility belt and a thick redneck accent, and Stoke hated him on sight. His name, according to the cheap plastic tag, J. T. Swoon. Hell kind of name was Swoon? Sounded like folks who married cousins to Stoke, people who lived in "hollers."

"Paperwork right here," Michelle said, and handed him a Palm Beach PD manila envelope with the name "John D. Smoke" printed on it in large letters. Swoon took out a sheaf of papers, glanced through them quickly, and nodded his head.

"Looks like it's all in purty good order, Detective. 'Less there's anything further I need to know about this here prisoner, I can begin processing this boy right now and you can skedaddle on back to the beach. Keep that nice tan a yours goin'."

Michelle rolled her eyes, gave Stoke a sweet look that said, *Sorry about this asshole, I get this all the time, don't worry about it.* She gave him a quick smile, turned around, and left before her face gave anything away.

"For some damn reason or other," the sergeant drawled when all the paperwork was done, "I can't lock you up yet. A suit over to the Admin Building has asked to see you. Something about a murder you allegedly committed up in Statesville, Georgia? A state trooper? You remember anything about that, boy? No? I'm talkin' to you, Smokehouse."

"I ain't got nothin' to say to you, cracker. Let's just get this over with."

"You call me 'cracker'?"

"You call me 'boy'?"

"You lookin' at hard time here, boy, that I can gar-an-tee. Hacks in here don't cotton to smart mouths. Sit your ass down over there on that bench. Guard'll be here momentarily to escort you over there—here he is now. Hey, Squirrel."

"Hey, J. T. This the one goin' over to Admin?"

"Yep, that's him. Calls himself Smokehouse. He's a big 'un, ain't he, Squirrel? You watch your damn ass with this one, son. Got a mouth on him, too."

"Les' go, boy," Squirrel said, and Stoke got to his feet.

The hot, humid air outside felt like a blast furnace. Miami, compared to the swampy Everglades, is Juneau in January. It was a long ten-minute walk over to the Admin Building and Stoke was soaked to the skin when they arrived. He was amazed at the size of the prison complex. It was shaped like a wheel, with cell blocks hanging off the end of each spoke. In the center of the hub was the ugly three-story building he was now entering.

They crossed the small lobby and took an elevator to the third floor. The guard, short, round, with a walrus moustache that obscured the lower half of his face, never said a word, which was just fine with Stoke. When the doors slid open, a big-bellied man in a short-sleeved white shirt and loud tie said, "I'll take over from here, Squirrel."

Squirrel gave this prison administrator his best shit-eating grin and said, "Looking good, sir. Like 'at tie yer wearin'. Sharp." It was obvious Squirrel didn't get a whole lot of face time at Admin, and when the doors closed on him, he was still smiling.

Warden Robb had a pretty brunette secretary in a tight pink sweater plucking at a computer just outside his office, but the warden himself was standing in the open doorway and motioned Stoke inside as soon as he appeared.

"Please come in," he said to Stoke, and went back into his office. The secretary swiveled her chair and looked up at Stoke as he passed. She looked like one of those tourists in New York, the first time they see the Empire State Building. They crane their heads back and back and just keep bending backward until they can see all the way to the top.

"You want to close the door, Mr. Jones?"

"Sure," Stoke said, and did.

"Well, I'm not going to say welcome to the Glades, but welcome to the Glades, sir."

"I appreciate that."

"Afraid I got some bad news for you, though."

"My friend Sharkey?"

"Yes, sir."

"Hurt? Dead?"

"Not dead. But it was close. He's over in the prison hospital. Sit down, will you? Pull that chair up."

"What happened, Warden?" Stoke said, sitting, silently condemning himself for not getting here sooner.

"Y'know, Mr. Jones, I been worried about that boy ever since he got here. Nice Cuban kid with a big smile. I had one of my most trusted guards keeping an eye on him. His name is Figg. Orson Figg. You remember that name if you find yourself in real trouble in here. He's the only guard you can trust and he knows who you are and why you're here."

"And my friend? What happened?"

"Yesterday, bunch of 'em Aryans caught him alone out in the yard. Before we could break it up, they'd stabbed him twenty-two times. Ice picks, mostly, couple of shiv wounds."

"Jesus."

"Amazing thing? By the time we'd ripped those goddamn White Aryans off him, he was still on his feet. Boy just wouldn't go down. Damnedest thing I ever saw."

"Sharkey?"

"One tough little rooster, I'd say. Wouldn't let anybody help him walk inside from the yard, neither. Shooed 'em all away. He just kept puttin' one foot in front of the other till he got inside, blood spurting from all those fresh holes in him. Once he was inside, out of sight of the population? Hell, he collapsed on the floor, unconscious."

"Can I see him?"

"Of course, but I'd wait. Get the inmates' attention you go see him first thing you get here. Word spreads like wildfire in here. Right about now, everybody in here's gabbing about the Statie you allegedly killed up in Claxton, Georgia. I'll get word to you when I think it's okay to visit. Don't worry about him, Mr. Jones. He'll recover. He just lost a helluva lot of blood out there in the yard, but no organs or major blood vessels were punctured."

"Thank you for taking care of him."

"These are my people in here, Mr. Jones. You wouldn't know it half the time, way they act, but they are. I know why you're in here, by the way, and I can tell you you're not a minute too soon either."

"How's that?"

"This Sword of Allah? Ones that blew up Jackson Memorial here a month or so back? Escapees? They got something big in the works. That's the hack grapevine anyhow."

"Bigger than Jackson?"

"Jackson Memorial was just practice, according to what I hear. Big, that's all I know. Something on a massive scale. I had a paid informant inside the Swords till about six months ago when he ended up dead. Wish to hell I knew more. Maybe you can find out, Mr. Jones. Nobody else can."

"That's why I'm here."

"You look like you can handle yourself."

"Still alive, anyway. That's something, I guess. I need to get inside the Sword. Get close to senior management, if you know what I mean."

"Yeah. But you got to let them come after you. You go after them, they get suspicious."

"Done this before, but thanks for the advice."

"Sounds right. Now, listen up. There's one inmate in here you definitely need to watch out for. Guy who controls the White Aryan Nations in the state of Florida. This boy is a three-hundred-pound ripped gorilla of a man, kickboxing, tai chi, karate, what have you, spends every waking moment pumping iron, a cunning psychopath who calls himself 'Bonecrusher.' "

"He one of the ones who stabbed my friend?"

The warden laughed. "Bonecrusher? Naw. Man doesn't operate that way. He's a specialist. He likes to break your back or your neck or both legs, or all three and then set your ass on fire, watch you fry. He knows he'll never get out of here alive and he don't mind the hole much, so he pretty much acts accordingly."

Stoke smiled.

"Warden, I'm not interested in the Aryan Nation. What I do need to know is who I need to get close to inside Sword of Allah? Who sits at the top of the pyramid? Who can tell me things I need to know in a way that I can believe what I'm hearing?"

"Good questions. The guy everyone thinks runs the Swords is a big mean sumbitch calls himself 'Ishtar.' The real brains belong to one of our beloved Gitmo transferees named Sheik Shiraz. Pakistani. Blew up that Israeli embassy in 2002. Smart little bastard, everybody calls him the imam. Talks like Yoda in *Star Wars,* know what I mean? Riddles. Very polite. All kinds of degrees from Islam U. or Islam you ain't. You get tight with the little guy, earn his trust, you have earned your government salary times ten, believe me."

"One more question, Warden, and I'll go to my cell and settle in and get comfy. Bottom line, what the hell do these people in here want? These Islamic fanatics? Call attention to their cause? Terrorize and intimidate our country's citizens? What? What is the Sword's ultimate objective?"

"Hell, that's an easy one. Kill Americans, Mr. Jones. Kill us like they did down at Jackson Memorial, kill our allies the Brits like they did at Heathrow airport a year or so back. They hate our country, our people, our way of life, and everything it stands for. And this is pure hatred with a passion that is almost inconceivable to ordinary people like you and me. They want to bring us to our knees, Mr. Jones."

"And they are everywhere."

"That's right. And then they want to cut our heads off with the Sword of Allah. If that's not enough, they want to die doing it."

"How about we begin at the end of their wish list, don't you think, Warden? They die doing it. That sounds good. Then we work our way backward from there? Start with that Fort Hood asshole. One who had Post-Traumatic Mass Murder Syndrome 'cause everybody was mean to him. Start with him."

The warden laughed, locking eyes with the big black man.

"I don't know you, sir. But by God I'm glad you're here. For whatever crazy personal reasons you may have for doing this, I can only say I admire your—"

"Called duty, Warden. Only thing worth living or dying for. Friend of mine named Alex Hawke taught me that a long, long time ago."

—

Stoke was in Cellblock D, the most secure of all the close custody wings at the Glades. It was also where the Sword of Allah members were housed. Keep the cancer contained as much as possible. It was a long, long walk to his cell, shuffling along in the ankle bracelets, and the wrist bracelets, and the little flip-flop slippers he wore with his bright orange prison garb.

"Open eight!" one of his two guards shouted, and the cell door slid back with a bang. They sat him down on his bunk and took off the ankle bracelets. They left the wrist cuffs on and sauntered back outside, waiting for the cell door to slam shut. The guards ruled the joint with a piratical swagger, Stoke saw, and a solid grasp of the principles of intimidation.

"Close eight!" the hack said, and motioned for Stoke to put his hands through the food tray slot. He did, and they removed his handcuffs. After they'd walked away, Stoke sat back down on the bunk, rubbing his bruised wrists, taking inventory. He was supposed to have shared this cell with Sharkey. But he'd been a day late and one shiv short, and the sons of bitches had gotten to him. He lay back on the thin mattress and put his hands behind his head, thinking things over.

Lot of work to do in the joint.

Whole lot of work to do.

He reached into the small duffel he kept under his bunk. Inside a hollowed-out hardcover copy of *Gravity's Rainbow,* the thickest book he'd been able to find at the used bookstore, was a shiv made out of a sharpened spoon and the melted plastic of seven toothbrushes, just like the one he'd made and given to Sharkey. In another big, hollow book, *The Teeth of the Tiger,* by Tom Clancy, one thousand dollars in twenties and hundreds.

He felt around inside the bag and pulled out his dog-eared copy of the Koran. He'd been reading it religiously every night since committing himself to incarceration in the Glades. He had a green highlighter and he was marking phrases he might just drop into the conversation if the opportunity presented itself, with Ishtar or one of his disciples.

The Koran was okay, a little harder to read and memorize than Bible scripture, though. *The Lord is my shepherd, I shall not want.* He'd remembered that psalm word for word since he memorized it when he was six years old. He said it a lot, when he was afraid, or even sad or lonely. It always helped. He thought all religions did that for people, and he'd really had a hard time finding the part in the Koran where it said hey, here's an idea, go out and murder innocent men, women, and children if you want a ticket to paradise.

Tonight, instead of reading silently to himself, he tried something a little different. Just in case anybody was listening, he recited the Muslim call to prayer in a loud whisper:

God is most great.
I testify that there is no god but God.
I testify that Muhammad is the Prophet of God.
Come to prayer.
Come to success.
God is most great.
There is no god but God.

He said it a few times, just to get the rhythm of it and let his words echo down the cell block. After a while he tired of religion and pulled out his paperback copy of *The Dreadful Lemon Sky.* That was the Travis McGee book he and Eddie's two-man book club was reading this week. What he liked most about it, *Lemon Sky,* as compared with the Koran, was you didn't have to underline or highlight anything.

You just got swept along by the master himself. There he goes, there's old Trav again, locking up the *Busted Flush,* setting the alarm, saying good-bye to his pal the Alabama Tiger, before going out on a knight's quest with Meyer, to find some poor woman's killer, after she showed up one night with ninety large and gave it to Trav for safekeeping. How's the Koran going to compete with literature like that? Or even the Bible for that matter? Luke, Matthew, and John—

those guys put together couldn't hold a candle to John D. MacDonald.

He got to page fifty-one, couldn't keep his eyes open, his mind concentrated on all this advice all these fanatic Arab cats were all so hepped up about. He was open-minded, hell, he'd tolerate just about anything, but he couldn't see what these people, these radical Muslims, these al Qaeda and Taliban suicidal underpants-bombing maniacs, what had they ever, and he meant *ever,* done to deserve anybody's attention, much less respect.

Let's see, he said to himself, holding up his hand with all five fingers raised. Had they ever built a single road, dammed up a single river, dug a single well to produce one damn bucket of water? No. Generated one single watt of electricity, built a single car, plane, boat, train, bicycle, or skateboard? No. Two fingers down. Okay, had they funded a single bank, constructed a single home, manufactured a single lifesaving medicine, hell, even a single product, written a single Pulitzer Prize–winning article, or a novel? Nope. Three down. Or maybe even composed one single damn song, choreographed one damn dance? Nope. Four down. Won a single election or even given a piano recital in all of their whole, long, bloody history?

No. Five down.

They killed people, that's it.

Stoke made a solemn promise to himself, right there in his cell. If he could, as long as he was still able and strong, he'd kill them first. He'd find the heart and rip it out. At least before they could kill any more of his own people.

Remember America? Folks had plain forgotten what that word stood for.

People who had a justifiable right to be proud of what they'd done. People who'd broken Hitler's back. Freed countless millions from the Soviets. Got Gorby to tear down that effing Wall. People who'd tried to make the world a better place. Fed billions of starving people around the world. Built homes for ones lost in floods or fires. Sent billions and billions of dollars of food and medicine all over the world, took on the dictators who wanted nothing but power. Fought for the right stuff. Fought for freedom. For the right of every man, woman, and child to be free.

Independence.

That's what he was talking about.

He wasn't talking about religious or political nuts who just wanted to blow airplanes out of the sky or put six million Jews into the oven, gas all those Kurds just because they were Kurds. No. He was talking about plain old patriotic Americans, simple as that.

With those semi-deep thoughts very much on his mind, Stokely Jones edged nearer to sleep.

First night in the Glades, Stoke slept like a baby in his mama's arms.

Second and third nights, not so much.

THIRTY-NINE

BELLE GLADE, FLORIDA

STOKE'S FIRST FEW DAYS IN THE SLAM passed pretty much without incident except for the time Chief Johnny Two Guns called Stoke's sainted mother a bad name and ended up in the prison hospital. Well, actually two guys ended up in the hospital that day. Chief Two Guns and the white-bread, butt-head Aryan who called himself the Bonecrusher.

This was to be the day Stoke learned that "clubbin' with the cons" wasn't all it was cracked up to be. Especially the con he'd nicknamed "Mr. Clean."

Bonecrusher was one crazy 1950s vintage cat, looked exactly like that good old TV Mr. Clean guy, now on steroids, even with the little gold hoop earring in his left ear. Stoke could still hear that jingle in his head: "Mr. Clean gets rid of dirt and grime and grease in just a minute."

Man was seriously juiced now, a violent, disturbed individual, and you didn't need a degree in shrinkology to notice he wasn't doing windows anymore.

Also, seemed like the Bonecrusher just plain didn't like black folks for some reason or other. Could have been something traumatic in his childhood. Peed in his jammies every night when Mommy tucked him in and turned out the light. Boom. Black. Scary. Or maybe he was just a natural-born dumb shithead from the day he was born. Anyway, Stoke had seen him around the yard surrounded by his crew, the White Aryans. He didn't seem like the type you just walk up to and say, "Hey, just a darn minute there, Mr. Bonecrusher, I don't understand why can't we all just get along."

What exactly happened that day was that Stoke was out in the part of the yard fenced off for lifting weights, minding his own damn business, when this Seminole Indian chief walks up and tells Stoke his time on the bench was up, and why didn't he go shoot hoops with the rest of the goddamn niggas?

Stoke naturally ignored him, kept bench-pressing, feeling the burn, really into it. The sun was brutal, and it had to be way over a hundred degrees out in the baking concrete yard. He didn't mind it. In fact, he'd decided to use his free time in the Glades to get back in shape. Serious shape.

He was doing the complete U.S. Navy SEAL physical training routine in his cell every night, and already he could feel his aging body starting to kick ass again. Feeling the SEAL edge, they called it. Stoke had a navy drill instructor when he was in special training down in the Keys; guy said something one day Stoke would never forget as long as he lived.

"The difference between combat and sport is that in combat you bury the guy who comes in second."

"You deaf, homes?" the Chief said to him, leaning over to pick up a twenty-pound dumbbell in his right hand.

"Try and keep your shit together, man, I don't want any trouble. I'll be done here in five minutes. Maybe less. Then it's all yours."

The Chief looked at Stoke like he was a new arrival from Mars.

"Hey! Sometimes, nigga, you get trouble whether you want it or not," the guy said, tossing the iron weight from one hand to the other like a tennis ball.

"That's true. Sometimes you do."

"Like, you got trouble now."

"I do? Me? I don't think so."

"You don't?"

"Nope."

"You don't think I could bring this dumbbell down on your ugly head so hard your brains squirt out your ears?"

"You're Johnny Two Guns, aren't you?" Stoke said, pumping out three fast reps in blinding succession.

"You got it, man." He pronounced it "main," trying to sound street. This from a swamp dog who'd killed his own mother with a tourist-shop tomahawk.

"How'd you get that name, Two Guns, I wonder?" Stoke asked, speaking now with some little effort between presses.

"My arms, man, look at 'em, you punkass bitch, what the hell you think? Chief Johnny Two Guns. That was the name I fought under. I'm the guy that knocked out Trevor 'the Animal' Garcia in the first round at the Hard Rock Casino in Vegas, man. Televised, man, high def."

"Really? That was you?"

"Bet your ass."

"I'm surprised."

"Yeah? Why's that?"

"I dunno. I figured maybe you, you know, went the other way. Batted for the other team, know what I'm saying?"

"What the hell you talking about? Baseball? I never played baseball! Didn't I just get done telling you I was a fighter?"

"Still."

"Still what?"

"You know that guard, squat little guy with the walrus moustache, button-popper belly, you know who I mean, what's his name, Squirrel?"

"Yeah, Squirrel, I know him. What about him?"

"Well, I was talking to him about you the other day and—hold on a second. Lemme just bang out these last few reps real fast, okay?"

Stoke did ten reps in quick succession, heaving the massive barbell up and down like it was only a couple of hundred pounds. "Okay, that's about five minutes. It's all yours, Chief."

"Screw it, man, tell me about Squirrel. Tell me what did that rabbit turd asslick say about me?"

"Well, like I say, me and Squirrel, we were just shooting the shit, you know, talking about this and that, and the other thing and, hell, I can't even remember why, but somehow your name came up."

"My name?"

"Yeah. Your name."

"And?"

"And Squirrel told me you were a pussy."

"Fuck! Squirrel told you that?"

"That's what the man said," Stoke said, easing the barbell up behind his head to the upright stands used for support. He sat up on the bench, catching his breath. He was drenched with sweat, mopping his face with a towel, when he saw the Seminole Chief step forward, a twenty-pounder in each hand now, clanging them together in front of his massive chest like marching band cymbals.

"You two think I'm a pussy? Huh? You and Squirrel, that right? I asked you a question. You think I'm a pussy?"

"Now look, Two Guns, how the hell would I know if you're a pussy or not? I just got here. I'm just reporting what Squirrel said, that's all. He thinks you're a pussy. Now I know Squirrel doesn't have a whole lot of high-end electronics in his attic, but still. Man's entitled to his opinion, right?"

"Here's my opinion, you stinking piece of dogshit. Your daddy was a polesmoker and your black-assed mama sucked donkey dicks down in Tijuana two bucks a shot. Okay? That's my opinion."

Stoke stood up, slowly and thoroughly wiping his hands dry with the towel. Carefully, concentrating on each finger.

This black man was a lot bigger than Two Guns thought he was, when he'd been lying there on the bench. A whole lot bigger.

"I want you to say that again, Chief. About my mother. Word for word."

"I said, your black-assed mama used to—"

"Here's an idea," a deep voice boomed from behind them. "Why don't you two bottom bitches take this bullshit elsewhere? I got work to do here."

It was the juiced-up Mr. Clean, aka the Bonecrusher, the White Supremacist Sharkey had warned him about.

Stoke smiled. An opportunity had presented itself and he was in a perfect mood to take advantage of it. Life was funny that way. It was why he never got bored. He couldn't wait to see what was going to happen next.

"Who the hell are you?" Stoke asked the new arrival. Man was pulling a torn prison-issue T-shirt over his close-cropped head of spiky, bleached blond hair. He had a bodybuilder's physique and the bulging blue eyes of a stone-crazy baby. Big red Nazi swastika tattooed on his forehead. One weird-looking dude, no doubt about it.

He did a bicep flex, pointed to it, and said, "This is who I am, bitch. Right here."

Stoke glanced at Chief Johnny Two Guns and smiled. "Know what, Chief? If those muscles of his were tits, I'd say they were store bought."

The Bonecrusher was so stunned by what he'd just heard, he was momentarily paralyzed.

"Here's my problem," Stoke said, seizing the moment, smiling as he moved quickly between the two of them, totally nonaggressive. "One of you two gentlemen just insulted my mother and the other one just called me a faggot. And, shit, I've only been here a week. This the way you treat newcomers? You two got to step your being polite game the fuck up, you understand what I'm sayin'? Otherwise, I can't be responsible, know what I'm sayin'?"

Bonecrusher laughed out loud. "Po-lite? Ah, hell, he ain't seen us being po-lite yet, has he, Chief?"

Now Two Guns was all smiles, clearly relieved to have timely backup, especially someone of the Bonecrusher's caliber.

Chief said, "Shit, this gutta thug player needs his black ass whupped, and I figure we just the right ones to do it? What d'you say?"

"I promise I won't crush his skull till after you put a fist through his liver," the Bonecrusher said.

They started for him.

Stoke gave them both a second to get comfortable with the idea of what they were about to do to him. Then he shot both hands out at blinding speed, one massive fist clamping around the throat of each one of them. He squeezed until they both started turning purple. When they were just about to pass out, he lifted them both about a foot off the ground, like lifting two babies out of a crib.

"Never, ever, come within fifty yards of me again, understand?" Stoke didn't even notice the gathering of yardbirds behind him, all come to witness this prison miracle in the making.

There were strangled grunts from the two dangling men.

"I'll take that as a yes," Stoke said.

And then he banged their two heads together with enormous force, forehead to forehead, knocking them both unconscious.

He released his grip and they both dropped like dead meat, collapsing to the blistering pavement, not moving a muscle.

"See that?" Stoke said to the two inert forms on the ground. "I tried to warn you two boys I'm bad for your health. Now you know."

A loud Klaxon horn sounded a thirty-second blast and Stoke knew it was time to head back to his cell. He jogged all the way across the yard, feeling good. He'd been saving the last three chapters of *Dreadful Lemon Sky* and was looking forward to reading them before chow time. Travis McGee and his pal Meyer were about to blow a pot-smoking ring wide open.

STOKE ALWAYS ATE ALONE IN THE MESS HALL, or "cafeteria" they called it here, like a damn high school. Nobody ever asked him to sit down and that was fine with him. Most of the time he could find a table with only one other guy and sometimes an empty table, like now. He set his tray down, pulled his Koran from under his arm, placed it reverentially on the table, and sat down on the steel bench.

Man, he was hungry.

He had to admit he'd been surprised by the prison chow. It wasn't good, but it wasn't any worse than what you'd get in most hospitals, either. Tonight, for instance, he was having baked chicken breast, rice pilaf, and carrots. Plus chocolate pudding. Not bad, he thought, taking a bite of chicken and opening the Koran to a dog-eared page.

He took the Koran to every single meal. Not because it was such a nail-biter or even a page-turner, but just because he figured it was good advertising. And he was learning interesting stuff too. You hear people all the time talking about what the Koran says. But, after reading it, he got the feeling most of these people doing all the talking? Never read it.

Like what the Koran says about infidels and what must be done about them, basically kill all of them. Stoke, who had loved the Lord with all his heart all his life, had never actually thought of himself as an infidel. But, since he was a Baptist, a Christian, he was definitely high on their hit list. And there was some really unpleasant stuff about women in there that would drive every woman he'd ever known completely apeshit if they took the time to read it. The other folks who didn't come off too well in the book were the Jews. Chief enemies on the Muslims' shit list, no doubt about that. Jews, Baptists, and women. Three bad enemies to have, he thought.

He finished his supper, but remained at the table, reading his book, underlining passages with his green highlighter.

"Good evening, my brother," somebody behind him said in a soft voice. "Do you mind if I sit down?"

He turned his head and saw a nice-looking young black kid, maybe twenty-three. Bone skinny. Round, wire-rim glasses perched on the end of his nose, like a college student. Clean-cut, shaved head, no gangsta bullshit karma here. A young black Gandhi. Stoke sorta liked him.

"No, son, sit down, sit down."

"Thanks," the boy said and put his tray down across from Stokely. He put his paper napkin in his lap and started in on his baked chicken. Didn't look up or say another word till he'd cleaned his plate and polished off his chocolate pudding. So Stoke just kept flipping pages and underlining, thinking if the kid had something to say, he'd get around to it. Or not.

"I've been sent to express our appreciation," the boy said quietly, not wishing to be heard.

Stoke looked up. "Me? Why?"

"For what you did today."

"What did I do?"

"Two of our most dangerous enemies now fear you. All of our enemies now fear you. The enemy of mine enemy is my friend."

"That's a good one. Where'd you learn that?"

"It is an ancient Arabic proverb."

"You a scholar?"

"I was. Now I'm a murderer, just like you."

"Who'd you kill?"

"Infidels. Nonbelievers. Aggressors. I blew up a U.S. Army recruiting station in Atlanta."

"I remember that. Who you think I murdered?"

"White state trooper up in Georgia. Pulled you over on I-84 for a busted taillight."

"I have killed. Yes, I have."

"Maybe those two in the yard, too."

"Well, I was just trying to knock some sense into their heads, that's all."

"We think you may have succeeded. We'll find out when they get out of the hospital. Certainly they will steer clear of you."

"They're in the hospital?"

"Concussions. Both of them."

"Damn, I didn't mean to knock sense into them that hard."

"If you'll excuse me, I need to be going. But before I do, I've been asked to invite you to attend a gathering. Friends of mine would like to meet you."

"A gathering? What kind of gathering?"

"We meet in the prison library reading room once a week. Tomorrow evening at six to be exact, this week. We discuss the great books. One in particular. May I tell my friends that you will attend our gathering?"

"What's your name, son?"

"I am Ali. What is yours?"

"Ali Baba," Stoke said, thinking fast, going with the first name that popped into his head.

"I welcome you, brother."

"Well, Ali, listen up, you tell your friends that I would be very grateful to be included in their reading group."

"*Inshallah,*" the boy said.

"*Inshallah,*" Stoke replied without a moment's hesitation, glad he'd learned that all-important phrase. *God willing.* That was the truth, in any religion.

The boy nodded and, without a word, rose and left the table. He looked pleased. He would tell the great imam that there was a new recruit. A most powerful soldier clearly ready to join the Army of God.

And Stoke would get some face time with the Wizard.

THEY CAME FOR HIM AT TWO in the morning. A hack unlocked his cell, walked in, and woke him up.

"Come with me," the guard said.

"Where?" Stoke asked, immediately awake. It was pitch-black and all he could see was a shape standing over him.

"You'll see."

They took him to the prison hospital. And a private visit with Sharkey in a single room, Stoke realized when the hack said, "Twenty minutes," and pulled the door closed.

"Hey, Stoke," came the thin, reedy voice from the hospital bed. Stoke crossed the small room and put a comforting hand on Sharkey's shoulder.

"Shark. Oh, man, I am so sorry."

"Shit. Don't be. You coming to the Glades is all I care about. They're moving me over to Good Samaritan Hospital in West Palm tomorrow. I told the warden I needed to see you tonight."

"Good. How're you feelin'?"

"Like something you drain spaghetti in."

"It's called a colander."

"Sí, es un colador en Español."

Stoke laughed. "You look pretty good, little perforated brother. Now, while we still have time, tell me about the shit you saw on the Wizard's computer."

"Stoke, I think they're gonna start killing kids."

"What?"

"Serious. I saw some shit on there about blowing up schoolhouses full of children. Some high school in Chicago. And school buses, shit like that."

"Jesus."

"Yeah. All they do, these Sword of Allah guys, is train how to be homegrown suicide bombers. Teach 'em to fly under the radar. Take poor kids from the cane fields, teenagers, fill them with religion, and show them how to blow shit up, including themselves."

"But, kids? Schools? Why do you say that?"

"I only had time to read a couple of his e-mails, but one of them freaked me straight out."

"What'd it say?"

"The children will die first."

"Was there a name? Who sent that e-mail, Sharkey? You remember?"

"Yeah, I remember. On a lot of e-mails. Got to be a code name. Smith."

"That's it? Smith?"

"Smith."

FORTY

BELLE GLADE, FLORIDA

THE MUSLIM GENTLEMEN'S READING SOCIETY MET at the far end of the prison library, behind all the stacks. There were about thirty hard-backed wooden chairs, like Stoke remembered from grade school, arranged in a semi-circle around a battered wooden podium. The imam, the little Yoda-like figure whom Sharkey had called the Wizard, was standing at the podium in a white robe, reading from the Koran. Standing next to him was his protector, the black Goliath Ishtar, arms folded across his chest, still as a statue, eyes ablaze with hate.

The audience was a strange mix of clean-cut young Muslim men, freshly arrived and beardless, who were staring at the imam like he'd just dropped down from paradise. The others were young black men, and boys, poor folk from the 'cane just outside the fence who'd come to learn about a religion that promised to justify and explain all the hate they felt toward their own country, its white rulers, its wars against the poor and downtrodden all over the world. Stoke saw the kid Ali, who'd invited him tonight, sitting one row back, and nodded to him.

The Wizard finished his reading, closed the Koran, and looked directly at Stokely. "Will Ali Baba rise?" he said in his weird little voice.

Stoke stood up.

"We welcome a new brother tonight," the imam said, "a new soldier in our worldwide jihad against the nonbelievers. Brother Ali Baba, have you something to say to us?"

"I have received a calling to fight the people until they say there is no God but Allah, and his prophet is Muhammad, peace be upon him."

Stoke sat down, and the imam continued.

"We are all servants of Allah. We do our duty of fighting for the sake of the religion of Allah. It is also our duty to send a call to all the people of this world to enjoy this great light and to embrace Islam and experience the happiness in Islam."

The audience all responded with some phrase in Arabic that Stoke didn't know so he just moved his mouth along with them. The imam picked up his Koran and stepped back from the podium.

"I now call upon our brother Ishtar to close this evening of praise and enlightenment. Let the truth be known."

Ishtar stepped up to the plate and got right down to it, clearly addressing the young black brothers in the audience. He said:

"You better watch what the fuck flies outta yo mouth
Or I'ma hijack a plane and fly into your house
Burn your apartment with your family tied to the couch
Slit your throat so you scream, only blood comes out
I see the world like it is, beyond the white and the black
The way the government downplays historical facts
Like the CIA trainin' terrorists to fight
Build bombs and sneak box cutters onto a flight
When I was a kid the Devil himself brought me a mike
But I refused the offer 'cause God sent me to strike
And you can't fathom the truth so you don't hear me
You think it's all just a fucking conspiracy theory

That's why conservative racists are all runnin' shit
And your iPhone is tapped by the federal government
I'm jammin' frequencies in ya brain when you speak to me
Technique will rip a rapper to pieces indecently
Pack ya weapons illegally, 'cause we ain't never hesitant
We snipe-scoping men in black surrounding the president."

AN HOUR LATER, STOKE, HAVING HEARD the Glades' poet laureate, Ishtar, let the truth be known, was sitting on one side of a two-inch-thick piece of Plexiglas looking at his beautiful Fancha on the other side, each talking on the prison phones provided. There was a long line of inmates to either side of him, all talking to their mamas or their wives or their girlfriends.

"How you doin', baby?" he asked her, putting his hand on the glass. She reached up and placed hers against his.

"Missing you. Tell me you're coming out soon."

"I am, I am. I'm getting close here. I'm on the inside of the bad guys, just what I came here to do."

"How long, honey?"

"Few days. A week at most."

"I saw the baby doctor today."

"Everything good?"

"It's all good, Stokely. As soon as you make it all good."

"Aw, baby, you know I will."

"How do I know?"

"Well, because when I say I will— Hold up a sec."

A woman had just taken a vacant seat about five chairs to the right of Fancha. It was that same shooter who'd tried to kill him twice, once in the street, once in his own damn apartment. She wasn't a blonde now. She had flame-red hair, cut short, but he'd know that face anywhere. She wasn't looking his way and Stoke could tell by the intense way she was talking on the phone and staring straight through the glass at somebody that she hadn't made him yet. He also knew she could glance his way at any second. He twisted his head slowly left to get a look at who she was talking to.

Ishtar.

"Baby, I gotta go. Now."

"I just got here. I drove all the way up from Miami to see you and you gotta go? Damn!"

"I'll explain later. I promise. But now— Oh shit."

She'd seen him. Her eyes went wide, and she stared straight at him. She started talking urgently into the phone indicating Stoke with a couple of head nods in his direction. Ishtar leaned forward and peered down the line until he saw Stokely.

His expression told Stoke all he needed to know. He'd been made. Completely busted. And he had barely minutes to do what he needed to do.

"I love you," he said to his fiancée and hung up the phone. He got to his feet slowly and tried to walk slowly toward the guard at the door; he could feel Ishtar's eyes burning a hole in his back every step of the way. The hack pulled the door open for him, and he said in the guy's ear, "White woman with short red hair. Talking to the huge black con. There's a warrant out on her. Miami-Dade PD. Murder and attempted murder. Arrest her soon as she leaves this room. Call it in right damn now before she makes a run for it."

Then he stepped outside into the green concrete corridor. A guard was assigned to escort him back to his cell.

"Listen to me," Stoke said quietly as they headed back to his cell block. "I am a federal agent placed inside this facility on a matter of national security. I've just been made by a con and I need to speak to a guard named Figg immediately. Okay?"

"Fuck you talkin' about, Smokehouse?"

"Call the warden, goddamn it. Tell him Mr. Jones is in trouble. Tell him I need Figg to meet me at the imam's cell in two minutes or less. Call him on your radio now or believe me, your career here is over."

Stoke looked the guy in the eyes until he got on his radio and asked to be patched through to the warden's office. Stoke was walking very fast and the guy had to hustle to keep up with him as he spoke.

"Okay," he said. "Sorry about that. Figg will be waiting for you."

"Appreciate that. Can I speak to Figg?"

"Yes, sir," he said, handing the walkie-talkie to Stoke.

"Sergeant Figg, the little imam must be immediately removed from his cell. Toss his cell now, before anyone gives him a heads-up. He's got a hidden laptop somewhere that contains vital national security intelligence. He'll scrub it clean if you don't get there right this second. Understand?"

The imam's cell was open when he got there two minutes later. Three corrections officers were tearing the place apart.

"Got it!" a guard said, holding up a small black Dell. It had been sealed in three watertight plastic bags and hidden inside the toilet tank. Not where you'd go to look for a computer, underwater.

"Thank you," Stoke said, taking the Dell. "Now if you could get me the hell out of here as quickly as possible? Also, have the warden immediately call the CIA agent-in-charge in Miami and relay what just happened, I'd appreciate it. I need an officer to drive me to Miami as well."

"Car will be waiting out front, Mr. Jones."

"Did you get the redheaded girl coming out?"

"We did. She's being Mirandized and charged right now."

"Man, this is turning out to be one fine day," Stoke said as he raced away, a guard on his heels to let him out of prison.

FORTY-ONE

COUNTY SLIGO, IRELAND

"COMMANDER HAWKE HIMSELF," the commanding officer of the British Army commando unit said, easily managing to make the greeting sound distinctly unfriendly. Alex ignored him and climbed in through the rear hatch of the black Saxon AT105C command vehicle. There wasn't a lot of room in these damned battle taxis, so Alex Hawke and Major Masterman assumed uncomfortably chummy positions.

There was a turret on top with a 7.62mm machine gun in the highly unlikely event any of the enemy combatants trapped inside the safe house ever got anywhere within a mile of the major's heavily armored hideout.

Hawke smiled at the army man, still fine-tuning exactly how he was going to go about this. Masterman smiled back, a man appallingly sure of himself. He was short, beefy, had narrow eyes the color of lead, a stubborn, cornerstone chin, and wore a moustache of the old wing commander variety.

Beneath the two men's smiles lurked a great deal of tension. Hawke let it build to an uncomfortable level, forcing Masterman to speak first.

"Everything all squared away up on the hill, I take it? Talked some sense into that pompous ass from Scotland Yard, did you?" the major asked. "And that pipsqueak policeman, what's his name, Drummond? Worked with him once. Talked about nothing but tea roses. Closet poofter if you ask me. I asked you a question about them, I believe."

Hawke looked at him, expressionless.

"Sorry. What did you say?" Hawke said.

"I asked you if you'd squared everything away with those two fools up on the hill."

"They're not happy, but they understand."

"And how about you? Do you understand?"

"Major Masterman, I know this is your operation. And that MI6 has no jurisdictional right to interfere or intercede on my behalf."

"Correct."

"But I must tell you, Major, that I absolutely insist on going into that safe house with the lads."

"And, as I said to you over an hour ago, I absolutely insist that you remain here with me in the command vehicle until we've accomplished our objective. Secured the house."

Hawke glared at the man, his eyes cold as winter rain, giving no hint of the furnace within. When he finally spoke, his voice was as sharp and hard-edged as Sheffield steel.

"Major, it is contrary to my nature to pull rank, but I'm afraid in the present circumstances, you leave me no other choice."

"Pull rank on *me*?" Masterman guffawed. "Is that what you said? You can't go high enough to pull rank on me, sir."

"I'm afraid I actually can. You serve in the Prince of Wales's Own Regiment of Yorkshire, according to your insignia."

"What of it?"

"I am here today at the express request of an old friend. He has entrusted me with finding the man or men who have threatened not only him, but his entire family. One of the men inside that house may have murdered my friend's godfather. I swore an oath to find that man. And I am honor bound to take direct action against him. Not after the fight. Now."

"Rubbish. I've never heard such a farcical fairy tale in all my life."

"I warn you, Major, do not ever insult me again. You've just called me a liar. Your entire career is on the line at this moment. I'm offering you one last chance to save it. Make your decision."

"Bollocks."

"As you wish. In the last half hour, I have spoken directly to my friend regarding this situation. He told me that should I encounter further difficulty in carrying out his explicit instructions, I was to call him on his private line immediately. I have that number on my mobile. Shall I ring it?"

"Of course, why not? This is rank insanity."

Alex pulled out his mobile and punched in Charles's private number. Masterman, seething and sputtering, seemed on the verge of spontaneous human combustion.

"Hello, sir, Hawke here. Still a bit of trouble at this end, I'm sorry to say . . . Yes, sir, Major Masterman is right here with me now."

Hawke listened for a few more moments and said, "He would like to speak with you, Major."

Masterman snatched the cell phone out of Hawke's hand.

He barked into the phone, "This is Major Milo Masterman, Prince of Wales's Own Regiment of Yorkshire. Who the bloody hell is this?"

Hawke watched the man listening to the famous voice at the other end, his eyes growing wider, his hand beginning to tremble uncontrollably, and his face turning the deepest shade of scarlet Alex had ever seen.

Hawke, having no wish to humiliate the man further, quickly made his exit and went to join the young platoon commander, Lieutenant Sebastian Bolt, who would soon be leading the attack on the safe house.

HAWKE FOUND BOLT IN THE MIDST of three or four commandos, leaders of the assault group, crouched behind some heavy underbrush, each man doing a last-minute check of gear and weapons. The assault would commence in exactly twenty-five minutes. A roughly drawn layout plan of the Barking Dog lay on the ground. One man held a pencil light while Lieutenant Bolt went through a final brief.

"Two teams, Yankee upstairs, Zulu down. You've all memorized the layout of this target. Three floors, central staircase. Two rooms right and two rooms left on the top two floors, here and here. One room left, one room right on the ground going in. Exits front and rear. Shoot like a surgeon when you acquire a target and verify he's armed."

He looked at each man, making eye contact one last time, waiting for each to nod.

"Night-vision goggles are a huge advantage here; use them. The enemy may be disoriented, but they are highly trained and highly motivated terrorist fighters. They kill innocent women and children, and they will be more than happy to kill you. You all know what to do, so let's do it! We go in twenty. Good hunting and good luck."

"Lieutenant Sebastian Bolt?" Hawke said, kneeling down beside him. He was blond, ruddy cheeked, and surprisingly young, and Hawke suddenly felt his age.

"Yes, sir, I am. You're Commander Hawke, aren't you? MI6? There was a pool as to whether or not you'd make it here in time. Or at all."

"I made it."

"Glad you did, sir, and honored. There's a rumor floating round you conceived and executed the hostage rescue aboard that Russian airship in the middle of the Atlantic. From a submarine. True?"

"I was there, yes. Now, how can I help?"

"Can you help us identify the terrorist leader known only as 'Smith'?"

"I cannot. No one on earth can, it seems. The invisible man."

"Then all you can do is help us kill or capture as many of these bastards as possible. Plain enough, sir?"

Hawke grinned at the eager-to-fight young lieutenant. "You're my kind of leader."

"We have the element of surprise in our favor, sir. Four of their sentries in the woods have been taken out silently in the last hour. None of them had a chance to use his radio."

"No one on the roof?"

"We've been watching that. You'd think they'd post a man up there. But, no. They did post an armed sentry out front. Stood by the door, smoked a fag or two, and went to bed about a half hour ago. All lights were extinguished. There has been no noise, no light, no sign of movement inside since."

"Lieutenant, if Smith is in there, I'd like very much to take him alive. In other words, I'd rather have prisoners than corpses."

"I understand. I'll get that message out immediately. We're using heavy loads, so a hit anywhere will take a man down without a kill."

Bolt, like all the troops, was wearing a battlefield commo set inside his helmet. An NVG device was mounted atop the helmet. He turned away and spoke quickly into his lip mike, passing on the new orders to his second in command.

He produced a similar Kevlar commo helmet for Hawke who donned it, pulling the flip-up NVGs into position and checking them. He noticed white circles painted around the tops of all the black helmets around him. The white paint popped, like something under black light, and he asked Bolt about it.

"Recently developed. Highly reflective through NVGs. You'll find it very handy once we're inside that house in the pitch-dark."

Hawke grinned. "Our troops look like angels with halos."

"That's the general idea," Bolt said, and looked at the digital countdown on his watch. "Helps you keep track of whose side you're on."

"The side of the angels."

"You got it, Commander."

"We go in twenty. I estimate a minimum of fifteen to twenty-five heavily armed IRA soldiers inside. All armed with AK-47s. We have microphones under the house and all we're getting is snoring. Safe to say we have the element of surprise."

"What kind of firepower do you have?" Hawke asked, checking his own M8 weapon, fitted with a noise suppressor, selecting a three-shot burst, and putting a round in the chamber. He also had a Kahr P9 9mm pistol in a Velcro holster strapped high on his right thigh.

"I've got two sections, twelve men in each, all armed with individual weapon IW-SA80s with noise suppressors, with the exception of my LMGs, light machine gunners. Each man also carries two 'Bullet Catcher' rifle grenades."

"Never heard of them."

"The grenade is simply pushed onto the muzzle of the barrel, and an ordinary 5.56mm round is fired into it. The grenade absorbs the bullet without damage and is projected toward the target up to 150 meters away."

"Good. You understand why I want to nix the mortar emplacements on the hillside?"

"Yes, sir. I heard from them and I agree with your assessment. We learn more from captured maps, documents, and laptops than we ever do from dead enemy combatants. I wonder. Did Major Masterman agree with that no-mortar decision, sir? I've received no direct orders from him on that."

"I didn't ask for his opinion."

"Radio must be down. I can't raise him."

Hawke didn't say a word.

"Anything wrong, sir?"

"Lieutenant Bolt, for the safety of your men and the success of this mission, I think it best if you immediately assume full command of this operation."

Lieutenant Bolt looked at Hawke carefully, thought a moment, then flipped up his tiny battlefield communicator mike and said, "Mortars, mortars. This is Bolt. Hold fire, repeat, mortars hold your fire until and unless you hear from me, personally. Roger that? The CO's radio is down, all orders during this operation will come directly from me. Over."

"Thanks," Hawke said, attaching a few more stun and smoke grenades to his utility belt.

"Fifteen minutes," Bolt said. "Sir, I suggest you stick with me and Yankee. Upon entry, we immediately mount the center stairs and clear the top two floors. Zulu, under the command of Second Lieutenant Hunter Foreman, will cover and clear the ground floor. He also has three of his LMG men posted outside at the rear and two sides of the building, covering those exits with machine guns."

"I'm with you, Lieutenant. I assume you're going in with flash-bangs and smoke grenades?"

"Yes. Both bangers and smokers through every window as well, upstairs and down. Maximum disorientation. They'll have enough time to pull their balaclavas over their faces and grab their AK-47s and that's about it before we come in shooting."

"Good," Hawke said.

Bolt's hidden commandos were creating so much warrior energy in the woods surrounding the Barking Dog you could cut it with a knife. Good energy. Killer energy. This was it, Alex thought, these were the moments that made staying alive a viable notion again. A novel concept, considering his recent state of mind. But he felt it, coursing through his veins, a liquid fire.

Hawke would find this bloody Smith tonight or the next, or the next. But he would find him and he would take him out, and he would do it for his future King and country.

FORTY-TWO

SLIGO, NORTHERN IRELAND

STAND BY, ZULU, YANKEE GOES GREEN in twenty seconds," Lieutenant Bolt said, silently raising the flat of his hand and motioning his squad to a halt. He and Hawke watched the digital timers on their wrists tick down to . . . four . . . three . . . two . . . one! Suddenly the muffled but deafening sound of the countless flash-bang grenades hurled inside the Barking Dog's windows could be heard. The blinding light and painfully high decibel level produced would disorient everyone inside and gain the assault teams precious seconds.

Bolt and Hawke ran in a low crouch toward the front entrance of the Barking Dog.

Standing to either side of the peeling and cracked front door, Bolt looked at Hawke as he prepared to kick the door in. Hawke nodded and Bolt saw that the man was more than ready. The icy hardness of the look in his eyes was actually disturbing to the young lieutenant. He'd seen warriors eager for battle before, but this was intensity of an entirely different order of magnitude.

Hawke said through clenched teeth, "Let's do it."

The force of Bolt's big boot split the wooden door and blew it off its hinges. The lieutenant immediately pulled the spoons on two smoke grenades and lobbed them inside the entrance hall. He dashed into the smoke-filled area and made for the center stairs at a full run. Hawke and the rest of Yankee were right behind him.

To Hawke's right and left were two large rooms. In each, Hawke saw large numbers of hooded men rising from the floor, AK-47s already in their hands.

The sound of the flash-bangs throughout the house and the splintered front door had roused the enemy, but by the time they were fully awake, reoriented, and had begun firing their weapons, all of Yankee section had raced up two flights of creaky wooden stairs, and gained the top floor.

"Zulu, go, go, go!" Bolt said.

The men of Zulu squad now started pouring inside, and seconds later a raging firefight began on either side of the stairs. Hawke glanced back down to the ground floor and all he could see in the billowing smoke below were glowing white halos and muzzle flashes. So far, mercifully, there were no fallen angels.

As previously agreed, Bolt went left at the top of the stairs and Hawke went right. Each man had six commandos covering his six. The low-ceilinged hallway had two closed doors and an open window at the far end. As Hawke approached it a smoke grenade came flying through. He reached out, caught it on the fly, and winged it back outside. He'd no need of more smoke in the hall now, just inside the two rooms he had to clear.

He looked back toward the stairs. Half his men were "stacked" outside the first closed door, lined up for dynamic entry into the room. Weapons at the ready, they waited for his signal. The other half was stacked right behind him at the door by the window.

He had just motioned one man forward to breach the door when he heard multiple staccato bursts of enemy automatic fire from the other end of the hall. Bolt's men were already engaged in clearing two of the four top-floor rooms.

The sound of fire, he knew, would make the terrorist combatants on the other side of his door trigger-happy to say the least. His men were going in with weapons suppressed. This bought you precious time while the bad guys were trying to figure out "what the hell was that and where did it come from?" Suppressors also keep muzzle blast to a minimum, assisting the entry team in situation awareness.

Yankee squad had been trained to the point of automatic response. The body automatically brought the weapon up to the ready. Trained endlessly in the fundamentals of sight alignment and trigger control, they now reflexively applied those two muscle-memory skills in the heat of combat. These British Army troops were as lethal a group of men as existed, taught to neutralize the hostile until he is no longer a threat.

"Yankee, go," Hawke said into his lip mike, signaling the other team's entry at the same moment his commando put his shoulder to the door, blowing it inward. He immediately rolled to his right, followed by Hawke and the balance of the team. Rule One was you never enter a room from the center of the doorway; that is called the Death Zone.

You go in from either side, low and fast, acquire targets, and hit them.

Which is what Hawke did to the man firing his AK-47 at him from the floor, the rounds zipping over Hawke's head and raining down plaster, as he began to lower the weapon for the kill. Hawke drew the P9 handgun with blinding speed and shot the man in the forehead in a single motion. There'd been no time for a body shot.

"Commander, behind you!" he heard one of his men shout and he whirled about to face a man three feet away with a gun pointed at his head. Hawke's instincts were operating at a level where he could see the man's finger applying pressure to the trigger. He was looking death right in the face when that face ceased to exist, the man's head literally disintegrating before his eyes. A halo from across the room had taken him out with a head shot.

Hawke estimated about ten armed men remaining in the room, half of them capable of getting off a shot before they were killed.

The IRA soldiers, disorganized and disoriented by the intensity of the surprise attack, were firing blindly and missing. Three more of them went down, and it was clear Yankee had achieved dominance in the room.

"The rest of you," Hawke shouted, swinging his M8 back and forth to cover them, "throw down your weapons! Now."

Seeing resistance was useless, they complied instantly, the AKs rattling to the floor.

"Hands up where I can see them. Everyone against the far wall. Good. Now turn and face it, putting your hands on the wall above your heads."

He now had seven prisoners on his hands. His only thought was that one of them might be Smith. He reached forward and yanked the balaclava off the head of the nearest man. A redheaded kid not much more than twenty stared at him with blinking blue eyes.

"Sergeant, cuff these men. Two of you stay here and cover these prisoners. The rest of you follow me," Hawke said, heading for the door. Once more in the hallway, he heard minimal fire and Lieutenant Bolt's voice screaming, "On the floor! Now, get on the fucking floor or you're fucking dead!"

Situation under control at that end, he thought, peering into the adjacent room. The shooting had ceased, but he saw two halos on the floor alongside the dead IRA men and the prisoners already with their hands cuffed behind them.

"Two of ours down in here, sir."

"How badly are they hurt, Sergeant?"

"It's Onslow, sir. Afraid he's dead. Gut shot. Bled out during the firefight. Afraid I didn't see him in time."

"Don't blame yourself, you were busy. How about the other soldier?"

"That's Briggs, sir. He'll make it, all right. Took a round, he did, blew out his shoulder."

"Prisoners secure?"

"Yes, sir. Five of them in here. And three down."

"Take them next door. Along the wall with the others."

To get to the other end of the hall, Hawke had to step over the body of a young British Army soldier who'd been shot in the back at the top of the stairs. He found Bolt in the farthest room, kneeling beside one of his men, who was badly wounded. He was holding the boy's hand.

Looking up at Hawke, he said, "Casualties?"

"Two dead, one wounded."

"Prisoners?"

"Twelve."

"Have a look in the room right there, Commander," Bolt said, pointing at a closed door. "See what happens to an IRA rat who gets caught."

Hawke kicked it open. The room was empty save for an unrecognizable human being tied to a chair. Obviously dead. There was not a square inch of his naked body that had not been ripped, burned, or beaten. Hawke crossed and looked carefully at the corpse, confirming his suspicions. Although the eyes were swollen shut, the nose smashed, and all the teeth broken or missing, the face was still faintly recognizable.

It was the IRA bomb maker, Thomas McMahon, the man who'd steered them to the Barking Dog for thirty pieces of silver.

"Zulu, Zulu, this is Yankee," Bolt said into his commo as Hawke returned. "What's your situation, Lieutenant Foreman?"

"We've secured the building, sir. All hostiles neutralized. We have four casualties, all wounded, no KIA. We have also recovered two laptops and numerous documents."

"Well done. Medics?"

"Just coming through the door."

"Send one up here, on the double. I've got a boy bleeding to death right here."

"Yes, sir, already on his way up."

"How many prisoners, total, down there? Ground floor and first?"

"Fifteen, sir."

"All right. I want all prisoners assembled in one room. You have a clear room down there?"

"Kitchen, sir. Clean as a whistle."

"Everyone hear that? I want all prisoners in the kitchen. Right now. Try and raise Major Masterman in the command vehicle. Tell him the house is secure."

"He's not in the command vehicle, sir. I just sent Nichols to inform him."

"Where the hell is he?"

"No one's quite sure, sir." At that moment a young medic came racing up the stairs, calling for Bolt. His face was a mask of terror.

"Lieutenant! We've got to evac immediately!"

"What?" Bolt said.

"Sir! I was attending a wounded hostile on the ground floor, desperate to be moved outside. He says the basement is a weapons cache. There is an explosive device down there on a timer. He says he saw another hostile trigger the timer just as he died!"

"Go!" Bolt said, screaming at the top of his lungs. "Everybody evac the premises right now! Take the wounded, leave the dead. There is a bomb in the cellar that could go off any second. I want every last man out of this house in twenty seconds or less!"

It was chaos. Wounded men screaming as they were bodily hauled down the stairs and out the front and rear entrances. Soldiers diving out of second-story windows, taking their chances of suffering a broken leg or worse. Hawke raced down the stairs, found two wounded British Army boys, and somehow managed to get both of them up onto his shoulders. He ran for the front door as fast as he could, leaping over the dead, hearing the cries of the two young men he carried, praying he wasn't injuring them further.

"Get as far away from the house as fast as you can!" Hawke heard Bolt shout in his headphones. "There are possibly tons of explosives down there!"

Hawke made it into the woods with his two casualties. He put them down as gently as he could before turning to look back at the Barking Dog Inn.

A young British soldier, his right arm hanging by a thread, was just coming through the front door when the house erupted in an earthshaking geyser of flame, debris, and thick, acrid smoke that climbed into the sky a hundred feet or more. When the smoke had cleared somewhat, Hawke saw a massive hole in the ground, almost a hundred feet across.

The Barking Dog had been vaporized.

And with it, enough arms and explosives to take down a large city.

TWENTY MINUTES LATER THE BRITISH Army and enemy wounded had received emergency first aid and were being MedEvaced to the HQ hospital in Sligo. The surviving prisoners had been placed under guard in a clearing in the forest beyond the cart path. Army vehicles had their lights aimed at the group of hooded terrorists, and soldiers with flashlights were everywhere.

Hawke and Bolt entered the clearing. Having been driven around the hill to the command vehicle, and found no trace of a CO to report to, they'd no choice but to return to the woods to interrogate the prisoners. Hawke thought that after his conversation with Prince Charles, Masterman had probably jumped off the nearest bridge.

"Commander," Bolt said to Hawke, "I think you and I should take a look first. We'll deal with them individually later back in the interrogation section at HQ. After those laptops have been vetted."

Hawke nodded and walked across the ground to the first prisoner in line. All of them had been cuffed.

He reached out and pulled the black balaclava off the man's head.

The man was dark-skinned and had a full black, unkempt beard. If this was an IRA killer, he surely didn't resemble one. Bolt took one look at the man and came rushing over. He ripped the hood off the second man in line. And found himself staring into another Arabic face.

"What in hell?" Bolt, stunned, said to Hawke. "Bloody al Qaeda in Northern Ireland?"

"Let's find out. Speak English?" Hawke said. For emphasis, he'd removed his assault knife from the sheath on his thigh and placed the tip under the man's chin.

The man murmured yes.

"Name?"

"Yusef Najeeb."

"Ah. One of the celebrated Najeebs of Londonderry, no doubt."

"No. From North Waziristan, Pakistan."

"Why the devil are you here?"

The man smiled. "We come to Northern Ireland to fight the oppressors alongside our brothers."

"Ah, your Catholic brothers. Where is Smith?"

"I don't know any Smith."

Hawke looked at Bolt. The lieutenant was just as amazed as he was.

Instead of further questions, Hawke simply went down the line removing the masks from each prisoner until he came to an IRA soldier. He put the blade of his knife across the man's throat. "I'm looking for a man named Smith. Has he been here?"

In a strangled voice, the terrorist said, "He was here. But he was gone before we came."

"You know him, then."

"I've heard of him, yeah."

"What does he look like?"

"No one ever sees him."

"I said, what does he look like? Someone must have seen him." Hawke pressed his point.

"Those who have seen him will not tell you his identity."

"Why would that be?"

"They are far more afraid of him than you."

When all had been unmasked, twenty-four of the prisoners were IRA, while fifteen were Middle Eastern terrorists. The implications of this one fact were enormous.

Hawke shot out a hand and grabbed the last Pakistani by the neck, pulling him out of his loose-fitting sandals.

"Who comes to Ireland to fight alongside their brothers? Taliban? Al Qaeda?"

"Sword of Allah, praise be to God."

Hawke was still scanning all the faces.

"Smith?" he asked the man again. "Which one of you has seen Smith?" he asked the second, and third, and the fourth.

He gave up after six or seven. Smith had to be in his seventies now. These were all boys and middle-aged men. If Smith had been here at all, he was long gone.

An hour later, Hawke and Sebastian Bolt were sitting inside the abandoned command vehicle of Major Milo Masterman. The sun had risen fully and with it came black clouds and a fierce rainstorm that beat against the steel roof above their heads. The major had simply disappeared. Troops had fanned out through the dense forest in search of him but so far with no result. Bolt was mystified. Hawke told him they should be searching the local pubs, not the woods.

Ambrose Congreve and Bulldog Drummond had had enough of the Barking Dog and had retired to their quarters at the Swan to get a few hours of sleep before taking up the matter of a thorough interrogation of the captured terrorists. Both had congratulated the two men now sipping hot coffee inside the APC for a job well done before catching a ride back to Sligo in a British Army vehicle.

"Sword of Allah," Bolt said. "I recall the name. Heathrow, no? Terminal Four a year or so ago, wasn't it? That despicable bombing?"

"Yes."

"Behind that monstrous attack in the States, as well. A Miami hospital, if memory serves."

"The same," Hawke replied.

"So my question is the same, Commander Hawke. What the

bloody hell are the Taliban doing in Northern Ireland? Fighting alongside the New IRA? It beggars belief."

"I think all these bastards are joining forces. And will go anywhere in the world, Lieutenant. Fight alongside anyone who hates Britain. Or America. Or the West in general. Remember, you had IRA bombers like McMahon training in Libya thirty years ago."

"They have the resources and the manpower to do this on a worldwide scale? Sword of Allah? That in itself is terrifying."

"It appears they do, doesn't it? The world's first transnational Islamic superpower, so to speak."

"You're right in the middle of this one, aren't you, Commander?"

"I am."

"What do you do now?"

"Defend the realm, of course."

FORTY-THREE

LONDON, PRESENT DAY

DAYBREAK. THE VENERABLE THAMES BARGE *PUDGE*, narrow of beam but with eighty feet of gleaming black hull on her waterline, was docked at Greenwich Pier. Her captain, Terrence Spencer, was a ruggedly put together seaman with a broad chest, heavily muscled shoulders, and a full red beard. He stood drinking a mug of steaming coffee just outside the low-roofed wheelhouse. Terry and his young charter client were watching the rental truck being unloaded.

Terry, like his dad and gramps before him, had been a Thames riverman since he was old enough to swim. He looked at the bearded lads offloading boxes of equipment from the lorry and shook his head. What a sorry lot. He thought he'd seen it all. He had chartered the old girl countless times over the years, anniversaries, weddings, retirement parties, but this bunch was a first, he had to say.

A rock-and-roll band. Called themselves Sunni and the Scimitars.

Clever, that.

"How much longer?" he asked the band's manager and lead

singer, Sunni, pronounced "Sonny." His full name was Sunni Khan. At one time, that would have been an unusual name for a *Pudge* client, Terry mused silently. But, now, almost eighty thousand Britons had the surname Khan. True, he had read it in the *Mirror.* That made Khan the eightieth-most-common surname in the United Kingdom. He'd looked up his own name, Spencer, just for fun. Number 147. Fancy that.

Sunni was a nice enough looking young kid, clean shaven, expensive leather jacket, even had a tie on. He was a student at LSE, he told Terry, and then said, London School of Economics, obviously for the brawny, brainless barge captain's edification. "Oh, is that what LSE stands for?" he asked the kid. "Always wondered about that. My daughter goes there."

"Sorry. No offense meant, sir."

"If you want to be on schedule, we need to get moving right away."

"Truck's almost empty, sir. I think you can plan to shove off in about twenty minutes or so. Sorry we're late. Few last-minute snags with the lorry rental."

The lorry had backed right up to the edge of the dock. Young toughs with beards and long stringy hair were still rolling large black boxes down the truck's ramp. Had the name of the band stenciled on each box in big white block letters: SUNNI AND THE SCIMITARS. Terry'd never heard of them, but then he'd stopped listening to music when Sinatra died.

Some of the lads were belowdecks in the midships hold, uncrating who knows what electronic gear, amplifiers, musical instruments, and such for the afternoon cruise upriver. There was to be a concert in the meadow across from Hampton Court. The band, Sunni had told him, intended to set up their instruments atop the large midships hatch cover. A floating concert was the idea he said, a new angle. Every ticket sold out.

Floating concert, my arse, Terry thought.

These clever blokes who'd booked *Pudge* for a full-day stint had no idea of his boat's historic significance. Nor, if they knew, he thought, would they bloody care. Foreigners, of course. No knowledge of British history. Didn't care. Hated the country, the people, the government, from what he'd read in the *Daily Mirror*.

Terry had an idea: if they didn't bloody like it here, didn't like our flag, our religion, our way of life, pack up and go home! He'd never express those feelings out loud of course, very un-PC as his wife would say. He was beginning to wonder about this whole PC movement. He thought it was ruining everything, especially the truth.

Pudge had played a historic, one might even say heroic, role in the evacuation of British troops at Dunkirk in World War II. Towed across the Channel by tugs for speed, the rescue barges were all rigged with sails to get them ashore upon release from the tugs. The crew of *Pudge* raised her sail just offshore and made a hard landing on the beach. She took on nearly three hundred soldiers. A bunch of the lads, under heavy fire, managed to shove her back into the sea, and get her under way toward home under sail.

Despite continuous strafing attacks by German dive-bombers, mine-infested waters, British destroyers being sunk to her right and left by countless batteries of heavy German guns on the cliffs, somehow, old *Pudge* had survived. She managed to make it all the way to Ramsgate and there delivered her precious cargo of human passengers safely ashore. Terry's grampa had been her captain then, not that anyone remembered such feats of heroism anymore.

And this lot of foreigners, his "clients," you think they knew beans about his dad? Fat bleeding chance. Born in Bedford during a 1918 Zeppelin airship raid, drama would follow him to the end of his days. In the Battle of Britain, he became a right legend, he did, posted to an American squadron flying P-51 Mustangs. He was known for flying just ten feet off the ground to avoid German radar, strafing enemy trains, boats, and military convoys, whatever he set his sights on.

But the truly amazing thing about his old man? He figured out how to take out the Nazi doodlebug flying bombs! He'd destroy them in flight by poking them with his wingtips! Now that was something. Earned him the nickname "Tip it in Terry" and national acclaim as one of Britain's most striking daredevils.

Maybe Sunni and the Scimitars could sing a song about *that*.

AN HOUR LATER, AFTER AN UNEVENTFUL CRUISE, *Pudge* was nearing the Lambeth Bridge. Sunni had stayed in the wheelhouse with Terry for the entire voyage, over in the corner whispering on his mobile most of the time, while the band members had come topside and stretched out atop the main hatch cover, getting some sun and talking quietly among themselves.

"Captain," Sunni said. "Unexpected stop. Seems my drummer slept in this morning and missed the lorry. He's waiting for us now on the Lambeth Pier just beyond the bridge."

Terry looked ahead, gauging his distance and the time it would take to slow the big barge. For some reason, he noticed, the band members had slid the big hatch open and disappeared down into the cavernous hold.

"Wish you'd told me sooner," Terry said, throwing the engines hard astern, slowing the big barge just as her bow passed under the busy Lambeth bridge. Water was boiling at her stern as he put the helm over to starboard and lined up on the pier. Sure enough, there was another scruffy musician waiting there.

Pudge's sole crewman had two lines ready and looped one neatly over the top of a bollard and cleated another as Terry eased her alongside the pier. It was a right nice piece of seamanship considering. The drummer leaped aboard and helped the mate free the lines. Terry gave her big diesels a bit of throttle and pulled away from the pier. No maritime traffic in either direction right now, so he headed right to the center of the river to begin the final leg of his journey up to Hampton Court. Be glad when it was over. Something about the whole charter had seemed wrong from the beginning. It was just too—

The captain felt cold steel pressure at the back of his skull and knew immediately that he had made a very terrible mistake. He heard the pistol, a round going into the chamber of the automatic.

"Full stop, Captain," Sunni Khan said. "Or I'll happily blow your brains out."

"Who the bloody hell are you people?" Terry roared, all of the pent-up anger at what was happening to his country bursting forth at once.

"Sword of Allah, Captain, that's what's happening."

"Sword of Allah. Right. Same blokes who killed all those hundreds of people at Heathrow last year."

"They died for a great cause."

"They died for shit, you filthy little bugger."

Sunni jammed the pistol painfully into his temple and said, "Stop this boat, Captain, now!"

Terry hauled back on the throttles and the boat slowed quickly to a stop.

"Now give her just enough forward throttle to hold her steady in place against the current. Do exactly as I say and you might live through this, Captain."

Terry did as he said. He wanted supper at home with the missus tonight and after that to hoist a few pints on the corner with his mates at the Bag of Nails. "If I go, I'm taking you with me, Sunni-Boy," he said.

He looked forward, scanning the bow, looking for Tim, his mate. That's when he saw the motionless body lying on the deck just aft of the midships hatch cover. Blood was pooling around his head. His mate was dead. The main hatch cover was now open and equipment was rapidly being handed up from below and mounted on the hatch cover. Looked like bloody pipes resting on a tripod, most of the stuff.

"Don't look like bloody musical instruments to me," he muttered.

"Mortars," Sunni said. "Russian Podnos 82mm mortars," he

informed the captain in a very casual way. "Not cheap, either, but perfect for this kind of short-range attack. Each mortar throws a three-kilogram fragmentation bomb a thousand yards at twenty rounds a minute. Keep your eyes open and you'll see the effect."

When Terry cast his eyes to the right to see what the mortars were aimed at, he thought, *Bloody hell.* They were going to blow up Thames House. It was the headquarters of MI5. *The very people who were charged with protecting us from these kinds of animals.*

All six mortars started firing rapidly and simultaneously. Each was targeted at different areas of the building, and the immediate effect was catastrophic. Giant hunks of concrete and glass were blasted away, whole sections of wall and roof started collapsing, and fire broke out everywhere, flames licking out of windows. *The death and injuries inside must be horrific,* Terry thought.

But the tide turned quickly against the Sword of Allah. Thames House was not quite as helpless as it looked. Return fire suddenly erupted from the roof of the giant building. Even though his precious barge was being riddled with lead, Terry cheered loudly for the men behind the guns up there.

The weapons atop Thames House were M61 Vulcan 20mm Gatling guns. And they trained their deadly fire on the stationary barge. These modern versions of the old Gatling guns were in fact six-barreled rotary cannons, each capable of firing more than six thousand rounds per minute.

Pudge was being ripped to pieces. But so were all the terrorists behind the mortars on the main hatch cover. Their bodies were literally shredded right before Terry's eyes, and what was left of their corpses was blown backward over the gunwales and into the river.

There was no more glass in the wheelhouse, and Terry was very surprised he was still alive. *Pudge* had been built of heavy steel, including the wheelhouse, and the rounds were pinging off. Sunni shouted, "Get her out of this fire!" For some bizarre reason, Sunni believed he could still escape the murderous hail of lead from the Thames House rooftop.

"Full astern," Sunni screamed above the thunderous fusillade from M15. "Back her down beneath the bridge and stay there!"

Terry looked over his shoulder. Amazingly enough, people had just stopped their cars on the bridge and gotten out to have a look. Insanity begets insanity.

He shouted, "It is over, you rank-smelling little moron! You'll never escape now!"

"Not quite over, Captain. I have loaded three 200-pound nitrate-peroxide bombs in the hold. I'm now going to take out the Lambeth Bridge and everyone on it."

"Timed-fuse or detonator?" Terry asked, seemingly on autopilot, having watched far more than just a few episodes of *Spooks* on the telly. Some part of his brain knew that if the answer was "detonator," he was going to ignore the bloody pistol and rip the little bastard's head off, then toss his fuckin' detonator overboard.

"Detonator," Sunni said, and patted his shirt pocket. "Right here in my . . . shit! I gave it to Rashid in case . . . shit!" Rashid, as they both knew, no longer existed.

At that moment, two Tornado Air Defense F3 fighter jets screamed just overhead, not twenty feet above the Lambeth Bridge and *Pudge*. You could see the deadly air-to-surface missiles hung in the shadows beneath their wings.

The Tornados were aircraft from the "Protection Wing" squadron based at RAF Marham. Marham was just one of dozens of World War II RAF fighter bases scattered around London. In the air 24/7, these Air Defense fighter jets provided the capital with an almost instantaneous air-strike response to any attack on the city.

Terry knew in that instant exactly what he had to do. He shoved the throttles full astern and she started to back downriver, taking her beneath the Lambeth Bridge.

Ahead in the far distance, still at unbelievably low altitude, he saw the two F3s go to afterburners, flying away from each other in opposite directions, carving incredibly tight turns to return to the river and the target slowly backing down into the shadow of the bridge.

"Get beneath the fucking bridge," Sunni shouted in his ear.

Sunni raced out of the wheelhouse, ran forward, and leaped down into the hold even though smoke was pouring out. Going below to hand-detonate the bombs once they were positioned directly beneath the center of the bridge, Terry thought as he reached for the throttles.

A VOICE CRACKLED in the lead pilot's headphones.

"Viper, this is Coldplay . . . completely cheesed, sir. No shot. Target appears stationary directly beneath the bridge . . . anticipate unacceptable collateral damage . . ."

"Affirmative. Sit tight."

Terrence Spencer put a lock on *Pudge*'s helm, securing the rudders in neutral position, and went to full power dead astern. *Pudge*'s powerful engines didn't disappoint, swiftly backing her down and out from under the bridge, headed downriver backward at about five knots.

"Target moving away from the bridge . . . Please advise, over."

"Thirty seconds," Viper advised. He wanted to give the target time enough to get well away from the crowded bridge.

"Thirty seconds, that's affirmative."

Coldplay had the target locked up. A beeping warning signal sounded inside his cockpit as he armed his missiles.

"Take it out, Coldplay. All yours."

"Roger that."

The lead fighter pilot's weapons were locked on to the old barge, now engulfed in flames and well beyond any danger to the bridge. He flipped the red safety up, then toggled the button that launched a single Sea Eagle air-to-surface missile from beneath his starboard wing. Almost instantly there was a muffled boom below, and Coldplay flipped his airplane left for a view of the now disintegrated target.

Just moments before the barge had erupted into a flaming ball of utter destruction, both pilots had seen a burning man race from the smoke-filled wheelhouse and leap over the gunwale into the river.

—

HE WAS BURNED OVER 30 percent of his body and unconscious when they pulled him from the river. The soles of his boots had been burned away, and the flesh on his feet came away in pieces. In the ambulance en route to St. Thomas Hospital, they also discovered seven bullet wounds in his arms, legs, and torso.

When Terrence Spencer awoke in his hospital bed, many hours later, the face of his missus of thirty years swam into view. She was standing over him, one small hand caressing his forehead, the other placed carefully on his bandaged chest.

"How are you feeling this fine morning, Cap'n Spencer?"

"Hello, my darlin'," he croaked, lifting his head from the pillow, his throat raw from all the damned tubes they'd jammed down it. "Unless you're a bloody angel, I'm still alive, I see. Ain't that something?"

"They say you'll be home in a month or so. Full recovery."

"Is that so?"

"They're calling you a hero, y'know. On the telly and in all the papers."

"Me? A hero? Bollocks. For what?"

"For what, he says? You only got the *Pudge* out from under the bridge before that huge bomb in her hold blew sky-high. That's what."

"Was a missile sunk the old *Pudge*. I saw it with me own eyes, I did, darlin'."

"That's not what the RAF was saying on *BBC World News* last evening. They're giving you the credit for saving all those people on the bridge whether you want it or not."

"No."

"Yes."

"Well, I had nothing to do with it, darlin'. It was *Pudge* that did it. All by herself, too. Nothing surprising about it, is there? Old girl did what she's always done, didn't she? Dunkirk? All these years?"

"And what is that?"

"She did her duty, love, the old *Pudge* did her sacred duty."

FORTY-FOUR

WASHINGTON'S CROSSING, PENNSYLVANIA

IT WAS THE VERY FIRST DAY of school and nobody in the house was very happy about it but mom. The kids had had a wonderful summer, maybe the best ever. Swimming and rafting on the Delaware River, exploring the woods, building a tree fort that could withstand the fiercest Indian attack, catching fireflies in a jar behind the house, and not doing a single lick of homework for three whole months. They had also read three books, but only because their mother had made attendance mandatory when she read aloud every night before bedtime.

She loved reading aloud, and this summer Trevor, his little sister Margaret, and her baby girl, six-year-old Barclay, had heard her declaim *Tom Sawyer, The Yearling,* and *Wind in the Willows,* in that order. Trevor, twelve, on his own, had knocked back *All Quiet on the Western Front.* The nightly readings would, of course, continue on through the winter and into the spring.

But summer had fled. And now the house, her great big beautiful house on the hill, was hers and hers alone! Her husband, Jay, a professor at the Woodrow Wilson School across the river at Princeton University, left the house every morning at six. Alice Milne had her house, and thus her life, back. Her plein air painting. Her beloved books. Her hours on the phone with friends and her mother. Her long walks with her German shepherd, Scout, in the woods, just the two of them, watching the leaves turn and fall as October rolled into November. And then the snow, beautiful snow.

"Up and at 'em!" she shouted from the top of the steps at seven fifteen that morning. "Breakfast in ten minutes, be there or be square!"

From down the hall, a chorus of groans and from little Barclay's room a simple exclamation of "No school! No way!"

She peeked into her daughter's room and said, "School. Way. It's first grade. First grade is totally awesome. It is waaaay better than kindergarten, trust me on this one, Barclay. Now get yourself dressed and come down and eat your breakfast, got it?"

"Oh, okay," Barclay said, sliding from the bed and padding into her bathroom in her pink nightie.

One down, Alice said to herself, moving along the hall to eight-year-old Margaret's room. Margaret was up, dressed, and sitting at her dressing table brushing her long blond hair.

"Morning, Margaret. Nice to see you up and dressed so early."

"Mother, do you think I've gotten prettier over the summer or uglier?" She leaned into the mirror and made a face at herself.

"What do you think?"

"Uglier."

"Wrong answer. You're the prettiest little girl in the whole world. And don't ever forget it." She pulled the door closed and went to check on Trevor.

Trevor was also dressed but not combing his hair because he didn't have any. He'd shaved it all off at the beginning of summer vacation. He had watched the war movie *Jarhead* so many times this summer he knew almost every line of dialogue by heart. He even had the U.S. Marine's distinctive patois down pat. Trevor Milne had literally metamorphosed himself into the Jake Gyllenhaal character, Swofford, and when he saw his mother standing in his doorway, he snapped to attention, saluted, and tooted "Reveille" with his lips just like in the movie.

Finishing the song, he saluted again and remained standing at attention, eyes straight ahead. The top sheet on his bed had military corners stretched so tight you could bounce a quarter off it. This was one of the benefits: a twelve-year-old who not only made his own bed, but also shined his shoes every night and kept his room absolutely immaculate.

"Breakfast in five, Corporal. Be there."

"Breakfast in five, sir!" Trevor said, snapping off a salute. "Hoo-rah!"

"It's the first day of school, Trevor. Maybe lose the camo pants and combat boots? You know, maybe ease into them during the semester? Good idea?"

"Welcome to the suck," he said, pausing for beat before adding, "sir!"

"You got it, Marine," she said, smiling as she pulled his door shut. It was amazing. She had actually gotten accustomed to being addressed as "Sir" by her twelve-year-old son.

Over the Fourth of July weekend, she and Jay had escaped for their annual romantic getaway to the Greenbrier Hotel in White Sulphur Springs, West Virginia. They'd left the kids with a babysitter, a seventeen-year-old day student at the Lawrenceville School just across the river. Trevor had clearly wrapped this poor girl, Annie, around his little finger. When she and Jay returned a full day earlier due to Jay's illness, they discovered that Trevor had moved every stick of furniture out of his room. Stored it all in the attic.

He had then covered the bare floor of his room with about an inch of sand he'd bought (having persuaded Annie to drive him to Home Depot) and pitched a pup tent in the middle of his room. Beside his tent was a Christmas tree stand with a sawed-off broomstick mounted in it. At the top, he'd hung an American flag. Models from Trevor's collection hung on fishing line from the ceiling, including B-1B bombers, B-52s, F-16 Fighting Falcons, and Black Hawk helicopters.

Trevor, of course, was first to appear in "mess hall," and Alice was happy to see he was wearing a pair of nicely pressed chinos and a starched khaki shirt. Not perfect, but better than camo. Margaret and Barclay followed shortly and seemed not only to have adjusted to the idea of school, but seemed almost giddy with excitement about it. Everybody wolfed down their breakfast, anxious to make the long trek down through the woods that led to the narrow rural road where the school bus would pick them up at the end of their driveway.

It was about a ten-minute hike, and Alice practically had to run to keep up with her children.

When they arrived at the road, the big yellow bus could be seen in the distance, cresting a hill about half a mile away.

"Armored personnel carrier at nine o'clock, sir," Trevor said, completely serious.

"Hostile or friendly?" Alice asked.

Trevor smiled and said, "Good question, Mom."

The bus finally rolled to a stop just in front of them. Since they were the last house on the route, it was packed with raucous, laughing children. Many of them pressed their faces against the windows and a couple stuck their tongues out, presumably at Trevor because he was sticking his out at them.

"Okay, team," she said, herding them toward the door. "I want everyone to behave, pay attention in class, and try to avoid food fights. I've already got enough laundry to deal with, thank you."

"Yes, Mother," Margaret said, mommy's little angel. Barclay said the same thing, even using her older sister's inflection. Then she reached up for one last hug as the school-bus door hissed open.

"Off you go," Alice said, looking up at the driver for the first time as the kids climbed aboard.

"Where's Mrs. Henderson?" she asked the dark-haired young man at the wheel.

"Called in sick. I'm the new substitute driver."

"Sick? She's been driving this bus since I was in sixth grade. Never sick a day in her life."

"Always a first time," the youth said, pulling the lever that closed the door.

The bus lurched away and then began the long climb up Potter's Hill, the highest point in Washington's Crossing.

She watched the bus moving away with a growing sense of uneasiness. A mother's instincts. She had not liked the young driver. Not liked anything about him. Not the way he spoke to her, the way he was dressed (a little cap on his head), or the way he failed to say "Good morning" the way Mrs. Henderson always did. Nor did she particularly care for the way he smiled at her as he pulled the door closed. There was something wrong with that smile, she thought, something dreadfully wrong.

She stood there, arms wrapped around herself, watching the bus accelerate up the steep hill, wondering if she was actually going crazy. Delusional? Paranoid?

No.

"Oh, my God!" she heard herself cry aloud.

Then she started running after the bus, screaming as loudly as she could for it to stop.

About a third of the way up the hill she simply ran out of breath. She'd been running as fast as she'd ever run in her life, but the hill was just too steep. The bus was nearing the top now, and she knew she'd never catch it. All she could do was stand there helplessly and watch it, praying she was only being silly, getting to be just as paranoid as everybody else in the country seemed to be lately.

When the bus reached the very top of the hill, red lights flashed and it seemed to pause for a moment.

The explosion sent shock waves rolling down the hill, staggering Alice Milne. She looked up to see a massive ball of fire and billowing black smoke where her children's yellow school bus had been just a split second earlier.

Alice Milne started running up the hill.

The blistering heat of the flaming bus seared her eyes as she reached the top of the hill and the roaring funeral pyre that was now reducing her children and her life to ashes.

FORTY-FIVE

ISLAMABAD, PAKISTAN

THE RED CRESCENT SOCIETY AMBULANCE rolled up Islamabad's Peshawar Road, nearing Golra Mor and the newly opened hospital. It was just after midnight. Any time after ten o'clock, the well-ordered, tree-lined streets of Islamabad were empty, save the occasional white cab or two. It was not a town for night owls. The only restaurant open at this hour was a highly controversial Pizza Hut that had opened in a nearby shopping mall.

Up front, the ambulance driver, Imran, and his paramedic first aider, Ali, were smoking cigarettes and talking, what else, politics. In the darkened rear of the vehicle, the occupant inside the heavy-duty dark green body bag wasn't talking at all.

Imran took a right into the wide entranceway of the new Quaid-e-Azam International Hospital. The ultramodern four-hundred-bed facility had only opened recently after endless construction delays, political infighting, and infrastructure difficulties. Something having to do with an underground parking garage was the street gossip. The wait had been worth it, though, most people thought. The radical, blue-mirrored architecture resembled something one might find in downtown Dubai rather than the capital of Pakistan.

A gift from a national hero. A fierce warlord named Sheik al-Rashad.

The ambulance stopped under the covered entrance to the Emergency Room. The two men inside got out in a hurry. They'd been held up at a security checkpoint for more than two hours and both were eager to get home. The driver said hello to the armed security guard as he swung open the rear doors.

The guard, Muhammad, was an old friend to ISI operative Imran, another ISI agent who'd been disgraced and lost his job. This is where the poor bastard had ended up. Driving an ambulance was shitty enough. The graveyard shift at a hospital was the bottom of the barrel. The paramedic helped the driver slide the body onto the bright yellow collapsible gurney.

"Late night, Imran," the guard said in English. "Looks like cold storage for that one."

The paramedic shook his head and whispered to the driver in Urdu, "Now there's a blinding glimpse of the obvious. No wonder they threw this idiot out of the secret service."

Imran said, "How do you know the secret service threw him out? How do you know he's still not working for them? How do you know they are not working for him? Once ISI, always ISI."

"I heard he got kicked out on his ass."

"Did you now? Do not believe everything you hear, brother. You will live longer."

The large-paned glass ER doors hissed open and the EMS team wheeled the gurney quickly past Registration, past the rows of elevator banks. And, finally, through a set of stainless-steel double doors above which hung a sign that read MORTUARY/RESTRICTED.

The morgue. The smell of death and decay. The myriad, nameless chemicals of the constantly processed dead. They passed through the dead-empty morgue and, as expected, no autopsies were being performed because of the late hour.

At the far end of the facility, beyond the morgue refrigerators, the grossing station, the histology supplies, and the necropsy equipment, there was a nearly invisible black glass panel in the wall. A card reader was next to the panel.

Imran swiped his card and the stainless-steel doors slid wide open. Once the gurney was inside, he swiped his card again, this time on an electronic reader that was the sole way to initiate descent.

The big Otis dropped smoothly at least three or four floors underground. Maybe more. The thing was so fast, so quiet, and so smooth, you really couldn't tell how far down you were going. Felt like a journey to the center of the earth.

They came to a soft landing. "Lands like a butterfly with sore feet, this elevator," the paramedic said. The driver placed the flat of his hand against the center of the door, a scanner read his palm print, and the glass panel slid silently into the floor, rising again after they'd passed through.

The doors opened with a soft electronic ping and they pushed the gurney out into the dimly lit space beyond. It was some kind of reception area, empty now except for one man sitting in the shadows.

"This all right?" the paramedic asked. The man was sitting at a desk with his feet propped up, smoking a cigarette. They'd parked the gurney about ten feet from a modern desk that looked like it had been carved out of a block of steel. The only light in the room was a desk lamp, and the man's face was not visible in the small pool of smoky white light it cast.

"Perfect."

"Will that be it for tonight, sir?"

"You realize I've been sitting here for two hours."

"Sorry, sir. Security checkpoint on the Rawalpindi Circle. Traffic was backed up for five miles."

"Sure it was. Good-night. Thank you."

They left without a word.

The man at the desk stared at the body bag in silence for a few seconds, puffing absently on his cigarette as if he had all the time in the world. He bent down and opened a drawer. Grabbing a liter of Johnnie Walker Blue by the neck, he unscrewed the cap and set it, and a Baccarat crystal tumbler, on the desktop. As he closed the drawer he caught a fluorescent glint of blued steel. The .45 automatic he always brought, no matter how cozy the circumstances.

He heard the sound of a zipper and swung his head around to regard the new arrival.

Looking at the body bag, he saw the wide nylon zipper sliding from the head down past where the waist would be, to just below the knees.

The corpse sat up and stared at him.

The man at the desk returned the stare, smiled, and said, "You look like you just came back from the dead."

"Two fucking hours," the corpse said in English. "I told that idiot Malik to route the driver on the back roads."

"You knew about the checkpoint?"

"It was *my* fucking checkpoint! Of course I knew about it."

"Scotch?"

"What is it?"

"Johnnie Blue."

"How much did you bring me?"

"They don't make trucks that big."

Abu al-Rashad, the lower half of his body still zipped into the body bag, was the most powerful man in Pakistan. He looked it, even in this ridiculous pose. Every inch the warrior, all six feet of him, his skin leathered and darkened by decades in the saddle and sun, his thick hair still jet black at forty, his white smile startling in the creases of his ruggedly handsome face. He was the kind of man who could take the skin off your hand with a simple handshake.

He threw back his head and laughed. "It is good to see you bearing gifts, my brother. A sign you are up to something big. Are you?"

"Let's go into your office and have a drink, shall we. I will tell you my plans."

"And then I will give you a tour of my new bunker. I have two other floors besides this one. Communications, battlefield command center, my bedroom suite with a suitably shy French maid, and a first-rate kitchen with a chef also from Paris. Even a movie theater."

"Built beneath a hospital so the Americans won't bomb you to paradise." Smith smiled. "Nor the Israelis."

"A little trick I learned from Hamas."

"Amazing. The Israelis *knew* the Hamas HQ was under the hospital in Gaza City and yet they didn't bomb it. I would have."

"You and me both, brother. Boom-boom."

"Well. You certainly seem to have your life exactly the way you want it for now."

"I do. Except for the fact that there's a fifty-million-dollar price tag on my head and I have to travel about my own country in a fucking rubber body bag."

SHEIK AL-RASHAD LOOKED AT SMITH, the Arab's large black eyes gleaming in the lighting hidden in the ceiling crown moldings. His office, deep inside a bunker beneath a civilian hospital, was paneled in ebony. His desk was of intricately carved ivory, depicting the life of the Prophet. He leaned back in his deep black leather desk chair, placing his hands behind his head. Having just heard what Smith intended to do, al-Rashad now said, "You, my beloved brother, are fucking insane."

Smith said, "That quaint premise was clearly established years ago, old friend. My only question to you is, are you or are you not willing to aid me on this latest, admittedly insane, but nonetheless potentially devastating operation of mine?"

"There was one question I have," the Sheik said and he wagged his head in the familiar Afghan way. Smith smiled at the ritualistic game they were playing.

Ah, the enigmatic smile of the wizened yet wise warlord. Could mean yes. Could mean your head. Could mean nothing at all. He gave the old devil a wry smile in return and they were both content to sit in silence for a time sipping their scotch. The bottle on the Sheik's magnificent carved desk was already half empty.

"Your question?"

"This idea of yours is fraught with risk. You could easily be killed or captured by the British. A catastrophe that would put all of our plans in jeopardy. Especially if you were captured and tortured."

"Yes."

"So. One wonders. Why do you yourself need to be personally involved at all? Surely the team can handle this without you."

"Perhaps, perhaps not. But I must be there. I'd pull the trigger if I had the skill. You will understand when I tell you this target holds great symbolic interest for me. This is no ordinary operation. It is intensely personal."

"I understand now. I agree. You must go. And if things should go wrong, you will take yourself out of the picture, of course."

"Of course. Cyanide is my constant companion."

The Sheik turned his eyes toward the ceiling, tapping the tips of his fingers together, clearly mulling this over. He thought like a chess player. It was the reason for his ascension to power in the void created by the absence of Osama bin Laden. He was always at least four moves ahead.

"It would be good public relations, naturally," Sheik al-Rashad admitted. "An explosive international media strike right to the heart of the enemy."

"Well put. And wholly accurate."

"It is not surprising that it is you who has conceived this assassination. You are always following your natural inclinations."

"Naturally. It is my sole destiny and what I live for. But I tell you. Not a bomb on this earth could rival the devastating effect this will have on our enemies."

"Not even the precious nuclear arsenal we will soon control at Islamabad?"

"All of those weapons will be in the hands of the Sword of Allah before we are done, brother. Only a matter of time."

"An extremely powerful nuclear device seems to have gone missing at the Islamabad nuclear weapons facility."

For the first time, Smith's face showed excitement.

"Good, excellent. Without a problem I hope?"

"The security guards at the airport storage facility were put in place by my ISI friends years ago. All of the guards' families are held at one of my bases in the mountains, under constant threat of death. No one will ever know how we are removing the weapons."

"We are so close now, brother, so very close," Smith said.

"How old is the boy now, by the way?" Al-Rashad asked, sipping from his glass.

"In his twenties."

"Old enough to fight, old enough to die."

"Yes. Old enough."

"I know very well why we, the glorious forces under my command, would glory in this particular invader's death. What I still cannot understand is why you, of all the people on this planet, would want to kill him. There is a good English word for it. What is it? Like a souk, sounds like, perhaps?"

"Bizarre?"

"Ah, yes. Bizarre."

"As I said, I have my private reasons. Deeply personal reasons. To me, they are not the least bit bizarre. It is my life's work. Leave it at that."

"Your precious reasons. All very mysterious. And always your gold to pay for them. It is, I assume, already in my vault at the bank in Basel?"

"Of course. It was in Switzerland a week ago. I'm surprised you received no confirmation."

"I have been out under the stars these last weeks. There are no confirmations there, only the almighty presence of Allah."

"I confirm that one million British pounds in gold bullion now sits quietly in your vault at La Roche and Co. in Basel."

"Your gold, your gold. Old friend, I must tell you something about gold. It is not so effective an inducement now, you know. Over the years, you and all the others—the Americans, Russians, the

Chinese—all of you have made me rich beyond imagining. Perhaps that was a mistake. Perhaps in hindsight, you should have kept the tiger hungry."

"Our business tonight is not about gold, brother."

"No. Of course not. Tonight is about . . . how do you put it in English . . . your vendetta."

"Are we not fortunate that, on so many occasions over the years, my personal reasons and yours have been in such perfect alignment?"

They both laughed deeply, remembering that they had long shared a certain sense of irony, a thread of humor that bound them, a connective tissue not common between their two cultures. It was one reason Smith was still alive after all these years. The all-powerful Sheik al-Rashad thought he was funny.

"Tell me more. Where is the boy now?"

"Afghanistan. Based in a U.K. forward operating base in Helmand. Serving as a spotter with the Blues and Royals regiment."

"And how do you know this?"

"It is my business to know everything."

"Impossible. My men, both my military and my intelligence operations, would have known of his arrival in the war zone."

"A very closely guarded secret, to be sure. All prearranged with the U.K. print and broadcast media who have entered into an understanding not to provide coverage. But he is here, serving on the front lines, that I assure you."

"Not Iraq? That's what the world was told by the Western media."

"No. At the last minute Iraq was deemed too dangerous. The British Army decided against it. But he was determined to fight. So. He has secretly been deployed to Afghanistan on condition that his whereabouts remain unknown."

"But *you* know," Al-Rashad said, smiling.

"I do. Known to be in Iraq, he would obviously have become a Taliban target. As the boy himself said, 'I would never want to put someone else's life in danger when they find themselves sitting in a foxhole next to the Bullet Magnet.' "

"The Bullet Magnet?" Sheik al-Rashad laughed. "Delicious! And this delusional Bullet Magnet thinks he is anonymous in Afghanistan?"

"No one knows the Magnet is here. Except, of course, for me. And now, you. With your help, I shall kill him. To maximum political effect, I can assure you."

"You are the strangest of men, my dear Mr. Smith. You know that, do you not?"

"I am not only stranger than you do conceive, brother, I am stranger than you *can* conceive."

"Tell me what you need, my friend," the Sheik said, "and it is yours."

"Primarily, I will need the sniper Khalid. Where is he now?"

"At my main training base in the Hindu Kush mountains."

"You once told me Khalid was the best Taliban sniper in existence."

"None deadlier, believe me."

"And he has the new weapon I sent months ago?"

"He has not let it out of his sight."

From Kandahar, Smith had arranged for the infamous sniper Khalid Hassan to be sent the very latest British sniper rifle, the L115A3, known by the British as simply the "long range rifle." Now in service with all U.K. combat units in Afghanistan, it was capable of killing with pinpoint accuracy at unheard-of ranges up to one mile. The new telescopic sight had twice the magnifying power of the older model. It could even cut through the heat haze off the desert floor.

"I am glad he received it."

"Received it? I think it receives him! I'm beginning to think he loves that damn gun. The two are never separated, keeps it in his bed when he sleeps. Between you and me, I suspect he fires it all day and fucks it all night."

Smith laughed. "He is having success with it, then?"

"Oh, yes. What a weapon! I tell you, it is devastating to enemy morale when a number of their fighters are suddenly shot in almost the same instant, and they cannot even see where the firing is coming from. They tend to withdraw most rapidly behind their lines. We will need more of these guns for the coming time, many more."

"I shall see that you get them."

"And what exactly will you require from me?"

"I will need provisions delivered to me at your camp in the south of Afghanistan, in Helmand Province near the town of Sangin. Food, water, weapons, and ammunition for a week. Horses and mules. A Furaya satellite phone and an automobile battery in my saddlebag to power it. My target has been under surveillance. He is on patrol most every day. He operates out of a small British forward operating base on the outskirts of Sangin. If all goes well, I anticipate a five- to seven-day mission at most. Weather will be a factor. High winds will delay us. But I am optimistic we shall succeed."

"*Inshallah.*"

"*Inshallah.*"

"Your request is granted. I will speak with General Machmud. Everything will be in readiness when you arrive at my small base camp. I look forward to your triumphant success, my friend and brother in arms. And the death of this . . . this infidel princeling . . . this Bullet Magnet, as he calls himself. Let Khalid Hassan's message of lead find the dead center of his heart."

FORTY-SIX

HELMAND PROVINCE, SOUTHERN AFGHANISTAN

UNDER A TATTERED TENT PITCHED beneath a vast black dome pricked with sharp, ice-white stars, they ate. The two men sat directly opposite each other on the stained Bokhara rug. They were drinking steaming potions of cardamom tea spiked with vodka and eating their meal of boiled mutton, raisins, onions, carrots, and rice. The sniper, his rifle close beside him on the Bokhara, ate in stolid silence.

This was fine with Smith. His man was a shooter, not a talker, and it bode well for the approaching mission.

Dressed in his well-worn Afghan mufti, an anonymous tunic over shapeless cotton trousers and the traditional *pako* headcover, Smith felt strangely at home inside the tent, the horses and mules tied outside. But there was a strong strain of the nomad in his blood, and he gladly went anywhere in the world his life might lead.

Beyond the tent, the surrounding landscape resembled the far side of the moon. U.S. Air Force B-52 long-range bombers and AC-130 Spectre gunships had been pounding these limestone mountains for days, raining death from above on entrenched Taliban fighters, their military bunkers and strongholds. Not the safest neighborhood perhaps, but fields of battle seldom were. Field was such an odd, incongruous word in the context of war, Smith thought, suggesting vast acres of green clover or bright red poppies, rather than rivers of blood.

Sangin, his destination, was a small Afghan town, with a population of less than fifteen thousand. The inhabitants were all Pashtun and all fiercely supportive of the Taliban. Sangin was also infamous as the center of the opium trade in southern Afghanistan. Since the summer of 2006 British, American, and Canadian troops had engaged in heavy fighting with Taliban insurgents and allied opium traffickers in the area.

Many had died on both sides. Recently, a large group of Taliban fighters attacked a UN convoy making its way up a narrow mountain pass. The convoy somehow reversed down the narrow twisting road, escaped, and was rescued by U.K. and Canadian forces supporting them. The frustrated Taliban attempted escape by crossing the Helmand River. Air support was called in. All were killed by a single two-thousand-pound bomb delivered by a USAF B-52 bomber based out of Saudi Arabia, completely out of sight, circling high above.

That bomb had been called in by a young British Army soldier acting as a forward air controller. His responsibility was calling in fighter jet support and bombing strikes on suspected Taliban targets. He also had the ability to provide the enemy's GPS coordinates for drone weapons to take them out. The job of the young FAC was critical, especially on battlefields where U.K. forces were typically outnumbered.

Bomber pilots circling above knew the young soldier as Widow Six Seven, never suspecting the voice crackling on the radio belonged to Second Lieutenant Harry Wales.

FORTY-EIGHT HOURS AFTER BIDDING SHEIK al-Rashad farewell in his Islamabad hospital sanctuary, Smith and his Talib sniper Khalid were making their way on horseback, traveling south through the footlands of the southern mountains. Reaching the Helmand River just as night fell, they crossed, then started upward again trekking silently through the dark night, their sure-footed mounts climbing toward the peak of a snow-covered mountain. Their destination was a cave whose mouth overlooked the small village of Sangin far below.

There were countless mountain caves here, deep and well fortified, built over the decades by the Taliban, first used against the Soviets and now the Americans and their British allies.

On an earlier exploration, traveling alone, Smith had discovered that one of these caves had a direct sightline to the heavily guarded front gate of the British Compound. He had spent two days in this perch, watching the comings and goings of the FAC patrols through high-powered binoculars, jotting down every bit of information he would need for his mission to succeed.

Three hours after fording the river, having climbed three thousand feet, the two men had reached that very cave.

The British Army's forward outpost on the outskirts of Sangin was clearly visible from their position, the lights of the town and the outlying camp twinkling below. The cave, nearly a mile from the British position, was the last place British Army spotters would be expecting a Taliban sniper to be setting up shop. Typical Talib snipers used AK-47s, and such weapons were hardly accurate at anywhere near such a distance. But Khalid was not a typical Talib sniper and his weapon was definitely not an AK-47.

Once inside the cave, the men ate hungrily, fed the animals, and, exhausted, bedded down for a few hours of sleep.

Smith and Khalid Hassan rose an hour before dawn to get themselves in position before daybreak. They wedged themselves into the surrounding rock formations protecting the cave. A flat, stable surface at the bottom of a narrow crevice provided an ideal rest location for Khalid's long-range weapon.

The kill would be from a distance no other Taliban or al Qaeda sniper Khalid knew could even conceive of. Nor would they. He would never speak of this to anyone. Almost a mile! He'd been told early on in his training that if he ever informed anyone of this most secret action, he and his family would be beheaded.

The sun rose, turning everything violent shades of red and gold. The sniper began the long process of sighting in his weapon, adjusting for distance, elevation, windage, humidity, and haze. This gun was a miracle and he'd no doubt, God willing, that he'd accomplish the mission.

Smith crouched beside him, just to his right, hidden behind the massive rock formation, a pair of high-powered binoculars hung round his neck. Both men had a plastic-coated color photo of the target taped around the outside of the left sleeve of their fur coats for quick reference. Khalid got the distinct feeling the man beside him would like to be taking the shot himself. He was glad there was only room for one of them at the bottom of the V-shaped crevice or the man would be asking to look through his telescopic sight.

Khalid began regulating his breathing. He was calm. Confident. Ready. All he needed now was a target.

In his British Army regiment, the Blues and Royals, Khalid's target was known as Cornet Wales. Prince Harry, the handsome young redheaded Royal whose raffishly smiling face had graced so many worldwide magazine and tabloid covers, was the youngest son of the Prince and the late Princess of Wales. He was third in line to inherit the throne of England, but he'd just been promoted to second lieutenant, an honor he treasured.

Khalid did not know the target's true identity, nor did he need to know.

All he needed to know was exactly what the target looked like. And that face was smiling up at him from his sleeve.

He'd studied numerous close-up photographs in the past month, memorizing every feature. Luckily, the target, due to his reddish complexion, had an easily recognizable face, one that would make his job much easier. Given the enormous magnification power of the new scope, he was not anticipating any difficulty once the target stepped outside the sandbag redoubts surrounding the base camp.

"Soldiers emerging from the redoubts," Khalid said quietly to his companion, the binoculars held to his eyes.

One hour after sunrise, six British soldiers had suddenly emerged from the camp. They moved slowly and began to spread out carefully. One of their number had lost two limbs the previous week when he'd stepped on a Taliban mine. Although the perimeter of the camp was swept almost continuously, it was the old Soviet-era mines that usually caused British casualties.

Khalid, sighted in on a troop, stopped breathing during that natural pause that comes between inhalation and exhalation. He extended the breath pause from the normal three seconds to ten seconds. This was his window and now it was wide open. He began moving the scope in minute increments from face to face among the soldiers, looking for the handsome red-cheeked boy.

No. No. No.

Yes.

Target acquired, he was relaxed, nearing his ten count, the stock welded to his cheek. He applied gentle pressure to the trigger as he centered the reticules carefully, bisecting the face of his target . . . and began the slow squeeze . . .

Khalid's expertly trained finger never finished pulling that trigger. His head exploded into a fine mist of blood, gristle, and bone and his body was thrown violently back against the stone face of the mountain wall behind him.

Smith, drenched in the sniper's blood, looked back at his grisly remains in shock. What the hell? He raised his binoculars and looked down to the valley. No shooters, no one looking up in his direction. Where had the shot come from? What the hell was this? Good God! He had to get out of here, now! He scrambled on hands and knees along the ledge behind the rock all the way down to the cave opening.

Inside the mouth of the cave, the two horses waited patiently.

He mounted the faster of the two, a fine Arabian the Sheik had ordered to be given him, spurred the animal's flanks, and headed toward the rear of the cave at a trot, the wavering beam of his flashlight illuminating the dark tunnel.

The cave he'd so carefully chosen was not a cave at all. Although, from the rough wooden-beamed exterior, it looked exactly like the countless others in these mountains.

The cave was actually a half-mile-long tunnel.

It had been built by the Taliban fighters for moments precisely like this one, when emergency escape from imminent attack by enemy forces was necessary. The tunnel had taken more than a year to complete. It burrowed all the way through the rugged mountain. At the other end, another anonymous cave mouth overlooked an entirely different valley.

He knew air support was being called in; it was happening now. USAF F-15Es would be streaking up and down this valley looking for Taliban on the run after the failed assassination attempt on Prince Harry. And troops from the Blues and Royals regiment would be racing up the mountainside in search of the dead sniper and any other enemy combatants who'd run for cover.

Eventually, they would find the corpse outside the cave where Khalid's horse remained, waiting for his dead master's return. But they would not find this entrance to the tunnel, carefully hidden for decades at the extreme rear of this deep cave. He reached it, reined in his horse, and dismounted.

Smith cursed himself as he pulled at the small boulders, clearing away an opening large just enough to accommodate horse and rider. He remounted the stallion and rode through the hole he'd made into the semi-darkness, the distant opening on the other side of the mountain soon visible as a tiny wavering disc of sunlight far ahead.

He'd made two very stupid mistakes. He'd not counted on the enemy spotters and snipers possibly surveilling the mountains above the camp with exactly the same powerful sniper scope and weapon Khalid had been using!

Unforgivable.

And, two, in his haste he'd left the very latest English sniper weapon available beside the dead sniper's body. Virtually impossible for anyone outside the British military to acquire. And yet this dead Taliban fighter had one, and they would assume he knew how to use it.

An English gun. An extremely rare and unusual weapon that could only have come from an English source. They could never trace it to him, of course. How could they? Still, it was a grievous lapse of judgment.

But now, for the first time in all these years of immaculate success, he'd left behind a bloody clue. He knew enough about clues to know that even one could be fatal. Especially with the full force of both British intelligence services arrayed against him.

He emerged into the hard light, dug his spurs into his horse's flanks, and raced toward the safety of Sheik al-Rashad's compound. Just four days ago, he and Khalid had decamped for the mountains above Tangin, supremely confident and sure of success.

As he galloped down and through the narrow valley, he took stock of his situation. He had always thought of himself, when he thought of himself, as a kind of magician. Or, better still, a composer. Yes, exactly that. A conductor orchestrating his own composition, a complex design he had been weaving since childhood, its dark threads, its potent symbols; all those myriad strands of his existence that required the dexterity of a true virtuoso in order to keep flowing.

This mistake, this frayed strand threatened everything; all of his meticulous plans now needed to be accelerated before they unraveled completely. He needed to step back and take a serious look at the fabric of his life. Hit the reset button. Make certain no more missteps were made in these few remaining weeks culminating in his ultimate objective. He could ill afford the one mistake he'd just made.

Still, perhaps the one, but no more.

FORTY-SEVEN

LONDON

Hawke and Sahira, delayed by traffic, arrived at the nurses' station a little after seven in the evening. Visitors' Hours ended at eight, so they would still have more than enough time for a visit.

"Lord Malmsey, please," Hawke said.

"Just one moment," the starchy nurse said, peering up at him over the tops of her silver-framed glasses. He must have passed muster because she was calling up the approved visitor register on her computer screen. "Your names?"

They gave them.

Just prior to the hospital visit, the two had enjoyed an early dinner at Tamarind in Mayfair, Hawke's favorite Indian restaurant. Sahira was dressed in black, a silk suit with white pearls at her neck, having attended three funerals that afternoon. In the soft light, he'd watched the burden of grief lift from her shoulders as the first scotch smoothed the rough edges off the day.

There had been no shortage of things to talk about. Sahira told Hawke the details of the river-based attack on MI5 and Hawke had given her a blow-by-blow account of storming an IRA safe house in

Northern Ireland called the Barking Dog. He kept his tale brief. He was more interested in an eyewitness account of the brazen attack on MI5 in central London. The message the terrorists had delivered that day was plain enough: all bets are off.

"Thank God you weren't hurt, Sahira," Hawke said when she finished, reaching across the table to cover her hand with his. An expression of genuine concern flickered across his face. And in that brief moment, despite all else, she knew that, at the very least, this man cared.

She looked at the big hand covering hers, smiled at his simple gesture of protection, and said, "Alex, what still rankles is how brazen it was. As if these damn people woke up, looked at each other, and said, 'Nothing on today, mates, let's sail up the river and blow up MI5.' Terrorism *works,* Alex. The people of London are *terrified.* That something like this could occur in broad daylight, on a bastion of British—"

"Very few alive remember the Blitz," Hawke said mildly.

"I suppose not."

"It's going to get much worse," Hawke said, "based on what your intelligence analysts decrypted in the computers we found at the IRA safe house."

"Yes, much worse." She thought for a moment and added, "It's amazing more of us weren't killed. There are two thousand people working at Thames House. We suffered seven deaths and thirty-two wounded. You know, it's so odd the way things work sometimes. Just ten minutes before the attack, Lord Malmsey asked that I come up to his office."

"Yes?"

"He's never done that before. I'm always summoned from on high by some anonymous secretary to some anonymous conference room. At any rate, he asked for an update on our latest IRA investigations and I gave him what I had, which, prior to your amazing discoveries in Ireland, was hardly substantial. He stood at the window with his back to me, gazing down at the river. I made some silly small talk and took the lift back down to my floor. Had I remained in his office another five minutes it could be me in that hospital room tonight, not him."

"Or both of you."

"Yes, I suppose you're right. He's lucky to be alive, you know. A razor-sharp shard of flying glass from his window sliced open the side of his neck, ear to chin. Nicked an artery. Were it not for Five's own first responders, he'd have bled out right there on his own office carpet."

"LORD MALMSEY IS JUST DOWN that long corridor on your left," the senior nurse said. "Near the end. You'll see two detectives outside his door. They know you're coming."

"How's his lordship faring?" Sahira asked.

"As well as can be expected. There are many others here, also wounded in the attack, who are not doing nearly so well. And those poor others who—"

"Thank you," Hawke said to the nurse, taking Sahira's arm and steering her down the hallway.

When they entered Lord Malmsey's room, they found Montague Thorne standing at the man's bedside, the two men engrossed in a quiet conversation in the dim light of a bedside lamp. Catching a glimpse of Hawke and Sahira, Thorne turned to greet them.

"Good evening," Thorne said with his warm smile. "I was just saying good-bye to our hero here. On my way out, actually."

Hawke shook his hand and said, "Monty. Please stay if you can. We're here to give Lord Malmsey an update on what we found in those laptops at the safe house."

"When did you return, Alex?" Thorne asked.

"About twelve hours ago. I wanted to be present when the army intel group interrogated some of the Arab terrorists as well as the IRA chaps who survived our assault on the safe house."

The smile on Thorne's face froze. "Did you say *Arab* terrorists? In Northern Ireland?"

"Yes."

"But, my God, that simply does not make any sense."

"Actually, the way these terror groups are forming unlikely international alliances against us, I was surprised not to find a few North Koreans or Venezuelans scattered among their number."

"Yes. At any rate, splendid job up there. No sign of our mysterious Mr. Smith, I don't suppose?"

"Apparently we just missed him."

"Rotten luck."

Sahira had gone to the foot of Malmsey's bed.

"Lord Malmsey, how are you feeling? You must be terribly tired. Shall we come back tomorrow morning?"

Lord Malmsey, whose entire neck was swathed in thick bandages, snorted, "After what Alex just told Monty? I should say not. Everyone please pull up a chair and gather round. Alex, would you mind telling the two distinguished gentlemen outside my room to close that door and let no one enter, no one at all, including doctors or nurses, for the next twenty minutes?"

"Yes, sir," Hawke said and stepped briefly out into the hallway to confer with the two detectives.

"Al Qaeda? In Northern Ireland?" Malmsey said. "The mind boggles."

"Extraordinary," Thorne said as Hawke returned and pulled up the last of the bedside chairs. "This is beginning to assume obscene proportions. In the decrypted analysis, Alex, any mention of this bastard Smith? The one who seems to be behind the threat to my old friend Charles and the two boys?"

"Yes, Monty. I'd hoped to find him inside. We found him all right, but inside the computers we took."

"We've got to stop this man, Alex. I'll do anything in my power to help you do so."

"Thank you, Monty, we can use all the help we can get at this point."

"Alex," Malmsey said, "my last report was you'd the house under surveillance. Trucks were coming and going, making deliveries, presumably weapons. Then what?"

Hawke told him, leaving out no pertinent details, except the run-in with Major Masterman and his subsequent mysterious disappearance. When he finished, Malmsey said, "The weapons cache. Were you able to determine the source?"

"Yes, by pawing through what remained after the explosion. The preponderance of weapons were out of Syria and Iran, sir. We also found old Stinger missiles, given by the Americans to the Taliban in the Soviet era."

Malmsey said, "Good Lord. And these Islamic terrorists you captured? What in hell are they doing in Ireland, for God's sake?"

"They slip in by way of Belfast Harbor, sir. Smuggled aboard merchant ships, tramp steamers, and the like. All young, all fresh and fervent, out of terror camps in northern Pakistan. Come to the aid of England's enemies in the struggle for justice."

"Al Qaeda? Taliban? Which?" Thorne asked.

"Both."

"Fighting side by side with IRA soldiers? It's incomprehensible."

"Indeed. One of the most astounding things we learned from the captured laptops was that, for want of a better phrase, some kind of super worldwide terror alliance has formed around their common enemy. I wouldn't be surprised to find Chavez or the Castro brothers, any enemy of the West, sending fighters to join their growing number. They see us as weak, tired of war, and they believe the time to strike has come. Look at America's southern border. It's not just Mexicans entering illegally. Every month hundreds of Iranians, Syrians, Yemeni, and North Koreans are caught by the Border Patrol."

"They have a name?"

"Sword of Allah. You'll recall we first heard that name from the group that claimed credit for the Terminal Four bombing. After years of infighting, the warlords in Afghanistan and Pakistan have united under one leader, identity currently unknown. But it is quite possible he has usurped the now impotent Osama bin Laden, now believed to be hiding in Tehran."

"To what end? Could you extract that level of intelligence from the enemy computers?" Montague asked, staring at Hawke.

"Yes, Monty, all exchanges have been successfully decrypted by the team at Five. These people are bent on *ummah,* a worldwide caliphate. The global domination of Islam. And they are ramping up for major attacks both here and in the United States. We're already seeing them here, of course, with the attacks on Heathrow, and now MI5. In the States, they've claimed credit for the hospital attack in Miami, and, more recently, the death of forty innocent schoolchildren in Pennsylvania at the hands of a suicide bomber."

"Despicable," Montague Thorne said.

"We found a video, sir, which has not yet been released. MI5 is currently trying to determine when it was made and where."

"What does it contain?"

"A hooded terrorist. Four more standing behind him with AK-47s. He's got a sword at the neck of one of the two female British tourists who mistakenly entered Iran some time ago. Innocent schoolteachers from Dorset who were tried and convicted as spies."

"What does he say?"

"Nothing, in the beginning. He simply decapitates the poor woman. The corpse is dragged away and replaced by the second woman, who is obviously hysterical and made to kneel. He places the knife at her throat and makes a brief speech in Urdu, which we've just translated. He says, and I'll paraphrase, that this is the fate suffered by all nonbelievers at the hands of Sword of Allah. The killing will continue until every last member of Western military personnel has left every last acre of sacred Arab soil. Then he looks into the camera as he raises his sword above the woman's head and says, 'We're waiting. But our patience is not infinite.' "

"And then he kills her," Sahira said.

"Bloody barbarians," Montague Throne said, shaking his head.

"There's more, sir," Sahira added. "We've identified those responsible for the attack on Thames House."

"Good work. How'd you manage that so quickly?"

"The terrorists themselves aided in our investigation. The mortars and the explosive device aboard the barge were delivered downriver by a hired truck. Whoever was driving the truck returned it to the agency to pick up his security deposit. On the off chance that he might just be stupid enough to do exactly that, the Metropolitan Police were waiting for him when he showed up."

"IRA, I suppose?"

"No, sir. Sword of Allah. All homegrown. Pakistani. And every one of them had a prison record. Petty theft, housebreaking. But they were converted to radical Islam while in prison, sir. It is absolutely epidemic. Both here and in America."

"One more thing and then we'll leave you in peace, sir," Hawke said. "There were two names that kept popping up in the preponderance of the Internet communications. You'll recognize the first from our meeting at Highgrove."

"Tell me."

"Smith, as I mentioned earlier."

Thorne exploded. "Smith? Good God. The man whom Congreve suspects of murdering Mountbatten."

"The same."

"And threatening the Prince of Wales," Thorne added.

Hawke said, "Yes. The 'Pawn' as he styles himself. I hoped to find him inside that safe house. And I did, in a manner of speaking. Encrypted in those salvaged laptops. Whoever he is, he is playing this game at the very highest levels. There was even an extremely angry exchange between this Smith and an IRA lieutenant over his failure in the attempt to murder Chief Inspector Congreve and me en route to Highgrove."

"You must be joking," Thorne said, incredulous.

"Astounding," Malmsey said.

"To say the very least," Hawke replied. "But let me assure you, sir, that I will run this fellow to ground and I will kill him before any harm befalls the Royal Family, or he kills me."

The room fell silent.

"And the second name, Alex? Scimitar?"

"Scimitar code name, obviously. We've no idea who he is at this point, but we will find out. That I can promise you, sir."

"Thank you all for coming," Malmsey said, his voice weary. "I'd say, despite the enormity of the challenges facing us, we're making good progress."

"But time is of the essence," Thorne said. "I'd like to put myself and all my resources at MI6 at your disposal, Lord Malmsey. Working together, in full cooperation, we just might crack this thing sooner rather than later."

"Your offer is both appreciated and accepted, Monty. Thank you."

"Good night, sir. Get well soon," Hawke said, getting to his feet.

Thorne and Sahira followed Hawke out into the corridor, leaving the director general of MI5 alone with his troubled thoughts. He'd always been on the hot seat. Somehow, he needed to find a way to get off.

Lord Malmsey's carefully ordered world seemed to be coming apart at the seams. Spinning out of control and there didn't seem to be a damn thing he could do about it. He reached over to his night table and buzzed the nurses' station. He told the duty nurse he wanted to see his doctor first on the morning rounds. He needed out of here, and he needed out now.

FORTY-EIGHT

INTERNATIONAL WATERS

STOKELY JONES TOLD HARRY BROCK HE needed a damn break right this minute. Harry silently nodded yes, and the two of them went up on deck to talk things over. The little guy down in the owner's stateroom wasn't going anywhere. He was tied to the chair, his wrists tightly bound behind him with, ouch, dental floss, a trick Stoke had learned with VC captives back in the shit.

Right about now, little Yoda down there was praying for a one-way ticket to paradise. But Stoke had no intention of letting this murderous child-killing bastard keep his hot date with seventy-two virgins.

"Martyr, my ass," Stoke had told Yoda right off. "This is America, asshole. Unlike you, we don't kill noncombatants. You're going to spend what's left of your sorry life in a prison that makes Abu Ghraib and Gitmo look like Mr. Roger's Neighborhood."

Cool salt air smelling faintly of iodine stung Stoke's eyes when he stepped out on deck. After the stink of sweat and cigarette smoke in the small, airless cabin below, it felt good just to breathe again. How long had they been at it, he wondered, looking at his watch. Three damn hours.

He'd grown weary of interrogating an arrogant man who'd blown up a hospital full of doctors, nurses, and sick people; more recently he had caused the deaths of nearly two hundred innocent schoolchildren in a series of school bus bombings—and showed not a trace of remorse for any of it. A man whose only regret was that he'd been stopped before he could kill more kids. A man who'd prefer to die rather than betray his religion of death.

These effing people were certifiable, no doubt about it. They were making babies faster than anybody else on the whole planet, then teaching them how to hate. And kill anybody who disagreed with them.

Great, huh?

Future's so bright, I got to wear shades.

"Good cop, bad cop thing? Just ain't working, Harry," Stoke finally said, hands on the varnished teak railing. He willed himself to relax, eyes gazing out over the deeply rolling swells of the blue Atlantic, ruffled whitecaps marching away to the horizon. The boat they were on, *Maiden Voyage,* a weather-beaten and barnacle-encrusted sixty-foot Viking sport-fishing boat, was a blind CIA charter out of Cracker Boy Marine over at Grove Key marina.

Stoke had four lines out, two from the outriggers and two off the stern. They were slowly moving south at idle speed, the helm on autopilot. Fishermen. Nobody would bother them.

Earlier, Stoke had taken *Maiden Voyage* through Government Cut into the Atlantic and out to a preset GPS waypoint beyond U.S. territorial waters. He'd deliberately established his destination four miles outside the United States' twelve-nautical-mile limit, just to be on the safe side. He was now in international waters, a good place to have unpleasant conversations like the one they were having with the imam from the Glades prison.

The terror kingpin's real name was Azir al-Wazar. Probably Arabic for Wizard of Oz, Stoke thought, and started calling the guy "Ozzie" just to piss him off.

"Got a better idea?" Harry said, lighting up a fresh unfiltered Camel. He'd stubbed the last one out in the little guy's left ear. Harry being Harry as usual, he only smoked on certain very special social occasions. Like rendition.

"Yeah, I got one, Harry. Bad cop, bad cop."

"I like it."

"Ozzie won't like it."

"Screw Ozzie. He murders schoolchildren on school buses, remember that little tidbit? Three buses in three states in the last three weeks. How many of our kids does he get to kill before we can, you know, really *torture* the dickhead?"

"Really pisses me off waterboarding is no longer politically correct," Stoke said. "I miss it already."

"Hopeless nostalgia, man, wasted energy. Listen. I saw a pair of really rusty pliers at the bait station back there in the stern. We could pull his goddamn tongue out, right? Put a big fish hook in it first and then yank—"

"Then he couldn't talk at all, Harry."

"Good point."

"You need your tongue to talk."

"Yeah, yeah, yeah. Whatever."

Stoke saw a baby dolphin suddenly surface about six feet away and then dive under the bow of boat, playing with them, surfacing on the other side before coming around again.

"I think I just got an idea," he said, smiling at Harry for the first time all afternoon.

"Spit it out. Look on your face, it's a really good one."

"Old navy tradition. Really old. Been around since the year 1560. But off the books for centuries so I doubt any of our more ladylike congressmen have passed any goddamn laws against it."

"Yeah? What is it?"

"Follow me," Stoke said heading aft for the stern cockpit where the big chrome fishing chair was and all the fishing gear was stowed. He did some quick mental calculations: the boat's beam; the draft. "C'mon, I'll show you how it works."

Harry flicked his smoke overboard, followed Stoke aft, and watched him opening hatch covers in the wide transom until he found the right one, a rope locker. He pulled out two big coils of thick white nylon line, each about thirty feet long, Harry guessed. Stoke quickly tied them together in a manner that suggested prior nautical experience.

Harry said, "Tie him up? With that? Whoa. But, yeah, very cool idea."

"Not tie him up, Harry."

"What then?"

"Go get his sorry ass. I'll show you right now."

Harry was back at the stern with Yoda in about five minutes. Boat was rocking pretty good in these big swells, and the Wizard was looking green about the gills. Shaky. Too bad they'd run out of Dramamine.

"Want to talk now, Ozzie?" Stoke asked him, leaning down until their noses were almost touching.

"How does one say 'go fuck yourself' in English?" he replied with his elfin smile. "Oh. I remember now. Go fuck yourself."

"Easy. Say it again, just one more time, and then try to say it without any teeth."

"There is no God but God," the imam smirked, and repeated his mantra for the hundredth time that day. His idea of name, rank, and serial number. This little dick was really getting on Stoke's nerves. He'd murdered, or caused to be murdered, nearly two hundred innocent American schoolchildren. And no one could legally lay a hand on him.

Stoke said, "Not what I had in mind, sportin' life." He backhanded the guy across the chops, rattling his teeth.

"One-track mind," Harry said, shaking his head in mock disgust.

"Cut his hands loose," Stoke said, fed up.

"Loose? Really? Why?"

"Just do it. He's going to need his hands."

"Just do it, Harry," Ozzie said, mimicking Stoke's accent and holding his hands up to be freed.

Harry did it. As he turned away, the crazy little killer took a swing at him. Harry laughed and swatted his fist away as if disposing of an annoying fly. "Listen up, pal," Brock said to him. "You fuck with a truck, you get run over."

"You mean . . . like the World Trade towers?"

Harry quickly turned his back to the imam, unwilling to give him the satisfaction of seeing the blazing anger in his eyes. As calmly as he could, he said to Stoke, "How about we just cut him into bite-sized pieces and feed him to the sharks?"

Stoke just stared back at Brock, so angry with the radical Muslim he didn't trust himself to speak.

As a result, neither man saw the terrorist snatch the fish knife from the bait station, lift up his prison garb orange shirt, and stick the blade inside his elastic waistband.

"Now what?" Brock said after a few long moments.

"We tie this line around his waist. Loop it around a couple of times. Okay, good. Now, nice and tight. He goes right in the middle. Need about twenty feet of line on either side of him."

"What the—"

"Trust me. Do it. Good. Oh, hold up, one more thing."

Stoke opened a locker full of scuba gear, dug through it, and pulled out a lead-weighted diver's belt. He cinched it good and tight around the guy's waist and tied the two ends of the nylon belt in a square knot.

"Perfect. Now we walk him forward to the bow. Ozzie? You cool with this? Good man."

Harry grabbed one end of the line and marched toward the bow. Stoke had the other end, bringing up the rear, Yoda in the middle, going along to get along.

"Now what?" Harry said, as they stood at the bow pulpit where the anchor was. Stoke grabbed the little guy by his scrawny neck and lifted him high above his head. Then he stepped out onto the pulpit projecting out from the bow.

"Okay, this is the good part. I'm just going to swing him around a little, like this, called the 'helicopter,' and then throw him in the ocean. Right off the front of the bow . . . Like that!"

"Cool!" Harry exclaimed, watching the guy splash down, disappear, and come up floundering, slapping the water to try and stay afloat; Harry was beginning to like this idea more and more.

"Pull him around to your side. Walk aft with the line. I'll ease my line to give you enough slack to do it. Don't let him sink."

"Why not?"

Stoke eased his line and went over to the opposite side of the boat, slowly feeding Harry some slack, the line disappearing under the boat, pulling his own end beneath the keel of the big Vike.

"Because that's not how you do this, Harry. Keep him afloat with your end of the line until I get over here in position. Okay, this is good right here." Stoke had stopped just forward of the wheelhouse, just about amidships.

"What the hell do we do now?"

"Keelhaul his ass. Just like the good old days. I bet nobody's done this in two hundred years. Maybe more."

"How does it work?"

"Hold on, let me tie my end to the railing over here."

Stoke did and then crossed over to Harry's side. He leaned way out over the starboard rail and saw Ozzie bobbing there, kept afloat by Harry's line.

"Here's a question, Ozzie," Stoke said. "Answer it and I'll think about not drowning you. Ready?"

"Ready," the terrorist said, nodding his head violently. Good sign. Some people just weren't comfortable out in the open seas with a life jacket made out of lead.

"Found a name in your computer, homes. Popped up a lot in fact. Somebody named Smith. Who the hell is Smith? You have ten seconds."

The guy shook his head no.

"Sink him," Stoke said. Harry eased his line and the little guy dropped like a rock. They both watched his bubbles for a minute or so.

"Okay, bring him up."

He popped to the surface, sputtering.

"Second question," Stoke said, bending over the rail. "Ready? Good. Another name that seemed to keep coming up in your electronic correspondence. A Sword of Allah bigwig code-named *Scimitar.* Tell me who he is and you can come back up."

"There is no God but God."

"Wrong answer. This time it's going to be a little tougher, okay, Ozzie?"

"What now?" Harry said. Stoke crossed back to the opposite port rail and untied his end of the line.

"We keelhaul him, that's what. There are two ways to do this. The bad way, and the really bad way."

"Talk to me."

"I'm going to pull him all the way under the boat's keel with my end of the line. Slowly. You feed me enough slack so that he just clears the bottom of the boat."

"And the really bad way?"

"You don't cut him any slack. That way, when I pull, he gets his ass bounced and scraped along about ten or twelve feet of really nasty, razor-sharp barnacles."

"Sounds unpleasant."

"Yeah. Do not try this one at home. Do it enough times and Ozzie won't have much skin left. First time, give him slack. We'll see what happens."

Stoke pulled on his end. The imam went down and disappeared under the boat on Harry's side, Brock feeding Stoke line. Stoke took his time reeling him in, looking at the sweep second hand on his watch, waiting to see the little bastard reappear in the water just below him.

He brought him up, sputtering and cursing.

"I'm going to wait until you finish throwing up all that seawater and ask you again. I don't want to alarm you, but all that splashing you're doing attracts sharks. Ready? Two names. Smith. And Scimitar."

"There is no God but—" He disappeared beneath the waves before he got it all out.

"Haul him back under, Harry. No slack this time."

"Fast or slow?"

"What do you think?"

Brock started slowly hauling away, singing a few bars of "Barnacle Bill, the Sailor."

FORTY-NINE

THEY HAULED HIM ABOARD AND STRETCHED him out on the teak foredeck. He was pretty bloody and chopped up from the barnacles. And, by the time Stoke reeled him in, the imam had experienced the thrill of ravenous sharks nipping at his heels because of all the blood in the water. Even now the sharks were circling the boat, looking for fresh meat. "Called keelhauling, Ozzie," Stoke said, "predates the Geneva Conventions by four hundred years. It's a bitch, ain't it?"

Stoke now took the freshwater wash-down hose and cleaned him up a little. Then they took him aft and sat him in the big chrome fishing chair. The imam sat there like a dazed and bloodied Neptune on his nautical throne, staring into space, his protruding eyes wide with real terror.

He now realized these two animals were capable of anything. This was not quite true, Stoke thought, but it was definitely the right impression to convey under the circumstances.

Stoke popped a cold Diet Coke snatched from the big cooler full of ice and underhanded Harry a frosty Bud. Both men sat on the gunwales and sipped their drinks, content to watch the dolphins play and let the imam think things over before they went back to work on him. About ten minutes later, having duly considered his situation, Ozzie started singing like a canary on crack.

"Smith," he croaked, his chin resting on his chest.

"Yeah, what about him?" Stoke said, looking up.

"Englishman. In Afghanistan."

"Okay, I'll bite. What's this Englishman doing in Afghanistan?"

"Assassination."

Stoke stood up and pulled a black leather notepad and pencil from his shirt pocket, then walked over and lifted the guy's chin up with his beard.

"Assassination of who?"

"Harry."

"Harry's not in Afghanistan. Harry's right here."

"No. Prince Harry. Son of Prince Charles."

Stoke looked back at Harry Brock who mouthed the words, *Ho-ly Shit!*

"Harry. That's the son who's serving in the British Army? Right?" Brock asked the prisoner.

"Yes."

"I thought he was in Iraq."

"No. Afghanistan."

"When is the attempt on his life?" Stoke said.

"Most imminent."

"You telling us the truth? If you're not, you're going right back under the boat. As many times as it takes."

"Truth. God's truth."

"Harry, on the off chance the little bastard really is telling the truth, you want to go get on the radio and call this in to Langley? Pentagon? This intel needs to get to the CO of the British Army forces in Afghanistan right now."

"You're right," Harry said, leaping to his feet and disappearing inside the wheelhouse.

"Okay, little buddy," Stoke said, pencil poised, "one more. Who the hell is this Scimitar I keep seeing?" The imam, who looked like a guy who'd just climbed out of a bathtub full of piranhas, gave Stoke the evil eye.

"He is known in my country as the Lion of the Punjab. His name is Sheik Abu al-Rashad."

"Sheik Abu al-Rashad. Good boy. I've heard that name. How high up? In the Sword of Allah organization?"

"Most high."

"High as you can go? Higher than bin Laden?"

"Yes."

"Where do I find this high and mighty Sheik?"

"Pakistan. Sometimes Afghanistan. Always on the move."

"Nomad, huh?"

"Precisely so. He travels light. Cave to cave, camp to camp."

"Where is he now?"

"Islamabad, I think."

"Where in Islamabad?"

"Hospital."

"Sick? Injured? Which hospital?"

"Don't know. That is the truth, I swear it."

Stoke grabbed his beard and lifted his face so that the guy was staring directly into Stoke's deadly serious eyes.

Nada.

"Okay, fine. On your feet. You're going scuba diving again without the scuba. See all those sharks swimming around the boat? They can't wait to see your bloody carcass back in the water."

"No! No!"

"All right. Take it from the top, one more time. What. Is. The. Name. Of. The. Hospital?"

"Quaid-e-Azam International Hospital."

"Spell it. Nice and slow," Stoke said, and copied it down letter for letter.

"You're absolutely sure about this hospital? I can go google it right now on my laptop."

"I speak the truth."

"We'll see about that. Where does this guy typically hang out when he's not in the hospital?"

"Mountains."

"Which mountains? You got some pretty serious peaks in Pakistan, right? Like, that's where K2 is, correct? Second-tallest mountain in the world."

"No. K2 is on the Chinese border with Pakistan. He's mostly in the mountains near Chitral. North-West Frontier Province. Malakand District. Where we fought Winston Churchill in 1885."

"Any particular mountain?"

"Yes."

"Does it have a name?"

"Wazizabad."

"Waz-iz-a-bad. Is that it?"

"Yes."

Stoke thrust the pad and pencil into his hands. "Draw me a map. Just rough. Put a black X where this Wazizabad mountain is, got that?"

The imam started drawing. He was actually a pretty good little artist, once he got into it. Had a horizon line, perspective, the whole deal.

Harry Brock stuck his head out the door.

"Hey, Stoke, you should come in here."

"I'm busy."

"I got through to the director at Langley, delivered the news. Now Alex Hawke is on the radio, patched through out here by the CIA station chief Miami. Says it's urgent."

"Hawke?" Stoke couldn't believe his ears.

"You heard me."

"Ozzie, you sit tight, buddy. I'll be right back. This is a fascinating conversation, so don't take this as an insult. Bossman on the phone, you know how that goes. Harry, will you babysit this badboy while I'm gone?"

—

"HEY, BOSS," STOKE SAID, PUTTING on the headphones and pushing the send button on the transmitter. "You're back! Man, it is great to hear your voice! You sound good."

"I am indeed, Stoke, but not surprisingly I need your help."

"Say the word. Where are you?"

"Cannons to the right, cannons to the left. I seem to be stuck in the middle. I'm in London now, but headed out to Pakistan. Like, yesterday. Urgent business requires my presence. Islamabad."

"What can I do?"

"I want you to be ready to go when I go. Start now. I'm going to need you over there. Things could get spicy fast. C wants me to ensure that all the Pakistani nukes are locked down. As you know, the local Pak government is not fond of us snooping around in their backyard. We'll be going in under the radar, needless to say."

"Boss, I was just there six months ago. Doing a small job for Brock, organizing transfers of F-34 aviation fuel to some supersecret U.S. airbase. F-34 is the stuff those Predator missile drones burn. Anyway, I got to know the town and some of the locals pretty well. I know one thing: don't trust a word the Pakistani Army generals tell you. Half of them are Taliban sympathizers. And the other half are on the fence."

"It's going to be tricky, all right. Your knowledge of the locals is a huge bonus, Stoke. Is Brock with you on that boat?"

"Yes, he is."

"You know how I feel about Harry. Always ready to give a helping hand to a man on a ledge a little higher up."

"I agree completely. We're in the same boat, so to speak."

"Sometimes I think he has the moral compass of a piece of driftwood. He could be useful to us, however. Good in a firefight. Do you agree? Your call."

"Yeah, we could use him all right. At least when he tells you he's got your back, he doesn't plan to stick a knife in it."

"Right. Tell him I'll be in touch with you guys the minute I've got a departure date scheduled. Be ready to roll at a moment's notice. Anything interesting going on aboard that fishing boat?"

"Yeah. We're interrogating a guy I met in prison. He's full of information and so was his laptop, some of it possibly true. Lot of chatter about the bombing at Heathrow, the attack on MI5 headquarters, et cetera. You ever heard of somebody named Smith?"

There was a long silence at Hawke's end of the line.

"Smith? Yes. I have definitely heard of him. What have you got?"

"Our guy says Smith's in Afghanistan right now. Aiming to kill the heir to the throne of England. Harry, the son of Prince Charles. You believe that?"

"I do now. I was just informed of an attempt on Prince Harry's life this morning. It failed. The sniper was killed and an accomplice escaped. Thanks to you, I now know who the accomplice was. Our friend Mr. Smith. And it makes sense of the fact that the shooter used the highly classified long-range British sniper rifle left at the scene."

"Sounds to me like you got a big hole in your bucket, boss, kinda leaks you're talking about."

"We certainly do. This intel is invaluable, Stoke, thank you. This Smith character must have connections at the highest levels of Britain's government. And he is deeply involved with Sword of Allah. One of our immediate tasks is to run him down."

"Sword of Allah took down Jackson Memorial Hospital here in Miami. It's the Sword that's blowing up school buses all over America. Another thing we found? About twenty radicalized homegrowns from a southside mosque in Chicago were all set to take down New Trier High School with AK-47s and suicide bomb belts. Almost five thousand kids in that school could have died. You believe that? FBI rounded up the killers just two days before they would have done it too."

"Appalling. We're dealing with the world's first, highly organized, megaterror group, Stoke. Recruiting and training in prisons. Forming allegiances with the IRA and the Communist governments in Cuba and Venezuela. Possibly the North Koreans, and God knows who else. Our job is to find and cut off the head so the body will die."

"I have more on them, boss. My songbird says the top dog in the entire Sword organization is somebody named Abu al-Rashad. Code-named Scimitar in all the encrypted Internet communications. I even think I might know where he is at the moment. In the Quaid-e-Azam hospital in Islamabad, sick or wounded, I don't know which."

"He was right about the assassination attempt on Prince Harry in Afghanistan. You've got him scared enough to start telling the truth. Good work. See what else you can get out of him. Whatever it takes."

"Will do."

"Please tell me, God forbid, you're not waterboarding this guy, Stoke. Politically incorrect in Washington, you know, even when the fate of the whole goddamn planet is at stake."

"Me? Waterboard? C'mon, boss, you know I'd never stoop that low."

"Stoke, I'll call you back in exactly one hour. I need to convey every word you just said to the directors of both MI5 and MI6. Stay near that radio."

Click.

Then Stoke heard Harry Brock cursing and screaming in pain.

WHEN STOKE STEPPED BACK OUT into the blazing sun, he saw Harry Brock clutching his gut, blood spurting between his fingers and pooling on the deck.

"He's got a knife!" Harry said, his eyes on the little guy, backing away. "Fucker tried to kill me."

"You okay?" Stoke asked him.

"Not really."

"Looks like a flesh wound."

"Hurts like a bitch though, trust me."

"Harry. Pay attention. You get that map he drew?"

"Yeah, I got it, that's when he knifed me, handing it over."

The master terrorist was backed up against the transom at the stern, nowhere to go, waving the rusty fish knife around as if daring Stokely to try to take it away from him. Stoke told him to relax. Then he put both his hands in the air and started slowly toward him in as nonthreatening a fashion as a man his size was capable of.

"Ozzie, listen up, partner. You're fighting way outside your weight division. Flyweights should not get into the ring with heavy-weights, it's a well-known fact. Ask anybody."

He spat out something unprintable in Farsi or whatever.

"Just throw the knife down and no one else has to get hurt," Stoke said. "Drop it on the deck and—"

Screaming the now all-too-familiar Islamic war cry, "Allahu Akbar!" the terrorist charged Stokely, the bloody fish knife raised above his head. Stoke calmly waited for him to strike, then shot out a plate-size hand and vice-clamped al-Wazar's right wrist just as his knife hand started down, pivoted, yanking his arm violently enough to dislocate his shoulder.

In a single, fluid motion Stoke whirled completely around, still gripping the man's wrist, and flung Azir al-Wazar high into the air, whereupon he dropped into a frothing frenzy of the bloodthirsty sharks still circling about twenty yards off *Maiden Voyage*'s stern.

"Hey, Stoke," Harry said, taking a front-row seat on top of the bait box. His fist pressed deep into his flesh wound to stanch the bleeding, he was watching with some interest the flashing fins circling ever nearer to the screeching and wailing terrorist, now flapping about like a pregnant pelican trying desperately to get airborne.

"Yeah?"

"I think you forgot to inform our little buddy out there of his Miranda rights."

"Did I? Damn, I think you're right, Harry."

Stoke lumbered up onto the wide teak transom, cupped his hands around his mouth, and called out to the man in the water now boiling with his own blood, the man who'd just tried to kill him and his pal Harry.

In a loud, clear voice, Stoke said, "You have the right to remain silent. Anything you say or do can be used against you in a court of law. You have the right to an attorney. If you cannot afford an attorney, one will be appointed to you. Do you understand these rights as they have been read to you?"

Stoke heard only a very garbled response.

"What'd he say?" Brock asked.

"Hard to tell. If I had to guess, I'd say he's going to exercise his right to remain silent."

FIFTY

BUCKINGHAMSHIRE

BRIXDEN HOUSE, ANCESTRAL HOME to Lady Diana Mars, and countless forebears both illustrious, nefarious, and notorious, was off the Taplow Common Road. Hawke slowed for the entrance gate, a massive black iron affair topped with numerous large gilded eagles atop marble columns, the birds sufficiently weathered over the centuries as to be discreetly unobtrusive.

Hawke rolled his gleaming black 1956 Ford Thunderbird to a stop just outside the gates and waited for the plainclothes detective to come out of the small guardhouse. While the man checked their names against the guest list, Hawke was content to sit and listen to the sweet rumble of the automobile.

The car had proved a worthy stand-in for the battle-scarred Locomotive, still undergoing massive bodywork after being pummeled with bullets in the assassination attempt. The T-Bird, as he lovingly called it, had the removable hardtop and he'd left the top at home so he and Sahira could enjoy the early August sunshine.

It was clear and unseasonably cool, with late afternoon sunlight like great bars of gold, laying upon the green hills and valleys.

He particularly liked the vintage American car for the lean beauty of its lines, its snarling mouth, and the single flaring nostril of the air intake centered on its bonnet. He'd replaced the stock Ford engine with a huge, low-revving Mercury V-8 of five-liter capacity, and the result was rock-solid performance; the T-Bird was definitely not a precision instrument like a good English sports car, but he counted that a virtue.

"Dr. Karim, Commander Hawke, welcome to Brixden House," the Scotland Yard man said, smiling as he ticked their names off against their identification and the big iron gates swung inward. "I hope you enjoy your evening."

"I'm sure we will," Hawke said, returning the professional smile. He put the car in gear, accelerated, and turned to Sahira to say, "Welcome to the infamous den of spies. You'll feel right at home."

Hawke motored slowly up the long, meandering drive. Sahira seemed to be enjoying the view over vast acres of parklike grounds offering occasional glimpses of classical statuary, sloping green lawns, lakes, and one or two small Greek temples.

"I'm sorry. Did you say 'den of spies'?" she asked a few moments later.

"I did. This place will be full of them tonight, but that's not what I meant. Over the years, Brixden House acquired a very sketchy reputation—you've heard of the 'Brixden Set'?"

"Not really, no."

"In the prewar years, a circle formed around Diana's great-grandmother, the Viscountess. Brixden House became a de facto salon for a right-wing, aristocratic group of politically influential individuals. The Viscountess hosted splendid parties for her friends, which surely included hot- and cold-running Germans, some of them undoubtedly spies. This Germanophile cabal was not only in favor of the appeasement of Adolf Hitler, but also of promoting friendly relations with Nazi Germany."

"Fascinating," she said, her eyes on the magnificent Italianate palace standing atop great chalk cliffs overlooking a graceful bend in the gently flowing Thames. Dusk was near, and every window, large or small, was blazing with light.

"Ah, but the best was yet to come. The 'Swinging Sixties' brought fresh scandal to the house. It was apparently the scene of wildly decadent sex parties. Including the one where Cabinet Minister John Profumo met and bedded Christine Keeler. A woman who just happened to be simultaneously sleeping with a Soviet agent. Profumo went down in flames and so did Harold Macmillan's government."

Sahira smiled. "Well, you've certainly given me a gold mine of information for dinner table conversation."

"Diana wouldn't mind, I assure you. She's a splendid lady, feet on the ground, a woman who seldom lets anyone or anything bother her. Ambrose is a very, very lucky man to have found her."

"He is lucky, isn't he, Alex? So very lucky," Sahira said, a sudden sadness in her eyes. It was, he thought, a shared sadness for both of them.

EVERY ROOM WAS ALIGHT WITH CHANDELIERS, flaming candles, sparkling diamonds, and bubbling crystal flutes of pink champagne; clinking wineglasses, laughter, and music filled every room with sounds of honest joy for the happy couple. In a far corner, a society band flung Gershwin memories into the smoke and chatter.

Hawke and Sahira made their way through the crowded great hall, a splendid room with its grand fireplace, soaring ceiling, and the famous John Singer Sargent portrait of Diana's great-grandmother that hung to the left of the wide hearth. People would turn to smile in appreciation when they entered new rooms. Hawke and Sahira saw in their eyes the flattering reflection, as if the two of them were some kind of double Narcissus.

Hands touched jeweled arms over and under the white tables. Under the spell of music, the vivid gowns and starched white shirtfronts swayed together, a vibrant rhythm of dancers circulating in the semidarkness of the candlelit ballroom. Among the passive observers around the edge of the floor, suits of gleaming armor stood guard against walls hung with faded tapestries and large gilt-framed portraits of Lady Diana's long forgotten royal ancestry.

Countless searching eyes instantly shifted toward the exquisite Indian woman on Hawke's arm. Sahira looked resplendent in a simple sari of blazing crimson embellished with gold embroidery. It was the first time Hawke had ever seen her with her dark hair up, held in place by two golden combs, and he had to admit it only made her all the more alluring.

"Ready?" Hawke asked her, looking for an opening in the crowd. He'd seen Diana and Ambrose across the room, receiving guests by the fireplace. Having plucked two champagne glasses from the liveried steward, he moved in their direction.

"Cover me, I'm going in," Hawke said.

"Go for it, champ," Sahira said with a laugh.

Hawke assumed his tried-and-true "Marvelous to see you!" smile and waded in, Sahira happily in tow. As he excused and beg-pardoned his way through the writhing mass of plunging necklines, enormous gems dangling from swanlike, lily-white necks, all the distinguished gents in white ties and tails, he saw looks of utter astonishment of the normally reserved countenances of polite London Society. Why on earth? Then he remembered.

He'd been missing in action for well over a year. Most of these people, upon seeing his face, must have thought a ghost now walked among them. "Was that Alex Hawke? We heard he was dead."

He didn't see Sir David Trulove in the crowd until the man reached out and put a hand on his forearm. C leaned in close to Hawke's ear and said, "Good evening. Need to speak. Rather urgent, I'm afraid. Can you slip away and meet me in, say, twenty minutes? I'll be waiting at the far end of the south terrace, overlooking the parterre and the river."

"Splendid idea, sir," Hawke said in a normal voice. "I should be delighted. Sahira and I just want to say a quick hello to the host and hostess."

"Good," C said, and turned back to the extraordinarily beautiful American wife of the Ambassador to the Court of St. James.

It took a good ten minutes for them to wade in and reach Ambrose and Diana.

"I must say you're beaming like a full moon," Hawke said to Congreve, shaking his dear friend's hand. Ambrose had introduced Sahira to Lady Mars and the two women had immediately engaged in a cheery conversation about charities or some such.

"I must count myself among the happiest of men," Congreve said, smiling, using that stilted lofty tone he adopted when the champers kicked in.

"As well you should, you old dragon," Hawke said, clapping his friend on the back. "As well you should."

"You should have seen her face when I produced the fabled rock at last, Alex. I think she was beginning to doubt the honor of my intentions."

"How long has it been since you first dropped to your knees and begged for her hand? Years, I think."

"Too long. I desperately wish I'd met her in my thirties, instead of my fifties."

"Beware of desperate wishes," Hawke said, looking quickly away.

"Alex, I'm so sorry. Please forgive me."

Hawke brightened and said, "Nothing to forgive. It's going to be a splendid evening, and we're all going to live happily ever after. I just want you to know one thing, in case, well, anything should happen. All my life, since I was a boy, you have done more for me than any friend could ever ask. And I will always love you for it, until the day I die."

"Alex, I don't know what to say. I only wish—"

"Don't say anything. It's just something I wanted you to know. In case something should ever happen."

With that, Hawke took Sahira's hand, and the two of them disappeared into the brilliant crowd.

HAWKE FOUND C STANDING ALONE at the stone balustrade, gazing out at the formal gardens now catching the dying rays of the sun. The silvery Thames below, winding through the wooded hills, made it a sight well worth gazing at.

"Lovely view, isn't it?" Hawke said, joining him.

"Lovely. You know, Alex, I've been standing here reflecting on the events of the last few months. We've never been particularly close. We're both given to broadsides, and thus there's been a distance. But. I have endlessly marveled at your . . . your, what shall we call it, your resurrection. And I've come to the conclusion that you are one of the very few men on earth I shall always have utter and complete faith in."

"Well, sir, that's kind of—"

"No, no, I don't mean it in that way. The Service, thank heaven, is full of brilliant, talented, and courageous men and women who execute their dangerous duties at the very highest levels imaginable."

"How did you mean it, then, sir?"

"Trust. It seems that every time I meet with someone, issue an order, confide in them, question them, I find myself wondering, Is this the one? Is this the traitor in our midst?"

"I understand completely. But I think one has to look beyond the Service as well. Beyond both Six and Five. MI5 reports to the Home Secretary, Lord Hume, as you well know. Perhaps someone on staff there, privy to the Home Secretary's every secret, is on a payroll somewhere. Or someone at Number Ten Downing. Anywhere in government, in fact."

"Yes, yes, of course you're right. At any rate, it's not why I asked you to join me. I'm afraid there is terrible news from Pakistan. I got a call on the drive out here."

"A fundamentalist military coup?"

"No. Worse yet. As you well know, Pakistani president Asif Ali Zadari recently released 'national command authority' over Pakistan's nuclear arsenal to Prime Minister Gilani, who won't really have control either. The real control is now in the hands of the army.

General Kayani, his top three-star general. As you know, 'military secure' is not necessarily totally secure. Everyone and his brother in HM government have been worried about nuclear security should the mullahs take over the country. While I have been far more worried about all those senior officers in the Pakistan Army who are caliphates. Men at the top of the chain of Pakistani military command who believe in a fundamentalist pan-Islamic state. And now my worst fears have been realized."

"Tell me."

"It was the CIA chief of station in Islamabad who rang me in transit. At least one powerful nuclear device has gone missing from the Pakistani nuclear arsenal."

"My God. How?"

"The CIA, as Abdul Dakkon stated in my office, have long suspected that some of the guards in the Islamabad underground storage facility were on the payroll of one or two of the most powerful Taliban warlords. Or that other rival warlords were holding the guards' families under threat of death should they not comply with their demands when the time came to seize control of the arsenal."

"And now the warlords have decided to act with impunity because they no longer fear retribution from the Pakistani Army."

"Exactly. They are putting us to the test, awaiting our reaction. We need to show a forceful response immediately. I called President McCloskey and informed him of MI6's plan to send a team to Islamabad. He backed it fully and offered the cooperation of the U.S. Air Force and units of the Marines operating nearby in Afghanistan."

"I'm prepared to go, sir, tonight if necessary."

"I knew you'd say that. I'm booking military transport for you, Sahira Karim, and Abdul Dakkon. You'll land at Shamsi, a top-secret U.S. Air Force base in Pakistan, thirty miles from the Afghan border. It's used primarily for launching the Predator drone missiles that observe and attack al Qaeda and Taliban militants on the Pakistan side of the border with Afghanistan. South Waziristan. Your operation will be based at Shamsi Air Force Base with the full cooperation of the USAF, the CIA, and the Marine Corps."

"I'd no idea the Yanks even had a base in Pakistan."

"No one does. That's why this whole operation must be conducted with absolute secrecy throughout its execution. The idea that Washington, or London, are running military operations, covert or otherwise, from Pakistani territory is, well, a hugely sensitive issue in that predominantly Muslim country. Both U.S. and Pakistani governments deny Shamsi's very existence."

"I understand, sir."

"You'll be fully briefed tomorrow. Identification of the location and identity of the warlord in possession of that weapon is mission critical. You leave for Pakistan in forty-eight hours. Are you completely comfortable with your team?"

"I'd like to add two men, sir, both of whom would be invaluable to me in this operation."

"Who are they?"

"Both Americans. Stokely Jones, former U.S. SEAL, and a man named Harry Brock, CIA field agent."

"I've seen both names in your past reports. I wholly agree. I want you to have them and absolutely anything else you need to find this weapon, neutralize it, and bring whoever was responsible for this lapse in security to light."

"I'll do my best."

"I know you will. And that, Alex, has always been good enough for me."

FIFTY-ONE

SHAMSI AIR FORCE BASE, PAKISTAN

The mammoth C-130 Hercules transport touched down at 3:15 in the morning, local time, its four huge engines howling as the reverse thrusters kicked in. The pilot braked hard enough to make the smoking tires screech like wounded banshees. The C-130 normally requires five thousand feet of runway to operate. The short Shamsi landing strip, used primarily for launching Predator drones, didn't even come close. The USAF pilot, Captain Alex Hufty, had strained against his harness as the end of the tarmac hove into view.

Hufty had been dealing with a 25-mph crosswind, which certainly added to the excitement in the cockpit. He was rapidly running out of runway.

"Shit," Hufty said, stopping just one word shy of the universal word every pilot used when they realized they'd run out of luck and altitude at the same moment.

"Next stop, sand," he heard his copilot mutter while he struggled to land the behemoth with about five hundred feet of paved surface remaining. The airplane slammed down hard, bounced once or twice, rocked, shuddered, and, finally, was still.

In the frigid belly of the beast, Alex Hawke stood up, stretched, and gathered his gear as the ramp was lowered to the runway. He'd popped a couple of Ambien shortly after takeoff and, surprisingly, they'd worked. Surprising because he'd been sleeping on a thin foam sleeping mat, the only thing between him and the ice-cold aluminum floor at thirty thousand feet.

"Ladies and gentlemen," Hawke looked around at his team and said, "welcome to Pakistan. Please be careful removing items from the overhead bins, as items may have shifted in flight."

"Nice landing," Harry Brock grumbled, getting to his feet. "Sweet."

Hawke looked at him and forced a grin. "Harry, if that landing is the worst thing that happens to you or any of us in this godforsaken place, I will personally kiss your arse in the department store window of your choosing."

"What the fuck, Alex? I was just saying."

"And one more thing, Harry. I know your fondness for the thoroughly exhausted F-word knows no bounds. So here's the deal. You don't say it in front of the lady here, right? Find another four-letter word for the duration of this mission."

"Like what?"

"Cuss would work. Four letters. Means cursing."

"Cuss?"

"Yeah. Like 'What the cuss?' " Hawke said.

"Or, like, 'Cuss you, mothercusser,' " Stoke said, laughing.

"Exactly. Try that, okay, Harry?" Hawke said.

Harry, no slouch when it came to taking Alex Hawke's temperature, wisely decided to keep his mouth shut after that little exchange. Instead, he helped Sahira with her gear and then slung his own backpack over his shoulder. Brock and Sahira were the first to make their way down the wide ramp at the plane's tail, followed by Stokely Jones, Abdul Dakkon, and Hawke himself.

It was bone cold in the desert and the white stars in the blackness above the mountain range looked sharp enough to prick your finger.

There was a convoy waiting for them, six Pakistani army vehicles, including three troop carriers full of soldiers and an armored personnel carrier. All parked in formation about a hundred feet away. Heavily armed Pakistani Army soldiers had already formed a perimeter around the C-130, and others were guarding the convoy.

Indian territory, Hawke thought, gazing out at the distant mountain range.

A burly American officer, a colonel, and another officer, Pakistani, strode across the tarmac from the operations building standing next to a large hangar. Inside the brilliantly lit interior, Hawke saw two sleek F-16 Fighting Falcons. Pilots called them "Vipers" because they resembled viper snakes. But also in honor of the *Battlestar Galactica* starfighters. Techs were mounting various missiles, bombs, and pods under the fighter jet's wings. And another crew was rolling out a Predator missile drone for launch.

"Commander Hawke?" the American officer said, making it a question.

"I'm Hawke," Alex said, walking toward him.

"Welcome, Commander. I'm Colonel Kevin Balfe, United States Air Force. I'm the nonexistent CO here at this nonexistent air force base. This gentleman is Captain Mahmood Shah of the Pakistan Army, who will be in charge of getting you and your team safely to the quarters in Islamabad arranged by Mr. Dakkon."

"A pleasure, sir," Shah said, and Hawke shook hands with both men.

"Judging by our method of transportation, Captain Shah, we should be safe enough," Hawke said, looking at the convoy. He'd expected a couple of Toyota Land Cruisers or something similar. Apparently not.

"We will make every effort to convey you safely to your destination, Commander. All of the comms equipment, food, water, and weapons MI6 requested are in the last truck. My men and I are happy to see you. We deeply appreciate your presence here. Under the present circumstances, of course."

"Of course."

"As you will soon see, this is no longer a stop-start battle of wavering ideals, Commander Hawke. It is now, without any doubt, a battle to the death for the very soul of Pakistan. You understand this?"

"I understand completely, Captain," Hawke said.

"You'll be traveling through Zazi territory en route, Commander," Captain Balfe said. "These are the guys responsible for 80 percent of the terrorist attacks in this region. Zazi's desert commandos have been on the offensive ever since we took out their leader, a warlord named Baitullah Mehsud with a Predator drone at the end of last summer."

Hawke turned to Captain Shah. "Captain, when Baitullah Mehsud was killed, who seized ultimate control of his armies and operations? I'm going to say a name. Sheik Abu al-Rashad."

Shah was dumbstruck. "How do you know this name?"

"It doesn't matter. But I do need to know the answer to my question."

"Sheik Abu al-Rashad is today perhaps the most powerful man in Pakistan. Every Taliban and al Qaeda leader in our country falls under his overarching command. If the government and the country falls, it will fall to him."

"That's all I needed to know. Thank you." Hawke had been engaged in counterterrorist operations long enough to know that the primary first step was knowing precisely who the enemy was.

A FEW HOURS LATER THE CONVOY was rolling through the endless desert when the armored personnel carrier Hawke and his team were riding in came to an abrupt stop. Hawke was sitting just behind and below the man in command of the vehicle.

"I thought I heard an explosion. What's happened?" Hawke asked.

The man driving said, "One minute, I'm getting information in my headphones right now, sir. It sounded like an IED."

"Cuss," Harry Brock said.

Two or three minutes later, the driver said, "The lead vehicle, a troop carrier, was taken out by an IED, Commander. Two of our soldiers killed, four wounded. It could have been much worse. Captain Shah informs me that the wreckage is being cleared and that troops are fanning out looking for the Zazi bombers. We are to proceed to our destination as soon as he gives us the 'all-clear.' "

"I feel like I'm on CNN," Harry said.

"You wish," Stoke said.

Everyone was silent for a few long minutes and then the APC driver said, "Our men have located the bomber's escape vehicle out in the desert and have called in its location to Shamsi AFB. They are launching a drone now."

A second or two later, the APC started rolling again, and three hours later the sun had risen. They were driving through the heart of Islamabad, en route to the hotel where Abdul Dakkon had booked them each a room. Hawke had come to think of the man as a one-armed magician. There was literally nothing he could not accomplish, no detail he had not considered, and the answer to every question was a big smile and an "Absolutely, sir!"

"What can you tell me about the hotel?" Hawke asked Abdul.

"The Punjab Palace? Well, first of all, sir, it is not a palace."

"No? What is it?"

"A Holiday Inn, sir. Renovated last year, with a new sign out front. I am sorry I cannot offer you the Marriott, sir. It was the only four-star hotel in Islamabad, but it was totally destroyed by a truck bomb."

"I remember that. Our thought at MI6 was that the bomber had intended to blow up President Asif Ali Zadari's residence a block away but was frightened off by the security cordons and so drove into the Marriott instead."

"This is absolutely correct, sir. But the Punjab is now slowly acquiring the same clientele, the same atmosphere. You may recall Rick's Café in the movie *Casablanca,* sir. That's what it is like. A neutral ground for the media, American diplomats, warlords, drug lords, peddlers of nuclear weapons, technology, and perhaps a few who fall into all those categories. The commodity in the Punjab is information, sir. In Pakistan, information is power. And power is a daily life-and-death struggle."

"Sounds like we should spend a lot of time in the bar," Harry said.

"It's not at all a very bad idea, sir," Abdul replied, peering out through a gun port. "No bars, but there are cafés, and a restaurant. Here you can get black-market whiskey in brown bags. I believe we are pulling over to transfer your team to the hired cars. We are near the Punjab now, it will only be a short ride from here. Ten minutes with no traffic."

The Punjab Palace was an undistinguished slab of 1970s architecture, and certainly no palace, Hawke thought as he climbed out of the car at the entrance. No different from any of the countless anonymous "business" hotels in every part of the world. The only difference was that in this one, the primary business was weapons of war and terror. There were security barriers out front, but they didn't look like they could stand up to a teenage martyr with a truck full of explosives and a death wish.

Hawke's team looked exactly as they should look, a bunch of travel-weary Western journalists. Each one had a plasti-coated "Press" ID card hanging from around the neck, each with a different news-gathering organization. The CIA had provided everything. Passports, driver's licenses, cash, even the clothing on their backs. Four large black nylon duffel bags containing weapons and gear for each of them were removed from the two hired cars.

A Punjab porter, obviously on Abdul's payroll, immediately loaded the bags onto a rolling cart. He and Abdul then took the bags to the rear entrance of the hotel. Dakkon had explained to Hawke that by avoiding the metal detector inside the revolving doors at the lobby entrance, Dakkon could personally deliver the "luggage" to their various rooms using the service elevator near the kitchen. "The guard at the rear is a friend of mine," Abdul said with a smile.

Hawke said, "Abdul Dakkon, little friend of all the world."

Dakkon lit up. "*Kim!* By Rudyard Kipling. My most favorite book, sir!"

"Mine too," Hawke said, clapping his new friend on the back.

Once everyone was checked in, Hawke suggested they all go to their rooms and get some real sleep and a hot shower and meet in the restaurant at seven that evening. He told Brock he had a few details to iron out and suggested the two of them go to the lobby coffee shop for a quick breakfast. Hawke instinctively sat facing the hotel entrance so he could keep an eye on anyone who came through the door.

He knew you minded your back in a country like this, especially when you suspected your movements were being compromised by a rat in the cupboard. A few minutes after they sat down, Abdul Dakkon joined them, giving Hawke a thumbs-up, his mission accomplished.

"Listen, Harry," Hawke said once they'd all ordered coffee, "you don't look so good."

"I don't?"

"You look peaked."

"What the cuss does 'peaked' mean, anyway?"

"Pronounced pee-kid. Sickly. You look sick. Let me take a look at that knife wound you got. Lift up your shirt."

"Jesus," Harry said, pulling up his violently colored Hawaiian aloha shirt. The wound was still puffy and red, looked like about twenty stitches to Hawke, healing normally.

"I think it's infected, Harry, you might have picked up a staph infection in the emergency room, happens all the time."

"Staph? That's not good, is it?"

"Nope. Fatal unless you get on some powerful antibiotics in a hurry. I think we'd better get you to an emergency room. Abdul, where's the nearest hospital? I was there a while back."

"Quaid-e-Azam? The International Hospital?"

"That's the one. Have you got your car here?"

"Yes, sir. It's valet parked. Full tank of gas, oil topped off and—"

"Let's go," Hawke said, throwing some money on the table. He was halfway across the lobby when some Pakistani "player" swung through the front doors, a self-important entourage in his wake, armed to the teeth, all of them simply ignoring the loud screeches of the metal detector. Hawke smiled. You just didn't see this kind of stuff at Claridge's.

"It is brand-new, sir," Abdul said as he swung his Toyota into the hospital entrance. "The most modern hospital in the country. The people here are very proud of it."

"I can see why," Hawke said.

"Sorry, sir, the outdoor parking lot is full. We will have to use the underground parking garage."

Abdul exited the lot and circled the entire building, looking for the underground entrance.

"I can't seem to find the entrance, sir. It must be somewhere." He was clearly embarrassed at this turn of events.

"You would think," Harry Brock said from the backseat.

Hawke said, "Maybe there is no underground garage, Abdul."

"Oh, no, sir. There was a big delay in construction. I read about it in the papers. Something about the structure of the underground garage. Load-bearing walls. I remember that clearly."

"Okay, let's just get Mr. Brock to the ER and then we'll go park the car anywhere we can. Okay with you, Harry? If we just drop you off? We'll come back for you shortly."

"Yeah, sure, whatever works. I am starting to feel kind of sick."

FIFTY-TWO

Abdul Dakkon said, "There is a VIP section on one of the very top floors of the main building. If Sheik Abu al-Rashad truly is a patient here, sir, that is most assuredly where we shall find him."

"Good. We'll start there. Drive around to the main entrance, please. I need to speak to Reception for a few moments before we have a good look around the property. I'd like you to wait at the curb. I don't imagine I'll be too long."

"Yes, sir. Absolutely. No problem."

Hawke walked straight past the two armed security guards and entered through the revolving doors. There was a newsstand in the lobby and he picked up a copy of this morning's *International News*, crossed to the reception desk, showed his press ID card, and asked for the VIP floor. The receptionist carefully examined his credentials, then gave him the floor number and pointed to a single elevator with yet another armed guard.

The doors opened on a small but extraordinarily lavish reception room. Quite empty of visitors. Behind a black granite semi-circle sat a very officious looking middle-aged woman. Sullen and sallow-faced, she did not look promising. Her black hair was pulled back severely, forming a slightly lopsided bun. Formidable, Hawke thought, attempting to disarm her with a smile.

"Yes?" she said before he could open his mouth to charm her.

"Good morning, madame. My name is Lord Alexander Hawke. I'm here from London on holiday and wanted to pop in and say hello to an old friend of mine. I think he is a patient here."

Without a word, she spun around to her computer keyboard.

"Patient's name?"

"Sheik Abu al-Rashad."

She typed it in.

"Sorry, no one here by that name."

"Sorry, I should think he would definitely be here on the VIP floor." Hawke had his eye on the surveillance camera, indiscreetly mounted in one corner and swinging back and forth through a ninety-degree angle. He'd have to make his moves accordingly.

"I'm quite sure he would be. If he were a patient in this hospital. Which he is not."

"Not here then, is he? Well, that's certainly a shock. Has he been here recently at all? As a patient, I mean. I've been told he's quite ill."

"What did you say your name was again?"

"Hawke. Lord Hawke."

"Surname 'Hawke,' given name, 'Lord'?" She went to another screen and started to type it in.

"Correct," Hawke replied, not bothering to correct her.

"The man you are inquiring about is known to everyone on staff here, Mr. Lord Hawke. His benevolent generosity built the very building you are now standing in. As a most gracious gift to our nation and the beloved city of his birth."

"Did he really? Built the hospital? Isn't that interesting? Never mentioned a word to me, but, of course, his modesty always becomes him. Well, thanks for your time, madame, I'll be off."

She didn't even look up as Hawke walked away.

"Oh," he said, pausing and looking back at her, "one more thing. I can't seem to find the underground parking garage. Could you possibly tell me where it is located?"

"Closed for repairs."

"Ah, that explains it. Well, where is the entrance?"

"Closed for repairs, too."

Hawke turned and crossed back to the counter, glancing up at the closed-circuit TV camera.

"You know, I have a very difficult time believing you. I have seen the architectural renderings the Sheik's architects used during construction. Which include an entrance to an underground facility. Perhaps we could have a more frank discussion if you took a look inside this newspaper."

He placed a folded copy of the *News* on the counter.

She eyed it suspiciously and said, "What is inside?"

"Have a look. It won't bite."

She took the paper, opened it, and a letter-sized manila envelope plopped on the desk in front of her.

"And what is this?" she asked, picking it up by a corner and giving it a shake. Curiosity most definitely piqued, he observed happily.

"That, my good woman, is fifty thousand dollars in small bills, all U.S. currency."

She looked around to see if they were alone, then ripped open the seal. The thick wad of hundred-dollar bills was secured with a heavy red rubber band. Looking nervously about, she thumbed through it, her eyes widening incredulously. Obviously, she'd never seen this much money in her life. Few had. It always had a positive effect on people. Her dark eyes involuntarily registered greed. It was all he needed to see.

Without warning, Hawke's hand flicked across the counter with blinding speed. He snatched the cash from her hands so quickly she rocked back in her chair in shock.

"About that mysterious underground garage," he said, slipping the wad into the pocket of his windbreaker.

"Yes? What about it?"

"I want to see it. I want you to tell me how to find the entrance to it. If you do, and I see it for myself, I shall return here and give you this money. Of course, if I discover you have lied, or alerted anyone about my inquiries, you will never see me or the money again. Understood?"

"Yes."

"Use that pencil and draw a simple diagram of where the entrance is located. Quickly, before someone comes."

As she drew, she told him, in an anxious whisper and with a good bit of detail, exactly where the entrance was located. She folded the map into a small square and placed it on the counter. "You'll need this, too," she said, placing a metallic silver electronic reader card on the counter. "After that, there are guards. You'll be on your own."

"Thanks so much," Hawke said, turning and then striding across the inlaid marble-floored room. He paused in midstride again and looked back at her.

"By the way, don't even think about picking up that phone. If you speak to anyone, or I encounter any unexpected problems, you will never see this money or your family again. Because you will be dead. And if not you, my men will find your family. In the event you keep silent and prove helpful, there is another ten thousand in it for you. Do we fully understand each other, madame? A simple yes or no will do. Now."

"Yes."

Hawke observed her carefully. She was telling the truth.

"Good. Let's hope so for your sake."

As Hawke rode the elevator down, the mental tumblers rapidly clicked into place. The Sheik had followed the same hallowed tradition the Hamas War Council had adopted during the Israeli conflict in Gaza City.

Hamas commanders had used the Shifa Hospital's basement as their communications center, issuing orders, paying salaries, and discussing war strategies. The hospital, the largest in Gaza City had been chosen to avoid being targeted by Israel's military, who knew the location. But it would have been impossible to take out without bombing. Or a massive ground operation and unacceptable civilian casualties.

"Let's go find Harry," Hawke said, climbing into the car. "Tonight's the night."

"You found out where the Sheik is hiding?"

"I did. It seems he's in the morgue."

FIFTY-THREE

THE TEAM STRUCK THAT VERY NIGHT, two hours before dawn. They'd neutralized two security guards standing outside the entrance. Hawke posted Abdul Dakkon outside wearing, as they all did, a headset and lip mike. His job was to alert them of any untoward activity at the hospital entrance. Dressed in a uniform identical to that of the hospital guards, he now cradled one of their Pak G3 assault rifles in his arms. Brock had advised him to select "full auto" and he had. The two unconscious guards, tightly bound and gagged, were in the bushes just behind him, silent as stones.

Hawke, Stokely, Sahira, and Brock had entered the completely empty hospital lobby at varying intervals. The three men were wearing doctors' robes with authentic name tags and stethoscopes round their necks. Beneath the traditional Pakistani medical garb, each man was heavily armed with automatic weapons, flash-bang and smoke grenades, and extra rounds of ammunition.

Hawke prayed they were sufficiently prepared. It had been difficult enough to plan this assault because no one had the remotest idea what to expect.

Sahira, primly dressed in a Muslim nurse's uniform, was now sitting at the reception desk where she would remain during the operation. That is, unless she heard otherwise from Hawke in her headset. A code word, "Boom!," meant the team had discovered the missing nuclear device in the underground bunker and needed her immediate threat assessment. The real receptionist had received the same treatment as the guards outside and was now peacefully supine beneath the counter at Sahira's feet.

Sahira kept her right hand out of sight beneath the counter.

In her lap was a very lethal pistol. Harry Brock had given it to her at the hotel. It was called "The Judge." It was a Taurus revolver capable of firing either .45 rounds, or .410 shotgun shells. Her gun was loaded with double-ought buckshot shells. In close quarters, nothing was deadlier than the Judge.

Giving her the loaded gun, Brock had said, "Remember, Sahira, in the eyes of Islamic militants, there are only two places for Muslim women. In the husband's home. And in the graveyard. Don't hesitate to use this thing."

The good news was that Islamabad rolled up its sidewalks at ten o'clock each evening and there was normally little to no walk-in traffic at the hospital at this hour. So far, their luck was holding.

Hawke led his team past the four banks of gleaming elevators. He turned right, entering a long hallway. At the end was a set of stainless-steel swinging doors. The sign above read MORTUARY/RESTRICTED.

Inside the green-tiled morgue, the stinging stench was immediate and almost overpowering. The myriad, nameless chemicals of the constantly processed dead. It was then that Hawke remembered the old trick of rubbing Vick's VapoRub under one's nose, but it was too late. At least the place was empty, just as Hawke had hoped it would be.

They quickly moved past the banks of stainless-steel refrigerators to an area where all the mortuary chemicals and supplies were stored. Hawke quickly located the black steel panel in the wall that the VIP receptionist had described. There was a card reader beside the panel. He swiped the silver card she'd given him and the doors slid open.

Inside the elevator was an identical card reader in place of any buttons. Hawke swiped his card once more and felt his heels lifting in his shoes as the elevator dropped swiftly and smoothly. It was a long ride and Hawke sensed they were going deeply underground. Deep enough so that no American bunker-buster bomb could ever penetrate.

Hawke pulled his SIG P226 Tactical pistol from his thigh holster and chambered a round. The other two did the same. All three weapons had three-inch barrels and were fitted with noise suppressors. And all three men wore Kevlar body armor under their flowing robes.

An electronic ping announced their arrival. They came to a gentle stop and the doors opened on a small room with four opaque white glass walls. Against one wall stood a single wooden chair. A gaunt, bearded man with a gun was seated in that chair.

The lone guard, shocked at their appearance, raised his AK and demanded to know what these three doctors were doing in a secure area.

Brock erupted into a flurry of furious Urdu and Pashtu epithets, barking at the man in loud gibberish, enough to distract him for a moment.

Simultaneously, Hawke brought up his pistol in one fluid movement and put a silent round into the guard's right eye. The man toppled from the chair and dropped to the floor, blood pouring from his wound, his weapon clattering on the polished white marble floor, even as the three men stepped out of the elevator.

"Okay," Harry Brock said, stepping nonchalantly over the corpse and looking around the bare room. "Now what? No doors, no nothing. This is it, huh? The Headquarters of the Evil Empire?"

"Has to be something here," Hawke said, running his hand over the smooth glass wall behind the chair. He moved to the adjacent wall to his right and repeated the process. "Stoke, check that wall to your left." Stoke did.

"Don't bother. Here it is," Hawke said.

"Here's what?" Brock asked.

"Biometric screening device. Compares stored images of fingerprints with anyone desiring access."

Hawke placed his hand against the barely visible screen and activated it. A green bar rolled down the small screen, scanning his five digits. It flashed red three times and then shut down.

"Stokely, do me a favor," Hawke said. "Bring that recently deceased fellow over here, will you please?"

"See that?" Stoke said to Harry as he dragged the corpse over to Hawke. "That's called using your head. Put the guard's hand on the screen, right, you see what the man's thinking?"

Hawke grabbed the corpse's right wrist as Stoke lifted the lifeless body from the floor. He carefully placed the man's hand flat against the screen and pressed. Again, the rolling green bar. Again, the five red flashes.

"Shit," Stoke said, and the three men looked at one another.

"He's wearing his watch on his right wrist," Hawke said. "He's a lefty. Bet on it."

Hawke placed the dead man's left hand on the screen, the green bar rolled down, and the entire glass wall suddenly slid into the floor. "That's what I'm talking about," Stoke said, peering into the dimly lit corridor that lay beyond the room. Light was visible through the cracks in a pair of double doors at the far end. Hawke held up his hand for silence and began speaking in a calm, low voice.

"Heads up. We stack up outside the door," Hawke said. "Me, Stoke, then Harry. Assume the door is locked. Assume there will be enemy fire from within. Possible booby traps. Who the hell knows. I'll fire a short burst at the latch and kick both doors open. Got it?"

The two men nodded silently.

"As soon as the doors are open, I drop to one knee and Stoke skip-bounces a concussion grenade hard off the floor into the room so they can't toss it back. Then, Stoke, throw one smoke and two frags. I'll provide covering fire while you do it. Then you stack up again. Our grenades go in, I issue the verbal alert, 'Frag out.' If I see any incoming enemy grenades, the verbal alert is 'Grenades.' Pick them up and heave them back. Clear?"

"Clear," Stoke said.

"Clear," Brock said.

"We go in with weapons in the ready-carry position. Full auto. I'll cross the threshold, go left, and clear my immediate area. Stoke, you enter immediately following, buttonhook, and clear the adjacent sector. Once we're in position, I shout, 'Next man in.' Brock moves to one side of the door and establishes a center sector of fire coverage. Got it?"

"Got it."

"We're going in now," Hawke said, the pumping adrenaline obvious in his voice. "Ready, go."

The three men moved quickly to the door and stacked up one behind the other. Hawke fired a short burst into the door latch, took a step back, and kicked it wide open. Hawke took a knee. Stoke pulled the pin on the concussion grenade and overhanded it off the marble floor so hard that it bounced twice going into the room. Then he threw the two fragmentation grenades and a smoke. A good bit of hell broke loose and then some.

A skeleton crew of Taliban militants had been manning a bank of monitors on the far wall. Hawke instantly scanned the command and control room, left to right. The two frag grenades had killed or severely incapacitated some of the men. But Hawke saw six more soldiers who'd been playing cards seated at a round table far to the right. All were stunned, but they had survived unharmed and quickly recovered. Seeing Hawke, then Stokely and Brock enter the room, they grabbed their weapons, threw the heavy wooden table over for cover, raised their AKs, and started firing wildly.

"On your right," Hawke said, seeing two men dive from behind the table and scramble for cover in a nearby alcove. "Smoke 'em, Harry, and go to cover."

Brock fired a sustained burst and the two men stopped shooting and living simultaneously. At that moment Harry sensed noise and movement from behind him. He whirled and saw the doors of another elevator opening into the room. Inside were three guys in green surgical scrubs carrying automatic weapons.

Harry began firing into the elevator car before the doors were fully opened. Two of the three Talibs inside never stood a chance. The third was unhurt and had Harry pinned down, crouching behind a very small wooden chair.

"Over here, mothercusser!" Stoke yelled at the last remaining elevator guy, diverting his focus away from Brock. "I'm putting a fatwa on your ugly ass!"

The guy looked wide-eyed at Stoke's yawning black muzzle and that was his last look ever. Stoke saw Hawke signal and hurled himself across the room to join him.

Stoke and Hawke took cover behind a large slab of marble being used as a desk. Rounds were taking chunks out of the stone. Hawke got Stoke's attention, mimicked pulling the pin on a grenade, and snatched one from his webbed utility belt. He pulled the pin and let the frag grenade "cook off" in his hand before heaving it over the upended table.

Stoke cringed at Hawke's decision. Cooking off grenades was an extremely dangerous thing to do since frag fuses were not completely reliable. On the other hand, this action eliminated any chance of the enemy hurling it back.

"One . . . two . . . and . . ." Hawke said before rising up and tossing it across the room where it dropped just behind the table. Ducking down as it exploded, he clapped both hands over his ears. The noise and concussion of the explosion was shattering in the closed quarters. Hawke looked at Stoke. "Ready?"

"Let's go."

Back to back, they moved out from behind the safety of the slab of marble swinging their weapons in opposite arcs, ready to kill anything that moved. Nothing was moving. There were four chopped-up bodies behind what was left of the heavy wooden table.

"Find a live one somewhere who speaks English," Hawke called out. "If you can."

"Over here," Brock said.

Hawke and Stoke converged on the guy. Chest wound sucking loudly. Hawke knelt beside him.

"You're going to be okay. You're in a hospital after all, we're getting medics down here right now. I need to know where Abu al-Rashad is. Is he one of the men in this room?"

"No-o," the guy wheezed, and you could hear air from deep inside the wound.

"Where is he now?"

"Office."

"Where is his office?"

"One floor above. That elevator there. Please help me. Am I dying?"

"We are here to neutralize a weapon the Sheik has taken from the Islamabad nuclear arsenal. Where is it? Here in this facility?"

"D-don't know . . ."

"I have help standing by on this radio. You want me to tell that doctor to hurry up?"

"Please, God. Please get me a doctor . . ."

"Is there another way out of this complex? A way for the Sheik to escape?"

"A hidden elevator. Drops down from the ceiling behind his desk. Leads to a door in the morgue."

"Where would he go? How does he travel?"

"In a body bag. Everywhere."

"Good God."

"Please help me. I don't want to die."

"No one does," Hawke said, getting to his feet. He looked at Stoke and Brock and said, "One floor up. We'll use the elevator with the three dead occupants."

It was the work of ten minutes to discover that whoever had been there had left in a hurry. Hawke found three half-empty plates of food and three cups of still warm tea on the desk in the Sheik's office.

He looked up at the ceiling and saw the faint outline of a square the size of a small elevator.

"Sahira," he said into his lip mike, "has anyone left the hospital?"

"No. But about ten minutes ago a Red Crescent ambulance pulled up outside and two medical technicians retrieved a corpse from the morgue and loaded it in the back. Did you find the weapon?"

"No. We have enemy wounded down here. Ring the hospital operator and tell them we need a trauma team down in the morgue. I will meet them there and direct them to the Sheik's underground bunker."

"Got it."

"Then go out and tell Abdul to call the ambassador at the U.S. Embassy residence. Use my name. Give him the situation here. Describe that ambulance and the two med techs in as much detail as you possibly can. And which direction it was headed."

"Don't tell me he—"

"Went out in that body bag? Yeah, that's exactly what he did. I need to know. Were the techs carrying anything?"

"No. Wait . . . Damn it!"

"What?"

"Alex, there was one of those UN corrugated aluminum coffins on the lower rack of the gurney, beneath the body. I thought that was a little odd, but since—"

"Our target has a nuclear weapon in that ambulance, Sahira. Not warheads, obviously, they wouldn't fit in the UN coffin. He's got a suitcase-sized device. Get Abdul to get his CIA contact to set up checkpoints and get Pak Army choppers in the air. We need to stop that ambulance before it leaves the city."

"I'm on it," Sahira said and dashed outside.

Hawke looked at Brock, and Harry saw red-hot anger flashing in the man's normally cool blue eyes.

"Say the F-word, Harry. Right now. This is a one-time-only opportunity."

Harry said it, all right.

Loud and clear enough for all of them.

FIFTY-FOUR

Muhammad Imran sped away from the hospital in the Red Crescent ambulance, leaving the staff and patients completely unaware of the ferocious drama that had just taken place deep belowground. He took the first entrance into the city's largest park. Inside the densely wooded area, in the predawn hours, there would be no vehicular traffic; and certainly no pedestrians out for a stroll.

Due to the seemingly endless power outages, most of the city was dark. Unless you lived in a section of the capital that housed some important minister, or retired generals, the chances were your street would have an interrupted electric supply at least twice a day. Imran believed the founder of Pakistan, the beloved Jinnah, was probably rolling in his grave over the current state of his country. Turmoil, to put it mildly. But Imran's employer, al-Rashad, would soon right all the wrongs, of that he had no doubt.

He drove the big white ambulance at very high speeds now, along the serpentine road leading to an ancient stone gate on the far side of the city. This arch was the entrance to Islamabad's "old town." It was all that remained of the original settlement of Saidpur.

The streets here were narrow and circuitous, with many dead ends, and the chances of being followed were minimal. The only thing he feared now were Pak Army or police helicopters with searchlights. But, so far, nothing in the sky, nor in the rearview mirror.

Muhammad Imran's knowledge that his ambulance now had, in addition to his powerful employer stuffed into a bag, one easily armed and detonated nuclear device two feet behind him was a bit worrisome. But he was sanguine. This night, or perhaps the next one, had always been his destiny. The Sheik had gathered him in, seduced the young ISI agent like the hypnotic imam he was, mesmerized him like so many countless thousands of Muslim jihadists.

Since the hospital's completion he and his constant companion, Ali, had practiced all of the Sheik's carefully planned and meticulously designed escape routes regularly. But this was the first time they'd executed the Islamabad hospital evac for real. All the plans were pretty much the same, although the level of menace had appreciated considerably, considering the fierce armed attack on what had previously been considered the ultimate secret bunker.

He doused his lights and took a hard right into a narrow, darkened, dead-end street. At the cul-de-sac stood a crumbling four-story warehouse, unoccupied for decades, with blacked-out windows. He couldn't see them, but he knew snipers were on the roof watching him and ready with rocket-propelled grenades affixed to the muzzles of their weapons should the Red Crescent ambulance ever be followed. An unseen electric eye caused a garage door in the warehouse to begin rising.

Imran drove inside the cavernous space and the three-inch-thick steel door closed swiftly behind him.

Fluorescent lights above automatically illuminated, revealing the Sheik's unique collection of antique and modern ambulances, plus a brand-new silver Rolls-Royce Phantom and a red Ferrari Italia. All of them, which were maintained by a staff of excellent mechanics, were always filled with petrol and ready to roll at a moment's notice.

Imran and Ali climbed out, went to the back of the vehicle, pulled open the rear door, and removed the gurney and its occupant. Ali unzipped the bag and a smiling al-Rashad sat upright and brought up a laugh from deep in his belly.

"Fooled the bastards, didn't we, my brothers? Americans. Or Brits. Or both. How in God's name do you suppose they found us?"

"Someone betrayed you, sir," Ali said, voicing his conviction.

Imran smiled. "Indeed we did fool them, however, sir. Which vehicle would you like to use for the continuation of the journey north to the mountains of Chitral?"

"The Battlewagon."

"We may well need her tonight, sire. A wise and inspired choice."

The Battlewagon, a nickname given the mechanical behemoth by the wily Englishman known only as Smith, when he made good use of her in Afghanistan some years ago, was a huge, heavily armored 1958 black Cadillac Landau hearse weighing nearly six thousand pounds. Its original V-8 engine had been replaced by a Mercedes-Benz 5.5-liter twin-turbocharged V-12 engine rated at 500 horsepower.

Powered by the same engine as the modern Maybach limousine, the hearse topped out at a shade less than 150 miles per hour and ran a 0-to-60 time of under twenty seconds. It was also equipped with all-wheel drive and the Range Rover air-suspension system for off-road driving.

It was heavily modified in other ways. Its armament included twin .50-cal machine guns invisibly mounted behind the dummy plastic chrome front grille, two gun ports for shooters on both left and right sides, and a wide rear door that dropped down from the roof to form a rock-stable battle platform.

On that platform, a swivel-mounted Dillon M134 Gatling gun could easily be mounted.

This state-of-the-art, lightweight, revolving six-barreled machine gun fired at a rate of three thousand rounds a minute. It could change the nature of any firefight in a heartbeat. It was this very weapon, the Sheik liked to tell close friends, that was turret mounted inside a special U.S. Secret Service Chevrolet Suburban. "You know, the one always trailing behind the American president's limousine like an intern in heat," he said.

The ambulance-mounted Gatling gun was the Sheik's favorite range weapon, and he longed desperately to use it on a real foe. Perhaps tonight his wishes would come true, he thought, dozing off as the miles reeled away, lulled to sleep by the hum of the big tires.

Imran kept his speed low and the hearse's lights doused for the initial hour of the journey. Reaching the main road north without being stopped at a single checkpoint, he snapped the headlights on and sped up. Fast, but not fast enough to attract unwanted attention. In front of him lay a long hard way over very bad roads, climbing thousands of feet from Islamabad toward the Sheik's impregnable mountain stronghold near Chitral in the mountains of northern Pakistan.

His secret mountaintop redoubt, called Wazizabad, had existed for centuries; honeycombed with miles of tunnels and cavernous caches of weapons and outfitted with twenty-first-century communications technology. All within a few days' ride of what had once been the scene of one of the most devastating defeats in the history of British Army warfare.

In 1838, an army of twenty-one thousand British and Indian troops had set out from the Punjab to take control of regions in Afghanistan. Four years later, in full retreat, the remaining British 16th Lancers force of sixteen thousand was caught on open, frozen ground and the treacherous gorges and passes along the Kabul River. In that single massacre, the British Army was reduced to forty men. Harassed by Ghilzai warriors, only one Briton survived. They let him live for one reason: he was sent back to tell the tale of what happens when foreign armies invade Afghanistan.

Occupying the top of one of the tallest peaks in all Pakistan, the exact location of the Sheik's fortified position known as Wazizabad still remained unknown despite countless attempts by the Sheik's countless enemies to find it.

Meanwhile, the great one rested, secure inside his dead man's bag, with some foodstuffs and a large bottle of water with a long tube to keep him hydrated as they climbed into the higher altitudes. He made not a sound from the rear of the hearse and Imran concluded he'd imbibed one of his special potions and fallen fast asleep, as was his wont on long journeys. Who could blame him? The fact that he was sleeping in extremely close proximity to a weapon of mass destruction would never even occur to him, much less keep him awake.

An hour later, they were well enough away from civilization to stop worrying about police roadblocks. All the driver Imran feared now was the appearance of American drones, gunships, and helicopters out looking for an unusual vehicle speeding northeast into the mountains bordering Afghanistan. If the Battlewagon happened to catch the attention of a Predator drone on the prowl, or a C130 Spectre circling at twenty thousand feet, the three men's lives would end in a spectacular fireball.

Five minutes later he crested a steep hill at high speed. Waiting at the bottom of the hill he saw a brightly lit Pak Army barricade across the road. There had to be fifty heavily armed soldiers surrounding the concrete barrier, their searchlights already trained on him, army M-113 armored vehicles with heavy machine-gun turrets already swiveling in their direction.

Imran thumbed his microphone and informed Sheik al-Rashad to prepare himself for an army stop and possible search. He slowed the vehicle, giving Ali time to scramble into the open space behind the front seat and be ready at the gun ports with his semiautomatic assault rifle. Under a blanket on the seat beside him, Imran had the most lethal battlefield weapon in the world today: an AA-12 automatic shotgun capable of rapid-fire 12-gauge shotgun shells or fragmentation grenades. It gave him a good feeling in close combat situations.

Imran slowed the Battlewagon to a crawl as he approached within a hundred yards of the barrier. Then he rolled to a stop, invoking the old warrior's rule "let them come to you." Twenty soldiers, assault rifles at the ready, approached the ambulance.

"Here they come. Fifty yards and closing," he said over the vehicle's intercom system. "Ready?"

"Ready," he heard the two men in the rear say, almost in unison.

"They're splitting up, ten to a side. Surrounding the vehicle. One soldier approaching me on the left, driver's-side window. Ali, cover my left, I've got the right side."

"Got it."

Imran smiled as he lowered his window. "Yes, sir, Sergeant," Imran said. "How can I help you?" The man had his weapon leveled directly at Imran's face. He had a powerful SureFire light attached to the lower rail of his weapon, using it to peer inside the front seat.

"Lower the other window," the sergeant said.

"Of course, sir," Imran replied and did.

"How many in the vehicle?"

"Just me sir. And a corpse in the rear."

"Destination?"

"Takim City," Imran said, naming the village of his birth. "The funeral is at sunrise."

Two soldiers were now at the passenger-side window, peering into the hearse with their weapons at the ready.

"We are going to search this vehicle. Keep your hands where I can see them and get out. Now."

"All right. Don't shoot. I'm getting out."

Hearing those words, Ali opened fire through the gun port, first taking out the sergeant standing outside Imran's window. Imran simultaneously raised the automatic shotgun and fired a long burst out the far window. The three or four soldiers outside simply disintegrated. He then floored the accelerator, using the trigger on the steering wheel to fire the twin .50-cal machine guns mounted behind the grille at soldiers blocking his way.

The soldiers returned fire, but the stunning surprise of an armed hearse caught many off guard and they died in a hail of bullets. Imran took a hard right turn and veered off the road, still accelerating in the sand as he headed straight for the barrier's end. Two armored vehicles opened up, but the rounds were no match for the Battlewagon's heavy armor and bulletproof glass. He did an end run around the barrier and, still firing the twin fifties, plowed through the mass of soldiers between him and the paved road. Ali, still at the gun port, was mowing down anyone in sight.

Throwing up a great wake of sand, the Battlewagon roared back onto the road north.

Six teams of two soldiers, mounted on powerful motorcycles with sidecars, were waiting for them on both sides of the road. As Imran desperately accelerated away, they tucked in behind him. Their powerful Kawasaki military motorcycles were more than fast enough to gain on the much heavier vehicle.

Soldiers in the armored sidecars began firing heavy machine guns at the escaping hearse, hundreds of rounds thudding off the armored rear door.

"They'll go for the tires next!" Imran shouted. "I'm lowering the platform, sire! Are you in position?"

"Go, go, go," al-Rashad screamed, and Imran knew that he was more than ready.

The platform lowered hydraulically, giving the Sheik time to get his hands on the weapon grips and triggers and slide forward onto the seat that swiveled with the gun itself. As soon as he felt the platform lock into place, he opened fire with the Gatling gun. The rotating barrels spat long, continuous jets of what looked like liquid fire. Since it was still dark, he could see exactly where he was shooting. He was methodical, first training his hail of lead on the motorcycle to his left. The thing was literally blasted off the road, exploding as it careened into the desert. Seeing the effect of this phenomenal weapon, the five other terrified riders began to brake and swerve.

The outcome for the five remaining motorcycles was immediate and devastating. Three more flaming machines went pinwheeling off into the desert on either side of the road, exploding into massive balls of fire that climbed fifty feet into the nighttime sky when their fuel tanks exploded.

"Our enemies are no more," al-Rashad announced proudly as he climbed out of the seat.

Imran raised the battle platform to its closed position and pushed the Battlewagon to its limits as he climbed the narrow rutted highway into the cold dark mountains. Now that they'd been identified, it was only a matter of time before the Predator drones and Cobra helicopter gunships would appear on the horizon along with the rising sun. Their own weapons useless against such enemies, Muhammad Imran knew it had now come down to a race against time. It was a race he had to win, and he flogged the Battlewagon like a demon out of hell up the twisting and deeply rutted road.

Forty minutes later, the somewhat battered Battlewagon, having encountered no aerial adversaries, rolled into a hidden cavern built into the side of a mountain by the Sheik himself over thirty years ago.

Waiting inside was a small army of veteran Taliban and al Qaeda fighters, Kalashnikovs slung over their shoulders, and many fine Arabian horses. The Sheik, protected by his men, would complete the journey to the secret stronghold on horseback, his precious cargo loaded onto the backs of the most primitive pack mules.

His cargo consisted of a small aluminum case measuring two feet by one and a half feet containing fissile material. The case weighed exactly 320 pounds. Inside this miniaturized nuclear device were a six-inch detonator and three coffee-can-sized aluminum canisters. Inside each canister was a single critical mass of plutonium (or U-235) at maximum density under normal conditions. To detonate, it was simply a matter of connecting all three and placing the device on a timer.

Or using a remote radio-controlled device.

The resulting explosion of this small case now strapped on a pack mule would be sufficient to take out the West End of London.

Humans in the immediate vicinity would likely die from the force of the conventional explosion itself. Survivors of the blast would die of radiation poisoning in the weeks afterward. Those farther away might suffer radiation sickness in the days and weeks after, and some of them might recover.

Al-Rashad smiled at the irony of it all, watching the incredibly sophisticated nuclear device being unloaded from the aluminum coffin and transferred to the waiting mules. Donning his ancient desert garb, a woolen tunic over baggy trousers, he marveled at how absurd warfare had become in the new century. Weapons worth millions still had to traverse the rugged mountains on the backs of mules. And corpses in body bags mysteriously came to life and made more corpses.

He shrugged into his heavy bearskin coat, a gift from a long-deceased Soviet colonel, and swung up into the saddle. He bade farewell to Muhammad Imran and Ali who were climbing into the back of a white Toyota Hilux truck for the long ride back to Islamabad.

An hour later he was riding at the vanguard of his column of heavily bearded fighters, welcoming the warming sun to another day in this earthly paradise. He was at his best when returning home to his mountains, and he sat tall in the saddle, a broad smile on his deeply war-weathered face.

Wazizabad.

It was his home, his fabled fortress, his castle. And before the sun set this day on the faces of these much loved mountains, turned them pink in the dying light, he would return once more to the unassailable sanctuary that had defined his real world for as long as he could remember.

FIFTY-FIVE

HAWKE HOVERED OVER THE SEVERELY wounded Pakistani Army officer in the cramped and bloodied rear of the military ambulance. The officer was still at the barricade, the scene of the horrific slaughter of many of his troops. Hawke had looked at the medic attending, and the man had looked back with a grave face, shaking his head no. The officer was obviously dying, but his dying words were of critical importance.

His voice broken and raspy, he strove mightily to tell Hawke what he needed to know. Upon learning of the bizarre hearse attack on the army barricade, Hawke and his team had immediately been airlifted to the scene by a CIA chopper pilot flying an unmarked Black Hawk. Hawke had no proof that Sheik al-Rashad had been inside that hearse, but he simply could not imagine it being anyone else.

"So, Captain, a black hearse, not a white ambulance, yes?"

"Y-yes . . . black . . . heavily armored."

"With weapons, you said. What will I be up against?"

"Fifty-caliber machine guns up front and . . . sorry, I can't seem to get enough . . . some kind of Gatling gun mounted at the rear . . . but . . . no concern of yours."

"No? Why?"

"This road north. It only lasts for . . . another hundred miles or so. Then . . . the . . . desert . . . and then the mountains."

"How will he proceed?"

"Horses . . . the only way up those narrow mountain trails. You need horses, camels, mules, Commander Hawke. Warhorses . . . and fighters. Seasoned desert fighters. Taliban war parties everywhere, returning since the army's 2008 offensive."

"Where is he heading?"

"Northwest of here. The provinces. Somewhere in the mountains near the village of Chitral. He has a . . . a command post there. Never been able to find it. There are endless mountains . . . hundreds of caves and tunnels . . . all look alike."

The medic put a hand on Hawke's shoulder. "I'm sorry, I have to put an end to this. It doesn't look good, but perhaps . . . you never know. But the captain needs his strength."

"I understand completely. I'd like to ask him just one more question. Is that all right?"

"Yes, one more."

Hawke bent even closer to the man, putting his lips near what was left of his left ear.

"Have you ever heard of a place called Wazizabad, Captain?"

"Y-yes . . . of course . . . a mythical name for one of the highest mountains . . . but I don't think you can . . . ascend. . . ."

Hawke knew better than to ask why not. He thanked the medic and let him get back to work.

"Commander," he heard the man whisper as he started to climb out of the ambulance.

"Yes, Captain?"

"Find . . . Lieutenant Amir, my second-in-command . . . in that ambulance . . . if he's still alive, he can help you. He knows those mountains. He can put together a small army of hard militia veterans

. . . men who have fought the Taliban for many years. God go with you, brother."

Hawke, having spoken to Lieutenant Amir, sprinted to the waiting helo, ducking his head as he climbed in and quickly settling into his vacant seat next to the pilot. He buckled himself in, put on his headset, and positioned his lip mike.

"Ever hear of someplace called 'Wazizabad'?" Hawke asked the young American flyer.

"No, sir."

"I have," Stoke said, leaning forward and squeezing Hawke's shoulder. "In fact, I've got a map of the place, boss."

THE EXPEDITION INTO THE NORTHERN provinces took Hawke and his new and very essential accomplice, Abdul Dakkon, three full days to organize and provision. Abdul's answer to every difficult logistical question was "Absolutely, sir!" or "Already done, sir!" Still, Hawke felt the pressure. He had his eye on his watch the entire time, knowing every moment lost meant the missing nuclear weapon might be lost to him forever.

He was also assisted in the time-compressed logistics of the operation by Lieutenant Amir, a small, handsome chap, a veteran, a much-decorated soldier who'd been wounded in the barricade attack, but who seemed impervious to pain. Hawke, in fact, had left him for dead in the Pak ambulance. Many of the men under his command had died in the barrage at the barricade and Amir was eager to seek retribution against the Taliban militants, to help Hawke mount an expedition into the provinces and run them to ground.

After many sat-phone consultations about the impending mission with C back in London, most of them at great length, Hawke's team had chosen the northernmost Pakistani Army outpost, Wanabah, an ancient enclosure of mud and stone, heavily guarded against the frequent Taliban attacks, to ready themselves for the impending journey on horseback. The outpost sat at the very edge of the desert they would have to cross before heading through the valley and up into some of the highest mountains on earth.

C's initial inclination, after consulting with the British Army forces in neighboring Afghanistan, and his CIA and Pentagon counterparts in Washington, had been to call in B-52s and drone airstrikes out of the secret Shamsi AFB to take out the objective. He thought it far too dangerous for Hawke and his small band of fighters to venture alone into a Taliban-infested area where thousands had died. "Pound that mountain into powder and come home safe, Alex," Sir David Trulove had said.

Hawke had patiently explained that there was no hard target yet, only endless mountain ranges. Any one of those mountains might be the command-and-control bunker of Abu al-Rashad, headquarters of the Lion of the Punjab. There would simply be no way to confirm his exact position, his actual presence, or that of the stolen nuclear device, without a boots-on-the-ground incursion and reconnoiter.

Hawke also pointed out that these mountains were home to many non-Taliban Pakistani villages, farmers, and goatherds. Their deaths at the hands of U.S. bombers, he said, would be morally and politically indefensible in the highly charged geopolitical climate of this region and this war.

C extracted a promise from Hawke that as soon as he had this confirmation, and the precise GPS coordinates of the enemy stronghold, he would call in strikes and let the U.S. Air Force do its job. Hawke had no choice but to agree. It was, after all, an order. Hawke's philosophy: always do exactly what you think is necessary and apologize later.

While satellite communications, ammunition, food stores, and water were being assembled for loading onto the camels and pack mules, crash courses were under way. Harry Brock was drilling the militia in the use of the U.S. M4 assault rifle on a makeshift shooting range while both Amir and the newly bearded Abdul Dakkon spent every minute of free time giving horseback riding instruction to the team.

Sahira, it turned out, was an equestrienne, a horsewoman all her life. She had no trouble controlling these fearsome horses, horses descended from the beasts Genghis Khan had ridden out of Mongolia. But camels, she soon learned, required other skills. Simply putting up with nasty, smelly, farting brutes being the least of it.

Lieutenant Amir, who had shed his army uniform for mufti and had asked to be called by his nickname, Patoo, worked with Sahira until she was comfortable with the camels. Or, at least, claimed she was comfortable. She didn't believe any human being could ever be comfortable with camels, and vice versa.

She wasn't one for complaining, Patoo noticed, and it made him somewhat less anxious about having such a beautiful young woman venture deep into enemy territory. He'd spoken to Hawke privately. Hawke understood his concern, but he said her presence would be critical should they find the stolen nuclear device.

Patoo conceded the point, but he looked Hawke straight in the eye and told the Englishman in no uncertain terms that, if she went along, under absolutely no circumstances should they allow the Taliban fighters to take this woman alive.

"You understand what that might mean, Commander Hawke?" Patoo said. "In extreme circumstances? Your obligation?"

Hawke looked at him for a very long time before replying, a searing image of Anastasia being loaded aboard the doomed airship flashing through his mind.

"Lieutenant, there are very few men alive who understand what you mean better than I."

Hawke was all too well aware that, in extremis, he himself would have to kill Sahira before letting her be taken captive. Patoo was right. This woman's unspeakably cruel death at the hands of these animals would be unthinkable. War. He'd given up this hell and tried to end his own life because of the overwhelming pain. Now, he was back in its grip and the heavy consequences were weighing upon him to the point where he had to just shove it all aside and concentrate on the job to be done. The job of the simple warrior.

Stokely Jones had already given their little expeditionary force a name: the Rat Patrol. Some bloody American TV show in the 1960s, he'd told Alex. Chaps in Jeeps with machine guns, three Yanks and one Brit, roaring around in the desert wreaking havoc on Field Marshal Rommel's Afrika Korps. Brock had picked the moniker up, and now everyone was using it.

Stokely Jones had never sat a horse in his whole damn life, and he obviously wasn't very happy about the idea either, Hawke noticed with a grin. The idea of Stoke finally encountering a foe who was bigger and stronger than he was made Stoke nuts.

"Look at him, eyeballing me like that," Stoke said to Patoo, who was holding the reins of a huge black Arabian, snorting, bucking, and pawing the sand. "Horse doesn't like me and I ain't too crazy about him, either. You think I could kick this horse's ass in a fair fight, Patoo?"

"No."

"Well, let's just hope it doesn't come to that," Stoke said, sticking his boot in the stirrup. "I pity this poor sonofabitch if he pisses me off."

"You see those hazy mountains in the distance beyond the desert, Mr. Jones?" Patoo said. "Many thousands of meters high. Freezing wind and icy ledges sometimes only one meter wide. You wish to walk up there, brother?"

Stokely got on the damn horse.

An hour later, as the air cooled dramatically and the setting sun shot red arrows of light streaking through the haze, Stokely and Harry Brock were racing each other across the sands, up and down the windblown dunes, shouting curses and laughing at each other, galloping hell-bent for leather around and around the army compound. Hawke looked up from the weapon he was cleaning and caught a glimpse of them through an opened window. He smiled. The team was coming together. And when a team makes a commitment to act as one, the sky's the limit.

Tonight the thirty grizzled Pak militia fighters who would accompany them were preparing a great feast around the bonfire in the center of the compound. Hawke was much reassured by the look of these battle-tested men. They'd been fighting the Taliban through the long, tough years, the house-to-house combat for control of strategic towns and villages.

Patoo and his militia were veterans of those cruel battles. He had told Hawke over dinner the first night, "Sir, every street battle in those days was like getting into a fistfight in a phone booth."

At dawn the little army led by Alex Hawke would mount up, ride out through the massive wooden doors of the army outpost, and begin their journey across the trackless desert toward the mountains waiting on the horizon.

"Eat, drink, and be merry, for tomorrow we ride," Hawke said softly to himself, smiling at the quaint old English homily before going back to work on his weapon, scrubbing the works of his M4 assault rifle with a toothbrush.

AT THAT PRECISE MOMENT, ANOTHER Englishman, fifty miles or so to the north of Hawke's position, was completing his ride. He and his camel herder had journeyed down from the mountains, his own horse slipping and sliding on the icy ledges where a single misstep might mean a death plunge of thousands of feet.

This particular mountain had, long before the existence of the written word, been known as Wazizabad.

Smith had made the journey down from the mountain many times, however, in far worse conditions, and so he was not overly concerned with death; or rather, not concerned with his own death, to be precise. The imminent death of others was a red fever in his brain; it was the only thing he lived for. He rode on.

Smith, ever the sensualist, enjoyed the occasional feel of level earth beneath him, the warmer temperatures of the lower altitudes, and the brilliant rays of the dying sun striking his cheeks. He rode toward the desert, through passes often so narrow he could barely scrape through. During the First Anglo-Afghan War in 1838, the British had marched an army of twenty-one thousand men through this same pass to retrieve "British honor" in Afghanistan.

He felt countless prying eyes pressing down upon him from the creases and crevasses, the deep folds in the earth and mountains, eyes judging his potential, weighing his possible net worth.

He drew comfort from the fact that certainly no one would mistake him for a wealthy Englishman. No, if anything he resembled a modern-day Lawrence of Arabia, riding tall in the saddle, swaddled head to toe in flowing white robes and blankets. Atop his head he wore a red-and-white-checkered scarf, wound round in a kind of turban.

His visit to the summit had been a brief one. A type of summit, really, with al-Rashad and one of his senior officers. He had traveled to the highest reaches of the Hindu Kush to see for himself that all was in readiness for what would be his ultimate strike. The time had come for him to drive a final, fatal stake into the very heart of the British Monarchy. And he had to see with his own eyes the men, the matériel, the final plans, and meet the man upon whose shoulders would rest the responsibility of ensuring that this time failure was not an option.

Six months earlier he had paid his old comrade the Lion of Punjab the princely sum of five million dollars. Money taken "off the books" from a secret slush fund he had access to at the Bank of England. Gold bullion had been placed in the vault of a small family bank in Basel, Switzerland. For that he had acquired the services of a certain Colonel Zazi, the second-most-powerful warlord in al-Rashad's universe, and his dedicated team of thirty young commandos whom he had been training here in the mountains for six long months. Zazi and his men were to be the backbone of his next operation. He had seen enough to satisfy himself that it was a backbone made of steel.

He looked back at the camel carrying his supplies in saddlebags cinched round his girth and smiled. Though he was a man of a certain age, his still youthful face was alight with a fire that might terrify the unsuspecting. The fire inside burned brightly and its fuel was pure evil. He was a man nearing the resolution of a destiny predetermined long ago. He knew his time was short; the fuse that was his life of vengeance was burning rapidly, and he spurred his steed onward.

High above the desert sands, white stars burned holes in the black sky. He rode on, urging his camel driver to keep up.

He had an appointment in Samarra and he was running a tad late.

In the distance, barely visible on an unmarked paved strip of desert, he could now make out a black, otherworldly silhouette. It was sleek and ominous in the starlight, a machine from another planet. Two orange ovals were aglow at the rear of the beast, heat from the two Rolls-Royce BR710 engines. As he drew closer, the shape-shifter resolved itself into the now quite unmistakable outline of a Gulfstream V.

Jet black paint, gleaming under starlight. No markings. Blacked-out windows. Air Incognito, he liked to call his airplane. If you listened very closely you could hear the low *shhhh* of its two powerful engines, even at this distance.

He was feeling very close to the end of his life's journey now, and the hour of true vengeance drew nigh.

The door lowered out of the fuselage as he steered his horse down the black macadam strip to the waiting aircraft. Two men in black jumpsuits, armed against possible attack, descended the steps and took up protective positions on either side of the staircase, swiveling their weapons through ninety degrees in either direction. The G-V was a juicy target, and now was the time for extreme vigilance.

Smith dismounted and turned the stallion's reins over to his camel driver. Then he turned toward the opened door of the aircraft where two more men waited, hovering just inside. Smith beckoned them.

"See to my luggage, please, gentlemen."

This done, Smith pulled a leather pouch from inside his blankets and produced a thick wad of Pakistani rupees. His camel driver accepted this generous consideration, mounted his animal, and was gone into the desert vastness in a blink.

The Englishman quickly climbed aboard, the two armed men right behind him. Smith settled into his accustomed leather recliner on the starboard side of the aircraft and nodded to the pretty attendant who strapped him in.

"May I bring you something?"

"A pillow and a blanket perhaps. I am tired," he said. "I will sleep now."

"Ready for takeoff, sir?"

"Oh. You have no idea how ready I am, darling."

Minutes later, the twin engines at the tail roared and the sleek black airplane surged ahead at full power, pressing the Englishman deeply into his seat, and suddenly lifted off into the nighttime sky. After a steep climb, it banked hard left.

It was headed west.

TWENTY-FOUR HOURS LATER, THE ENGLISHMAN made a satellite telephone call to Sheik al-Rashad. "Hello, my brother," Smith said. "I just wanted you to know that I arrived safely."

"Brother, are you calling on a secure line?"

Smith laughed. "Yes, I certainly am. It is perhaps the most secure line in the entire world."

"Good. How may I be of further service to you?"

"It is I who wishes to be of service. I am calling you with a warning. First, is your Islamabad luggage still in your possession?"

"It is. I am expecting a courier in the next few days. He will then smuggle it directly into the belly of the Great Satan, as we discussed. The weapon will be detonated in the center of the designated American metropolis to maximum effect. And I anticipate it will come as something of a shock to the laughable nation of infidels who have grown so complacent, so pitifully weak."

Smith laughed. "A wake-up call so to speak."

"Yes, brother. But tell me. You mentioned a warning."

"Yes. I am calling to warn you about the man who forced your hasty departure from the hospital at Islamabad. As of this moment he is crossing the northern desert with a small army of heavily armed fighters, headed for the mountains mounted on horseback. Perhaps thirty or so. He is coming after you."

"Does he know where I am?"

"I'm afraid that he does."

"Precisely?"

"Yes."

"Then I must hurry and prepare a welcoming committee for this troublesome pest. We will ensure that he receives a very warm reception at Wazizabad."

"Brother, listen carefully to me. Do not take this man lightly. His name is Alex Hawke. MI6. He is one of the most effective and most lethal counterterrorists in the Western world. The Russians, the Chinese, the Cubans, all have confronted him, and all have regretted it. I would go so far as to say he is perhaps the most dangerous man alive. Many have underestimated him over the years, and all paid dearly, most of them with their lives."

"Ah, I see. So, I will heighten my security and use extra caution. I am capable of surprises of my own. I deeply appreciate this warning, my brother. Peace be with you."

"And also with you."

FIFTY-SIX

THE RAT PATROL RODE OUT at dawn; the desert air was frigid but bracing. Hawke rode a chestnut stallion standing fifteen hands at the head of his ragtag army. His weapon was in a leather scabbard mounted on the right side of his saddle. For some reason, during the night, Patoo had braided a scarlet pom-pom into the coarse hair at his animal's forehead, giving his steed a more warlike appearance. Hawke had named the stallion "Copenhagen" after the magnificent chestnut warhorse that carried Wellington to victory at Waterloo.

Hawke was followed by his now deeply trusted aide-de-camp, Abdul "Absolutely!" Dakkon, followed by Sahira. Behind her rode Stokely Jones on a huge white horse he had now taken to calling "Snowball," even though the horse's proclivity for biting humans and other horses made this innocuous name ill-fitting.

The previous night Hawke had ordered Sahira to keep her mount between his and Stokely's at all times as they crossed a desert valley. This high desert valley was still considered one of the most dangerous places on earth. But U.S. drones had made it a deadly place for Taliban or al Qaeda enemy fighters as well.

One hoped.

One thing, religious fervor aside, kept the insurgents fighting. Vengeance. Nearly all Taliban were ethnic Pashtuns who subscribed to an age-old code of conduct called Pashtunwali. One of its strictest rules was eye-for-an-eye revenge. Most Taliban had had many kinsmen killed in the war. Or imprisoned, or humiliated by Coalition searches of their family compounds. Most sought payback against those who had inflicted pain and dishonor upon their relatives.

"I want to die in the jihad," a fighter once told Hawke in Iraq, "not as a sick old man under a blanket at home."

Behind Stokely rode the bulk of the thirty leather-tough militia fighters under the command of Patoo. Next were the numerous camels and pack mules heavily laden with great leather satchels containing weapons, bottles of water, ammunition, comms gear, food, and other necessary provisions.

Bringing up the rear was Harry Brock, riding with five of the most seasoned desert fighters he'd handpicked from the whole crew. All of them had radios with orders from Hawke to immediately report anything even remotely suspicious. Harry was behaving himself, thank God. Stoke said, "Just you wait, boss. Sooner or later, he'll cop an attitude. Extreme pissed-off-ness or extreme bored-ness, one or the other." But so far, Brock had been a model citizen, if not a model soldier.

Hawke had assigned Harry and his five-man squad to act as skirmishers. It would be their responsibility to ride out and repel any attack by a small contingent of Taliban or al Qaeda warriors, keeping them away from the main body of the expedition. "Outriders" Harry had dubbed them.

Hawke was well aware that there were many warring factions under the command of various warlords in the Pakistan-Afghanistan border region. They constantly switched sides whenever their team appeared to be losing. But the skirmishes in these valleys were usually internecine, battles between the Taliban leaders themselves—or when the enemy was occupied countering attacks by the Pakistani army or the ferocious anti-Taliban militia armies.

The deliberately ragtag group he was leading would not normally generate much excitement among Taliban forces. Hawke's men and sole woman were all dressed like Bedouins over their flak vests. He hoped that was the image they presented, at any rate. Thanks to the commanding officer at the U.S. base at Shamsi, the assault team was blessed with enormous firepower in the event of an attack. Each and every one of Hawke's men was equipped with an M4A1 assault rifle within easy reach from the scabbards attached to their saddles.

These state-of-the-art weapons had a rate of fire of 700–950 rounds per minute. Accessories included an M203 grenade launcher, a laser system, reflex sight, and night-vision optics. Since sand penetrates everything, they had even been provided with baby wipes to clean their bullets with, making sure they were free from grit that could cause a rifle to jam.

About an hour into the journey, soon after the long caravan forded a wide and swollen river without incident, Patoo treated everyone to a bit of spontaneous poetry, using his radio to transmit it. For such a small man, he had a big, deep, sonorous voice.

"Cannon to the right of them, cannon to the left of them, cannon in front of them, volley'd and thundered. Stormed at with shot and shell, boldly they rode and well, into the jaws of Death, into the mouth of Hell . . . rode the six hundred," Patoo intoned.

There was a long moment of silence on the radio.

"Thanks, Patoo, 'jaws of death,' yeah, that was motivating, very inspirational," Brock finally said over the radio, his voice dripping sarcasm.

"You scared, Harry?" Stoke asked right back.

"Just cranky. Give me a chance to kill some Talib assholes who seriously deserve it and I'll be all better."

"So, scared or semi-scared?"

"Lemme tell you something, pal. Right now you couldn't shove a hot buttered pin up my sphincter."

"Yeah, you're scared. Heebie-jeebies, that's what—"

"From now on," Hawke interrupted, "everybody shuts the hell

up. Radio silence unless there's a threat or a hostile I need to know about. You'd think that was understood."

They rode on in silence, duly chastened.

THE FIRST DAY'S JOURNEY WAS relatively uneventful. They rode past many ruins, mud huts, and deserted villages. At one point, traversing through a small copse of fig trees, they disturbed a pair of antelopes who bounded away and were soon lost to sight. But, later, they did encounter one rather troubling demonstration of the truly bizarre quality of desert warfare.

Around five o'clock that afternoon, they came upon a small, bullet-riddled British fort, early nineteenth century by the looks of it, the forlorn outpost looming up just off to the column's right. The fort was star shaped, crumbling, but certainly still standing. Curiously enough, there was a thin wisp of grey smoke rising from a crack in the dome-shaped roof.

Hawke raised a hand, signaling a halt, and grabbed his radio.

"Stoke, you, Brock, and Patoo. Dismount. Let's go have a look inside. Abdul, you stay with the lady. Shoot anyone who threatens either of you."

The first thing they saw was a battered white Toyota Land Cruiser parked at a crazy angle on the far side of the building. There was a nice line of bullet holes stitched above the truck's rear wheel. It was the kind of vehicle the Taliban used in the desert. It didn't mean they necessarily were Talibs inside, but it didn't mean they weren't, either.

"Heads up," Hawke said quietly. "We stack up at the entrance. On me. Stoke, ready a flash-bang. Go."

Weapons at the ready, they silently moved around to the entrance.

There was no door, just an arched opening. They entered with caution, prepared for anything. Except what they found.

In the center of the main chamber of the centuries-old building, the smoldering embers of a cook fire sent smoke curling up to the ceiling. A charred joint of meat was on the spit, still dripping fat.

In each corner was a crumpled man, all of them breathing, but dead to the world. Each had an AK either cradled in his arms or splayed across his lap. The pungent smell of hashish and burned mutton lingered. And there was an empty liter of Johnnie Walker on the stone floor next to a half-eaten leg of roast mutton and a jug of water.

"Sure look like unholy warriors to me, boss," Stoke said, carefully removing their weapons without waking them.

Hawke said, "Wake that big one up, Patoo. Use the water jug."

Patoo picked up the jug and emptied it directly into the face of the largest of the four men. He sputtered, fluttered his eyelids, and stared up in some amazement at the man standing over him with an empty jug in his hand. When he reached for his missing AK, Patoo snatched his own 9mm pistol from the web holster on his thigh and pressed the muzzle against the man's forehead.

"Relax," he said to the man, first in Urdu, then in Punjabi.

"Ask him what he's doing here," Hawke told Patoo.

Patoo asked and the man spat something back.

"He is telling me to go have sex with myself, sir," Patoo told Hawke, his face apologetic for the obscenity.

"What the hell is this?" Stoke asked, picking up a blood-encrusted military shirt from a pile of similar clothing scattered on a stone stairwell. "Looks like British Army uniforms. Three or four of them. And British weapons."

Hawke took the shirt from him and examined the insignia on the sleeve. Then he saw bullet holes below the breast pocket.

"British Royal Marines, 3rd Commando Brigade," Hawke said. "Operating in Helmand Province across the Afghan border. That means these guys are militants who killed and stripped four of our troops of their uniforms and weapons. Bastards."

"Martyrs who fled across the Pakistani border to plan a suicide attack on a British outpost in Afghanistan, I'd say," Brock said, holding a suicide bomb vest aloft. "Hara-kiri. I got me a satchel full of fake British Army IDs over here, boss. Not to mention four more bomb-packed suicide vests. These four assholes were about to go back to Afghanistan on a mission, just a guess. Decided to get wasted before heading back across the border to blow themselves up and kill Brits."

"Make all their dreams come true, Harry," Hawke said, a look of abject disgust for the drunken look of hatred on the big Talib's face as Hawke headed for the door.

"What do you mean?"

"You said they wanted to get wasted, Harry. So waste them."

"Cool," Harry Brock said, as Hawke walked out of the fort, headed for his horse.

Four short bursts of automatic weapon fire reverberated inside the fort. Then Brock, Jones, and Patoo, grim-faced, emerged from the old fort and mounted up.

"Done," Brock said to Hawke before swinging up into his saddle. Hawke kept his eyes straight ahead, gazing into the distance. Shooting unarmed men was not something he approved of. But neither was blowing up unsuspecting British soldiers. It was war. Tough shit.

"Good," Hawke said.

And then they rode on, into the darkness. Into the jaws of death.

THE RAT PATROL SLEPT UNDER THE STARS that night. The three-part military sleeping bags, good to minus forty degrees, kept them all from freezing to death. At least they were bedded down in the lee of a massive curving sand dune. The towering dune provided protection from the howling wind and stinging sand that would have made getting any sleep at all impossible. And protected the horses, camels, and mules as well.

Hawke had assigned Brock and Patoo's skirmishers to form a perimeter around the makeshift camp. The seven men had dug shallow rifle pits in the sand and mounted their automatic weapons on tripods. Once this was done, Hawke walked the perimeter twice before attempting sleep. He checked to see that all the horses, camels, and mules were tethered and secure in one spot. The whole damn thing was far from perfect, but it was the best he could do under the circumstances.

ALEX HAWKE LAY ON HIS BACK, hands clasped behind his head, gazing up at the crystal clear constellations, thinking about what lay in front of them and subconsciously calculating their chances of survival. C's words of warning about the danger he faced kept reverberating in his brain no matter how hard he tried to sublimate them. The presence of a civilian woman, especially one he cared for, didn't help matters. He'd faced dangerous situations before, but, somehow, this one felt— A figure swaddled in blankets was approaching him through the darkness.

"I couldn't sleep."

"Sahira."

"I want to be with you tonight, Alex. Do you mind?"

"Climb in this bag with me right now or I'm going to sleep without you."

"I was hoping you would say that."

Hawke pulled down the nylon slider that secured the bag and made room for her. She crawled inside and he resecured the bag against the chill.

"Cozy," she said, embracing him, holding him against her body.

"Very."

"Are you mad at me for doing this?"

"Are you insane?"

"It's very unprofessional of me."

"So kiss me and I won't tell Lord Malmsey."

"Oh, Alex, I have missed you so since—"

"Ssh. More kissing, less talking."

He held her very close. She liked the pressure of his hand, urging her even closer. She cupped his cheeks with her palms, kissing him at last, but in a taunting way that made him want to kiss her brutally, take her now. Some women liked to be taken that way, roughly, and he suspected she was one of them. Lips, open a little in hunger, fed upon each other. His hands were two thieves: one holding her fast while the other made a desperate search; a hurried, clumsy thief pulling at buttons, tearing at openings.

"Do you think we can do this inside this thing?" she whispered.

"You're about to find out."

"You seem very determined."

"You've no idea."

Fingers under her clothes, "Yes . . . oh, yes."

"Be still a moment," he said, and she complied.

"We're going to make it through this alive, aren't we, Alex?"

"Of course we are," he whispered into her ear as his body slowly slipped deep inside hers. "Of course we are."

FOUR HOURS LATER, ALEX HAWKE was awakened by Harry Brock. The man was kneeling beside him, squeezing his shoulder. Hawke opened his eyes, blinded by the light of the rising desert sun.

"Harry? What's going on?"

"Bad news, chief. We got a bunch of horsemen headed our way. Full gallop."

"How the hell do you know that?"

"Patoo. Little guy puts his ear to the ground every sixty seconds or so. Been doing it all frigging night. This time he picked up riders. Lots of them. Damn it. Some shepherd or goatherd must have spotted us and told the bad guys we were coming."

"Number of bad guys?"

"A very large group, he says. Very, very large."

"How far out?"

"Thirty minutes. Maybe twenty. Do you think we can outrun them?"

"Only if we left all the camels, mules, ammunition, and supplies behind. Which we clearly can't do."

"Yeah, right. So we can't run and we can't hide. Shit. Now what?"

Hawke said, "Look, I've got an idea. Get Stoke and Patoo. Meet me at the base of the dune where all the livestock and horses are penned. Two minutes. Have Patoo get all the militia fighters up and ready and scared silly. Order them to use their pack shovels and start building a five-foot-high berm. Circular. Radius of thirty feet. And tell them to build it far enough away from this dune that we can't take fire from above. And make sure all the horses are tethered safely on the other side of that dune. We're not going anywhere without them."

"Done."

"Got it all? Hurry."

Harry was gone.

Sahira peeked out from under the zipped-up bag. "What can I do, Alex?"

"How are you doing with your M4 rifle?"

"I'd say, comfortable."

"Ever killed a man?"

"Of course not."

"Get ready, then, darling. Every bullet helps."

FIFTY-SEVEN

Hawke, Abdul Dakkon, and a number of solemn-faced Pakistani militia fighters led some of the livestock, the maximum number of mules and camels they thought they could spare, around the circular berm now being constructed by their brethren, who were digging madly. Hawke had never seen men move with such ferocious alacrity in his life. Like a scared sailor with a bucket on a sinking ship. The thing was about three feet high and thirty feet across. And it was almost complete.

Patoo was prone in the center of the ring, his ear to the ground.

"Patoo," Hawke said, "how long?"

"Another twenty minutes if we're lucky, sir."

"Well, then I guess we have to be lucky," Hawke said, with a reassuring smile.

Hawke then ordered the men to tether the big animals nose to tail in a large circle all around the exterior circumference of the makeshift redoubt, putting a space of about two feet between each camel or mule. When this was done, he pulled his pistol and told the others to do the same.

"Now comes the hard part," Hawke said, walking over to the nearest camel. First, he removed the leather saddlebags from the animal and threw them to the ground. Then he put his pistol to the side of the beast's head and pulled the trigger. The camel shuddered and dropped right on top of the berm. Hawke then cinched the saddlebags to the camel's carcass facing outward. All those leather packs and saddles full of water and canned goods would afford a little more protection.

He turned and beckoned Patoo toward him.

"Patoo, I want you to go make sure absolutely every one of your men is armed to the teeth, has plenty of ammunition, and is positioned shoulder to shoulder inside this circle in five minutes. Run!"

"Yes, sir!"

"This is how you do it," he said to his men, moving on to the next mule, raising his pistol to the animal's head and repeating the process. In five minutes he, Brock, Stoke, and a couple of others had killed all the animals, creating a makeshift breastworks around the diameter that now stood about five feet in height. High enough to provide protection, low enough to fire over. It was hardly an ideal fortification, Hawke thought, surveying it, but it would simply have to do under the circumstances.

At least he'd fight with good men at his side.

One look at the dark-eyed and heavily bearded militia and he knew Patoo had chosen his small band of fighters carefully. Hawke had been constantly studying them, assessing their willingness to fight when things got spicy.

Then he'd seen the looks on their faces as the battle drew nigh. He'd never seen such volcanic hatred in men's eyes. These were men—and boys—who'd seen the Taliban stone their sisters and mothers to death for sport, or cut off the fingers of anyone caught smoking. Seen Taliban thugs drag their fathers and brothers from their houses into the streets. Where they were castrated and then beheaded and left to rot where they died. Their brothers' heads mounted on pikes on the roads that led into their villages, welcoming them home with empty eye sockets.

At night, the Taliban would roam the streets, amusing themselves with a game they laughingly called the "Dance of the Dead."

They would prop a beheaded corpse upright and pour gasoline into the open neck. When they set them afire, the dead would jerk their limbs spasmodically and kick their hideously bent legs outward before collapsing into the street. This blasphemy, the self-righteous Taliban seemed to find endlessly amusing.

The militiamen now standing with Hawke had seen this kind of thing happen to their families for decades. They would fight to the last man.

Five minutes later, Hawke's entire army was in readiness, standing side by side inside the perimeter of the hastily built breastworks. The tension was palpable and Hawke stepped to the center. He felt it necessary to say a few words.

"We are reasonably well protected. We have enormous firepower and unlimited ammunition. The men who are coming for us will be on horseback and they will fight to the death, which, for them, is the ultimate reward. I want each of you to pick individual targets and stay with them until the kill before moving on to the next. Make every shot count. Shoot the horses out from under them if necessary. When the fighters get up, kill them quickly before they can charge us on foot. I guess that's it. Good luck, God bless you, and good shooting."

He went silently around the circle, shaking hands with each and every one of them, looking them in the eye, showing his confidence in them with his eyes and his smile. When he got to Sahira, he held her hand a little longer and bent his head toward her ear.

"Listen carefully. I am sure we will be all right. But if the worst should happen, you should know that under no circumstances will I let these barbarians take you alive. Do you clearly understand what I am saying? What I will have to do?"

"I do, Alex. And I appreciate your concern."

"It's more than concern, Sahira," Hawke said with a gentle smile before walking away to take his place among the men standing at the breastworks.

—

THEY SAW THE RISING CLOUD of dust long before they heard the thunderous pounding of hoofbeats drawing nearer. Stokely Jones, who was standing to Hawke's immediate right, was leaning over the berm, peering through a pair of tripod-mounted, extremely high-powered Zeiss 8X30 binocs, his well-used M24 SWS sniper rifle at the ready beside him.

He would see the enemy long before the enemy saw the tiny band of fighters taking a desperate stand behind a pitiful mound of sand, the carcasses of dead animals, and old leather saddlebags. Stoke was a trained ex–SEAL sniper and it was said he could shoot the wings off a firefly at a hundred paces. He would start picking off the enemy in the vanguard as soon as they appeared in his lenses. The opposition's day always got off to a bad start seeing their commanding officers toppling from their saddles before they'd seen, or even engaged, the foe.

"See anything yet?" Hawke asked Stoke. He'd been looking around at his defenders, all of them doing last-minute weapons checks, adjusting their Kevlar flak vests for the tenth time, getting mentally prepared for battle.

Praying.

"Just the dust cloud," Stoke said. "Big damn dust cloud, though, and moving fast in this direction."

"As soon as you acquire a target, start shooting. Pick off as many of the obvious commanders as you can. As soon as the main body is in range of our weapons, I'll give the order to fire at will."

Hawke saw Abdul at the breastworks, speaking quietly with Sahira. Earlier that morning he'd asked his reliable new friend to stick by her during the battle, no matter what, afford her all the protection he could. Dakkon had proven his bravery and loyalty beyond question. Hawke knew the man would lay down his life for any of them.

Harry Brock, at his station to Hawke's left, had pulled a battered harmonica from his vest pocket and was playing it softly.

Hawke recognized the plaintive American Civil War tune, even recalled some of the lyrics, sung to him as a child long ago by his American mother. "Mine eyes have seen the glory of the coming of the Lord . . ."

"What's that song called, Harry?" Hawke asked.

" 'The Battle Hymn of the Republic.' "

"It's lovely. Don't stop."

Harry played on as the massive twister of swirling dust and sand drew nearer and nearer.

Faces appeared out of the dust, hard faces with hooded black eyes and tangled black beards, tattered robes flapping wildly behind them in the wind. Glittering belts of ammo criss-crossed their chests. Their mouths were torn black holes in their fierce faces; but their murderous war cries went unheard, obliterated by the pounding hooves and the sudden explosion of gunfire.

At the forefront of the charge was a big bearded man in flowing black robes that were wildly whipping and snapping behind him. The commander was beating his horse, urging his steed to gallop even faster. He had his rifle raised above his head, exhorting his troops onward with fierce battle cries.

"Who is that man leading the charge, Patoo?" Hawke asked.

"That is the legendary Colonel Abu Zazi, sir. He is Sheik al-Rashad's brilliant and brutal second in command. He was born in the United Kingdom and graduated with honors from Royal Military Academy Sandhurst. He is now responsible for the worst of the suicide bombings in Pakistan and Afghanistan. He leads an alliance of Taliban, Punjabi militants, al Qaeda, and the former Mehsud fighters."

"He looks fearsome enough, I'd say."

Dakkon said, "Colonel Zazi has a price on his head of US$5 million, sir. He was among the assassins who murdered Pakistan's beloved premier Benazir Bhutto."

Looking through his binoculars, Hawke clearly saw the face of his enemy. And knew beyond any shadow of a doubt that he was in for the fight of his life. Outwardly he awaited the battle with composure and confidence. This was one of those times that called for stern tranquillity.

"Now I know how General George Armstrong Custer must have felt," Harry Brock said, firing as rapidly as he could. The mad horde of wildly galloping Taliban fighters, shouting and screaming their war cries, had completely encircled them. There had to be at least a hundred of them, riding around and around at full gallop, directing the fire of their AK-47s at the vastly outnumbered men inside the pathetic and hastily built fortification.

It may have been pathetic, but it seemed to be working, Hawke thought, as he slammed another mag into his weapon, welded the stock to his cheek, and rapidly killed as many men as he could before pausing to reload. Bullets filled the air, whistling overhead, thudding into the berm, and sometimes finding his men. He already had two of his fearless militiamen dead, and four badly wounded.

But Patoo's gravely wounded Pakistani militiamen stood their ground and kept fighting. They were not fighting for their lives, Hawke knew. They were fighting for the very soul of their country. And they were fighting in the memory of their fathers, their mothers, their sisters, their brothers, all victims of the vicious Taliban jihadists.

Hawke believed he could ask for no finer men than those who fought at his side.

Stokely had taken to firing RPGs into the ground in the midst of the charging Taliban horses. His objective, Hawke saw, was not only to take out the horses, but to create large craters with the exploding grenades. This caused a great many of the horses to stumble when the unexpected hole appeared suddenly, and they went down, throwing their riders to the ground and making them much easier targets.

"Where the hell'd you learn that, Stoke?" Hawke shouted over the deafening roar of gunfire.

"I didn't," Stoke said. "I just made it up."

Hawke laughed and took out a large number of fighters who were stumbling around looking for their AKs after being thrown from their mounts. Some of the militia fighters had seen what Stokely was doing and began doing the same thing. One man fired RPGs, the two men to either side of him concentrating their fire on the thrown fighters as they scrambled to their feet.

The firefight raged on for ninety blistering minutes.

The now-diminished enemy forces showed little sign of retreat, continuing to pour it on. Brock thought he was in one of those battles where the bad guys just kept turning the volume up, and it was getting louder and louder. They had at least three or four KIAs inside the redoubt now, and many more wounded still standing at their stations. Brock began to wonder how much longer they could withstand this withering assault.

And then the brave little man to his left, Patoo, was killed, the incoming round tearing away most of his throat, blood spouting out in gouts as he lay sprawled on his back on the ground, no chance. The militiamen had lost their brother and leader.

Brock saw Hawke register Patoo's death, saw the devastated look on his face. And then Hawke was going about inside the circle, walking right through the hail of bullets whistling across the compound at head height, encouraging Patoo's men to stand up to their duty and not let the bastards whip them. He never once sheltered his own person, and Harry could not see how he escaped being killed.

Hawke was one of the bravest men he'd ever seen in a fight and he'd seen one hell of a lot of brave men.

"Harry!" Stoke shouted. "Above you!"

Brock whirled around to see a Talib fighter standing atop the berm with a sword in his hand, a demonic look on his face, and clearly ready to relieve Harry of his head. Guy must have crawled on his belly up to the berm when Brock was kneeling and reloading, trying to comfort the dying Patoo at the same time. No time to get his rifle up, so he whipped his sidearm out of the holster on his thigh and brought it to bear on the man just as the sword blade started its deadly arc toward him.

He shot the guy in the face, causing him to drop his sword and pitch backward onto the blood-soaked sand.

When Harry got back to his feet, he saw an amazing thing.

The enemy seemed to be withdrawing. They had taken severe casualties, had probably lost more than half their original force, and it looked like the bad guys didn't like the heat and were getting out of the kitchen. At least, temporarily.

"Keep firing until they're out of range," Hawke said to Stokely, before expending an entire mag at full auto on the retreating foe. "Then use sniper sights and see what you can do to the rear guard."

Brock said, between bursts of automatic fire, "A good victory, I'd say, chief. How the hell did we survive that?"

Hawke, reloading, said grimly, "Right. Another victory like that one and we'll all be dirt-napping throughout eternity, Harry. We are now officially in what we used to call in the Royal Navy, 'the Deep Severe.' "

"What do you think, boss?" Stoke said, pausing to reload. Then he saw Hawke had his radio out and was desperately trying to raise somebody, anybody, to come to their aid. "Bloody thing doesn't work! We're in a dead zone," he said, and he threw the radio to the ground in frustration, before regaining his composure.

"They'll be back," Hawke said, still firing at the last of the retreating enemy. "They're only nursing their wounds, regathering for the next assault. Pausing to regroup and replenish their ammunition. The commander, Zazi, if he's still alive, is at this moment coming up with a new strategy of attack."

"Well, we can hold them off," Brock said, trying to convince himself.

"I don't think so, Harry. We're still seriously outnumbered. If I were Colonel Zazi, I'd be telling the troops to bunch the horses up flank to flank, charge straight at us, en masse, and simply overrun our position."

"Yeah, that'd probably work."

"Harry, listen up. I don't know how much time we've got before they come back at us. Here's what I want you to do. These radios are useless. You've still got the sat-phone satchel? Tell me it's not all shot up?"

"Right here. Looks intact, I think."

"You need to take it and leave the compound. Right now. Go to the top of that dune, set it up, and try to call in some help. You may not raise anybody, but you've got to try, it's the only chance we've got. The B-52s just across the border in Afghani airspace can't help from that altitude, but if they could send in a nearby AC-130 gunship from over there, we might get through this. You'll get a lot of bureaucratic crap about invading Pakistan airspace. Don't listen. Give them our approximate position and the strength of the enemy and tell them just how bloody serious this is. Tell them we've got our guys dying out here . . . we need help before we get overwhelmed. Go, Harry, go. Godspeed."

HARRY BROCK, AT THE TOP of the giant sand dune, set the range finder next to the satellite phone in the sand beside him. He pulled out his map and spread it out, using the spidery legs of the sat phone to keep the map from blowing away. Then he looked out across the valley they had passed through. He looked to the mountains on either side, their prominent features, the way they funneled down to their present position, matched that with where they'd built their defensive perimeter. He could still see the old British fort in the hazy distance. He absorbed it all, creating a map in his mind.

Then he looked down at his real map, transposing the features in his mind on to the elevation lines fanned across the paper. He did this many times, looking back and forth between the valley and the map until he located the position on the paper that matched the features he saw with his eyes until he had a fix on their position. He pulled out his small spiral notebook and wrote down the position's grid coordinates. These would be the numbers he would radio up to anyone he could raise and—

He heard a clink of metal and grabbed his weapon. Five armed Taliban fighters were just starting the long climb up the dune.

MINUTES LATER HAWKE HEARD the rattle of heavy automatic weapon fire coming from the direction where Harry had disappeared behind the dune. At least three or four weapons firing simultaneously. Hawke figured Harry had surprised a Taliban squad mounting the back face of the dune on foot. Planning to use the dune's elevation to fire down into the redoubt.

Harry was probably dead.

And no help was on the way.

They'd stand alone.

ONE HOUR LATER THE ENEMY force returned with a vengeance, riding en masse, just the way Hawke had predicted. He'd pulled every man who could still fight to the forward rim of the circle facing the onslaught. Stokely had patched up the wounded militia guys and now, God only knew how, they were back on their feet at the ramparts. They all started firing RPGs the instant the Taliban horsemen got within range, eleven hundred meters. It had some effect, a lot of horses went down, but it was not nearly enough to even slow the charge.

"Full auto," Hawke shouted up and down the line. "Keep pouring fire into them, throw as much lead out there as you possibly can."

And they did, but still the enemy kept coming, and their intentions were clear. They would simply roll right over the flimsy fortification. Then wheel, return, and kill every single one of them with blades or bullets.

Hawke looked over at Sahira, firing her weapon with an intensity he'd never imagined she was capable of. Abdul Dakkon stood beside her, cleanly picking off anyone directing fire in their direction. Hawke called her name and she looked over at him.

He shook his head and mouthed the words, *I'm so sorry*.

He saw the tears rolling down her cheeks and his heart broke and once again he felt that stabbing—

"Look! The top of the dune!" he heard Stokely shout. "Holy mother of God, will you just take a look at that!"

Hawke whirled just in time to see an armored U.S. Army Humvee come flying over the top of the massive dune and go skidding down the face of it, throwing out waves of sand. It was followed by a second, a third, and then a fourth! The four vehicles immediately whirled toward the enemy, raced across the desert, and inserted themselves directly between Hawke's team and the charging Taliban horsemen.

Hatches flew open in the roof of each vehicle, and soldiers manning M240 7.62mm machine guns opened up on the now-terrified horsemen. The Humvee was also equipped with an MK19 40mm grenade launcher now firing a variety of grenades at an effective range of more than two thousand yards. The Americans were launching them into the enemy at a rate of sixty rounds per minute.

The Taliban force, shocked and disoriented, either died in the saddle or turned and ran. Most of them died. The Humvees charged in pursuit of the retreating enemy, and Hawke knew their fate was sealed.

He looked up into the vast blue sky above and thanked whoever was up there. It was over.

Hawke, deeply moved by the courage he'd just witnessed, went around the little compound with Stokely. While Stoke, who had extensive battlefield medical experience thanks to Vietnam, tended the newly wounded, Hawke embraced each man in turn, saying to each, "Well done. I shall always remember your courage."

When he came to Sahira, he embraced her, too. He whispered into her ear, "I told you we'd be all right."

"I didn't believe you," she said.

"Frankly, I didn't either."

—

WHEN HE WAS SATISFIED THAT EVERYTHING possible was being done to care for his dead and wounded, Hawke left the compound and headed behind the dune to retrieve the body of Harry Brock.

He found Harry lying spread-eagled on his back, high on the back face of the dune next to his satellite radio and his rifle. Blood was seeping from his multiple wounds into the sand. Below him were five Taliban, sprawled on the back of the dune, dead.

"Hey, chief," Harry said, blinking his eyes in the harsh sunlight and smiling through the pain up at his friend Hawke. Blood was trickling from the corners of his mouth. He seemed to be drifting in and out of consciousness from loss of blood.

"You okay, Harry?"

"Couple of holes, that's all. We beat those bastards?"

"Yeah, we beat 'em, Harry."

"We don't pick fights, we finish 'em. Ain't that right, boss?"

"That's right, Harry."

Hawke knelt in the sand, slid his hands under the man, rose to his feet, and started down the wide face of the dune with Brock in his arms. Harry was clearly in pain and, mercifully, he'd passed out again.

"The cavalry showed up, Harry," Hawke said to his unconscious friend. "You did your duty. I hope to God you make it, old friend."

FIFTY-EIGHT

THEY CLIMBED HIGHER INTO THE MOUNTAINS. Fewer men, fewer horses, fewer supplies. The Rat Patrol they'd called themselves. Now, hair stringy, their beards coarse and foul, they'd been reduced to brushing their teeth with their fingers; all of them had begun to reek. The riding, if you could call it that, was nightmarish on the narrow, icy mountain trails. Snow, wind-whipped off the mountains, made visibility poor to nil. The fact that the horses could even keep their footing was miraculous. The cold at this altitude, nearly ten thousand feet, was deadening. Hawke hadn't felt the reins in his hands in hours.

The four Humvees had provided a reassuring escort through the tribal badlands to the foothills of the very mountains where Osama bin Laden was rumored to be hiding. The U.S. Army had also secretly entered Pakistani airspace, sending in a big Chinook helicopter to evacuate the dead and wounded in the tiny compound where they'd made their stand. Hawke had held a brief prayer service for Patoo and the others who had died as the chopper descended out of the red haze of early evening in the desert.

When it came time for Harry Brock's stretcher to be loaded aboard the helo, Brock had insisted he was fit to fight, but Hawke had insisted he clearly was not. Hawke had won that round, mainly because Brock was so weak from loss of blood that he couldn't sustain the argument. He and Stoke had been there when Harry's stretcher went aboard. Both men shook his hand, expressing deep gratitude for all he had done to save so many lives.

"I can't stay and fight?" Brock asked weakly.

"No, Harry," Hawke said.

"Cuss," Harry said and disappeared inside the big helo.

THEY'D LOCATED THE MOUNTAIN CALLED Wazizabad using the crude hand-drawn map Stokely had extracted out of the diminutive prison imam. The one who'd waived his legal rights sixteen miles out in the Atlantic off Miami.

The distinct features of the formerly mythical mountain's peak on the map exactly matched what they were all looking at. It was a majestic, threatening thing, a jagged pyramid of rock that scratched the sky, clad in ice and snow, its upper reaches swathed in dull grey clouds and whirlwinds of blown snow.

This, Hawke wanted to believe, meant they were looking in the right place. But the Pakistani imam Stoke had busted in the Glades Prison wasn't stupid. If he'd spent a lot of time in this region, he could have easily drawn the shape of the mountain he remembered most clearly.

He was not a man to give up hope. But they'd been climbing the mountain since daybreak and were now nearing the pinnacle. So far, they'd seen nothing that would indicate the rabbit warren of tunnels supposedly inside this mountain.

An hour later, as the sun was setting, the western skies were turning purple and gold. But just as the temperatures began plummeting, hope rose. They had finally reached something that might be the entrance to a tunnel. They'd almost missed it in the growing darkness. The entrance had been cleverly disguised with boulders, but a ray of sharp sunlight pierced a small fissure in the rock and illuminated what looked to Hawke like the inside of a tunnel.

Hawke raised a hand for the long line of men and horses in his wake to halt. He dismounted, and, with the help of Stoke and Dakkon, began pulling away the heavy boulders that blocked whatever lay beyond. Hawke watched Stoke shoving a huge boulder aside and realized that without his enormous strength, this effort would have been impossible. Soon they'd created a hole large enough for a man to squirm his way through. Abdul was the obvious choice as he was the smallest of the three. Hawke handed him his SureFire flashlight and Dakkon climbed up and disappeared.

A moment later they saw his smiling face looking down at them. He crawled out and dropped to the trail.

"A tunnel, sir! Maybe the mother of all tunnels!"

Hawke ordered more men to dismount and remove all obstacles to the entrance. When the work was finally done, he entered the tunnel alone, his weapon in hand, his finger on the trigger, his SureFire mounted to the bottom rail of his M4. He walked about twenty yards into the darkness, looking at the ground for any signs of activity, recent or otherwise. Hawke knew this was simply the first of many such tunnels they would expect to encounter, since his map indicated the entire top of the mountain was honeycombed with tunnels and caverns both natural and man-made.

But this one would certainly do. Night was falling rapidly and so was the temperature. It had been a very long day, and shelter from the wind and cold beat the hell out of a night outside on the trail.

The nearly frozen, saddle-sore riders were indifferent about where this hole in the side of the mountain might lead. If it took them into the heart of the enemy lair, fine. But all they cared about at this moment was getting off the damned horses and out of the frigid blasts of air that had buffeted them every painful step of the way up.

The tunnel entrance, thank God, was also large enough to accommodate the horses. Hawke had a couple of his men lead them inside, tether them together, then water and feed them an abundant meal of the hay they carried. Hawke saw to it that the shivering steeds were also covered with heavy woolen blankets. He wanted them rested and strong in the highly likely event the team might need to beat a hasty retreat down the mountain.

They all squatted around a small fire and ate, gulping great draughts of warm tea as soon as the animals had been cared for. Then they unrolled the three-part sleeping bags and prepared to bed down on hard rock for the night, with hopes of getting some much needed rest. Having survived the Taliban attack, and climbing ten thousand grueling feet up a frozen rockpile on horseback, they were nearing the point of exhaustion.

So were Stokely and Hawke, but they could not responsibly bed down without a more complete recon of the tunnel to make sure their squad was safe, at least for the night. Stoke had the powerful SureFire lighting system mounted on the bottom rail of his weapon, too, and they used the powerful beams to make their way cautiously, deeper and deeper into the mountain called Wazizabad.

After about a mile without incident, they came to a fork. The tunnel to the left led downward, while the one to the right angled up. They decided to place guards here on four-hour shifts. The team would return the next morning and see where the upward-leading right-hand tunnel might lead them.

"I'm feeling we're close," Stoke said to Hawke, as they trudged back to the mouth of the tunnel. "You feel close, boss?"

"I will. When I'm staring at this murderous bastard over the sights of my gun."

"I don't see how the Rat Patrol will ever find this baby-killing a-hole Rashad, boss. This damn mountain is just one big maze. You took science class just like me. You put rats in a maze, they get all disoriented and shit trying to find the cheese. I hope you've got an idea how we're going to navigate this maze because I sure as hell don't."

"Yeah. I do have an idea, Stoke."

"You plan to share it with the grunts?"

"Sahira will lead us right to him, Stoke. Trust me."

"Sahira? How does she know any more about this place than we do?"

"She doesn't."

"Oh. Well, that clears that up. I guess I can just relax now. About finding a damn needle-nosed prick in a haystack, I mean."

"Yeah, Stoke, actually you can."

Stoke couldn't see Hawke's face in the darkness, but he knew the man had a big grin plastered on his kisser.

"Stoke, do me a favor. Find two good militiamen and post them on guard back at the fork. They'll be relieved in four hours by two more. Tell them my radio will be on all night if they see or hear anything out of the ordinary."

"Aye-aye, skipper."

Weary of bloodshed, wind, and weather, Hawke climbed into his military sleeping bag and was instantly asleep. Peace on earth, at least until tomorrow.

HAWKE, SAHIRA, AND STOKELY WERE up at first light. The rising sun flooded the cave mouth with rose-gold light. The three began unloading weapons and equipment chosen by a very accommodating Special Forces weapons specialist at Shamsi AFB. The first item they uncrated was Sahira's tracked UGV. This unmanned, remote-controlled ground vehicle, about the size and shape of a child's pedal car, was essentially guns, cameras, and sensors on tank tracks.

Although it was not widely known, there were currently more than six thousand combat robots in use in Iraq and Afghanistan. The model Sahira had requested was one she had helped to design. It was a British combat-bot, one specifically for tunnel warfare. It had sensors that could detect and analyze poison gas and bacterial agents. It was also designed to detect radioactive materials, which was the reason she needed it for this mission.

The UGV was also equipped with turret-mounted twin M249 light machine guns and multiple night-vision cameras, fore and aft. In the tunnels, "Ugg"—as Sahira had dubbed it—would be used to peek around corners and send a live video feed of hostile areas and investigate suspected bombs without needless exposure of personnel. It had the ability to locate or bypass threat obstacles in buildings, bunkers, and tunnels.

It could also identify and neutralize improvised explosive devices, or IEDs. Ugg was basically a robot soldier, packing serious heat, just like the ground troops. And, as Hawke had once heard a Royal Marine commando in combat say, "A robot can shoot second."

Ugg was able to follow inserted GPS waypoints, breach ditches, climb stairs, and navigate the most cramped conditions on its own. Robots were fearless. But Ugg was not an autonomous killer. Only a human could make it kill another human. If and when deadly autonomy ever came to robots, it would come on little cat's feet. Still, Ugg could take small-arms fire and survive to fight again. And it could be repaired easily, unlike a soldier or a Marine.

Hawke now had under his command twelve men, one woman, and the very sophisticated robot she'd designed. It was the minimum he would go in with, but he felt it was sufficient. He was sure this Sheik al-Rashad would have his primary stronghold well guarded. Hawke's team would have, he still hoped, some small advantage of surprise. In addition to Ugg, his fighters would be in full Kevlar body armor, with flip-down NVGs on their helmets to pierce the darkness of the tunnels. They would be carrying weapons vastly superior to the Kalashnikovs of the enemy.

And, unlike the Sheik's bunch of presumptively bored "Imperial Guards," they hadn't been sitting around idle, watching DVDs and playing pinochle for months on end. Hawke's team had been out there killing and getting killed; and that kind of thing had a way of sharpening your warrior senses.

"All right," Hawke said to the gathered assault team, "we're going to take this mountain today. Everyone knows what to do. Let's go do it."

The team moved forward, following Alex Hawke into the absolute darkness of the tunnel.

Hawke felt good. But to describe him as "overconfident" at this point would be a vast overstatement. He knew he was once again taking these people into harm's way and that mortal danger could be lurking around every corner. When the team came to the first fork in the underground stronghold, Hawke signaled the team to follow him into the right-hand tunnel.

THE TUNNEL ANGLED UPWARD, SOMETIMES steeply. Hawke, with Sahira and Abdul Dakkon immediately behind him, stayed in the lead. The militia fighters behind him, sensing a day of reckoning with the supreme Taliban leadership, were alert, composed, and spoiling for vengeance, eager for a fight. Stokely Jones, who brought up the rear, was constantly looking over his shoulder for any stealthy hostiles who might approach from behind.

Sahira had her primary weapon slung over her shoulder. In her hands was the remote controller for the armed UGV. A single joystick controlled Ugg's direction, forward, backward, left or right. The machine could also pivot 360 degrees on its axis. A second toggle rotated the turrets and elevated the barrels on the twin machine guns. In the center of the controller was a four-inch black-and-white screen displaying what the small, matte-black war-bot was seeing.

When the tunnel curved blindly in any direction, Hawke would halt the team and Sahira would send Ugg ahead to ascertain that no enemy guards, bombs, or IEDs lay in wait for them. Not to mention poison gas or airborne bacterial agents.

They trudged on endlessly in the cramped and fetid blackness, taking only the tunnels that seemed to lead toward the mountaintop, expecting enemy gunfire to erupt at any second within the deadly confines of the narrow tunnels. At least they were climbing toward their target, Hawke thought. Common sense told him the Sheik's stronghold would be higher, not lower. Sooner or later, they would encounter resistance and he was ready for—

Contact.

Ugg had picked up something.

Just around a bend up ahead, some kind of light. Hawke signaled a halt. Sahira brought the robot to a quick, silent stop just before it entered a large cavern that seemed full of misty red light. She looked closely at the tiny monitor, using the digital zoom as the war-bot went into target acquisition mode. Then she toggled Ugg forward very slowly until it was just far enough inside the lighted area for a recon.

The forward camera did a 360. It was a huge, natural cavern. Massive stalactites, glistening with shiny black obsidian, hung down from the dark heights above. Their sharp tips, steadily dripping water, were maybe thirty feet overhead. As were the tiny red lights up in the mist. Stalagmites reached up from the rocky ground, a small forest of them, through which ran a swiftly flowing stream of clear water, about two feet wide, the water level exactly that of the cavern floor.

The cavern was empty, save for two very alert, armed, and uniformed guards on the far right. Because Ugg remained in semi-darkness, the tiny camera lens extended before him on a long, telescoping rod, the guards had not spotted the war-bot. The guards stood at attention to either side of what appeared from this angle to be a round, steel vault built into a wall of solid natural stone.

The two men had their weapons at shoulder arms. Ugg had its sights on them now and was flashing a "Fire?" icon at the top of the screen. The battle-bot's twin machine guns could easily take them out, but Sahira knew Hawke didn't want the sound of automatic weapons echoing down the tunnels.

Hawke drew his sidearm from his thigh holster. He always kept a parabellum round chambered at times like this, and a full mag. He fitted the noise suppressor to his weapon, stepped silently out from the darkness at the edge of the cavern, raised his pistol and fired twice, *phut-phut,* two head shots.

The guards crumpled to the ground, and he motioned the team forward into the cavern.

"Maybe this is the Sheik's back door," Sahira said.

"Let's hope so," Hawke replied. "We certainly wouldn't want to come in through the front."

It was a vault. A massive round titanium door stood between them and whatever was on the other side. Hawke put the radius of the vault door at about fifteen feet. "Same handprint recognition pad," Abdul said, staring at the print screener mounted on the right.

"May I offer you a hand, sir?" Abdul said, looking up at Hawke and taking one of the newly dead guards by the wrist.

"Please," Alex said, and Abdul lifted the right hand of one of the corpses and placed it against the screen, activating it. Digital lights in the center of the round door began flashing. The large stainless-steel wheel at the center instantly spun through any number of combinations. A second later, the door suddenly swung open with a hiss, perhaps four inches.

The moment the door opened, Ugg's radiation detector began to beep softly for the first time. Sahira looked closely at Ugg's controller and studied the readouts the bot was analyzing, saying softly to herself, "This door has a lead shield."

"Talk to me, Sahira," Hawke said.

"Gamma rays," Sahira said. "We're on it. The nuclear device has got to be somewhere inside this vault. Although this is a very weak signal. The weapon may be shielded. Or located somewhere well beyond this location."

Abdul and Stokely swung the perfectly balanced one-ton door open just enough to allow the bot inside. Sahira used Ugg's joystick and tank treads to send it climbing up and over the rounded threshold of the vault's entrance. Once inside, she stopped it and looked at the readouts. "No human thermal heat, no gas, no bacteria," she said. "Trace radiation."

"What's in there, Sahira?" Hawke asked.

"Gold," she said, matter-of-factly.

"Go," Hawke said to his team, standing back and waiting as they entered before stepping inside.

Gold. An Egyptian pharaoh's fantasy hoard of gold. Endless gold, row after endless row of gold ingots and bars neatly stacked upon endless metal shelves, shelves that stretched off into the darkness and rose up to the dimly lit twenty-foot ceiling. Hawke made a quick calculation and estimated he was standing within six feet of many billions of dollars. Now he knew how al-Rashad funded his worldwide jihad, blowing up airports, schools, hospitals. He literally had limitless resources.

And that was just what he could see through his NVG goggles. He saw a dim rectangle of light at the end of one of the golden corridors and signaled his team to follow. The rectangle looked like an exit.

Ugg was first to exit the gold vault and looked both ways, the radioactivity sensor beeping noticeably louder now. A second later, Sahira, studying her monitor for hostiles, called out to the team stacked up at the door, "Clear! Go!"

NEAR THE END OF THIS NEW TUNNEL they came to a barrier. Not a physical barrier, but an ever-shifting spiderweb of red laser beams, constantly in motion. There was simply no way a human being could penetrate this barrier without causing every alarm inside the mountain to start screaming.

Sahira touched Alex's forearm. "Look all the way through the web. The beams are emanating from some kind of device mounted on the wall at the end of this tunnel. Take the device out, and we're clear."

"Right. But we can't get to it to disarm it."

"No, we can't. But Ugg can."

"Ugg can't get under the lowest beam. The turrets are too high."

"Maybe not. Watch this."

Sahira pressed a toggle switch on the controller and the bot instantly lowered itself until its underside was less than a half inch off the ground.

"How the hell?" Hawke said.

"Air suspension. I designed him with bladders that raise or lower him twelve inches."

"Wizard."

"Heartbreaker."

"Let's see what your little Ugg can do, shall we?"

"As you wish," she replied and pushed the joystick forward. The bot moved swiftly and silently beneath the lowest of the brilliant red beams, clearing by perhaps half an inch. Hawke and Sahira peered at the screen as the wall-mounted device came into view. "Now what?" Hawke said.

"Two options. I can use his robotic arm to open the device and sever the laser's power supply. Or I can fire a quick burst of automatic fire and destroy the whole thing."

"The former. The less noise we make, the better."

Hawke watched Ugg's mechanical arm extend, pry open the metal lid exposing the inner workings of the laser device, and use its finely articulated claw to carefully separate and disconnect the tangled myriad of wires. It clipped several with its wire cutters. Then it reconnected one red-coated wire to a new terminal before cutting one final connection.

"What's it doing now?" Hawke asked. "I mean you. What are you doing now?"

"Preventing any disruption of the status alert signal from going to the alarm systems when the power is cut off. Watch."

Ugg's pincers found the power cable and cut it cleanly. The laser beams disappeared instantaneously. The tunnel was clear. And there were no alarms.

"Good work. Let's go," Hawke said, moving rapidly to catch up with Ugg, the machine already disappearing around the next bend. Sahira suddenly clutched his arm.

"Alex! Stop!"

"What?"

"Look." She held up the controller. On the screen was another unmanned robot coming rapidly toward Ugg.

"That looks identical to the one you designed!" Hawke said.

"It *is* one of the ones I designed," Sahira said in utter disbelief.

"How many were manufactured?"

"Only a handful."

"So how the hell does this Sheik of Araby end up with one of our highly classified British robots in his personal arsenal?"

"I have absolutely no idea. Only someone who has access to the highest—"

She was interrupted by the resounding rattle of machine-gun fire.

"The other one is shooting at Ugg! Shoot back!" Hawke said.

Sahira's fingers flew all over the controls, blindingly fast, sending Ugg careening all over the tunnel while managing to keep both barrels of the machine guns pouring lead into its twin. The enemy bot tried to reverse away but Ugg accelerated, chasing down the evil twin and giving it both barrels, blasting it to pieces until almost nothing but the tracks remained, grinding to a smoking, sparking, frazzled halt.

Hawke smiled at the ridiculous sensation he was experiencing. He suddenly found himself wanting to cheer for a bloody machine!

FIFTY-NINE

THE SMILE DIDN'T LAST LONG. After an hour of climbing, always upward in the dark, the team entered a new stretch of tunnel, trailing along behind the wounded but victorious Ugg. Ugg's radioactive warning beeps had become much louder now, especially when it had passed the opening of a fresh tunnel leading off to the left. Sahira desperately wanted to explore it, but Hawke insisted they keep moving until they engaged the enemy.

He knew his men were tired and hungry. They'd been inside this bloody beehive for almost five hours without a break. But he knew better than to pause; he'd learned that the hard way once in Cuba. It had cost lives and he'd never forgiven himself.

This was the first lighted stretch of tunnel they'd encountered, and Hawke was proceeding with extreme caution. After the robotic battle, there was no chance the enemy was still unaware of their presence inside the mountain stronghold. It was only a matter of time before they would run up against some form of armed resistance. And, lacking any intel at all about the number and quality of troops guarding al-Rashad, he simply had no idea of what magnitude of force he was up against.

Just then Hawke caught movement out of the corner of his eye. Above and to the right. He looked up and saw a small security camera pivoting back and forth. He could even see the iris of the lens closing and opening as it paused and stared at him and his small assault force. This tunnel section was illuminated, and the rock walls appeared to be weeping water, two small ditches to either side carrying the water downward. Hawke was trying to figure out where all this water was coming from. It had to be snowmelt, runoff caused by the sun as it rose in the sky.

It was now only a matter of minutes before they'd meet the enemy, whoever the devil they were.

Hawke raised a hand and halted the team as Sahira sent the machine out for a peek around another blind corner. She stared at the small screen in shock.

"Oh my God, Alex, look."

It was a large phalanx of guards, Imperial Guards by the look of their splendid gold-braided epaulets and uniforms. Gold braid and scarlet sashes, turbans of silk the same shade of red. There had to be at least fifty of them. Quite possibly more. They were marching in tight formation toward Hawke's position, so many men that they were filling the tunnel, advancing shoulder to shoulder toward where Hawke's men were holding, awaiting orders.

Hawke turned toward his men, speaking quickly and clearly.

"Enemy soldiers coming down the tunnel. Roughly fifty. We've got maybe four minutes until they reach us. Sahira, you and Abdul, go back and check the tunnel we passed where Ugg got excited. But Ugg has to stay with us, I need him. Can you manage without his detection capabilities?"

"No problem. I brought a backup handheld device in case he was destroyed. Here's his primary controller. Are you comfortable operating it?"

"Yes. Go back to that tunnel, Sahira. Now. Find that bloody nuke. Stoke, I know your great god of war, Sun Tzu, would disapprove, but I say we attack, not stand and defend. They now know how small a force we are and will not be expecting aggression from us."

"Agree."

"We send Ugg out first, open fire with his twin guns to slow them down, create panic and disorder in the front ranks. The second his ammo's completely expended, I'll step out and throw three smoke grenades into the main body, blinding them, filling the space with smoke. Then we round the corner and enter the tunnel as one unit, moving as fast as we can right into them, simply firing ahead, covering quads, side to side, knowing we'll hit them because inside a tunnel they've nowhere else to go. With me?"

"All the way."

"Each man fires two weapons simultaneously, doubling our firepower. Rifle in one hand, sidearm in the other. Don't stop. Just roll right into and over them until we break through at the rear of their formation. Then turn and fire at them as we retreat to find our true target. Yes or no?"

"Yes."

Hawke toggled the fire control, opening up on the advancing phalanx with both barrels, swinging Ugg's turrets from side to side with murderous fire at this range. As men went down, troops surging forward from behind stepped over their dead and wounded only to be killed themselves. There were screams and shouts of confusion from the enemy. Hawke stepped out into the tunnel and heaved three cooked-off grenades into the midst of the enemy, instantly filling the space with thick white smoke.

"Good," Hawke said to his men. "We bunch up, stay glued to each other, move as a single unit and only fire outward at chest high level, got it?"

Every man looked at him, grim but determined, and nodded yes.

"Good. Let's knife through these troops and go find that child-killing bastard and do what we came here for. Go! Go! Go!"

Hawke, his men tightly gathered behind him, rounded the bend and waded as one into the swirling smoke, firing into it with everything they had, knowing their rounds were finding targets because the enemy had nowhere to run, nowhere to hide.

There was withering return fire, and Hawke sensed they were taking heavy casualties. But the enemy was surprised and completely disoriented at the sudden and vicious attack. They were firing wildly, killing more of their own than the invaders. Still, his militiamen were dying, falling around him. For every five feet he advanced, Hawke sensed losing two men.

Hawke felt like he was moving against a human tide of agony, mowing down whatever was in front of him, his boots slipping and sliding in the endless blood and gore that lay before him. It was as if time itself was paused, and this horrific journey through the tunnel of death would never end—but he finally broke free of the writhing mass of dead and dying bodies—and emerged, grateful to be alive, into clear air.

He looked over his shoulder at the swirling smoke. The most terrifying thing in combat is to be a leader who glances behind him and finds no one there. Then he saw Stoke emerge, saw him slap in a fresh mag, then whirl around and fire into the few enemy who remained on their feet. Hawke waited for more of his own men to emerge, fearful that all but Stoke had died in the firestorm.

But here came two, stumbling, one supporting the other. They looked shell-shocked from the carnage in such a confined space. He waited another minute. Only one more member of his militia came out of the smoke and blood. His team now numbered five. Ragged, reeking men, eyes blood red with smoke, now drenched in blood from head to toe. Five would have to do.

And Stokely Jones? Stoke was at least three more men all by himself, Hawke told himself.

So, counting Stoke, make it eight.

THE TUNNEL TURNED FROM ROUGH stone to smooth white marble. There were classical pillars and pilasters and pediments. There were heavily carved doors of solid bronze, and niches in the polished stone walls, each one with a bust or torso of great antiquity. Soft recessed lighting now illuminated hidden coves and architectural features, and Persian tapestries hung in great profusion.

It was like a dream after the nightmare they'd just come through, like coming up from the dark stygian underworld and into the Kingdom of the Sun.

Massive bronze double doors, a rampant lion carved into each one, stood at the far end of this brilliant passageway. Beyond them, he had no doubt, waited the master of this brilliant domain. The Lion of the Punjab, Sheik Abu al-Rashad.

Hawke held the keys to the Kingdom in his hand, a weapon capable of penetrating virtually any door ever conceived and now he'd get a chance to use it. He pulled the rocket-propelled slug from his web belt and affixed it to the muzzle of his M4. Unlike a grenade designed to effect a maximum kill radius, this explosive round was designed to punch a hole one foot across in three feet of steel-reinforced concrete. As far as he knew, it had never been used against doors like these but what the hell.

"You know the drill," he said to his four-man squad, and they stacked up behind him, weapons reloaded, and prepared to face whatever they found on the other side. Stoke took one look at the size of the grenade on the end of Hawke's gun, put a finger to his lips, and waved everybody back.

"As Adam said to Eve, 'Step back, baby, I got no idea just how big this damn thing is gonna get.' "

Hawke laughed out loud. It was just what they all needed. Hawke held the weapon six feet from the great locks where the double doors joined and pulled the trigger. The resulting shock wave buffeted him back, almost knocking him off his feet. The two doors blew inward with tremendous force. Had they not weighed so much, they would surely have been blown off their hinges.

As it was, the great doors simply smashed into the walls to either side of the entrance, causing, Hawke saw, massive damage to a portion of the Sheik's exquisite art collection.

"Picasso?" Hawke said to the man who had to be the Sheik as he entered, his .45 automatic pistol leveled in the middle of al-Rashad's chest. The man was seated and wisely had both of his hands on the desk in front of him. The room was exquisite, high white walls reaching up to a barrel-vaulted ceiling, floors of Persian marble inlaid with semi-precious stones, and tapestries woven in silver and gold thread hung from many of the walls.

"Dubuffet, to be precise."

"What the hell, they all look the same to me," Alex said, wiping somebody's blood out of his eyes with the back of his hand.

"Lord Hawke," al-Rashad said, smiling at him above the great expanse of his ebony and ivory desk. Stoke had swung inside the great room on Alex's heels, pivoting left and right with his weapon, covering Hawke and ensuring that the room was clear and that the target was all alone. He was. Stoke signaled, and the three remaining militiamen entered, taking up positions that covered both the entrance and egress, and the target himself.

"Sheik Abu al-Rashad," Hawke said, "so sorry to drop in unexpectedly."

"You come highly recommended, your lordship. And I must admit I'm impressed with your grand entrance. Nothing like it has ever been even remotely attempted."

"Really? Recommended by whom, may I ask?"

"Our mutual friend, of course. Mr. Smith."

"Ah, the ubiquitous Mr. Smith. Odd, we've never met. After all these years. Pity."

"He certainly knows you."

"Then I'm afraid Mr. Smith has me at a disadvantage."

"He does indeed."

"Meaning?"

"Meaning he is about to change the course of British history. And there is absolutely nothing you can do about it."

"Hardly merits discussion then, does it?"

"I suppose not. You are here looking for the missing device? Or simply to kill me?"

"Both."

"Good. In that case we shall mount on golden wings and fly to the gates of paradise together."

"I think not."

"I think so," the man said, raising his right hand and revealing something cradled in his palm. It was a shiny black metal object the size and shape of a pack of cigarettes.

"This is the detonator for the one-kiloton device. I have just depressed the button. It's now armed. If you care to shoot me, which I'm sure you do, my finger will obviously release the trigger. I will accept my martyrdom with joy. You, and everyone remaining alive inside this mountain, will die instantly. Why, my God, it will be spectacular. We'll blow the whole top of Wazizabad to the skies. Glorious."

"And if I don't shoot?"

"Your life will go on. You will bear witness. We stand here at the threshold of a new world order, Lord Hawke. A caliphate. A world where Sharia law is the rule of all nations. The new Golden Age of Islam. Do you believe in God, Lord Hawke?"

"I believe this moment in time is no accident."

"I honor you in this belief."

"Stoke?" Hawke said, looking his old friend in the eye. "What do you think?"

"Tough call, boss."

"Yeah."

"I think we do our duty and that's the end of it. We've always known we'd have to go sometime. At least this way, we go out in a blaze of glory, knowing we did what we had to do."

"You remember Admiral Lord Nelson's last words, as he lay dying on *Victory*'s deck in supreme triumph, having defeated the French at Trafalgar?"

"Tell me, boss."

"Thank God I have done my duty."

"Yeah. That's what it's all about."

"Ever since I was a child I've always thought that is how I would like to go out. A fine way to die, doing your duty."

Hawke raised the pistol, aiming it at the man's head.

"Don't take this the wrong way, boss. One last thing. I love you like a brother. Always have. Always will."

"I return it tenfold, Stoke."

Hawke said a brief silent prayer and squeezed the trigger.

Abu al-Rashad, who'd never once believed this man Hawke would willingly commit suicide, died with that thought still firing in his perforated brain.

Alex Hawke, who, a split second earlier, was prepared to lay down his life for his country, was staggered to find himself still alive. Al-Rashad's brains were spattered on the wall behind him. The little black controller fell from his hand and clattered harmlessly across the marble floor.

Hawke, dumbstruck, heard a voice behind him.

"All right then, you two lovebirds. Abdul and I found that dirty nuke," Sahira said from the doorway.

"You found it?" Hawke said. It seemed like he'd sent her off to look for it a lifetime ago.

"At the end of that tunnel back where Ugg lit up. We disabled it about five minutes ago."

"Only five minutes?" Stoke said, incredulous.

"Is that a problem for you?"

"Could have been a little bit, yeah."

Hawke and Stoke stared at Sahira in utter disbelief at how precisely they'd cheated death. And then the two men started smiling, grinning at her, lunging toward each other and embracing, pounding on each other's backs, convulsed with joyous laughter.

As Churchill once said, it wasn't the beginning of the end, but at least it was the end of the beginning.

SIXTY

BALMORAL CASTLE, SCOTLAND

A LONE MAN WALKED THROUGH THE DEEP and dusky Scottish wood. The forest floor was mossy and springy under his feet. It was early evening and he walked slowly beneath towering dark giants with massive limbs; he walked with a thoughtful gait, not stealthy, but somewhat self-consciously, almost as if he were being watched. He was, of course, but he was a recognizable figure on the property and so posed no threat. He wore his wool stocking cap low on his brow, hiding his predatory smile and his dark, shining eyes.

There were countless tiny security cameras nesting like small black birds in the trees above; and everywhere there were, too, unseen heat, sound, and movement sensors scattered throughout the property. His heart was pounding against his rib cage hard enough to splinter bones, but he was quite sure even the most sophisticated sensors couldn't pick up a heartbeat.

He was singing softly to his unseen audience as he walked, singing the words of Scotland's favorite son, Robbie Burns.

Gin a body meet a body
Comin' thro' the rye

Gin a body kiss a body
Need a body cry?
Yet a' the lads they smile at me
When comin' thro' the rye!

In the gloaming, a purple stillness fell over the trackless forests, the moors, and the placid rivers of the Balmoral estates. He walked on among the black trunks of magnificent specimen trees, many of them centuries old, some of them even planted by Prince Albert himself. He savored every step of this journey.

He had waited a lifetime for this night and this moment in time. As a small boy, he had foreseen this. All of his life, no matter what the dim and distant future held, a final reckoning was coming.

His heart quickened as he saw faint light ahead, deep in the woods. He slowed his pace now. He was approaching a small two-story lodge from whence came the light in the forest. It was built of rough-hewn logs, beneath a lichen-covered slate roof; smoke was curling from stone chimneys at either end. It looked like any one of dozens of such cabins and lodges, built over the centuries on the estate.

But this particular structure was quite unlike all those others. This unlikely spot was the nerve center of Balmoral Security Operations, home of Balmoral's state-of-the-art PIDS: the Perimeter Intrusion Detection System. It was run by SO15, now officially called the Counter Terrorism Command. This was a recently merged version of the old Special Branch, established in 1883, and the much newer Anti-Terrorist Branch, both divisions of Scotland Yard.

Working closely with agents of Lord Malmsey, the director general of MI5, the detectives stationed here on the property were responsible for the safety and protection of Her Majesty the Queen and all members of the Royal Family in residence at Balmoral Castle for summer holiday.

And here in this cottage a four-man team worked round the clock. They manned a formidable surveillance operation that ensured that there were no breaches of the security perimeter protecting the

Queen and her family. It was a full-time job and, to their credit, no one had ever penetrated their fail-safe systems.

Smith well knew Balmoral was the Queen's favorite place on earth. As had it been her mother's and grandmother's before her. It held a special place in Her Majesty's heart because here alone did she feel completely secure. At a safe remove from the world, she could jounce along the miles of rutted roads at the wheel of her battered Range Rover, left in peace to do as she wished, surrounded by her horses, her beloved Corgis, and of course her family. They had weathered many storms in the decade prior, but now at last it seemed tranquillity had settled in for good.

And Smith had long ago decided that it would be this haven, this paradise bequeathed to her by her ancestor Queen Victoria, where he would pay the Windsor family one final and terrible visit.

In the autumn of 1842, Queen Victoria, and her new husband, Prince Albert, paid their first visit to Scotland. They were so struck with the majestic beauty of the Highlands, they resolved to return again and again. For years, Victoria and Albert always depended on the kindness of friends who would graciously open their castles and estates to the enormously popular Royal couple.

Meanwhile, the Queen's physician, Sir James Clark, had recently been the guest of Sir Robert Gordon at his small castle, Balmoral, which lay to the east of the Grampian Mountains just beside the river Dee. Queen Victoria received many glowing reports from Sir James, not only about the magnificent scenery, but about the air, which he described as having "an unusual dryness and purity."

By 1848, Sir Robert Gordon had died, and the lease was for sale. Queen Victoria snapped it up, and so it was that in the autumn of that year, she and Prince Albert arrived to take possession of a property that they had never seen. They were not disappointed. In her diary that first evening, when the house was still all around her, the

Queen described a "pretty little castle in the old Scottish style, surrounded by beautiful wooded hills."

"It is so calm and so solitary," she wrote, "it does one good as one gazes around; and the pure mountain air is most refreshing. All seems to breathe freedom and peace, and to make one forget the world and its sad turmoils. The scenery all around is the finest I have seen anywhere. You can walk forever and the wildness and solitariness of everything is so delightful, so refreshing. And the local people are so good and so kind and so simple."

TODAY, THE QUEEN'S PRIVATE ESTATES, owned by the Crown, extend to just over fifty thousand acres, with sporting privileges leased on a further twelve thousand acres. The majority of the land is heather-clad hill-ground overlying granite. More fertile land lies along the south bank of the river Dee and is used for farming and forestry. The ground on the property is dramatic. It rises very steeply in parts, up to the top of the Lochnagar massif, which, at almost four thousand feet, dominates the entire area.

Every August and September, Her Royal Majesty Queen Elizabeth, the Duke of Edinburgh, the Prince of Wales, his wife, and his two heirs, Wills and Harry, abandon London and take up residence for a peaceful month or so at Balmoral Castle. There the Royal Family are able to escape the glare of the public eye and enjoy walkabouts, shooting, stalking the great fourteen-point bucks that roamed the moors. There was also boating and fishing on Loch Muick, a name the Queen was said to dislike intensely because it meant "pigs."

Charles had awoken that bright morning with a fine sense of anticipation. His wife, the Duchess of Cornwall, known here in Scotland as the Duchess of Rothesay, was not present. She was in London with her own son Tom, Charles's godson, who had suddenly taken ill. But both of the Prince of Wales's boys were home on leave from the military; and all looked forward to a magnificent day out in the country air with close friends and family.

Today was a very special day, the historic Glorious Twelfth. The Twelfth of August, celebrated each year, marks the opening of the shooting season for red grouse throughout the United Kingdom. As Prince Charles had a number of friends who were keen shots, it was his habit to invite them to Balmoral for a day out on the moors, shooting the driven birds. Afterward they would celebrate with a great game feast that evening with all members of the Royal Family and their guests in attendance. Even now, the kitchen staff was putting final touches on the evening's grand banquet.

SMITH WAS ABOUT A HUNDRED FEET from the cottage when he suddenly staggered and clenched his chest in agony. Stricken, he put a hand out to brace himself against a tree. After only a few moments, he made his way with difficulty to the side entrance.

Smith mounted the stone steps and rapped on the weathered wooden door. His face set in a rictus of pain, he was clutching desperately at his chest, breathing heavily, pounding again upon the heavily secured door.

"Yes, sir?" a Special Branch detective said, opening the door slightly and regarding him carefully in the dim light. "You all right, sir? Don't look well at all, I'm afraid."

"John. Dear old John. I say. Can . . . can you help me please. I—I think I may be having a bloody heart attack. There's a good fellow . . ." With that he pitched forward through the door and the man inside caught him in his arms. The three other officers manning the complex were staring at him, openmouthed, as he removed the leather satchel that hung by a strap from his shoulder and let it drop to the floor.

"Good lord, sir, steady on! We'll get on to the house physician immediately!"

He groaned in pain and the man called John stretched him out on the floor, before heading back to the console and the emergency telephone. "Won't be a moment, sir. Doc's always on call. Be here in two shakes of a lamb's tail, he will."

"That won't be at all necessary I'm afraid," Smith said in a suddenly strong voice.

All four spun around to see Smith on his feet, breathing normally, with a long-barreled .357 magnum revolver pointed in their direction.

"All of you, put your hands in the air where I can see them. Out of your chairs. Now! Everyone together in the center of the room. Turn and form a line, facing the wall."

They stared in horror at the large-caliber pistol in the man's hand, affixed with a silencer. They had no choice but to comply, not even a split second to send out a silent alarm. They simply did what he said.

"Noses to the wall, hands behind your backs," he said calmly, quickly binding them all with plastic cuffs. "Good. Now, how many of you are on duty in this facility at the moment? Anyone sleeping upstairs?"

"Just the four of us," the man named John said, furious anger rising in his voice. How could he have been so stupid? He had been trained never to open that door to anyone, not under any circumstances.

"You will never get away with whatever you have in mind, you know. You have no bloody idea what you're up against," John said.

"Really? Now how would you know that? In truth, I know exactly what I'm up against. Which means I've no further use for you lot. Except for you, John. Please step away from your colleagues and sit on the floor, back against the wall."

"Oh, God, no, please don't—"

Smith stepped up to each of the three remaining men in turn and put a bullet in the back of each skull without a word. He looked at his watch and moved to the console, looking at the monitors mounted above. He quickly located the one he wanted, a screen that displayed views of the main entrance to the estate from many angles. As he watched, a large delivery van rolled to a stop outside the black wrought-iron gates.

The lorry, even here in the Highlands of Scotland, was instantly recognizable. It bore the trademark of Harrods, the world-famous department store in Knightsbridge. You would see vans from the emporium often enough on the roads in Aberdeenshire. On the A93 between Braemar and Crathie, and on the secondary roads hereabouts, up from London, usually delivering treasures from around the world to the area's great country houses.

The van was painted in Harrods signature livery, a shade called "Harrods Green," a bespoke color that most closely resembled a metallic army green, and featured the familiar handwritten script, *Harrods,* in gold leaf on both sides and the rear.

Harrods, as it happened, was owned by the father of Dodi al Fayed, the Egyptian playboy who had courted and then died in a car crash in Paris with the Princess of Wales. In a famous trial, Mohamed al Fayed had publicly and vociferously blamed the death of his son and Diana on the Royal Family and MI6. He had lost.

That this particular van now stood waiting at the gates of the Royals' most sacrosanct of hideaways presented not a small bit of delicious irony for the always ironic Smith. The wolf, in sheep's clothing, was once more at the door.

Smith located the master control that opened the main gate. He hit the marked button and the big black gates swung open. The green van rolled inside the estate proper and the gates quickly closed behind it. Instead of proceeding along the main road to the castle, the driver veered off to the left, taking a narrow lane through the thick woods that came to an end at the Security HQ car park. There were a number of other vehicles, mostly open trucks with four-wheel drive for getting about the property in any weather.

Smith was outside waiting anxiously when the truck finally appeared out of the darkness and pulled into a spot next to a pair of mud-spattered Land Rover Defenders. He smiled at the sight of the satellite video dish now being raised atop the truck's roof. Inside the van were all the electronics necessary to broadcast live television throughout the U.K. from this remote location.

The driver's door swung open and out climbed his old friend from school days back home, a lanky chap dressed in a Harrods delivery uniform. His name was Hurri Singh. He'd been one of the most highly decorated heroes in the Pak Army, and one of the few men on earth he completely trusted. They embraced warmly, clapping each other on the back.

"No problems on the way up from London, I trust?" Smith said.

"None at all."

The two walked to the rear of the van and Singh opened the padlocks that sealed the double doors. He swung them open to reveal thirty heavily armed men, ten in civilian clothes, ten in perfect copies of Balmoral security uniforms, and ten commandos in full camo. They were seated along benches opposite each other.

Their eyes were eager; they were aggressive young men recruited from the poorer, more radical Muslim neighborhoods of London, all screened for intelligence, courage, and religious fervor. Once identified, they'd then been sent to the mountains of northwest Pakistan. There, under the aegis of Sheik Abu al-Rashad, in a terror camp operated out of the bunker at Wazizabad, they'd been through six months of heavy military/terror training.

One of Abu al-Rashad's most trusted veteran commando officers, a graduate of Sandhurst, had supervised these U.K. fighters during the preparation for this Balmoral operation, going so far as to construct a mock-up of the castle's interiors. His name was Colonel Abu Zazi. The burly, bearded desert fighter climbed down out of the truck and embraced Smith.

It was Zazi who would lead the critical phase of the attack.

The storming of Balmoral Castle.

SIXTY-ONE

ALL THIRTY OF THE YOUNG HOMEGROWN U.K. terrorists gathered around Smith at the main control console, listening carefully to his every word. No one paid the slightest attention to the three bloodied corpses crumpled against the rear wall. Although the fighters were barely out of their teens, they were all about focus. Tonight would be the realization of all their months of training in the mountains of Pakistan. And, finally, vengeance for the deprivations and humiliations heaped upon their families since arriving in the United Kingdom decades earlier. Not to mention the daily murder of their brothers by invaders in the mountains of Pakistan and Afghanistan.

It had fallen to these boys, these angry children of Islam, to deliver a blow of unprecedented magnitude against the infidels and their supreme rulers.

Ten of the young fighters were dressed in photographically precise reproductions of the Balmoral Security Forces uniform, right down to the buttons. They would be first to take action and Smith addressed them as a group.

"As you well know, your first objective will be to neutralize the Balmoral security guards and the Raytheon PIDS surveillance system of electronic fencing and sensors. Ten Balmoral security guards are all currently at their posts throughout the forests surrounding the castle. Ten monitoring stations, each not much larger than a small garage, are all linked directly to this command center. At the Wazizabad camp, you were provided with maps of the Balmoral estate, indicating the location of each station and its designated number. They have the maps, Colonel Zazi?"

"Of course."

"Good. When I give the order, you ten will proceed to your assigned stations in the vehicles outside, clear?"

"Clear, sir," they all replied in their oddly unaccented English.

"Do not deviate from your assigned routes through the woods. Each station is equipped with TV monitors displaying live feeds from the many closed-circuit cameras in every guard's assigned sector. In addition, as you know, they constantly monitor the various hard-wired sensors designed to alert them to any suspicious human presence on the grounds. Yes?"

They all nodded in unison.

"My old friend John over there on the floor is going to provide cover for your approach. John has a lovely family living right here on the estate, not five miles distant. So John is going to make an announcement to the on-duty security officers. When you arrive on station, you will look like an electrician and you'll be expected. In that satchel over there are dark green Balmoral electrical engineering jumpsuits and caps to be worn low over your faces."

"One question," Hurri said.

"Yes?"

"The glass in those forest stations? Bulletproof?"

"Good question. Should have been covered in training. Yes, it is. You will need to get the security officer inside to admit you. Big smile as you rap on the window. Remember, they are armed too. Anything else? No? Good. As soon as John's announcement is made, move out. John? We're ready for you now."

Two of the young terrorists dragged the bound chief of security over to the console and placed him in a chair in front of a microphone. Then they removed his cuffs.

Smith sat on the edge of the console looking down at the chief of security, now in a state of shock.

"Do exactly as I say, John. Should you deviate from the script, I assure you, two of these men will go directly to your home and kill your entire family. The children first. You know that I will do it, don't you, John?"

He nodded, tears in his eyes, a broken man.

"First, John, I want you to shut off all the power to every single motion, heat, audio, and thermal sensor within the perimeter. Do it now."

Like an automaton, John reached forward and pulled back on four bright red levers. All of the sensor readouts above were suddenly extinguished. "Good. Now do exactly the same with all the security cameras. Power them all down."

When that was done, Smith placed a handwritten script in front of the man and bent the microphone toward him.

"You're going to make this announcement. You're going to do it with a pistol at your head so you don't make any stupid mistakes. And you are going to sound as natural as possible under the circumstances. Let's do a rehearsal, shall we? Read it first without the live microphone."

He got through it, with only a slight tremor in his voice. In his mind, he saw nothing but the faces of his beloved family.

"Good enough. Try to give it a more 'just a minor glitch, lads,' attitude this time, will you? Now we'll turn the mike on and do it for real."

The man leaned into the microphone and spoke.

"Heads up, lads. Bit of a cock-up here with the electrical system as you've no doubt noticed. Some sort of a short between your stations and the main circuit breakers. I've already alerted Engineering staff and a team of electricians are on their way to restore power. They'll need to check the connections inside each of your stations.

We shouldn't be down for more than a few minutes, they tell me. No worries, lads. Everyone read me loud and clear?"

The ten officers could be heard over the speaker system, all responding in the affirmative. Smith switched the microphone off.

"Now, John, I want you to shut down the officers' interstation communications. Cellular has already been jammed; I can't have them talking to each other. As soon as those boys have shut this compound down, we'll move on to Colonel Zazi and Phase Two. In an hour or so. As General Singh will inform you, John, you still have a role to play. That's why you're still alive."

"Bugger it," the man murmured. His mind was racing in all directions, searching for a way to save his beloved Queen. But every thought was a dead end.

"Colonel Zazi, your men are fully briefed and ready to go?"

"Indeed. We only await your orders."

"Good. Have them use this time for a final weapons check."

From this moment forward, Hurri Singh would take over here in the command and control post and the ten stations soon under his control. The ten men who'd been sent out on the grounds to neutralize the Balmoral Security team had been trained to replace the dead guards at their individual stations. All of the cameras and sensors would then be restored to full power. Balmoral would once more become impenetrable, but the fox was now guarding the henhouse.

CONGREVE WAS AGOG. HERE HE was, at Balmoral Castle of all places, standing around in a kilt (first time ever in a bloody skirt, he believed) and HRH, the Duke of Edinburgh, was about to tell him and his fiancée, Lady Diana Mars . . . a joke.

"Are you quite sure you haven't heard this?" HRH asked them both, lowering his voice and leaning toward them conspiratorially.

"Quite sure, sir," Diana said, cool as the proverbial cucumber. "Please. Do go on."

"Well," Prince Philip said, lowering his voice, "as I was saying, this chap from Chilton had won the Lotto, a billion pounds for life or something, and this other chap, his mate, says to him, 'Wotsit, Harry? You have a fairy godmother in your family?' And Harry looks at him and says, 'No. But we do have an uncle we keep a pretty close eye on!' "

Congreve, who had not expected to laugh, chuckled so forcefully he spilled a drop or two of champagne on the tartan carpeting. Diana, bless her soul, tittered marvelously and smiled at the Duke with something akin to, if not precisely flirtation, then something close to it.

"Lovely to have you both here at Balmoral, Chief Inspector, Lady Mars," he said, before moving on to other, perhaps more fertile valleys. There were some lovely swans about this evening and he quite enjoyed their company.

"Got off quite a good one, HRH did, didn't you think?" Diana asked Ambrose.

"Yes, yes, dear, very good indeed," he replied, looking around the room. All the bejeweled ladies were in splendid evening gowns, and all the gents were decked out in kilts and sporrans, the full regalia. It was called "Scottish Black Tie" and worn in honor of the Glorious Twelfth.

Congreve surveyed the company, secretly pleased to find himself in such esteemed society. An abundance of famous faces, anyway, some more esteemed than others. He was delighted to see the Queen over in the corner beside a grand piano covered with silver-framed photographs. She was wearing a deep blue silk suit with an astounding diamond brooch at her shoulder. And she was sipping her drink, which gossip had it, was always gin and Dubonnet. She was lovely in person, Ambrose thought, her eyes alight, smiling as she conversed with those around her, always paying strict attention to whatever was being said to her. That alone put her on a pinnacle in Congreve's estimation.

When Diana had told him about the invitation to Scotland, he was taken aback. Not that he and Prince Charles hadn't gotten on awfully well at Highgrove, garden chat, dahlias, and all that, but still. A weekend at Balmoral? Heady stuff. "Seems that Charles and I hit it off quite well at Highgrove, Diana," Ambrose had said, a bit puffed up.

"It's not *Charles* who invited us, silly," she said. "Camilla and I are first cousins. Didn't I ever mention that to you at all?"

"Not really, dear, no."

"Oh, look, darling! There's Charles over there by the fire. So sweet, laughing with his two boys. I must say he looks very happy. And Wills and Harry. Aren't they handsome, darling? Not hard to see why all the girls are gaga over them, is it?"

At any rate, here they were. Alex Hawke was supposed to be here as well, but he'd been tied up in northern Pakistan a few extra days. He had been interrogating prisoners captured when he'd managed to find and disarm the missing nuclear device stolen from the Islamabad arsenal. He was currently on an RAF command bomber, headed home, but probably would not make the weekend.

As it was, Ambrose hardly knew a soul. He estimated about thirty guests for dinner. Mostly Royals, whom Diana knew, shooting friends of Charles's like Montague Thorne, a charming fellow whom he'd met and thoroughly enjoyed at Highgrove, plus lots of ministers of this and that up from London, including his good friend, C, Sir David Trulove, and Lord Malmsey of MI5. Earlier, Ambrose and Trulove had cornered Lord Malmsey and given him a detailed but enhanced account of their daring raid on the Rastafarian stronghold on Nonsuch Island in Bermuda. Suitably impressed, Ambrose thought he was, too.

At precisely eight, a Scottish piper in full fig appeared in the reception room, his plaintive tune announcing that dinner was served. Ambrose took Diana's hand, noticing with some pride his mother's diamond sparkling on her finger, and they made their way to the dining room.

The Queen's love of all things Scottish was evident everywhere.

The table was splendidly set, of course, a very long stretch of mahogany, beneath high ceilings with classic molding, vivid tartan draperies on the tall bay windows, red leather dining chairs, and massive gilt-framed Highland landscapes by Landseer on the walls and above the hearth where a fire was roaring against the evening chill.

The Queen herself was seated at the far end of the table to Congreve's right. To his left, Prince Philip was holding court at the other end, with his grandsons nearby on either side. Diana had been seated next to Prince Charles near the middle of the table. It was odd, but Congreve found he simply could not take his eyes off the Queen. He'd found Her Majesty very dear, in fact, as kind a person as one could imagine. He'd even managed to have a bit of surprising conversation with her when he'd been presented in the receiving line earlier.

"You're retired, I understand, Chief Inspector," Queen Elizabeth had said after he'd shaken her hand and bowed politely.

"I am, ma'am," he'd replied, stunned that she knew anything at all about him.

"How are you finding it?"

"Well, ma'am, people are still shooting at me."

"Are they really? One must always remember to duck, mustn't one?"

AMBROSE CONGREVE WAS ABOUT TO TUCK into his first taste of the celebrated haggis (a near-mythical Scottish dish that was definitely an acquired taste) when the bustling and festive dining room was suddenly plunged into utter and complete darkness.

All the lights went out at once, and not just those in the dining room, it appeared, but the pantry, the adjacent drawing room, everywhere. It was as if someone had just pulled the plug on the entirety of Balmoral Castle.

"Stay calm, everyone," a heavily accented but authoritative male voice announced, and indeed everyone was. There was the usual twittering and titter of nervous laughter that accompanies such incidents. Ambrose heard and felt the presence of men moving quickly toward the right end of the table and assumed they were house detectives moving to protect Her Royal Majesty.

The lights flickered once or twice and then came back on. It was as if they'd all gone to sleep to awaken in another world.

In that moment or two it took for the guests' eyes to reacquaint themselves with light, someone, a woman, screamed in horror at the top of her lungs.

There was a large, bearded man standing beside the Queen, and he had a pistol to her head.

The Queen had gone rigid, clearly in a state of shock, staring straight ahead, her hands clasped resolutely in her lap. Congreve worried that this desperate situation could easily trigger a heart attack in an eighty-five-year-old woman, especially one who had suffered much heartache here at the end of her long life.

Up and down the table, heads swiveled in shock and there were more shouts of alarm as the reality of what was happening hit the guests full-on, like some nightmarish force of nature.

Armed men now stood in every doorway of the room. And more were entering every second. They arrayed themselves around the table, waving the muzzles of their heavy black machine guns at the seated guests, shouting at everyone to stay seated and be quiet.

The heavily bearded man threatening the Queen slammed his huge fist down on the table, causing all the china and crystal to jump and shatter, glasses breaking, red wine spreading like so much spilt blood across the pure white field of linen stretching out before Her Majesty.

"Quiet!" the large man roared at them. "You will be quiet! Now!"

The screaming subsided to be replaced by quiet sobbing as the guests stared at each other and their beloved sovereign in abject horror. Many of the women held their napkins to their eyes, unable to look at the terrifying scene that confronted them. Many husbands put their arms around their wives, whispering reassuring words in their ears.

"I am Colonel Zazi," the big man said, speaking in a surprisingly clipped British accent. "I am a warrior in the great jihadi army known throughout the world as the Sword of Allah. As of this moment, my men have seized complete control of this castle and the surrounding grounds. This is a fait accompli. No one is coming to save you. They are all dead. They are all—"

"You bloody barbarians are stark raving mad!"

It was Prince Philip, struggling to rise from his chair, his face white with rage as the men to either side roughly shoved him back into his seat. His two grandsons, Wills and Harry, enraged at seeing their grandfather treated in this brutal fashion, started to rise, but their father, Charles, called their names and shook his head, urging them to sit and be calm.

"I shall make an announcement," the big man said, when the rage subsided a bit. "You people seated at this table are, as of this moment, political prisoners of the Sword of Allah. And shall remain so until, and if, our demands are met. But there are members of this household in whom we have no strategic interest. The staff, housekeeping, the secretaries, the kitchen—you, in the green jacket by the fire—what is your name?"

"Higgins, sir."

"What do you do here, Higgins?"

"I have the honor to be one of Her Majesty's footmen, sir."

"Can you cook?"

"A little, sir."

"You now have the honor of working for me. These people are going to need food and drink for a few days. See that they get it."

"Indeed, sir."

"Higgins, you have exactly ten minutes to inform all the household staff members that they are free to leave by the main entrance to the grounds. Those you tell should tell as many of the others as they can find. Go now. Tell them that my men have orders to shoot anyone who remains inside these walls ten minutes from now. Do you understand?"

"I do, sir, yes."

"I suggest you hurry along, Higgins. Get while the getting is good, as they say."

Higgins fled, first into the kitchen, where horrified staff peered out from behind half-closed doors. Ambrose could hear him shouting at them, urging them to race throughout the castle, find everyone they could, and get them all out at once.

"Now then," Zazi said, removing his 9mm pistol from the Queen of England's temple and slipping it into a black nylon holster on his right hip. Congreve noticed that on his other hip he wore a battle sword in a scabbard. It did not reassure him. "We are going to move you to another location. I strongly suggest you do this in an orderly fashion and in complete silence. If any one of my men gives you an order, follow it immediately. Understood? On your feet. Form a single line at the door to the right at the far end of the dining room. Then we will proceed."

Ambrose reached under the table and took Diana's hand, squeezing it gently in reassurance. He leaned over and kissed a shining spot on her cheek where a tear had been. When he looked up at her face, he saw that she was crying softly, but she smiled at him through her tears and he knew that she would have the strength to get through this nightmare.

At this point, it was all he dared hope for.

SIXTY-TWO

THINGS WERE GOING HELLWARD FAST. Descending the curving stone steps down into the castle's dank cellar was unnerving at best. It was as dark and cold as a crypt despite the season. All Congreve could think of was the fate of the Romanovs, the Royal Family of Russia. Tsar Nicholas, his wife, Alexandra, and their young children.

In the summer of 1918, after suffering house arrest at Ekateringburg for months, they were herded down to the basement in the middle of the night. Twelve Red Army soldiers entered with rifles and murdered the whole family in cold blood. The young princesses, whose nurses had sewn the crown jewels of Russia into their blouses, had to be finished off with bayonets. The bullets had ricocheted off the gemstones.

In the long Balmoral hallways that the forlorn and terrified hostages had traversed en route to the cellar entrance, they'd seen the splayed bodies of several Special Branch bodyguards and detectives, their throats slashed from ear to ear before they could even fire a warning shot. The jihadists had simply swarmed inside and overwhelmed them.

Congreve wondered how the terrorists had made it past the castle entrance until he saw the body of his old Scotland Yard colleague John Iverson sprawled in the entrance hall. John had for years been chief of security here at Balmoral. Clearly Iverson had been forced to trick the SO15 men on the door into opening it.

The terrorists, all little more than boys with beards and guns, kept shouting and prodding them along with their weapons, heedless of how difficult it was to keep one's footing on the worn stone, especially in the semi-darkness. Ambrose kept one steady hand on Diana's shoulder as she preceded him downward. From time to time, she would reach up and cover his hand with hers. It helped both of them.

They both assumed they were all going to die; he believed most of the guests felt the same way. But Congreve knew this was still purely a fluid hostage situation, in other words, a negotiation. And that this high-stakes drama had a long way to go until the final curtain.

It would certainly not be pleasant. But if they had a little luck, they all might just survive. The British Army, the Special Air Service (SAS), and the legions of counterterrorist operatives at both MI5 and MI6 would not look fondly upon the Monarch and Britain's Royal Family being held captive in a basement.

The cellar itself was an enormous warren of rooms and alcoves, filled to overflowing with the detritus of centuries. Furniture, primarily, but also art, bicycles, and baby prams from another era; there were endless shelves of old books, towers of Persian rugs that reached the ceiling, a lot of it the former property of Queen Victoria.

A vaulted hallway finally opened up into a cavernous room that appeared to be inhabited by ghosts. Sheets covered retired Victorian furniture of every possible description, sofas, chaises, deep armchairs, and ornate gilded side chairs. A dim, misty light from exposed bulbs mounted in ceiling sockets provided the sole illumination, and it was hardly cheery.

Zazi informed them that this room would be their new home for the foreseeable future and that they should make themselves comfortable on any of the furniture they found suitable. His hostility seemed to have diminished now that they had descended three flights of steps and entered a closed environment in which he had far more control. With himself and the armed men keeping watch over the hostages, he didn't anticipate too many problems maintaining order.

Once everyone had ripped away the sheets and settled into the furniture of their choice, two of the young fighters began distributing large plastic bottles of Highland Springs water, a gesture most took to be grounds for optimism. The Royal Family was seated apart from the guests, in a small alcove off the main room. Charles and his two sons moved furniture around, making sure everyone was as comfortable as possible under the circumstances.

Ambrose could see the Queen from where he and Diana were seated on a deep-cushioned velvet sofa. Her majesty was seated on a large silk brocade settee next to the Duke of Edinburgh. Surprisingly, Zazi had allowed her beloved Welsh Corgis to accompany her and they lay quietly at her feet. Her composed face and posture in this calamitous moment could only be described as stoic, if not serene.

Her uncanny ability to rise above this situation only confirmed Ambrose Congreve's long-held belief that it was her poise, her selflessness, her personal courage, and her enormous strength of character and dignity that had enabled her to lead her country so nobly for nearly sixty years. She had, in fact, become a British institution, and the reason was never more apparent than now.

Ambrose still recalled hearing her on the BBC *Children's Hour* radio program when he was a young boy. Addressing the children of the nation in the darkest hours of World War II, the fourteen-year-old Princess Elizabeth had said, "We are trying to do all we can to help our gallant sailors, soldiers, and airmen, and we are trying, too, to bear our share of the danger and sadness of war. We know, every one of us, that in the end all will be well."

—

"Do you think you can sleep, darling?" Diana asked him some time later, maybe hours, her voice barely above a whisper.

"No, but I want you to," he said, putting a small velvet pillow in his lap for her to rest her head upon. He removed his dinner jacket and placed it round her shoulders, as she lay her head upon the pillow. A few minutes later, she was snoring softly as he gently stroked the hair at her temples.

Looking about, he saw that many of his fellow guests had been able to find their way to slumber. He could only attribute it to the reassuring presence of the Queen. One look at her and they seemed to believe, every one of them, that in the end all would be well. A few moments later, Ambrose himself drifted off, his arm draped protectively around the woman he loved.

Next morning, Ambrose awoke with a start. The noise nearby had not woken Diana and he decided to let her sleep for as long as she could. Some of the others around him were awake, red-eyed, and still in a state of shock. The sight they'd awoken to didn't help matters much.

Colonel Zazi had cleared a space along one wall. It was an all-too-familiar scene. A banner now hung on the wall, white with Arabic script in red surrounding the depiction of a large red sword, dripping blood. A professional-grade video camera on a tripod had been erected, and many heavy cables ran across the floor and toward the staircase. Congreve had to believe they were going to do a live broadcast on British television.

There were a number of very bright lights, all on tall standards. A large, ornate, and heavily gilded chair with a crimson cushion had been placed before the banner.

Colonel Zazi was at this very moment escorting the Queen onto this bizarre "set." Three of his men kept their weapons trained on the Queen's family who remained seated in their alcove, and all of whom were plainly enraged by this treatment of the Sovereign. Once she was seated, Zazi handed her a handwritten sheet of paper. She put on her glasses, read it silently, and nodded at the colonel. Two of the young terrorists, now with hoods covering their heads, stood to either side of her thronelike chair, AKs cradled in their arms.

Zazi stepped to one side and told the cameraman to focus on him alone. He looked into the lens and began speaking in his deep baritone.

"My name is Colonel Zazi. I am a soldier in the greatest army on earth, the Sword of Allah. I am speaking to you this morning from Balmoral, Scotland. Last night, my soldiers and I took over the Royal residence—the house and grounds are now wholly under my control. We have also taken hostages, who are watching and listening to me at this moment. They include ministers and Members of Parliament, the heads of both MI5 and MI6, and many members of the Royal Family. I have drafted a list of demands that I wish to deliver to the prime minister, Mr. Edward Weed. You will hear those demands in a moment. If they sound familiar, it is because they were issued over a year ago by my martyred brother Abu Mahmood at Heathrow airport. Much blood was shed and yet still our just and righteous demands went unmet.

"So now I have raised the stakes considerably. Should you not heed our call, Mr. Prime Minister, I will begin taking the lives of not only your highest-ranking government officials, but members of your beloved Royal Family. These executions, beheadings, will take place in this room, televised daily, until I hear directly from the prime minister. Once he accedes to our demands and demonstrates convincingly that he is removing every member of British armed forces from sacred Arab soil, I will halt the executions and release the remaining hostages.

"I have asked a member of the Royal Family to read my complete statement and list of demands. You have shown in the past that you will not listen to us. But perhaps you will listen to your beloved Sovereign."

The cameraman panned the camera around and moved in for a tight close-up of Her Majesty the Queen. Ambrose was astounded to see that she looked every bit as composed as she did every twenty-fifth of December when she delivered her annual Christmas message to the nation on television.

"Good morning," she said calmly, holding up the single sheet of paper given her by the colonel. "I have been asked by Colonel Zazi to read to you his statement. However, I have chosen instead to make a statement of my own."

With that, she ripped the sheet of paper into shreds and let the pieces flutter to the floor. Ambrose felt like leaping to his feet and cheering. Clearly she knew her very life was at stake, and she was prepared to lay it down for her country.

"Do you want me to cut, sir?" the cameraman whispered to Zazi, standing right beside him.

"No," he whispered back. "Keep rolling. It'll make good television."

"Today," she continued, "it is self-evident that a special kind of courage is required of all of us. The courage to stand up for all that is good and right. True and honest. The kind of courage that will show the world that we in Britain are not afraid of the future . . . not afraid of tyrants and religious despots whose evangelism is expressed through the wanton murder of innocent men, women, and children around the world. It has always been easy to hate and destroy. To build and cherish is far more difficult.

"I know that I cannot lead you into battle as did monarchs of old. I can only give you my heart and my sincere devotion to these old islands and all our people. I still believe in our great qualities and strengths. Our marks and our scars we carry with us—and remind us of this—that no matter how dark the night, nor how wicked the storm, we have always come through. And we always shall."

The room fell into shocked silence.

Everyone looked at the enraged Zazi to see what he would do. His face was empurpled with rage, and he had his hand quivering on the hilt of his sword. He stared at the Queen and she returned his stare with unbending courage. After a few moments of this standoff, it was clear who had won the first round.

At first there was only a slight ripple of applause from a distant corner of the room. But it grew louder with each passing second. More and more joined in, clapping loudly now, the applause resounding and reverberating, and soon they were getting to their feet, all of them, and giving their Queen the tribute she deserved.

"Silence! All of you! Silence!"

An angry Zazi stepped in front of the camera and shouted orders for silence, which went unheard in the thunderous applause. It was not until one of the young terrorists fired his AK-47 continuously into the ceiling, raining plaster down on their heads that, slowly, the applause abated and the hostages returned to their seats. Zazi looked at his cameraman. "Are we still rolling?" he asked.

"Yes, sir."

Zazi stepped back onto the "set," standing directly in front of the Queen.

"There is a price to be paid for defiance," Zazi said into the lens, barely able to keep himself under control. Motioning to one of the terrorists, he pulled his pistol from his holster and chambered a round.

"That one there," he said. "In the green dress and the emeralds. Bring her to me."

There was a noisy struggle off camera. An angry man shouting, then pleading. A moment later a hysterical elderly woman, begging for her life, was dragged by the wrists by two of the bearded killers. She was dropped to the stone floor at Zazi's feet.

"Up on your knees, woman!" he shouted into the poor woman's face.

Sobbing, she struggled to get to her knees. Pressing her palms together as if in prayer, tears coursing down her cheeks, she looked up into Zazi's eyes, pleading for her life.

Zazi turned his head toward the Queen.

"That price, Your Royal Majesty, is a bullet to this old woman's head."

He pulled the trigger.

Then he looked into the camera and said, "Cut."

A THOUSAND MILES TO THE EAST, flying at maximum altitude, thirty-two thousand feet, Alex Hawke was sound asleep in his seat aboard the RAF Hercules C-130J transport plane that carried Stokely and him back to England. It was freezing inside the fuselage of the giant aircraft and they had wrapped themselves in the Afghan blankets they'd strapped to the back of their saddles on the journey up into the Hindu Kush mountains.

Sahira had returned to Islamabad after the Wazizabad Mountain incident. She'd been assigned by MI5 to spend a month assisting the Pakistani government in finding out how and why a nuclear device had been removed from Pakistan's heavily guarded arsenal. And how they could prevent a recurrence from ever happening.

A young airman was bending over Hawke, squeezing his shoulder and repeating his name. Somehow, Alex dredged himself up from the depths of his exhaustion, opened his eyes and stared, bewildered, at the face looming over him.

"Yes?" he said, not fully aware of where he was.

"Sir, Captain Davies has asked that you come forward to the cockpit. He has an urgent message for you."

"What is it?" Hawke asked, struggling to come fully awake.

"He didn't say, sir. Just that he needed to speak with you immediately."

"I'm right behind you," Hawke said, getting to his feet and following the airman as he made his way forward. When he entered the cockpit, he saw the pilot turn to face him in the red glow of his instruments.

"Commander, sorry to disturb your sleep but I'm afraid it's most urgent."

"Not at all. What is it?"

"You're not going to believe it, sir. I've just been on the radio with my commanding officer. It seems that an armed wing of the Taliban called the Sword of Allah has stormed Balmoral Castle and taken everyone inside hostage."

"Everyone? Good Lord."

"Yes, sir. All the guests, and the entire Royal Family. The Queen herself, sir. Prince Philip, Prince Charles, and his two sons . . . all of them."

Hawke was stunned.

"It's not possible."

"I'm afraid it is. They've already killed one hostage, a much loved lady-in-waiting to Her Majesty, Lady Fiona Hicks. The Queen, with Pakistani gunmen to either side, gave a statement on the BBC. It is a hostage situation and the terrorists are threatening to keep killing one a day on live television until Prime Minister Weed agrees to their demands. The first deadline is tomorrow at midnight, Greenwich Mean Time."

"And our response?"

"Forces are mobilizing and disembarking for Scotland as we speak, sir."

"Captain, listen. There is no time to waste. I need to be put in immediate contact with MI6 to organize a hostage rescue team. And, most importantly, I need to see that BBC video of the Queen. Perhaps I can visually identify exactly where she's being held inside the castle. I need to speak with Sir David Trulove. Tell him exactly what I will need to—"

"Sorry, sir. Sir David is one of the hostages. As well as Lord Malmsey of MI5."

"All right," Hawke said, thinking rapidly, "what is the RAF station nearest to Balmoral?"

"RAF Aberdeenshire, I believe, sir."

"Can we divert there?"

"In this case? Certainly. I'd set this behemoth down right outside Balmoral's front gates if I could."

"Get the SAS director of special forces on the radio. Tell him we need him now. And we need that BBC video ready to screen as soon as we touch down. He needs to start putting an SAS paratroop squadron together at RAF Aberdeenshire immediately. What's our ETA there?"

"I could have you on the ground in less than two hours, Commander."

"It'll have to do. If you've got any extra horses under those wings, now would be a good time to use them. When someone's holding a gun to your Sovereign's head, every minute counts."

SIXTY-THREE

HE TRIED TO GO BACK TO SLEEP, but it was useless. In the dim light of the cellar he could see that most of the hostages were asleep, or pretending to be. He looked at his watch. Three in the morning. His nerves were shot and he needed sleep badly. He put his head back down on the sofa cushion and tried to will away the boyhood images that kept flooding into his fevered brain. Since he could not stop them, he let them come. Perhaps with them would come sleep. . . .

TABU BABAR RUSHED ACROSS THE TREE-SHADED courtyard, already thronged with teeming crowds straining forward. The ten-year-old student had traveled by rail from his school to Delhi, and his country's trains were notoriously late. The streets surrounding the Viceroy's House were already jammed to overflowing with hundreds of thousands come out to have a look at the latest gentleman arrived from England to lord it over them, Lord Louis Mountbatten.

Were it not for Tabu's honey-toned skin, you could easily have mistaken him for a young Etonian. In his heart of hearts, that is exactly who he was. He certainly dressed the part: starched white shirt and striped bow tie, trousers held aloft with matching braces. He had gleaming black hair, slicked back in waves, thick black brows, and a long, straight nose between two penetrating black eyes.

His school, Mayo, was the "Eton of India." But, even in this rarefied air, Tabu was something of a rare bird. He was a devout Moslem, from the overwhelmingly Moslem town of Lahore, and yet his every mannerism, his every word and gesture, bespoke an English sensibility so convincing his classmates called him "Sahib," or even "your lordship," or "your grace," bowing from the waist with a feigned deference that evoked howls of laughter once he was safely out of earshot.

In Mayo's hallowed halls and paneled libraries, an extremely wealthy Moslem boy like Tabu could easily indulge himself in Anglophile fantasies of Elizabethan castles, of knights of old and Coldstream Guards, the grandeur of royalty, and a small boy's noble ideal of a manly English aristocrat. All of these idealistic notions Tabu had invested in the singular person of his great hero. This was the man who, in a short while, would become the new Viceroy of India, Lord Louis Mountbatten, the man who would save his beloved country from self-destruction.

India's countless millions of Hindus, Sikhs, and Moslems were on the brink of a religious war that would dwarf anything since the Crusades. Even isolated within the high walls of his small school, inflamed religious fervor brewing outside could pit schoolmate against schoolmate. There had been fights at school and many boys had been hospitalized.

A half million already stood in the broiling sun. Above the crowds atop his lamppost perch, he now had a bird's-eye view of the very spot where the new Viceroy's coach would soon arrive. The crowd was shouting now, and surging forward, a near riot, but Tabu was safely perched above it all.

And there he was at last.

He looked like a Hollywood film star in his immaculate white naval uniform. Serene, smiling, his adoring wife, Edwina, beside him, Louis Mountbatten, Earl of Burma, rode up to the foot of the grand palace steps to lay claim to Viceroy House. Tabu's eyes were riveted on the man who had come at last to preserve the peace. To save his beloved country from becoming one vast boiling cauldron of hatred and blood.

Long after the Mountbattens had mounted the marble steps and disappeared inside the palace, and the cheering crowds had dissipated, Tabu clung to his precarious spot, prolonging this historic moment of hope for as long as he could . . . here, finally, was a powerful man who could save India. A great diplomat who could bring Nehru, Gandhi, and Jinnah to their senses. Who could prevent his beloved India from tearing itself to shreds.

ONE NIGHT, MANY LONG MONTHS later at Mayo, Tabu had felt a rough hand on his shoulder, shaking him violently awake.

"What is it?" he said, rubbing sleep from his eyes.

"You must go, get out of here at once," Sindhu, his only Hindu friend, said. "Grab what you can, Tabu, and run! For your life, my dear boy."

"What is happening?"

"The English. They have left us. As of the stroke of midnight tonight, India is free! And all hell has broken loose, believe me."

"Mountbatten has left us? Abandoned India? Impossible."

"Yes, stealing away like a thief in the night is your great hero, and already the angry mobs are turning the streets red with blood. It is open religious warfare now, Tabu, everywhere. Moslem against Hindu against Sikh. A religious slaughter tearing the country apart."

"He's done nothing to stop it, has he, Sindhu? Mountbatten was our last hope. And now he's left India to drown in a sea of blood!"

"Tabu, listen! There is no time for this now. One floor below us, a group of fifth-form Hindu boys are going from room to room, hacking Moslem students to death in their beds with swords. I heard your name mentioned. They won't be so kind to you, I fear, Little Sahib."

Tabu leaped out of bed and started throwing his beloved books and clothing into his old leather portmanteau.

"How long have I got, Sindhu?"

"Ten minutes if you're lucky. They are still killing boys on the floor below. You'll have to go out the window. It's a ten-foot drop from the roof to the wall, five feet to the ground. Be careful not to break anything when you leap, my dear friend, or you're surely dead."

"But where shall I go, Sindhu? I've nowhere to go!"

"Home! Your newly created homeland of Pakistan. Make your way to the central train station. There is a train for Lahore at midnight. You're the fastest boy at school. If you run as fast as ever you can, you just might make it before the clock strikes twelve."

Tabu heaved his bulging bag out the window and, with a farewell wave to his friend, followed it. When he hit the ground, he tucked and rolled into a crouch and managed not to break any bones. He jumped to his feet and ran for his life. There were fires everywhere, flames licking into the black skies. His fury knew no bounds now. Betrayal and shame and fear were indistinguishable in his mind.

As he ran, Tabu Babar felt a lifetime of boyhood hopes and dreams slowly falling away from him, running like dirty water, sloshing along the filthy gutter and disappearing down the drain.

Tabu ran out into the thick of the screaming mobs, dodging this way and that. In his emotional fever, he ran for the station blindly, hoping for a bullet or a blade to end his agony. He was without hope, now. He wanted to leave this world. He'd lost everything; and now he felt he might be losing his mind as well.

Strangely, this was a kind of comfort. Hope had been lost and replaced by a kind of hot lust.

A fervent dream of revenge now settled into his brain and, with it, an odd sense of peace in all the madness around him. He would survive. And he would make them pay.

The streets were a nightmare, but the great black fortress called the New Delhi train terminal was a raving madhouse. He stood gasping at the scene before him. Every Moslem in the city it now seemed wanted to escape to their new homeland of Pakistan. Somehow, Tabu made it to the platform for the Lahore-bound train just as the big station clock bonged twelve. The train was still there, thanks be to Allah, huffing and puffing, billowing clouds of steam rising from beneath its great iron wheels.

This was always an obscenely noisy place. But now, the cacophony threatened to overwhelm him. The cavernous black hall, with its maze of iron girders above, was overflowing with clamor and shouting, almost drowning out the cries of the countless water and sweetmeat vendors, the useless barks of policemen, the shrill cries of women snatching up baskets and herding their children and husbands forward on the mobbed platforms.

The throngs were clambering over one another to board third-class railcars already full to overflowing. Women and children were simply flung aside by bigger, stronger refugees. Fights were breaking out and the few police stood idly by, laughing as they finally gave up and turned a blind eye to the inter-Moslem violence before them.

Tabu looked at his bag chockablock with his cherished books and knew he had no choice but to leave it behind. He flung it onto the glimmering tracks beneath the wheels, and in a sudden flash of rage, ripped off his little English schoolboy cap and hurled it onto the tracks as well. Books be damned. Mayo be damned. England be damned!

THE TRAIN CARS WERE PACKED, jammed with desperate people hanging out the windows just to breathe in the stifling night air.

He raced back to the rear of the train and clambered up the metal ladder to the roof of the very last car. There were many others already there, and a smiling family made room for him. Somehow they'd managed to get a pair of family goats up top with them and the animals were bleating in fear.

The patriarch of the family, the ancient grandfather, looked at Tabu's rumpled school uniform and said, "English school?"

Tabu nodded.

"You like English, boy? You like this Mountbatten? This noble lord who deserts us in the middle of the night? After swearing to keep our poor country whole and at peace? Who now treats us like so many swatted flies?"

Even Tabu was surprised by the violence of his own response. He slammed his fist down on the roof of the train hard enough to dent it and screamed in anguish.

"Mountbatten is a false god, a bloody liar! A betrayer! Devil! They are all devils, these English! Let Almighty Allah take these English far, far away! May they never even *smell* paradise!"

The family moved away slightly, thinking him surely mad. And perhaps, he realized for the first time, he truly had gone mad.

Far ahead, a plaintive locomotive whistle blew and the old train lurched and creaked forward, slowly at first, gradually gaining momentum. There was the familiar deep chugging noise, a rattling of the couplings, and the squeak of the iron wheels, but Tabu heard a strange sound echoing off the iron roof of the great station.

A loud staccato noise.

He looked behind him at the throngs of swarming people left stranded on the platform, and understood the noise. Mobs in red turbans, a vicious Hindu sect, were firing machine guns into the helpless crowd of Moslem men, women, and children left behind. Screaming, they jumped down onto the tracks and ran for safety, but many, many died.

Bitter tears coursed down Tabu's cheeks as he looked at the sprawling dead and dying he was leaving behind. With them died his lifelong dreams, his hopes of making a fine life for himself on that cherished green island called England; the one precious ideal he had held so strongly in his young heart was now seeping into the ground with the blood of his slaughtered brothers.

The journey to Lahore was almost more than Tabu could bear. Beside the tracks, along roads twisting through the most fertile part of what was once India, the Punjab, he saw what must be millions of Moslems, most walking, the elderly or infirm in ox-drawn carts, women with babies in their arms, furniture piled high upon their backs, all bound for the newly partitioned Moslem nation of Pakistan.

Tabu learned that countless tens of thousands of these Moslem immigrants had been slaughtered by violent sects of Hindus and Sikhs waiting in ambush along the great trek north. This was the legacy that his great hero, Lord Louis Mountbatten, had left behind. And then he was home. . . .

The Babar ancestral home, *Putrajaya,* was one of the great landmarks of the city of Lahore. The monumental palace was set inside a vast parkland of exquisite gardens, fountains, and beautiful flower-choked lagoons, all protected by a high wall surrounding the entire property. For some reason, no guards were on station and the entrance gate was not closed. It was flung wide open, and intuition made Tabu enter with caution.

As he started to move slowly along the drive toward the house, and then crossing open ground, everything suddenly began to make horrible sense.

He saw two men, dressed in the familiar garb of the Mahadi sect, dragging his young sister of sixteen down the white marble steps of the entrance. She was screaming and trying to twist away, but the men were huge and overpowering. Tabu, knowing any attempt at rescue would only result in the death of both him and his sister, retreated quickly into the trees before he could be seen. Three more Mahadi appeared, and they had his mother and father. Both were bruised and bleeding. And now smoke was pouring from the countless windows on the upper floors. His boyhood home was afire, his boyhood was afire.

Tabu fled, his home a funeral pyre, and ran for the main gate of *Putrajaya,* praying a Mahadi would put a rifle bullet in his back before he reached the road. For days afterward he would aimlessly wander the streets of Lahore, scrounging for food, trying to make sense of what had become of his once charmed life. He went to the homes of relatives and found them charred ruins, found sticklike corpses inside. Nowhere left to turn, hungry and afraid, he lived the hand-to-mouth life of a street urchin.

One day, a withered old crone took pity on him. The streets were too dangerous for a boy so young and pretty, she said. She would take him to a wonderful orphanage. A place of safety, a refuge where poor boys would find hot food and shelter. When Tabu saw the man who ran the orphanage put five filthy rupees into the hand of the old woman, Tabu knew he'd just been sold into a life of slavery.

They took you in, all right, and put food in your belly and a roof over your head. After a while, though, when they thought you were ready, they'd come in the night, steal you sleeping from your bed, and ferret you down to the cellar. There, under harsh lights, they would bind you to a blood-soaked butcher's block. Then, as you stared up in horror, they would do one of two things, sometimes both if you had been a trouble.

They would either lop off one of your hands with a filthy cleaver, and then plunge your bloody stump into hot pitch. Or someone would carefully pour a tablespoon full of boiling acid into one of your eyes. He would then scoop the jelly out of the socket with the same hot spoon as you screamed until you were hoarse.

It was, of course, simply a matter of good business. Out in the streets, the one-handed, or the one-eyed, beggar boy was far more productive, these savages, these saviors, these "defenders of the poor" had learned. They had studied the charitable habits of the influx of European grandees and grand dames to a fare-thee-well. And they knew what worked.

And these roaming saints of the streets, always in search of hopeless orphans, were nothing if not good businessmen. They had soon realized there was money to make off the downtrodden. You just needed to keep trodding them down at a steady clip, and clip one wing. So simple.

A one-eyed Tabu would now join the swarming floodtide of thousands of India's half-blinded children surging through the narrow confines of every city, holding out his or her remaining hand for a rupee, please, sir, one rupee, sir, only one, sir. Please.

How terribly swift had been his fall from grace, from a life of knowledge, privilege, and comfort.

It had taken less than a month.

Tabu Babar, only yesterday a brilliant boy who'd foreseen a brilliant future for himself, perhaps as a successful banker in the "City" of London, or a famous barrister, now occupied life's lowest rung.

Untouchable.

Until, that is, in a squalid back street of Lahore, he'd managed to catch the attention of, and been touched lovingly by, an enormously wealthy Englishwoman named Lady Braeburn Thorne.

He was no longer untouchable. Oh, no.

He was touched again and again and again . . .

HE MUST HAVE DOZED OFF for he awoke with a start. Sir David Trulove was squeezing his upper arm tightly enough to hurt. He cracked an eye, saw Sir David leaning in toward him with a crooked grin on his deeply lined face. "Have a look," C said.

"What on earth?"

"Down there. At your feet."

He looked down and saw one of the young terrorists crumpled on his back, a great red gash in his neck still pumping great gouts of dark blood.

"How did—?"

Sir David held up a long blade he must have hidden somewhere upon his person. It was dripping blood. He casually swiped it across his trousers and stuck it back in a sheath round his ankle. Old bugger had no end of tricks up his trousers.

"He fell asleep right in front of me. Drugs must have worn off," C whispered. "These guards are all buzzing with methamphetamines, but not a few are bloody dozing off as time goes by. Except for our esteemed colonel over there. Look at him, drugged to the gills, having a go at one of the young belles of the ball. Probably promised her the earth and moon by the looks of things."

Zazi was positioned squarely behind a naked blonde, the girl bent forward over the cushioned back of a chair with her broad and gleaming white rump high in the air. All you could see was the colonel's muscular back, glistening with sweat even in the murky light as he labored over her, thrusting himself ever more rapidly into this gullible girl whose voice could be heard, moaning her appreciation for her captor's deepest expressions of affection.

Trulove reached down and snatched the AK from the dead terrorist on the floor and stood up in a single, athletic motion. He aimed at the jihadi colonel's back, his finger tightening on the trigger—suddenly a hand pressing down on his forearm and—

"No! Don't!"

"What?" C said, oblivious, opening fire, his lethal burst cutting Zazi nearly in half at this range, before he swung his head around to confront this bloody naysayer.

Trulove, astonished, was looking into the ugly snout of the Markov 9mm pistol, not two feet away, as it spat two rounds into his chest, his blood spattering the face of his assailant before he went down.

"OH, MY GOD," CHARLES SAID, looking across the room at his old and trusted friend, now revealed as a traitor and a madman. A monster, now revealed for what he was, standing in a haze of gun smoke, a ghostly blue figure beneath the misty bulbs above. The Prince of Wales had just watched one of his oldest friends murder the director of MI6 in cold blood. So had the boys. It defied all belief. But he'd seen it. Everyone had.

Montague Thorne, gun in hand, walked slowly toward the Prince of Wales, weaving his way through the maze of furniture and terrified hostages, his free hand swiping the blood spatter from his eyes until he stood before the Prince of Wales flanked by his two sons, standing there silently, with his aristocratic nose and his vulgar heart.

"Monty. Oh my God, Monty, why? Who are you? *What* are you?"

Montague Thorne smiled, red blood on his white teeth as he spoke.

"I am what I have always been, Charles. You've seen my signature. A pawn. Just a little black pawn in the game. The Great Game as you people call it. The human chess game you and your family have played for years in my part of the world. Our blood is on your hands, just as yours is on mine. I've been playing my own little game all these years, you see, devoted my whole life to it. Moves and countermoves on the great board. The time draws nigh for the pawn's final move."

"What in God's name do you intend, Monty?"

"Pawn takes Queen, Charles. However else did you think this game could end?"

SIXTY-FOUR

The good news, Stoke thought, was they'd gotten very lucky with the weather: a storm had rolled in. Heavy fog with intermittent rain. That meant it would be a lot harder for any enemy shooters on the ground to hit them once they'd deployed their chutes. There was also a lot of booming thunder around them that would mask the *thwump-thwump* of the rotor blades when they descended from their current altitude.

The bad news, Stoke realized, was with the heavy ground fog at night, it might be a hell of a lot harder to spot the LZ, or, if you missed the landing zone, find another good spot to land on the rooftops of Balmoral Castle without breaking your damn leg or worse. Stoke had never seen so many damn chimneys on one house in his whole damn life.

"How are you feeling, big man?" Hawke, who was seated next to him, asked, just loud enough to be heard over the noise of the twin rotors.

"My pucker factor is rising a little."

"Really? Why?"

"What you said to me back there in the hangar at Stornoway."

"Which part, Stoke?"

"The part where you said, and I quote, 'This is the big one, Stoke, the counterterrorist Lifetime Achievement Award, so get ready. It won't look good on either of our résumés if we come back from this mission with a dead Queen.' "

"Oh, right. I did say that, didn't I? Well, it's true, isn't it?"

"Damn straight it's true. That's why my pucker factor is so elevated."

Hawke said, "And another thing, Stokely. Don't shoot my best friend Ambrose Congreve if you can possibly avoid it, all right?"

"I thought *I* was your best friend."

"You are."

"How's that work again?"

"It's a tie, all right? A dead heat."

"Don't say dead anything, okay?"

"Look. We can do this, Stoke. These SAS Special Projects troops are the best- trained counterterrorist outfit in the world. You've never worked with anybody remotely as good as these guys at this kind of thing. Seriously, Stoke. They wrote the book."

"Hell I haven't. I'm telling you, man, the U.S. Navy SEALs are as good as anybody in the whole damn world. Maybe these guys wrote the book, but the SEALs? They made the movie and the movie is better."

"You're right. It's a tie, okay?"

"Yeah. I guess."

At the stroke of midnight, Hawke's chosen mode of transportation, a matte-black Royal Air Force Chinook HC2 helicopter with no RAF insignia, had arrived on station at its insertion point, five thousand feet directly above Balmoral Castle. The tandem-rotor Chinook carries up to fifty-five troops and, because this might be a casualty evacuation, twenty-four stretchers. There were two RAF medical officers aboard, too, with full trauma emergency capabilities.

Early on in the planning at RAF Stornoway, Hawke had decided this had to be a nighttime operation. The Chinook's cockpit had full nighttime capability when operated with night-vision goggles. The helo was armed, too, with two M134 six-barreled miniguns, one in each front side window, and an M60D heavy machine gun on the ramp. It was the perfect aircraft to conduct a low-level night operation in a hostile environment.

At this moment, the Chinook, flying IFR, on instruments, with no visible lights, was hovering, an invisible black-bellied monster hiding in the soup.

In the belly of the beast, in addition to the mission commander, Alex Hawke, and his colleague, Stokely Jones, there were two fourteen-man squads of SAS counterterrorist commandos known as SP teams. They specialized in assault and hostage rescue missions. They were all checking and rechecking their gear and weapons, sitting directly across from each other on the canvas cargo sling seats that ran up and down the interior fuselage of the Chinook.

All were wearing one-piece assault suits made of flame-retardant Nomex 3, bulletproof armored waistcoats, ceramic armor plates covering the front, back, and groin, and an armored helmet capable of stopping a 9mm round at close range.

The weapons they carried included the HK MP5 submachine gun, the SIG Sauer P226 pistol, and Remington shotguns loaded with "hattan" rounds designed to shoot off door hinges without putting hostages at risk. From their utility belts hung stun grenades, flash-bang grenades, and smokers.

The SAS had two ways of going into a hostage situation: quiet or noisy. Hawke had insisted they go in quiet; thus, their weapons were all carrying noise suppressors. And he'd added two of the SAS's very best snipers to the team.

One lucky troop would jump with a very cumbersome "Harvey Wallbanger" in his arms. This wall-breaching device fired a water-filled plastic projectile at high velocity, causing a breach. The projectile immediately lost all kinetic energy once the breach was made. Much safer, and quieter, than explosives.

In addition, each troop carried a postcard-sized blueprint of the enemy-occupied stronghold to be assaulted, plasti-cuffs, and glow sticks filled with chemicals that glow when the sticks were snapped. These would be used to mark an area as "cleared."

Numerous SAS sniper teams were already in place on the ground. They were arrayed around the Balmoral estate's perimeter. And they were more than ready to take out any "X-rays," as terrorists were called, once an assault was launched to rescue the "Yankees," which is what the SAS called all hostages, including, for the very first time, the entire Royal Family of England. A little irony there, Hawke thought, Royal Yankees.

A blowup of a recent aerial photograph of the castle from directly above was taped to the bulkhead of the cargo hold where the troops were waiting for the jump order. A red circle marked an area of the roof large enough for the big Chinook to set down. This was also the designated LZ, a one-hundred-square-yard landing zone, for the paratroopers. The waiting troops had been studying the aerial photo carefully, looking for a good bail-out spot if for some reason they missed the LZ entirely.

DIRECTLY BENEATH THE CHOPPER and Balmoral Castle, three stories underground, Ambrose Congreve was spoon-feeding his friend Sir David Trulove hot cream of tomato soup. This, courtesy of Higgins up in the kitchen. C, the crusty old gent, having taken two bullets at extremely close range, was very lucky to be alive. The credit went to one of his fellow hostages, Lady Beale, who happened to be a volunteer nurse at St. Thomas's Hospital in London. The two slugs had narrowly missed his heart en route to passing through his body. Lady Beale had torn her purple silk skirt into strips to use as temporary bandages for the director of MI6.

It had been an extremely long and difficult day.

The killing of Colonel Zazi had had a predictable result on the mood down in the cellar. The terrorists, having seen their heroic leader shot dead, had become much harsher in their treatment of the prisoners. Prior to Zazi's death, the young killers had pretty much ignored their aristocratic captives. Now that he was dead, they went out of their way to shout at, kick, and insult them at every opportunity.

As if that were not enough, there was the infamous "Mr. Smith."

Ambrose could scarcely imagine how Prince Charles must be feeling. Shattered, to say the very least. To learn, to *discover,* that one of one's closest friends, trusted beyond measure, beyond any faint shadow of doubt for decades, a very senior member of the nation's key intelligence service, had in fact murdered the Prince of Wales's beloved godfather, Lord Mountbatten. And, in a stunning revelation, to learn he'd killed the mother of his children, Diana, as well. It simply had to be beyond devastating for him and the boys.

The monster, this Mr. Smith now unmasked as the MI6 heir apparent, Montague Thorne, had even laughed while describing to the Queen in great detail how he had masterminded the horrific fire at Windsor Castle. And then, gloating, told Prince Charles and his two sons just how close he'd come to assassinating Prince Harry in Afghanistan only one month earlier!

Harry, enraged upon hearing this, jumped to his feet and spat out, "But we almost assassinated *you,* didn't we, Thorne, you filthy bastard! How's your idiot sniper doing? Is he feeling better?" This earned him a vicious backhand blow to the side of his head. For a moment, everyone in the cellar held their breath, looking at the madman Thorne, knowing they all were teetering on the thin edge of chaos and mass murder. But Monty had only laughed and walked away.

Ambrose reached into the pocket of his dinner jacket and felt the comforting presence of Sir David's knife, still crusty with blood. He'd managed to secret it away before his jailers were any the wiser. Now, if he could only find the chance to use it . . .

SIXTY-FIVE

THE JUMPMASTER SHOUTED, "GET READY!" and Stoke, like everyone else, checked the harness of his parachute for the tenth time. It was shortly before midnight. A few minutes later the man bellowed "Stand up!" then "Check equipment!" and, finally, "Stand in the door!" At this final order Hawke and Stoke moved to the ramp at the rear of the aircraft. The SAS troops were right behind them.

The big bird shuddered and quailed, and Stoke felt the pilot begin his descent straight down from five thousand feet to two thousand feet, the altitude at which they would jump. The descent was fairly rapid, about three hundred feet per minute he guessed, and then they were hovering again. The ramp was lowered and a blast of wet air whistled into the hold as the first troops moved into position.

A green light began flashing on the overhead.

"Go! Go! Go!" the jumpmaster shouted, and Hawke and Stoke bolted to the edge of the ramp and hurled themselves out into the night air. The SAS troops rapidly moved out onto the ramp and, just seconds after Alex and Stokely jumped, followed.

Stoke pulled his rip cord immediately, waiting for the sensation of the chute slipping out of his backpack and separating. A second later, he was yanked skyward by his harness, always a nice, cozy feeling.

He looked down between his boots. There was patchy fog, but he saw the roof and identified the LZ where he was supposed to land. It was a large area of flat roof surrounded by four chimneys. He tugged on his guidelines a bit, lining up for it, and saw that Alex Hawke, who'd been just in front of him, was flaring up for a landing.

Damn!

There was an X-ray with an AK-47 standing guard on the roof not fifty feet beneath Hawke's feet. Had Hawke seen him too?

The guard was gazing out to the Grampian Mountains, day-dreaming or something. Luckily, he was facing away from Hawke. And Stoke. But at the last second something caught the man's eye. The whole sky above the castle was filled with parachutes. He spun around bringing his weapon up.

Hawke, to Stoke's great relief, had already pulled his silenced SIG pistol. He was still about forty feet above the rooftop and swinging under his canopy. Hawke managed to acquire his target and take the man out with a single head shot before he could kill any paratroopers. Moments later, Hawke's boots hit the roof. When Stoke dropped in, Alex was already gathering his chute and moving away, clearing the LZ for the new arrivals who were landing all around them.

Minutes later, Stoke and the assault team were happily standing on the roof of Balmoral Castle. No one was hurt, no one was shooting at them, no one had a clue. Hawke called for a head count. After every man on the roof had sounded off, he pulled down the lip mike inside his helmet and said to the Chinook pilot, "Rattler One, Rattler One, this is Warlord. Twenty-eight out and twenty-eight down, safe and sound, roger?"

"Roger that, Warlord. Pretty good shot from a swinging harness, by the way."

"Got lucky. We're going in."

"Uh, roger, Warlord, this is Rattler One, we acknowledge, sir. We will remain at zero-two-thousand until LZ is completely clear, then set the bird down and await any wounded Yankees for emergency med evac. We'll keep her spooled up for a quick exfil, don't worry. Rattler One, standing by, over. Godspeed, Warlord."

"Roger, Rattler One, over," Hawke said into his lip mike, moving quickly across the tar-papered rooftop toward a weathered wooden door set between two chimneys. He remembered this door from his childhood. It was never locked then, it was not locked now. "How'd you know about this door?" Stoke asked.

"I spent half my boyhood playing cowboys and Indians in this house. I know every square inch of it."

"Go, go, go!" Hawke said to the SAS commandos and they didn't need further encouragement.

THEY MADE THEIR WAY DOWN the steps leading to the attic. Hawke had never truly appreciated night-vision goggles until this very moment. The team was snaking silently through the dark attic rooms, a powerful, lethal force that he truly believed could overcome any conceivable obstacle.

Hawke led them to the staircase leading to the top floor of the castle. He raised his palm for a halt, pulled the door open, stepped outside, and did a quick recon of the long corridor. As he remembered, this floor was primarily devoted to storage, laundry, pressing, and staff quarters.

"Clear," he said, returning, snapping a glow stick and tossing it. The team swiftly moved down the long corridor to the next staircase. When he reached the bottom stair and an open door, he was about to step out into the hallway when he saw the guard sitting at the top of the next staircase, his AK-47 across his lap, smoking a cigarette and gazing off into space.

Hawke stepped back and whispered, "Guard. Mine."

The pale green carpeting underfoot was very deep, and Hawke approached the man with great stealth. He had his pistol out should the man spot him, but he much preferred to use the assault knife carried in his other hand. He got behind him without incident, reached down and clamped his hand over the man's mouth, yanked his head back to expose the throat beneath the beard, and slit it from ear to ear.

He turned and saw Stoke's face back at the door and motioned for the team to follow him. They reached the ground floor without further inconvenience, pausing halfway down the stairway and listening for noise of any kind. Only a silence resounded from the grand old rooms he'd loved to explore as a boy.

The SAS lads did a full sweep of the entire floor. Clear. The hostages were being held down in the cellar, just as Hawke had surmised upon seeing the queen's BBC video. The low, curved, white-plastered ceiling, the dim, naked bulbs above her head, even the white-painted brick wall behind the Sword of Allah banner.

He was quite sure the terrorists, with their limited knowledge of the castle interior, would have used the main stairs to the cellar. But there was another staircase, one very few people even knew existed, a very narrow, steep, and seldom-used staircase. The door to it was hidden behind a Chinese screen in the butler's pantry. These stairs were reserved solely for the yeoman of the cellar to ferry wine up from the Queen's wine cellar. And, luckily enough, it was at the exact opposite end of the house from the main stairs.

Hawke had spent a good deal of time hiding in that wine cellar. A good deal of time hiding in every nook and cranny in the entire house. And there was a way one could pass from the wine cellar out into the main rooms of the cellar. Which meant they might get very lucky and have the element of surprise.

Hawke signaled the team to follow him and went left. They were headed for the kitchen and from there to the butler's pantry and the secret staircase. Hawke paused at the kitchen door. There was someone in there, he heard china rattling. He halted the squad and pushed through the swinging doors with the muzzle of his HK leading the way.

"Higgins," Hawke said quietly.

"I recognize that voice," the man said. The elderly fellow turned with a smile on his face. "My goodness, your lordship, how long it's been."

"Yes. We'll talk later, Higgins. We've come to rescue the hostages. You know where they are, of course?"

"Oh, yes, m'lord. They're all down in the cellar. I've been charged with keeping them fed. I'm up and down stairs from morning till midnight. Awful down there. I've been in service to Her Majesty for my entire life. She has never treated me with anything but respect and kindness. And I tell you it's frightful, sir, disgraceful the way those men are treating our Monarch."

"Hold on a tick, Higgins, I'll be right back."

Hawke went back through the doors.

"Stoke, we just got lucky. Member of the household staff in there. Knows exactly where they're keeping the Yankees. Let's go get these bastards."

Returning to the kitchen and seeing Higgins again gave Hawke an idea.

"Higgins, we need a piece of paper and a pen, pencil, anything. I want you to make a drawing of the section of the cellar where the hostages are being held. I want you to use an RF to indicate precisely where each member of the Royal Family is located. Use an O for a hostage and an X for a terrorist. Try to place them all exactly where they were the last time you saw them."

"Yes, m'lord," Higgins said, pulling out a drawer with a legal pad and a box of ballpoints. As he sketched, Hawke peppered him with questions. Were the hostages bound in any way? Had any member of the Royal Family been harmed? Exactly how many terrorists was he dealing with? Were any of them wearing suicide vests?

"Here you are, your lordship, best I can do, no artist I'm afraid."

"It's perfect. I recognize this space. It's the very large area filled entirely with furniture. The one with little alcoves along the south wall. The big room near the main staircase, correct? All the way at the other end of the house?"

"That's the one all right, sir," Higgins said, eyeing the SAS troops. "This lot looks like they can take care of themselves."

"It's Her Royal Majesty these men want to take care of, Higgins. The Royal Family and all those other poor innocent people down there. What's the Queen's favorite cocktail, Higgins? Gin and something as I recall . . ."

"Gin and Dubonnet, sir, all she ever drinks."

"I'd have one ready for her, Higgins. I think she'll be most appreciative."

"I will indeed, sir. Jolly good idea."

"Any more dead or wounded?"

"In addition to Lady Beale, I'm afraid they've shot your colleague, Sir David Trulove, m'lord. Didn't want you to be shocked, sir."

Hawke, stunned to the core, showed nothing. "Let's go get 'em," he said, headed for the pantry.

HAWKE COULD HEAR A LOW rumble of voices before he could see anyone. With the aid of night vision, they'd slipped through most of the pitch-black cellar without a sound. He turned and signaled the two SAS snipers to join him. They had prearranged the commencement of the operation.

Hawke, Stoke, and two SAS snipers would advance toward the enemy first, moving to within one hundred yards of the location where the hostages were held. From Higgins's drawing, Hawke had seen that the snipers would have a clear shot at the Royals' alcove. First, the snipers would use silenced weapons to neutralize any terrorists guarding the Queen and her family.

Hawke could feel the presence of the SAS team gathering just behind his position. Their coiled-up energy was palpable. They were spoiling for a fight and they were about to get one.

There were two guards in close proximity to the Queen. One on either side of the alcove, both holding AK-47s. The two terrorists were clearly on edge, probably very high on the massive amounts of methamphetamines they used to stay awake. The two snipers dropped to one knee, sighting in on their targets. Both men nodded, a signal to Hawke that they had acquired and were ready to fire.

HAWKE LOOKED AROUND AT THE TROOPS gathered immediately behind him. He held up three fingers. Three seconds until "go." Simultaneously, he lightly tapped the top of each sniper's helmet. They fired on the signal. A nearly invisible muzzle flash, two silent *pffts*, and two clean head shots later, the two targets dropped like sacks of dirt.

"Go, go, go!" Hawke shouted, entering the room, already firing at targets he'd chosen.

In they went.

The terrorists began spraying bullets wildly as the hostages, screaming in fear for their lives, put their heads down or dove to the floor. Hawke spotted Ambrose Congreve and Diana Mars to his right and began moving in that direction, taking out anyone who got in his way. Congreve spotted him in the fiery chaos and screamed, "Alex! Montague is Smith! Watch out for him!"

Hawke was momentarily stunned by disbelief.

Montague Thorne was Smith?

A lot of tumblers started clicking into place as Hawke scanned the room, looking for him. He heard fire coming from the direction of the Queen's alcove and whirled in that direction, smiling at what he saw there. Prince William and Prince Harry had immediately grabbed the weapons of the two dead guards and were now on their feet, joining the battle. Prince Charles had moved to his mother, shielding her with his body, putting himself between her and the guns.

Hawke saw Stoke, too, now standing shoulder to shoulder with the two young princes, all three of them forming a protective cordon of lethal fire around the Queen and her family. It was a brilliant idea and Hawke damned himself for not thinking of it. But this was why you needed Stoke; he instinctively did the right things in battle.

The air was filled with lead. The SAS troops were going about their business with deadly precision, calming prisoners even as they fired short bursts that always found their targets. These incredibly brave men practiced 365 days a year for precisely this kind of situation and it showed. The room had filled with choking gun smoke, making visibility difficult, but Hawke saw two middle-aged women in satin gowns suddenly rise from their hiding place with the obvious idea of making a run for it.

They almost made it.

A terrorist, little more than a boy, saw the fleeing women, whirled, and fired a sustained burst that simply tore them both apart. Furious, Hawke ran toward him, and instantly and brutally returned the favor with his assault knife. His blood was up now, he was keenly alive, and doing exactly what he'd been born to do.

Hawke sensed movement behind him and spun to see a bad guy swinging his gun up and aiming, not at him, but at Ambrose and Diana. Hawke raised his gun to fire, but Congreve beat him to the punch. Ambrose simply exploded off the divan, dove at the man, knocking his AK aside with one hand and plunging a knife directly into the man's heart with the other.

Seconds later, Hawke knelt at Congreve's side.

"Are you both all right?"

"Let you know when it's over. Alex, you've got to find Montague. This is his operation now. He shot Sir David, for God's sake."

"I'll find him."

Hawke stood and scanned the room, trying to pierce the veil of smoke and see the face of the man who'd betrayed them all. There was still sporadic fire, but the battle was winding down and there was little doubt as to who'd won. And then he saw the demonic "Mr. Smith," stealing ever closer to Stoke and the two princes in a low crouch, using the furniture to conceal his advance. His intentions could not have been clearer. Another second or two and he'd have a shot at all three.

And then, a clear shot at the Queen.

"Montague Thorne!" Hawke called out as loudly as he could.

Their eyes met.

Seeing Hawke had him in his sights, Thorne dropped and rolled behind a heavy sofa. Hawke moved toward him, firing into the sofa, then saw Thorne on his feet, running through the scrim of smoke and disappearing into the blackness, headed for the main staircase.

HAWKE REACHED THE BOTTOM of the steps just as Thorne reached the top and raced away to the right. Emerging at the top, Alex saw the traitor about to duck into the nearest room, the Queen's Library. Hawke had his pistol in his hand and fired at him. But he missed and the man ran into the room. He was trapped but he didn't know it. The Library had only one door, the one he'd just entered.

Thorne quick-peeked around the door and fired a short burst at Hawke. Alex returned fire and ducked back out of sight. Then he raced into the next room and the next after that until he entered the small, walnut-paneled office. Here the Queen answered her correspondence, wrote letters of thanks, or offered condolences. The office shared a common wall with the Library where Thorne had taken refuge, but it also had its own little secret.

Hawke hurried behind the desk and pushed ever so gently on a wide wooden panel, almost invisible, in the center of the wall. On the other side of the panel were bookshelves full of books from floor to ceiling. Perfectly balanced, it made not a sound as it swung inward.

Hawke, pistol in hand, peered into the Queen's Library.

Thorne had his back to him. He was still hiding beside the door he'd entered, weapon at the ready, fully expecting Hawke to appear at any moment. Thorne didn't know it, of course, but he just had.

Hawke stepped silently into the room and pointed his pistol at the back of the monster's head.

"Thorne," he said, just loud enough to be heard.

Montague whirled, bringing his weapon up.

Their eyes locked.

"You're dead," Hawke said.

And pulled the trigger.

EPILOGUE

HAWKESMOOR, GLOUCESTERSHIRE

It was on a nasty November evening some months after the Balmoral affair that Alex Hawke received a most intriguing phone call. Because the call would ultimately have enormous significance in his life, he could recall every detail surrounding it.

He remembered, for instance, that he had been sublimely stretched out on the worn leather sofa in his dimly lit library. Remembered four solid walls of leather-bound books disappearing up into the darkness near the ceiling. And that the dying embers of a fire were in need of a good stoking.

But he was far too comfortable and engrossed in *The Volcano Lover,* a novel about his hero Lord Nelson and Emma Hamilton, to move. He would read a few pages, drift off to sleep, awake, and read a few more. Bliss.

And then, across the room and sitting atop his desk, the bloody telephone rang.

It rang, and rang, and then it rang again.

He determined to let it ring off the bloody hook if need be.

Nor did he wish to disturb dear old Pelham, last seen ensconced in the butler's pantry, perched atop his ageless stool, round gold glasses precariously hanging on the tip of his nose, working on his latest needlepoint masterpiece while frozen snippets of rain beat against the windowpanes.

Still, he must have dozed off, for suddenly Pelham was standing above him saying something about a telephone call. Most urgent, gentleman wouldn't identify himself, said he must speak with Lord Hawke immediately.

With a sigh, Hawke rose from the sofa and padded over to his desk to pick up the damn phone. Pelham vanished from the room just as Alex said, "Hello?"

"Alex?"

"Indeed I am. And who are you?"

"It's Halter."

"Halter! Good Lord, it's been aeons."

Stefan Halter was a don at Cambridge. He also worked for both MI6 and the Russian KGB; he was the longest and most successful double agent in the history of the British service. He was a good man, brilliant, and he had saved Hawke's life once, risking his own, on a remote Swedish island. In hindsight, Hawke might well have preferred to die.

"Alex, we need to see each other. I have certain information that I must share with you. I'm not at all comfortable discussing this business on the phone."

"I understand. Would you like to come to Hawkesmoor? We could do some shooting, mix business with pleasure."

"It's not a good idea for me to be seen in England at the moment. I'm sure you'll understand."

"Yes. I'll come to you then. Where are you? Not Moscow?"

"No. I've a small chalet in Switzerland. Should I manage to live long enough to retire in one piece, it will be my home."

"Done. How do I get there?"

"You still have your beautiful little airplane?"

"Guilty as charged, your honor."

"Good. The nearest airport is Lucerne."

HAWKE CAUGHT A TAXI AT THE AIRPORT and went directly to the ferry docks on Lake Lucerne, just across the way from the main railway station. Halter had told him there was a boat called the *Unterwalden* departing promptly at noon and tickets could easily be had at the *Vierwaldstättersee* office right on the quay.

Halter had promised a very pleasant trip down Switzerland's most beautiful lake, emerald green and clear as gin. When Hawke heard the distinctive shriek of a steam whistle and saw the *Unterwalden* arriving at the dock, he knew why he was in for a pleasant voyage.

She was a large, 1902-vintage paddle-wheel steamer, one that obviously had been impeccably restored. He was one of the first aboard. Mounting the stairs to the first class dining room for lunch, he saw that the modern designers had encased the ship's engine room and the two huge steam engines entirely in Plexiglas.

Gazing down into the pristine engine room, you could see the pulsing of the massive polished steel connecting rods that drove the paddle wheels, and even the man on the throttle, taking orders from three brass horns linked to the bridge. Hawke, transfixed by the sheer beauty and elegance of this century-old technology, almost missed the first seating for lunch.

His table by the curved window offered splendid views of the Alps as the paddle wheeler zigzagged across the green lake, stopping at one tiny storybook village after another. The snowcapped Alps and thick green forests, laden with snow, marched right down to the lakeshore everywhere you looked. For perhaps the first time in his life, he felt thoroughly enchanted. Hawke imagined that there might be somewhere on the planet he'd like to live besides England.

When the announcement came over the P.A. system that the next stop would be his destination, Vitznau, he was almost disappointed. He would have been more than happy to remain aboard and continue on to the southern tip of the lake.

At Vitznau, Halter had instructed, he was to board one of the small trains that left every hour at quarter past. The rail station was a five-minute walk from the dock. He was startled to see that the tracks ascended the mountain at a nearly vertical angle. Slightly nervous about such a steep ascent, he asked the ticket master how the trains did it.

"This is the oldest cog railway in the world, sir," the kindly man told him in perfect English. "Built in 1898."

"Ah," Hawke said, not overwhelmingly reassured, gazing out the window at the steep incline.

"Don't worry," the man said with a smile. "Our little steam engines may look old-fashioned, and they are over one hundred years old, but they will get you safely to the top, I promise."

Like the steamship, the arriving Swiss train was a marvel. The engine, huffing and puffing steam as it descended into the station, was a lovely thing of brass and dark forest green, as were the uniforms of the two conductors. The cars themselves were bright red, which seemed to be the favorite color of the Swiss.

Hawke gleefully bought his ticket and climbed aboard, more than ready for his ascent. Travel here in Switzerland, all of it, was not just getting from one place to another, he mused; it was all a glorious adventure. As the little train wound its way up the mountain, he heard cowbells clanging away as the livestock munched hay in and around countless farms. Every chalet was a delight, with brightly colored shutters and doors, and trim under the eaves.

It took the train about an hour to reach the top, through some of the most spectacular scenery on earth. When he reached the tiny town of Rigi and climbed down from his car, he saw Halter waving to him from the platform. Professor Stefanovich Halter was hard to miss in a crowd. He was a tall, big man, a rugged bear of a fellow with sharp, dark eyes beneath wild bushy black eyebrows.

And he was wearing the brightest red ski parka Hawke had ever seen, not to mention a large black mink Cossack trapper hat perched atop his head. He moved surprisingly gracefully for such a big man as he hurried along the platform toward Hawke.

"Welcome to the top of the world," he said, extending his hand. For a dyed-in-the-wool Muscovite, Halter had a pitch-perfect Oxbridge accent, the product of a boyhood at Eton and Cambridge.

Hawke shook his hand warmly and said, "I warn you now, Halter, I may never leave. It is too glorious for words."

"It is rather pretty, isn't it. Look at the two tallest mountains over there beyond the lake. That's the Eiger to the left, and beyond that the Jungfrau. You've come on the perfect day. Cool and clear. We've been besieged with snow all month. Shall we be off? Don't tell me that's all the luggage you've brought?"

Hawke slung his black nylon duffel bag over his shoulder and said, "I assume you don't dress for dinner up here, do you? I'm afraid I didn't bring a dinner jacket."

Halter laughed and said, "Follow me, Alex, your carriage awaits. My God, it's good to see you. You look marvelous by the way. I heard you went through a rough patch out in Bermuda."

Hawke ignored that and said, "Would you mind terribly if we stopped at a Realtor's office en route to your chalet? I should very much like to buy a house. Before sundown if possible."

"Not at all. Brought your checkbook?"

"As a matter of fact, I did."

They started off, walking through the streets of the picturesque hamlet.

"Ah, here we are," Halter said, as the two men rounded the back of a small *gasthaus* where diners sat on an upper deck enjoying the amazing views, the sunshine, and great glass steins of beer.

"This is yours?" Hawke said, looking at the lovely red sleigh behind two sturdy Swiss dray horses that very closely resembled palominos.

"Only way to get around up here. I cannot abide those horrid snowmobiles, and thank heaven there are few of them about up at the summit."

Hawke climbed inside after tossing his duffel behind the bench seat. Halter flicked the reins and they were off. The horses were beautifully tacked with a surfeit of gleaming silver sleigh bells that tinkled merrily as they made their way through the snowy wood.

"Do your comrades at the Kremlin know about this place?"

"Alex, you are the first and only person I have even told about this house, much less invited for a visit."

Twenty minutes later Halter reined in the horses, stopping just below a small but exquisite Swiss chalet. It had bright red shutters with decorative cutouts on every window, a steep pitched roof, and lots of carved Swiss imagery under the eave of the top floor.

"It's perfect, Stefan."

"With all due modesty, I must agree. Let's hurry inside and get you some food and drink, shall we?"

Once inside, sitting before a roaring fire in an ancient stone hearth, Halter took a sip of lager and looked carefully at his old friend.

"Alex, what I'm about to tell you will most certainly be a shock to you. I was shocked myself and that's a difficult thing to do. But I want you to hear me out before you respond. And I want you to know beforehand that what I tell you may well turn out to be pure fabrication. Misinformation designed by the KGB for purely political reasons. Do you understand?"

"Yes," Hawke said, his heart suddenly trip-hammering inside his rib cage. "Tell me."

"Anastasia may still be alive."

"What?" Hawke felt as if he'd been struck in the heart by a giant wielding a sledgehammer.

"She may not have died in the airship explosion in Sweden."

"But that's—"

"I know, impossible. We both saw her loaded aboard on the stretcher minutes before the explosion. At least, we saw *someone* carried on board. The body was concealed beneath a fur blanket."

"Yes, but we saw her arm slip down. The white ermine jacket she'd worn to the Nobel—"

"I know, I know. But apparently it may not have been her. I'm told the housekeeper at the summer house, for whatever reason, donned the ermine jacket, covered herself with the blanket, and had herself— Alex? Are you all right?"

Hawke had gone as still as death and as pale as wax. He covered his eyes with his trembling hands and, his voice breaking, said, "This cannot be true, Stefan. It simply cannot! I saw what I saw. I saw what I saw."

"Let me get you something. Brandy? Schnapps?"

"Brandy, please. I can't, I really just cannot deal with this, you know. After all this time. All this grief. All this goddamn pain I've been carrying around for—for—what? And now I'm finally—what? What am I, Stefan?"

"Drink this. Let's not talk for a few minutes. Do you want to walk around in the snow for a bit? Take some deep breaths of cold air? Might help."

"No. I want to hear it all. I'm all right."

"You're in shock, Alex. Perhaps we should speak after dinner and—"

"No! I want to hear it all! Right now. Every damn bit of it."

"All right. I'll tell you all I've heard. The KGB went to Sweden immediately after the tsar's death. Went to his house. Searched it. They claim they found Anastasia hiding in the cellar. Barely alive. She'd attempted suicide. Rat poison. But they got her to the clinic on the mainland in time."

"And then?"

"Returned her to Moscow. Lubyanka Prison. She was there for a year. They . . . coerced a confession from her. Treason against the state. She was tried and condemned to death by hanging."

"God. Oh, my God."

"You remember General Kuragin?"

"Of course. The little town in Sweden. The man who cut off his own left hand to avert suspicion. Betrayed the tsar. Gave us the code to the Beta machine."

"Yes. At the last minute, Kuragin interceded in her behalf. Saved her life. If I had to guess, I'd say Putin was behind it in some way."

"Putin?"

"Yes. After the tsar's death he was one of many political prisoners freed from Energetika Prison. He's been restored to power as you well know. Saving Anastasia could have been Putin's way of retaliating against those who'd betrayed him in favor of Count Korsakov. I really don't know the details, but she was released into General Kuragin's custody."

"Where is she now?"

"The KGB took possession of the tsar's country estate. You've been there, Jasna Polana. They use it for winter military training exercises, high-level meetings, entertaining visiting dignitaries, whatever. General Kuragin has retired. He lives there now, running the place, so to speak. So does she. Under lock and key. Constant guard. The place has become an armed fortress."

Hawke stood up, went to the hearth, and put both hands on the mantelpiece, facing away from Halter. Tears were coursing down his cheeks. His breathing was very shallow, and he was shaking badly as he tried to compose himself.

Halter waited silently for the question he knew was coming. It was some time before Hawke gained sufficient control of his emotions to ask it.

"And what about—what about my son?"

"Alive. He was born in Lubyanka Prison. He is now with his mother at Jasna Polana."

"He would be—how old now?"

"Almost two, Alex."

Hawke's heart was in his throat as he said, "One last question, Stefan."

"Anything."

"Who told you all of this?"

"General Kuragin."

"Kuragin. I was afraid you'd say that."

"Why?"

"Because, Stefan, you and I are the only two men on earth who know that General Kuragin betrayed his tsar and his country for fifty million dollars in a Swiss bank."

"And now he wants both witnesses to his treason eliminated."

"It's a possibility we must consider."

Hawke turned and faced his friend.

"I-I don't know what to say, Stefan. I don't know whether to believe this or not. I'm terrified of believing it. And terrified of *not* believing it."

"I've felt the very same way ever since learning about this. There were times when I thought I'd never be able to tell you all this."

"I killed Korsakov, Russia's beloved tsar. I'm sure the Kremlin wants me dead. I'm still amazed they never came after me in Bermuda. I was expecting a bullet to the head every single day."

"Yes. This could well be a very elaborate KGB ruse. Ordered by Kuragin. A trap, with Anastasia and her child as the perfect bait. A way to bring you to them while exacting a horrible emotional punishment upon you before he silences the voice that can bring him down. They are certainly capable of concocting such a monstrous assassination."

"I am returning to Russia. If Anastasia and my son are alive, I promise you I will find them and I will bring them out. Or happily die trying."

"I know, Alex. I knew you would feel that way. I'm of course prepared to help you in any way possible, from inside the Kremlin. And, if you'll allow me, even going with you to bring them out if you want me."

"And expose yourself? After all these brilliant years? You cannot do that. England needs you alive, right where you are."

"It would be a glorious way to end my career, I believe. Helping you to find the two of them. All of us coming out together."

Hawke's heart caught in his throat. His eyes were brimming with more tears he fought hard not to spill.

"Thank you—thank you, Stefan, that's all—all I can say. If I might borrow your cheery red parka, I would like to go for a very, very long walk in your beautiful Alps."

So saying, Hawke strode to the door, grabbed Halter's parka from the rack, and stepped outside into the howling wind and whirling snow without another word.

What was there left to say, really?